WELCOME TO WESTVILLE

WELCOME TO WESTVILLE

A NOVEL

RYDER JONES

REMNANT HEART PUBLISHING

REMNANT HEART PUBLISHING

remnantheart.com

This book is a work of fiction. Any references to historical events, real people, or real places are used fictitiously. Other names, characters, places, and events are products of the author's imagination, and any resemblance to actual events, places, or persons, living or dead, is entirely coincidental.

Cover Design by Christian Storm, Edited by Justin Tiemeyer

ISBN (KDP Hardback): 979-8-9926643-5-5
ISBN (Paperback): 979-8-9926643-0-0
ISBN (e-Book) 979-8-9926643-2-4

For information about special discounts for bulk purchases, please contact Remnant Heart Publishing: ryder@remnantheart.com

Manufactured in the United States of America

"If you gaze long enough into an abyss, the abyss gazes back into you"

—FREDRICH NIETZSCHE

"And what rough beast, its hour come round at last, slouches towards Bethlehem to be born?"

— FROM 'THE SECOND COMING'
BY WILLIAM BUTLER YEATS

WELCOME TO WESTVILLE

FRIDAY NIGHT LIGHTS

1

The walls were too thin for secrets.

Millie Thompson drowned out the yelling with the sharp edge of Alanis Morissette's voice. She paced in tight circles, headphones clamped over her ears, while her parents threw words like knives—bouncing off walls, slicing through her bedroom door. Her father said he *"had it under control,"* while her mother sounded very convinced he did not—whatever *it* was.

Millie knew something was wrong. She had for a while now.

The sour stench of alcohol clung to her father's breath most mornings when he dropped her off at school. *"Have a good day, Millie girl,"* he'd say, and she'd pretend not to notice. Pretended not to smell the proof of late nights and bad choices.

She lowered her headphones, set the yellow Discman on the dresser, and pulled her blonde hair back into a ponytail as a tinny chorus leaked through the foam pads around her neck.

She wanted to believe it was all going to be alright—just like the song said.

But Millie could not know what was coming.

No one could have.

2

The Slate River lay placid under a dying autumn sun, a red seam splitting the surface.

Millie moved through crisp air thick with a musk of damp leaves. She skirted past the old high school through the parking lot, its broken windows gaping like dead eyes in the dusk, partly demolished and mostly forgotten, and looking more like a haunted house every day. She struck out down the riverwalk. Ahead, the Westville Showboat sat steeped in the shallows, its grand red wheel useless as a broken clock.

She crossed Main Street, cutting through the parking lot, then stepped onto the train trestle, where the river roared out of the dam, frothing and spilling over the banks in a slow, steady creep. Her grandpa's company, PRINCE Milling, loomed on the far side of the river, tall silos and fat grain bins standing like sentinels against the darkening sky. In theory, her dad would take it over one day. She shook away an encroaching churn in her gut as she thought about that, passing the looming concrete mills buildings as the tracks came back onto solid ground.

Millie banked left toward the fairgrounds and the football field. The town turned out in force as usual for the Redhawks. Millie didn't really care about football much; it was an escape just to be with her friends and not think, for a while.

The old stadium lights reminded her of six-eyed insects atop their splintered stick bodies, shining over the bleachers as dusk took hold, revealing shadows of old townies and students alike heading for food, beverage and bathrooms as little kids chased each other screaming.

She spotted Olivia leaning against the worn white and red paint of the concession building, interjecting herself into Kyle's flirtation with a couple of sophomore girls.

His pale cheeks were flushing though Millie could tell he was doing his level best to stay smooth, wiping a hand over gelled, messy brown hair. He stared pins and needles at Olivia, as she raised an aluminum wrapped hot dog eyeing it thoughtfully under the yellow stadium light.

"I'll say this for Kyle Anderson, he really knows how to handle a wiener."

Olivia passed it off to the taller girl whose face was screwed up in a mess of confusion. Then they looked over at Kyle, and snickered.

Olivia beamed with pride as the pair walked back to the bleachers. Kyle, rosy-cheeked and glaring, tightened his concessions apron behind the counter and when his mother wasn't looking flipped a shakily rigid middle finger.

Millie snickered. "They didn't deserve you anyway."

"Mil!" Liv said, grinning. "I was just telling Kyle he's found his true calling."

"Maybe," Kyle shot back. "Or maybe I'll get a job as a busboy down at Fischer's."

"What, so you can creep on my sister?"

"Why else?"

"Dude, she's like, seventeen years older than you."

"And age is but a number."

Kyle's mom called him away, and he trudged off.

"You love riling him up, don't you?" Millie said, shaking her head.

Liv shrugged. "Easy target."

That was what Millie liked about Olivia—how she just *said* things. Did things without thinking. No hesitation. It got her into trouble, but there was freedom in that.

Liv's eyes flicked to the Discman in Millie's hand. "Like the album?"

Millie nodded. "Yeah. It's maybe just a little better than Amy Grant."

"Told you." Liv smirked, then dropped her voice. "So, I've been thinking . . ."

Millie recognized that tone. It meant trouble. "We're not ditching the game."

Liv rolled her eyes. "Come on, why not?"

"Because I told my parents this is where I'd be."

"And what if I told you we don't have to go far?"

"For what?"

"Brett Huizenga and some others invited us down by the river."

Millie's stomach tightened. "Liv, come on."

"We'll just go for a little bit. Back before halftime. No one will know we left."

Millie hesitated. Before she could say no, Liv grabbed her hand and tugged her away from the field, back toward the tracks.

Millie wrenched her hand free. "Why does everything have to change just because we're in high school?"

Liv turned, brushing a wild red curl from her face. "It doesn't have to. But if some cute boys want to hang out—"

"Brett isn't cute. And did they even invite me, or just you?"

"I may have mentioned you'd be joining me."

Millie offered a weak smile and followed. Already she found herself wishing time would rush ahead to next week. On Halloween there would be no other option other than what had become hard and fast tradition: Liv and her, along with Kyle and Austin, stuffing pillowcases full of strangers' candy and then camping out in her living room watching *Hocus Pocus* for the thirty-second time while stuffing their faces. Things could just be how they used to be. Plus with friends around it usually stopped her parents from fighting—at least for a night.

They reached the river. A small group of upperclassmen, mostly guys, huddled in the dark, their laughter sharp, edged with something mean. Brett Huizenga stood in the center, as greasy as ever, like he'd washed his face with a slice of pizza.

"Who's your friend?" Brett asked, his eyes trailing over Millie.

Liv shot her a quick, apologetic look. "This is Millie Thompson."

"Wait—Thompson?" Brett's head flicked toward the PRINCE Milling sign glowing through the trees. His lips curled into something that wasn't quite a smile. "Damn. We're in the presence of Westville royalty." He gave an exaggerated bow.

Millie flushed. "Not exactly."

"She's cool," Liv said quickly.

Brett's smirk faded, his voice turning cold. "Yeah? 'Cause her old man fired mine four months ago."

Millie's stomach twisted.

"My dad doesn't run the company," she muttered. It was true—technically. But her dad did run the floor and handled a lot of the employees, so he probably *had* fired Brett's father.

He shoved a bottle of Jack Daniel's toward her, the cap off, its sharp scent burning her nose. It reminded her of her dad's breath some mornings.

"I'm good," she managed, through a roil of sudden nausea.

"She doesn't really—" Olivia started, but Brett pushed the bottle closer.

"What are you, a nark?"

"No," Millie said, her voice quieter. "I just don't—"

Olivia grabbed the bottle, took a hearty swig. Her face scrunched, and she wheezed out a cough then pointed to Millie. "She's allergic."

Brett stared between the two of them for a beat. "Whatever," he snorted, shrugging and headed toward the others, lighting up joints by the river. Millie swallowed hard, watching the thin wisps of smoke rise into the air, mixing with the cold dampness of the evening.

"I shouldn't be here."

Liv sighed. "Come on, Mil. Just loosen up for once."

"It's not—I just don't want to be here."

"You drag me to that youth group every Sunday, and I don't complain."

"You do, just not out loud."

"Maybe because I don't want to talk about that stuff."

"What stuff?"

"If God gave two shits about me or my dad, he wouldn't have let him suffer like that."

Millie's chest tightened. She remembered Mr. Fischer's face, gaunt and pained, lying in a downstairs bedroom, back in the springtime when warmth and beauty poured through the cracks of winter's last days.

"I'm sorry, Liv."

Her friend shook her head, sniffing. "You don't get it. You have a perfect life. Perfect family."

Millie felt a barb of pain in her chest. "You don't know that."

Olivia wiped her face and took another swig. "Look, just stay and hang out this once. If we hate it, we'll never do it again."

Millie shook her head. "I'm going back."

"Seriously?"

"Yeah. Seriously."

3

Millie walked back alone under a sky bruising into violet, the last embers of daylight smoldering behind bloated gray clouds. The air smelled of damp concrete and something stale from the river, and every sound was sharper—the crunch of her shoes on gravel, the low murmur of the football game behind her, a metallic shunt as a piece of automated mill machinery kicked on nearby.

Something red flickered at the edge of her vision, jagged motion. Her heart lurched.

She stiffened; her breath catching in her throat. Her eyes tracked up past the towering concrete silos, to the culprit.

The crimson neon PRINCE sign glowed through the night haze. Same as always. The light hummed faintly, its reflection wobbling in the visible shard of the Slate river's dark surface far off to her right.

Millie let out a slow breath, unclenching her fists. Stupid. The same sign she'd seen every night of her life.

So why had it startled her like that?

She stopped, pulling off her headphones. Listened.

The wind pushed a brittle leaf across the tracks. Somewhere far off a dog barked, and the mill's ventilation sighed.

A horn honked, Millie's stomach dropping like a lead ball and heart leaping at once.

The white Methodist Church minibus idled just ahead, and the driver's side window rolled down. A grinning, heavyset face with a gray-white beard. Howard Meyers, one of her youth group leaders and a bus driver for the school system.

He wheezed out a laugh. "Whew, that got you good."

"Hey, Mr. Meyers," Millie said, offering an obligatory smile. She took off the other ear of her headphones.

"What kind of mischief are you getting into tonight, young lady?" he asked.

Millie would usually joke back with him. His sense of humor lacked any sort of nuance, but she couldn't help playing along. Olivia, on the other hand, had never been amused when she'd come along with Millie to the small youth group. The thought of her friend soured Millie.

She forced a casual tone. "Just headed home." Then added, "Game's pretty much over anyway," to cut off any further questioning.

Mr. Meyers nodded. "Them Hawks are gettin' after 'em this year, huh?"

"Yeah," she said, though she hadn't been paying attention, just assumed.

"Well, I'll see ya Sunday night then."

"Yeah."

"I can give you a lift," he offered. "Been shuttlin' folks back and forth from the school lot."

"That's okay," Millie said quickly. She didn't feel like talking, not even to someone as kind and familiar as Mr. Meyers.

He studied her for a second and nodded. "All right. Just straight home, though, you hear?"

Millie gave him a small salute. "Got it."

He chuckled and rolled up the window, the minibus lumbering forward, red taillights swallowing into the dark.

Millie turned back toward the tracks, slipping her headphones on.

But she didn't press play at first.

She just listened to the night for a while.

4

Millie walked clear past her street and wanted to keep going as she came to the end of the album.

Right now, the most jagged pill to swallow would have been going home.

Not yet.

She passed rows of two-story houses, until the street emptied out into Elmwood Cemetery. She kept to the concrete path that hugged a black chain link fence, through which she could see the factory down near the river, cars bathed in strange radioactive yellow given off by cyclopean parking lot lights. Slowly, the fragile comfort of knowing she was surrounded by warm bodies within nearby homes bled out, replaced with creeping loneliness.

To her right, gravestones stood solemn and cold, some smooth and polished, others jagged with time, the moonlight tracing their names in silver. Further along the middle path, she'd find her grandparents' graves, which they visited every year.

A deep cold night had settled fast, like it had been waiting underground, biding its time until the sun gave up the luminous ghost of day. Millie breathed warm air into her hands, watching the vapor curl upward. The final track's hypnotic chant looped in her ears, a refrain telling her it was time to 'wake up' and 'get out of here'.

She couldn't help but agree.

An oppressive feeling crawled through her veins and settled in her chest, making it harder to breathe. She turned on the path that cut through the cemetery, looking to Harrison Street, which would lead her back home, where she suddenly wanted to be very badly.

When she turned right on the dirt part of her road—her house only a few blocks away— she was blinded by headlights. Millie flinched, throwing an arm up against the glare. She couldn't make out the kind of vehicle. Bigger than a car. A truck or large van maybe.

But it wasn't moving.

Millie slipped off her headphones, her skin prickling.

It just sat there watching her—if a vehicle could watch—which made her wonder just who was behind the wheel and why *they* were staring at her. She walked briskly along the shoulder, keeping as far as she could to the side.

She just needed to get past, and get home.

The engine coughed to life—a guttural, diesel growl.

It lurched forward, then stopped. Waiting. Watching.

Millie heard her pulse acutely in her eardrums now, and her arms shook. The engine revved again, this time with a vengeful scrape of tires on dirt as it careened toward her.

Millie ran.

She didn't think—just moved, sprinting into the dark as the vehicle roared behind her, its headlights throwing sporadic shadows over the graves and trees.

She glanced back.

It was toying with her, coming close enough to terrify, slamming the brakes, letting her think—just for a second—that she had a chance.

Her lungs burned. The road narrowed to a dead-end. The old Boy Scout cabin loomed ahead, barely lit by a single flickering blue-white streetlamp.

She veered toward it, sprinting across the grass circle in the dirt turn-around and vaulted over the rusted metal gate into the trees. Branches whipped at her face as she tore through the narrow two-track path, running blind.

Millie was yanked back like a dog on a short leash, her body twisting.

Her headphone cord had caught on something, the Discman flying off into the dark. She stumbled, her foot snagging on a root or a rock and a pop thrummed though her whole body.

She tasted dirt, felt searing, wide pain around her kneecap.

Headlights shone on her as the vehicle idled outside the tree line.

"Leave me alone!" Her voice broke when she yelled, and she barely recognized it.

The engine shut off, and so did the lights.

Quiet. Dark. She stared into the void of the windshield.

A red light bloomed on the other side, and cold dread pooled in her gut.

She worked her ankle free and despite the torture of every step got up and ran limping through the woods. She came out into the clearing, tears streaking down her cheeks now.

She forced herself forward.

She just wanted to go home.

With bleary eyes she stumbled through the trees, hands shaking violently.

She broke into a clearing, the river ahead glinting faintly between the trees under clouded moonbeams. The North Country trail was just ahead, she could take that into the woods and get out onto a different road. Her throbbing knee said otherwise.

Then she heard it: a deep, groaning creak. Like all the trees were bending under a weight that would break them. Like bones cracking under pressure.

She stopped, turned slowly, and saw it.

A glaring red circle emerged from the woods. It grew larger until it seared through the many spindles of tree trunks, shooting blades of crimson light.

Something moved inside.

A wrongly twisted figure like a shadow, pulling itself forward with deliberate jerking movements, long skeletal limbs, and jagged protrusions from its head—like antlers.

Millie's heart seized. A hissing sound grew deafening like the screech of a boiling teapot, freezing her where she stood and piercing her every pore.

She wanted to run, but she couldn't move.

So she screamed instead. And knew, somehow, no one could hear.

THE GUILTY ONES

D.C.B. Interview Transcript

Incident Report
Interview Series 3: The Westville Incursion

Lochlear: Date is December, 31st 1996 — 10:48 AM. This is Special Agent Stephen Lochlear. Please state your full name for the record.

Benson: It's Casey Benson--for the tenth time.

Lochlear: Your *full* name.

Benson: Casey. Alan. Benson.

Lochlear: I understand your frustration Mr. Benson, but this is necessary. An incursion of this scale re-quires absolute diligence. We need to know exactly how the events of these past few months unfolded.

Benson: You call diligence leaving a girl to rot while your people played spy games in my town?

Lochlear: The situation left us no better choice than to adhere to our protocols.

Benson: Don't feed me your bureaucratic bullshit."

Lochlear: Mr. Benson, please calm down. The sooner we finish, the sooner you can return home. Things can start to go back to normal.

Benson: You don't believe that. You can't honestly think we're ever going back to normal after what happened.

Lochlear: I do. Because I have to. And so do you and everyone in Westville who witnessed what happened. I think you know that.

Benson: Fine. Let's just get this over with.

Lochlear: Good. Now, from the beginning.

17

1

OCTOBER 26TH, 1996

Westville wasn't the kind of place where people went missing—until one frigid October morning, it suddenly was.

Casey Benson turned onto M-12, the dim, lifeless glow of the *Family Affair Supermarket* sign slipping from his rear view, as the neglected speed gun rolled listless in the passenger seat. A grand total of three cars had passed in the last two hours, and the temperature plunged like the speed limit coming into town, the Indian summer breaking like a brittle bone.

The weathermen hadn't warned about the coming snap, and usually, they got all hot and bothered about that sort of thing. But Casey felt the cold clawing at him now through his open window.

He twisted the radio dial away from the drone of political chatter—Dole, Clinton, Perot. China trying to influence the election. Static gave way to a story on a severe tornado outbreak overnight in South Dakota and Nebraska, and finally to the slow gallop of *'One Headlight'* by The Wallflowers. Casey exhaled, eyes flicking to the pale green glow of the clock.

6:56 a.m.

The department was understaffed; taking the nightshifts was doing a number on him and his sleep. Plus, this time of year, everything was dark.

The mornings were black and nights blacker, and right now, there was only the faintest gray-yellow bruise on the horizon hinting at dawn.

The Caprice patrol car had V8s with a hell of a kick, and he sympathized with the poor townies he had to pull over. It was too easy for him to speed coming into town, careening over the railroad tracks at 55 instead of 30. Fog crawled over the road, rolling low as Westville stretched awake in pieces. Hardware and auto parts galore, fast food and pizza, Herb's lumber and used car dealerships. A small town starter set that Westville never broke out of.

Casey slowed at the blinking red light.

Two warring gas stations stubbornly stood at opposite corners of the town's main intersection—Shell on one side, Marathon on the other—still and quiet. The hulking grain bins of PRINCE Milling loomed overhead, skeletal steel trusses and angled downspouts crisscrossing between them. If Westville had a skyline, this was it—a row of towering concrete silos, the six-letter crimson neon declaring *PRINCE* like a beacon.

He rubbed his brow tracing rough skin on the scar there.

The dispatch radio crackled. He ignored it—he was only minutes from the station anyway.

The tires hissed on pavement as he rolled forward, past the first block of historic buildings housing the two-story antique mall, a tax office and more, and more antique and trinket shops. Between those, the five-and-dime on the corner of Water St. and the comic book shop across from it, Westville was a bustling hub of commerce.

Cold mist rose off the rushing dam as he hit the bridge, vapors snaking around the newest silo under construction, sheets of plastic draped over it like a veil. Ahead, the rolling fog cast a ghostly glow over black iron street lamps that lined the half-mile run of Main Street.

The radio squawked impatiently again, but with an odd burst of static— almost like a whisper. Casey frowned, glancing at the receiver.

Silence.

Then a harsh hiss as Gail's honking voice came through:

"Benson, you copy?"

He startled, and grabbed the radio. "Yeah, I'm here. Heading your way. Over."

Another brief squelch.

Then— "I've been trying to stave her off, but Ruth Potter's blowing up the line with another noise complaint. Want to check it out? Over."

Casey let out a slow breath.

His stomach growled, and his eyes burned at the thought of extending his shift. He could already feel food and rest slipping away.

"Not really, but I'm on my way."

Gail's smirk was audible.

"Copy. You'll get your reward in heaven."

Casey snorted, as he turned left at City Hall.

"God's work, huh? Over."

He passed the station, shooting it a baleful glance.

Who needed sleep anyway?

2

Ruth Potter's place was just past Elmwood Cemetery, where Harrison gave up on pavement.

Casey had lost track of how many noise complaints dragged him here—or any officer lucky enough.

The old yellow two-story stirred up memories: his dad mowing her lawn—another side job to make ends meet—while Casey sat on the back steps, eating gas station Oreos. They always tasted like chemicals thanks to the cloud of mosquito spray Mrs. Potter insisted on dousing him with, her voice sharp as she scolded him to hold out his arms—and to let her get behind his knees, too.

He pulled in behind her Buick Century, the rusted car leaning to one side, victim of a flat tire that had probably been that way for months.

She didn't drive anymore, far as he knew. Since Bob passed, her kids carted her around.

Casey barely had time to unbuckle before the front door swung open, hinges shrieking. Ruth Potter stepped onto the sagging porch, wrapped in a floral housecoat, gray hair piled haphazardly atop her head like cotton candy gone wrong.

"About time, Officer," she barked, cutting through morning fog.

Casey grinned, shutting the patrol car door.

"You can call me Casey, you know."

She huffed, arms crossed over her narrow chest. "Well, I wish I didn't have to call you at all."

"Noise complaint?"

"Them kids were at it again," she said, eyes flashing. "Hollerin' like they got nothing better to do."

Probably didn't. High schoolers in Westville late on a Friday night meant bad decisions in the woods.

He nodded anyway, suppressing a yawn, looking toward the tree line across the road.

"By the Scout cabin?"

She lifted a quavering finger, her voice dropping to a mutter. "Saw a red light over in the woods on the hill, too."

Casey squinted toward the dark forest bordering her property. The land sloped down to the river, and beyond that, the hills of the North Country Trail. The Boy Scout cabin had been a teen haunt for as long as he could remember.

"Red, huh?"

"Yep. Flickering in and out. Better not have been fireworks." Her lips pressed into a thin line. "Damn kids'll set a blaze."

Nothing changed in Westville. Same boredom, same reckless midnight activities. He and Joe Thompson had been no different, setting off a dozen road flares stolen from PRINCE Milling's rigs, just because. Joe's dad made sure he didn't leave the house for weeks.

"I'll check it out, Mrs. Potter."

She narrowed her eyes. "You do that. And call me Ruth, dammit."

"Right," he said, smirking as he climbed back into the patrol car.

He wrote up her report, tapping his pen against the clipboard in time with the engine's idle. His brain felt like fogged glass, the strain of consecutive night shifts making everything slower, heavier.

He thought about just heading back to the station.

But Ruth Potter would be watching from the window, making sure he did a proper loop past the cabin. She was persnickety like that.

He sighed and threw the car in reverse.

Just for show.

The dirt road dead-ended at a turnaround, the Boy Scout cabin perched on a low hill to the right. A rusted gate, padlocked but laughably easy to climb, shrouded in fog creeping up from the river.

Casey had scattered teenagers from this spot before, his headlights flashing through the woods, their laughter turning to panicked curses as they bolted. Sergeant Gordy Reynolds had once likened it to spritzing an ornery cat with a spray bottle.

Casey rolled down the window, letting the cold air rush in.

For a second—he thought he heard something.

A low groan. Maybe a dead tree shifting.

The gravel crunching under his tires drowned it out.

Nothing looked out of place.

He exhaled, turned the wheel, and pulled back toward town.

As he headed back down Harrison, a dog stood on the shoulder where the dirt met pavement. Ears pricked, eyes locked on the tree line, like it was listening to something only it could hear.

Casey glanced at the dog in his rearview, a shiver running through him as he rolled up the window.

3

Casey pulled into the station, just as tired and hungrier, the garage door rattling down behind him.

The hum of fluorescent lights buzzed overhead, and from Johnson's cubicle, a boombox crackled, Metallica playing at a moderate volume on K-ROCK 94.9.

Things were quiet. Relatively.

Gail sat behind the reception desk, a jar of peanuts and candy corn perched precariously near the edge. It never seemed to empty, so either it was going stale, or she had a sweet tooth and refilled it when no one was looking. She was focused on her daily crossword.

"How's Ruth?" she asked, smirking.

"Thoroughly annoyed, surprisingly sharp, and ears like a bat."

"Maybe we should hire her, then."

"No argument there."

Casey caught Travis Johnson—the department rookie—up to speed on the night's events. Which, aside from the cold snap and the false kegger, was a whole lot of nothing.

He was finishing the last of his coffee when Travis cleared his throat.

"You used to go out with Allison Fischer, right?"

Casey clenched. "We talked for a while," he lied. It had been more than that. And it didn't end well.

"Thought about asking her out."

Casey paused, glancing up. "A little old for you, huh?"

Travis grinned, rubbing a hyper hand over his blonde buzzcut. "I'll take that as a yes." He proceeded to back out of the kitchen in exaggerated display—and promptly crashed into Sergeant Gordy Reynolds.

"Watch your six, son," Reynolds said.

"Sorry, Sarge."

Reynolds nodded at Casey. "Another night in the trenches, eh, Benson?"

"Something like that."

The Sergeant refilled his maize-and-blue U of M mug, glancing to a copy of the Westville Ledger with a headline that read '*DNR Investigating Deer Decapitation*.' He pulled a McMuffin from a crinkling McDonald's bag, unwrapped it and bit into it with a grotesquely loud, wet chew.

Casey thought of his time in Chicago when headlines screamed about shootings, muggings, and murder. In Westville, some decapitated deer ranked as major foul play.

Creepy? Sure. But Casey had no reason to think much of it.

"Well, Benson," Travis barked, heading toward the garage, "I'll make up for your share of the ticket quota this morning."

He walked with a stocky arms-out gait and Casey swore he ordered his uniform one size too small on purpose. He had won the department MCOLES fitness challenge, granted, but given his only real competition at this point was Casey, it wasn't saying much.

"Have at it," Casey called after him. Reynolds shook his head.

After clocking out, Casey changed in the locker room, swapping his uniform for a flannel, undershirt, and jeans. He ran a hand through his matted brown hair—probably getting too long for department standards—and caught the twitch of his left eyebrow in the mirror.

He'd had it ever since he fractured his orbital bone on a rusty trampoline at twelve, leaving him with a slight droop of his left eyelid—ptosis, the doctor had called it. His dad had taken the diagnosis with skepticism, as if waiting for a punchline that never came.

There wasn't much to do about it. So, Casey learned to live with it.

The running joke had been that it knocked him smart, since his academic aptitude went from mediocre to advanced in a hurry not long after. Casey never felt all that smart, more like he guessed right a lot and went with his first impulse. He didn't study nearly as hard as his fastidious older sister Mel, much to her chagrin. Truth was, he'd just decided to try—maybe to make up for the way his new look bothered him.

Nineteen years on, the crooked brow was just another mark of the past— wanted or not.

His thoughts drifted—unwanted—to the roadside memorial he'd passed earlier that morning. A white cross, a wreath of dead, dried flowers.

He shook the image away, grabbed his bag, and headed for the door.

"Benson, watch the phones for a minute?"

Gail didn't wait for an answer, already hobbling off toward the ladies' room.

"Sure thing," Casey muttered to no one. His stomach growled. Eggs and bacon at Fischer's sounded good. Maybe a waffle or two.

But Aly was probably working. And truth be told, he didn't have the energy.

Still, Travis's comment had stirred something up in him.

She'd been back in town six months now, ever since her dad passed, helping her mom run the restaurant. He hadn't seen much of her since the funeral—and before that, it had been two years since he broke things off. In a town of three thousand, though, you couldn't avoid each other forever.

The sharp trill of the phone cut through the silence. Casey let out a resigned sigh, picked up the receiver.

"Westville Police Department, Officer Benson speaking."

A beat of static-laden silence. Then a shaky inhale.

A woman's voice, tight with panic.

"Casey? It's Erin."

Erin Thompson.

Casey's first thought was Joe, passed out behind Riverbend again. Or worse—his car in a ditch or wrapped around a tree.

Westville had seen its share of tragic wrecks but he pushed down the worst assumption.

"Hey. Everything alright? Joe okay?"

"What? I mean—it's not Joe."

Her voice wavered.

"Erin, what's going on?"

A sharp breath. Then—

"God, I'm sorry . . . Millie."

A cold weight settled in Casey's gut.

"She didn't come home last night. I—I don't know where she is."

His mind spun.

"Maybe she stayed over at a friend's and forgot to tell you."

"I've called everyone. I don't know what to do."

Casey gripped the phone tighter. "I'll be right there."

4

Olivia Fischer woke with the taste of sick in her mouth.

She groaned and rolled over, every inch of her body protesting. The moment she moved, a thick wave of nausea surged up her throat, punishment for the cocktail of weed and cheap whiskey Brett Huizenga had stolen from his dad's liquor cabinet.

Her tongue felt like sandpaper, her palette sour, and when she breathed in deep a skunky stench clung to her nostrils. She reached for her matted red curls, pulled them close, and sniffed.

Yep. Biggest offender.

She rubbed her face, trying to piece together where Friday night ended and Saturday morning began. The blue curtains in her room were slightly drawn, and through the gap, gray light cut through, making her wonder just how late she'd slept in.

The house was too quiet.

For a second, panic flared—then she remembered.

Kathy (Mom) was out of town.

That was the whole reason she'd let loose last night, the reason she'd felt bold enough to down Jack Daniel's like she wasn't fourteen and stupid. Normally, by now, she would have poked her head in, fresh from opening the restaurant, nagging Olivia to get up, get dressed, be useful.

But if Kathy was with Aunt Stacy this weekend, that meant Aly was running the restaurant in her absence. Her jaw clenched at the thought of her much older sister, who'd moved back from Lansing permanently to help Mom run things after Dad died.

Six months already, she thought, choking down the realization.

Some part of her knew she should feel more than she did. But truth be told, by the time he was gone, she'd been ready for him to be. Or at least, that's what she told herself. Well before he got sick he and Kathy had been nothing but at each other's throats, stressed over the restaurant and who knew what else. After that, dad hadn't been himself the whole last year.

Brain cancer as it turned out, was a bitch.

Olivia shoved those thoughts away, blowing a tangled mess of curls out of her face. The silence pressed in around her, thick and suffocating, amplifying the pounding in her skull. She let her mind drift back to the night before.

Brett. Matt. Some sophomore girls whose names she never bothered remembering.

And—

Millie.

The thought hit her like a slap, and Olivia bolted upright—only to immediately regret it as her stomach churned violently.

She closed her eyes, replaying their argument.

You just had to have your fun, didn't you, Liv?

Her throat tightened. She needed to fix this.

And she knew exactly how to do it: *O.C.P.*

The two of them. Four months ago on a hot July afternoon. Riding in the back of Mr. Thompson's new truck from the Lakeshore with the windows down, screaming along to Naughty by Nature until their voices gave out, clutching their gas station loot.

"You down with O.C.P.?" Millie sang, waving her half-eaten Oatmeal Creme Pie in the air like a microphone.

Olivia had nearly choked on hers, laughing so hard she couldn't breathe. *"Yeah, you know me!"*

She'd needed to laugh, then.

Olivia swung her legs over the bed and grabbed her hoodie, her stomach a knotted mess, but a couple of Little Debbie's and a shared Coke slush could mend any rift between them.

Millie would probably roll her eyes, make some snide remark about them being laced with last night's weed, and Olivia would grin and say, "If only." Olivia would come back to youth group—pretend to take it seriously—before deciding she was over it.

It was sort of their routine.

Olivia dragged herself out of bed, ignoring the protest in her skull, and threw her hair into a painful ponytail with a teal scrunchie. She cracked the window, wincing against the gray morning glare, and stuck her hand out into the chill, and a soup of fog.

She grabbed cargo jeans from the floor, sniffed her windbreaker, gagged, and swapped it for a salmon Reebok sweatshirt over her Green Day tee.

Then—without thinking twice—she grabbed her bike and headed out.

The cold wet air slapped her awake as she pedaled toward the 7-11.

Ahead fog hung thick, swallowing the Main Street buildings in gray haze. She squinted up at the PRINCE sign, its red glow bleeding through the mist, and crossed just as a pickup roared through the fog with headlights off.

She swerved, heart lurching, and called after the driver in a creative combo of curses that probably made her prudish grandmother roll over in her grave-- God rest her soul.

By the time she rolled up to the convenience store, she had her breath back.

She grabbed OCPs, Coke slush, and two straws.

The perfect peace offering.

As she headed for the Thompsons', something settled in her gut—cold and heavy, making her shiver. Maybe it was the cold snap. Maybe it was the guilt, heavy and sour, from ditching Millie and indulging in last night's whiskey and weed. She hadn't hated the way it felt at first—the warmth, the looseness— right up until she'd thrown up on Brett's shoes. But as she rode further past the old high school and banked onto Millie's street, a creeping dread clawed at the edges of her thoughts, growing stronger with every stroke of the pedals.

Olivia skidded to a halt.

A police car sat parked in front of the house. Her chest tightened as she stood there, legs akimbo over her bike, frozen.

Why the hell was there a cop here?

The cold she'd been trying to ignore now felt brutal, like ice sinking into her skin.

She felt sick all over again.

Olivia slunk around the side of the house, heart hammering. Some part of her screamed to turn back, but she couldn't. She reached the backyard, creeping toward Millie's slider door. Her breath fogged the glass as she peered inside.

Millie's room was empty. Pristine. The bed was made—neat and perfect, just like Millie always kept it.

Her stomach dropped.

So where is she?

From inside the house, she heard voices.

Adult voices. Serious voices.

Her pulse pounded in her ears and every nerve in her body screamed for her to listen. But something told her she wouldn't like what she was about to hear.

5

Within three minutes of hanging up the phone, Casey was walking up to the front porch of Joe and Erin's house, a two-story historic home four blocks from the station.

Reynolds hadn't liked him taking the call—he was already over his hours, out of uniform—but everyone else was tied up, and Chief Hart was off for the day hunting up north. He took the cruiser since technically it *was* police business. His own boat of a vehicle—grandpa's old silver '71 Monte Carlo— sat in the drive at his duplex. He walked the mile to the station most days when he could, and to most places in Westville. It helped him think, and sometimes helped his migraines.

Casey knocked, though he didn't need to.

Joe had offered him the spare bedroom when he'd first moved back, and said he could stay as long as he needed. It would've saved Casey from renting, but it became apparent quickly that Joe and Erin had enough to work through without him haunting their hallway. He felt for his friend, knowing that he'd wanted to get out of this town with Erin, but when they got pregnant just out of high school it seemed to have sealed Joe's fate as heir apparent to the PRINCE throne.

Inside, Erin was in her blue scrubs, just off a shift at the nursing home or late for one.

She was yelling at someone over the cordless phone, voice sharp, frustration crackling through every syllable, before slamming it down. The plastic receiver toppled to the floor, and Erin slapped a hand against the counter, her jaw clenched so tight it looked like it might crack.

Casey walked over, picked up the phone, and set it back on the receiver.

Erin exhaled sharply, wiping her eyes. "Didn't hear you come in."

"That Joe?" Casey asked, nodding toward the phone, though he already knew.

Erin gave a tight nod. "He's on his way."

Casey sighed. "So Millie wasn't planning on staying anywhere last night?"

"No. And if she was, she would've told us." Erin's voice wavered. "This isn't like her."

Casey agreed. Millie, for all intents and purposes, might as well have been his honorary niece. And Millie was not reckless. She wasn't the sneaking-off, lying-to-her-parents kind of kid.

"How long's it been since you saw her?"

"She left here for the football game around six."

Right. Games were being played down at Birch Field by the fairgrounds one more season, since the new stadium wasn't finished yet.

"Who was supposed to pick her up?"

Erin hesitated. Glanced at the phone.

"...It was supposed to be Joe."

Casey's stomach turned.

He already knew where this was going, but he hoped he was wrong.

Three weeks ago, Roger Osmond at Riverbend Saloon had called the station saying Joe was passed out in the men's bathroom. Casey had picked him up, like too many times before.

"I know, Case. I know," Joe muttered, wiping his mouth after puking on the side of the road.

"Erin needs you sober. So does Millie."

"Don't tell me what my family needs."

"Well, maybe you need to hear it."

Joe had stayed quiet after that, until they pulled up to the house.

"You're a good friend, man."

"I'd rather not be the kind of friend who has to pick you up outside a bar."

"I'll be better."

"You need me to take you to get the truck tomorrow?"

"I'll figure it out."

Casey had hoped that he would. That it would be the last time. Apparently, it wasn't.

He forced himself back into the present.

"So Joe wasn't around last night."

Erin shook her head. "No. He was up at the cabin, 'clearing his head' again." She really laid on the flair with the air quotes. "I couldn't reach him."

"Who would she have been with at the game?"

"She said she was meeting Liv."

Casey frowned.

Then it clicked. Aly's younger sister.

Erin's voice tightened. "What do we do now?"

"First we should file a report."

Erin nodded, eyes glistening. He grabbed the phone, calling Gail at the station. "We're coming in. Let Reynolds know."

Erin sighed. "Let me grab some things."

Casey nodded, leaned against the counter near the fridge. He winced against a blooming, fatigue induced headache. Then something slapped to the floor.

Three fridge magnets had slid down. The biggest, a ceramic green frog holding an umbrella and a thermometer fell to the ground completely, cracking off one bulbous eye. It had clipped a polaroid photo of Millie with none other than Olivia Fischer, posing and laughing on the train trestles by the dam.

Casey replaced the magnet on the fridge, and set the eye on the counter, as Erin reappeared from down the hall. They walked out the door just as Joe's new blue Ford roared down the street. He parked it crooked, left it running, and jumped out.

Joe had the Thompson height and a few inches on Casey. When they were kids he was the far superior athlete, Casey chasing his stats on the basketball team and in general much less confident, cool and collected than his friend who had essentially been the figurative and literal 'Prince' of Westville High. Even with the increase of flab that too much alcohol often brought with it, Joe was undoubtedly stronger, though Casey had tried to buckle down since becoming a cop, having picked up running and biking again.

Joe had also inherited his dad's receding hairline, retaining a thin covering of blonde.

Casey at least had fuller hair. Small victories.

Right now, his friend looked like hell—bags under his eyes, a slack look to his mouth, and moving slow. Probably more than just a bad night's sleep.

Joe pulled Erin into a hug, and for a moment, she fought it until she folded, body racked with sobs.

Casey might have been pissed as hell at Joe, but now wasn't the time.

"We were heading to the station to file a report," he said, voice even.

Erin shoved Joe off, stepping back.

"Dammit, Joe. Why do you do this?"

"Erin—"

"Just don't."

Erin bit her lip, sidestepped as Joe reached for her shoulder, and climbed into the passenger seat of the truck and slammed the door.

Joe ran a big hand down his face.

"…I'm sorry, Case."

Casey shook his head and tried to offer his best consolatory smile, and glanced toward the passenger side door where Erin sat. "Don't apologize to me."

Joe sighed. "Right."

Casey nodded. "Meet you at the station."

He got in his car and pulled away, mind already running through the next steps. They needed to talk to anyone who might have seen Millie last.

And right now, that looked like Olivia Fischer.

His brow twitched as he banked left. He hadn't mentioned to Erin or Joe the sinking feeling he had as Ruth Potter's noise complaint clawed at the edge of his mind.

A red light flickering in the woods.

Kids partying and yelling by the cabin.

Or maybe just *one* kid screaming.

He didn't want to think that way. The friend in him refused to entertain it. But then, thinking in best-case scenarios wasn't part of a cop's job.

Still, he pushed the thought down. Not yet. It wasn't the next logical step.

They needed to talk to anyone who might have been the last to see Millie.

They'd start with Olivia.

6

The pickup snarled out of the drive.

Olivia crouched low by the fence, pulse hammering, hoping they wouldn't spot her bike.

She peered around the corner, catching a glimpse of Mrs. Thompson's face in the passenger seat—red, twisted, crumpled with something Olivia didn't want to name.

She wanted to believe that Millie was in the backseat of that pickup.

Or in the cop car, ready to tell them everything.

If it meant ratting Olivia out for smoking pot and drinking stolen whiskey down by the dam—hell, that would have been better.

Because it would mean she was safe.

But Olivia knew what she'd heard. Hangover or not, she knew.

Millie hadn't come home last night.

Her stomach twisted violently, and she thought she was going to vomit all over her Vans.

She swore percussively under her breath, remounted her bike, and tore away from the house, pedaling toward downtown.

I should've just gone back with her.

She thought of those news stories of girls gone missing. Her chest tightened.

As she neared the police station, paranoia spiked. She yanked the handlebars, veering hard onto the riverwalk, cutting across Main Street, pushing toward the woods near the river behind the row of historic buildings where the train tracks crossed the water.

The farther she went, the colder she felt.

Then she screeched to a halt.

A postcard-perfect view stretched before her—a snapshot from someplace called Reality, Michigan.

Welcome back, Olivia Fischer.

The train trestles stretched over the frothing river, the dam roaring beneath. The sound drowned out everything else.

Later, Olivia would realize this was the last place anyone had seen Millie Thompson.

Later, she would realize that last night, she had done more than just make a stupid mistake.

She had damned Millie Thompson.

1

Fischer's Café was no exception to the rule in Westville: the more the outside world changed, the more things stayed locked in a time capsule of old routines and miraculously preserved locales.

The bell hanging over the door gave a pitiful hollow ring as Casey stepped into the restaurant, cueing the familiar din of breakfast chatter over Melissa Ethridge growling *I'm The Only One* through old speakers on either side of the restaurant. The greasy scent of diner comfort food hit him—a heady mix of sizzling bacon, onions, and poorly ventilated, sodium-laced air mingling with a stale, acrid cigarette smoke bellowed by black-lunged patrons.

Then there were the clowns, which, for reasons beyond human comprehension, Fischer's was chock-full of.

Framed portraits lined the walls—an array of middle-aged men in white makeup with red noses and lips—some pouting, others gleefully glaring down at customers in the booths. One leered like a madman. Porcelain figurines filled a glass display case—tiny, 1950s-style cartoonish jesters and ring leaders frozen mid-laugh, eyes glossy and soulless.

As a kid, Casey had imagined them coming to life at night, creeping out of their see-through prison, kitchen knives in tiny hands to lie in wait for their human jailers.

As a 31-year-old gun-carrying cop, the thought still creeped him out a little. He'd sometimes fantasized about taking a few of them to the makeshift shooting range above the station in the old community theater, to see how well they stood up to a .40 cal Glock—just to put the nightmare to bed.

But these days, what really gave him pause was Aly Fischer.

He'd been avoiding her for months, steering clear on the days she worked, keeping an eye out for that lime-green Volkswagen Beetle in the lot. Hard to miss. A week ago, she'd been in a fender bender, something Travis had responded to, hence his sudden interest. For now, she was sharing her mom's old woody station wagon.

Today, though, he needed to see her. He needed to know if her sister had been with Millie last night—and if she'd seen her come home. Otherwise, they could be looking at two missing girls, not just one. Worst-case scenarios. One of the joys of the job.

He scanned the restaurant—both the smoking and nonsmoking sections which were separated by a grand total of about fifteen feet and said second-hand smoke permeating every corner regardless—for Aly's signature blonde ponytail, bobbing purposefully as she worked. Not seeing her, he stepped up to the host stand. A longtime waitress named Julie, whose tan weathered skin stretched taut over a wiry frame, flashed him a grin that was more like an exasperated grimace.

"Usual table's open," she said, nodding toward the booth on the left.

"Not staying, actually," Casey said, though a sudden dull blade of hunger prodded at him. He peered over Julie's shoulder to the food window and into the kitchen. "Aly on today?"

Julie's painted-on eyebrow arched. "What am I, chopped liver?"

Casey sighed and flashed a smile. "Just the usual to-go, thanks."

That was when he caught the sound of Aly's voice among the mingling chatter, hacking chuckles of old town curmudgeons, and the chaotic din of young families with screaming toddlers. A voice that had a way of making him feel lighter. Even now, with Millie missing, Erin falling to pieces at the station, and Joe probably barely holding it together.

It loosened something inside him.

He followed the sound toward the non-smoking section, nearly colliding with her as she rounded the corner. She stopped short, a curse dying on her lips.

"Sorry, I—" She looked up, recognition flaring in her green eyes. "...Casey."

"Hey."

"Haven't seen you around here lately."

It wasn't a question, but had the unspoken edge of one. He thought it best not to mention he'd been actively avoiding her. "Been putting in a lot of hours." At least that wasn't a lie.

"I can tell," she said. Probably thinking he looked like hell, which was how he felt.

She moved past him to the food window, balancing two plates on her arm and scraping the remains into the trash with notable vigor.

Casey followed, and stood awkwardly in the doorway.

"I need to ask you something," he said.

Aly narrowed her eyes in the way that often came with a wry smirk. Not this time. Right now she just looked guarded, like she was looking at a stranger. Maybe she was.

"I'm not sure now's the time," she said, grabbing two more plates of eggs and bacon off the warmer, and a third with a whipped cream smothered waffle probably to abate the screeching toddler behind them.

He raised his voice over the noise. "It's not about—" He exhaled. "Look, do you know where your sister is?"

"Probably home," she said slowly. "Sleeping like the dead. The usual for a Saturday." Aly skirted past him, but paused. "...Why?"

"Millie Thompson is missing. Looks like Olivia might've been one of the last to see her."

The plates wavered in her hands and her green eyes flashed.

"When?"

8

A few minutes later, they sat in a booth near the back entrance of the restaurant.

When Julie dropped off his food 'to-go', she rolled her eyes. Casey wolfed down some scrambled eggs, scraping the bottom of the Styrofoam container with a plastic fork.

He filled Aly in. Told her that Erin called just after his shift, that Joe had been by her place earlier looking for Millie. He'd knocked. No answer. Erin had called too. Aly frowned, got up, and went to the kitchen phone.

When she came back, her face was drawn tight. "They already checked with the Andersons?"

"As far as I know. Can you think of anywhere else she'd be on a Saturday?"

"These days, she's usually with Millie. Riding their bikes. Maybe the bowling alley?"

Casey washed down the last bite of bacon with coffee and glanced at the tacky clown clock on the wall—a bozo-esque figurine with ruffled sleeves and gloved fingers pointed tauntingly as seconds ticked away. 10:37 a.m. Roughly fourteen hours missing.

He exhaled sharply, rubbing his left temple.

"I've gotta go."

Aly blinked. "Where?"

"The Boy Scout cabin. Ruth Potter called in a noise complaint this morning. She thought she heard kids partying out there again."

Aly's expression darkened and she crossed her arms.

"You think it was them?"

"I don't know." He pushed back from the table. "But that's all I've got."

Aly frowned in a way that would put most smiles to shame. "What do you want me to do?" she asked.

Casey realized then that it was the most they'd talked since her dad died— and before that, it had been almost a year. He had wanted to apologize for the way things ended. Or rather, didn't end—just sort of faded into nothing. He wanted to say something. But it was hard, maybe pointless, to apologize when you knew nothing was going to change, and the tick of the clock pushed him forward.

"Find your sister," Casey said. "Make sure she's safe. Take her to the station. We need to see if she knows anything about Millie."

Aly hesitated. Just for a second.

Then—a sharp nod.

Casey muttered a quick thanks, already heading for the front door.

The bell over the entrance coughed out a weak, pitiful ring behind him.

9

Olivia pushed her bike down the sidewalk, the chain clicking laboriously. Mist rose from the roaring dam, seeping over rooftops of Main Street buildings then curling into trees of fading fall colors along the river.

On the other side of the street, the Showboat was a listless ghost ship, steam rising as if something simmered under the dark waters of the Slate. She paused and watched water frothing beneath trestles with muted fury, and she felt a lurch in her stomach.

Come on Millie, where are you?

The thought ricocheted inside her skull, bouncing like a pinball, triggering uglier thoughts.

Why had she chosen those idiot boys over Millie? All she got out of it was a pounding head and reeking hair.

She tried to shake it off, but the feeling clung to her, heavy as the damp fog.

If they'd walked back together, maybe Millie wouldn't be—

She shoved the worst thoughts away.

She was just . . . somewhere else.

Somewhere.

She kept moving, her black and white checkered Vans scraping against the worn sidewalk. At any moment, she expected a cop car to pull up, sirens blaring, ready to haul her in. They'd tell her they knew—about the fight (for some reason), about the party (seemed more plausible), about her being the last person to see Millie before she disappeared (probably true).

A bleak future of scenarios flashed in her mind. No driver's license, no job, and the weight of knowing her best friend was gone because of her.

Okay, maybe that was extreme.

But maybe not.

She thought about what she would have done, granted Millie wouldn't ditch her for boys. Still, trying to suspend disbelief, she thought that she probably would have sulked around for a while and gone home. But if Millie *had* just gone for a walk to clear her head, she wouldn't have stayed out all night. Millie was careful, cautious.

In other words, she wasn't like Olivia.

The possibilities gnawed. Either Millie had gotten hurt—or someone had hurt her.

As Olivia reached the end of the historic district she turned and found herself staring up at the many silos and bins of PRINCE Milling, where train tracks snaked over the concrete on the road to the fairgrounds.

She didn't know what she was hoping to find. She'd seen Millie walking across the trestles last night on the way to the game, so this was probably the way she'd have gone back.

Olivia followed the tracks toward the river. Signs posted around the yard warned about trespassing, but she ignored them.

What's the point? she asked herself. *I'm not going to find anything. I'm just doing this to make myself feel better.*

Millie was going to show up, crying and apologizing to her parents. They'd sit together later, laugh about how ridiculous it all was. Olivia would apologize for being an idiot, and Millie would forgive her because that's what they did. Everything would go back to how it was before.

Olivia walked past graffitied train cars, their colors muted in the foggy overcast day. Over the hum of the mill she heard the distant screech of brakes and the hollow clang of metal. A train rumbled somewhere down the line.

There was a shuddering.

She turned toward what she thought was the loading dock, as the doors of a freight elevator opened with a grinding whine. A single red light in a metal cage flickered overhead at the top of the stairs. A shabby looking man in a gray PRINCE Milling shirt emerged from the elevator. He walked toward some kind of vehicle covered in a tarp.

Olivia felt a hitch in her chest. A feeling she probably shouldn't be there and probably shouldn't step closer. *Could be the trespassing signs, Liv.*

But she did anyway.

The man turned her direction immediately.

"Can I help you?" he called out.

"No, I'm good," she said. But she didn't move. Something kept her there.

He walked out of the loading dock, and into the pale, overcast light of day, far enough into the road that it forced her back a little. She could see the dark bags under his eyes, greasy brown thinning hair lined with flecks of gray. She glanced at the red name tag under the red crown logo that read 'Ethan.'

"You shouldn't be here, kid," his voice low and gravelly. 'Ethan' didn't just look at her like she didn't belong there—he looked at her as if she'd done something deeply offensive to him personally. She glanced down at his pant legs—dirty—and his boots, caked with mud.

This is a mill, not a farm.

"What's with the dirt?" she wanted to say.

What she said instead was, "Sorry. Just . . . looking for something I lost."

"Hm," he murmured, wiping his nose with a hard sniff. "On the train tracks?"

"I don't know where. If I did, I wouldn't be looking."

Olivia immediately regretted the smart remark, especially when he took a couple of steps closer.

"Alright, yeah. I'm going," she muttered.

He didn't move a muscle. "That'd be best."

Olivia backed away, her pulse quickening.

When she glanced over her shoulder, he was watching her, eyes drilling into the back of her skull like he was trying to examine her brain matter.

Back on the sidewalk, Olivia felt that catch in her chest again. Something about that guy bothered her. She thought of his boots.

What had he been up to? Maybe she was just being paranoid. Probably, that was it.

She just needed to talk to somebody. She thought of Kyle and Austin. Maybe they'd seen Millie at the game after their fight.

Olivia walked her bike over to the Shell station and rummaged in her pockets for enough spare change to use the dingy old payphone around the back. She dialed Austin's number first because it was the one she had memorized, but when he didn't answer, she grabbed the phonebook and searched for 'Anderson'.

Kyle had just moved several months back, and their family had gotten a new number. Luckily, this happened to be the new phonebook.

The phone rang and rang, and the line went dead. Not even an answering machine. She managed to scrape together just enough change for one last call.

Come on, come on. "Pick up, dumbass," she hissed.

No answer, and no more coins. She slammed the phone back on the receiver.

Then it hit her. She wasn't sure why she hadn't thought of it before.

Kyle had joined that bowling league on Saturday mornings—at least that's what he told his parents—so he and Austin could meet there and play arcade games.

She hoped to God that's where they were.

Olivia climbed back onto her bike, glancing one last time toward the mill loading dock.

The overhead door groaned shut. And standing just inside the darkened dock, shadowed by the overhang—Ethan watched her ride away.

10

Olivia sailed down the sidewalk, her white-knuckled grip locked on the handlebars.

The wind whipped her hair, cold air stinging her face, but she barely felt it. She blew past Valley View Trailer Park, tucked behind a row of tall pine-like trees, an oversized hedgerow that acted as a curtain or fence depending on who you asked.

She drew a deep breath. *Focus on the next thing.*

A mile ahead just before the bowling alley, the over-tall sign for *Boon's Salvage Yard* poked out where tractors and junkers went to die.

Olivia hated that place—a graveyard for decrepit cars, their rusted husks piled high, waiting to be picked clean. The ending of *The Brave Little Toaster* ran through her mind—cars singing as their lives flashed before their headlights, right before the compactor crushed them into nothing. A horror movie for kids if there ever was one.

Except Boon's didn't have a massive, magnetized trash compactor—thank God.

Olivia gripped the handles so tight the skin of her palms stretched and stung.

OK, something else.

A familiar tan station wagon pulled up beside her onto the shoulder of the road.

"Liv!" Aly's voice came sharp and urgent from the driver's side window. "Get in. We need to talk."

Olivia swallowed. At this point, she needed to talk to someone—anyone. But her sister . . . no. She wouldn't understand. She never did, and Olivia didn't want a lecture.

"Not right now," Olivia said, pedaling harder. "I have somewhere to be."

Anywhere but in that car with her.

She banked hard, veering into the trailer park, cutting through to Rowe Street. Her sister followed.

Aly leaned out the window, voice cutting through the cold.

"Liv, stop. It's about Millie."

Olivia skidded to a halt.

The words were ice down her spine. The whole town was going to hear soon.

"I know," Olivia muttered, kicking at the pavement. Her voice cracked. "I—I don't know what to do."

Aly's voice softened. "You can start by getting in the car."

Olivia tossed her bike in the back and climbed into the passenger seat. Aly shook her head, pulling onto the road.

"You should've come to the restaurant."

"Wasn't hungry."

Aly shot her a look. "Don't be a smartass."

She glanced over, but Olivia pretended to look out the window, watching the Rocky Lake Apartments, the dog park, the pieces of Westville blurring past.

"Were you with her last night?"

Olivia swallowed hard.

"Yeah."

She clenched her hands into fists in her lap.

"We got into a fight . . . and she walked off on her own."

The truth tasted bitter. The memory of Millie's retreating figure, swallowed by the night—it wouldn't leave her head. Her chest tightened as Aly turned toward Main Street, toward downtown.

". . . Where are we going?"

Aly hesitated. "To the police station." Her grip tightened on the wheel. "They want to ask some questions."

So this was it.

The Westville Police Station wasn't big or imposing.

Then—Olivia saw them.

Millie's parents. Huddled in the small kitchenette, whispering, their faces pale, eyes red. Mrs. Thompson met her gaze—and Olivia's own worry tightened around her throat, making her eyes burn hot.

Keep it together, Olivia.

She clenched her jaw, turning away. She couldn't break down. Not yet.

The questions came fast. She tried to hold it in.

But then—she cried.

She told them everything. She told them about the fight, about the party, about Millie walking away. She gave them names. Names of every kid who'd been by the river last night.

She thought—*this is it.*

This is the worst of it. Ripping off the Band-Aid.

That once they had more information, they'd find Millie.

She didn't realize this was only the beginning.

That Millie's disappearance would be the first crack in a dam of secrets that would flood Westville. And no one was prepared.

Least of all Olivia Fischer.

11

He'd been suppressing the instinct ever since Erin's call came through.

But there was a sinking certainty now, that this was more than anyone was willing to admit—that Millie Thompson hadn't just wandered off or decided to crash at a friend's place.

As the morning dragged on, dread coiled tighter in Casey's gut, the statistics of missing kids circling his mind; like a cruel, broken carousel.

48 hours.

After that the odds were slim at best and better described as grim. His unease only deepened when he pulled back into the dirt turnaround near the old Boy Scout cabin.

He wondered if it counted as deja vu if he'd been there only hours earlier, though the fog had retreated toward the riverbank and seeped into the woods. Now, Casey could see what he hadn't before—or what he hadn't wanted to.

The rusted gate leading back to Scout Park was slightly ajar. The chain hung limp, clattering against the red iron as the breeze picked up. The padlock lay in the dirt, sheared clean through. Casey knelt, running his thumb along the jagged edges of the metal—sharp and biting.

That's when he noticed the deep tire tracks. A heavy vehicle had been through here. He pushed the gate open, wrapped the broken padlock in one of his loose gloves and slipped it into his jacket pocket.

His eyes narrowed as he stepped further down the two-track that spilled out into the clearing. He examined the leaf-choked forest floor and traced the winding trail, lingering mist from the river weaving between trees like spider's thread.

"Anyone out there?" he called. Heavy silence pressed back. He tried again. "Millie?" Calling her name made it real.

Only his voice returned, echoing back, her name distorted and haunting.

A chill ran through him, raising the hairs on the back of his neck. The forest deathly still.

Casey turned back, and he saw it.

A neon yellow and gray Sony Discman lying in the fog-damp grass, lid open. A CD—a black disc with white text reading *Jagged Little Pill.* Black headphones lay tangled beside it, the cord limp and haphazard.

He put one knee down in damp grass and grabbed the Discman, an image careening into his mind: Millie, sitting on the back porch of Joe's place the week before, waving at him as he walked into the yard. "Hey, Uncle Nut-Case!" she'd shouted, wearing the same headphones he now held in his trembling hands, the yellow CD player resting in her lap.

Casey's brow twitched, then ached, and he felt the sudden swelling pang of a migraine.

Spots took over his vision as he stood, the fleshy black of closed eyelids, swelling to strange, pixelated shades of violet and red. He regained his orientation as worst-case scenarios bled in—less paranoia now and more real possibility.

He swore under his breath, stormed back to the patrol car. He yanked open the driver's side door, the radio crackling faintly.

"This is Benson. I found—"

The words barely left his mouth when a strange sound drifted through the woods—a soft hiss, distant, like air leaking from a tire.

The hissing grew louder, morphing into something sharper—static on a detuned radio. Then came a low groaning, as if the trees were bowing to a gale force wind that wasn't there.

A cold shiver crawled up Casey's spine, as something red flashed in his periphery near the trees.

He spun around. Nothing.

It was faint when it came, almost inaudible—a whisper. It brushed past his ear, chilling, garbled and sounding like a tape being rewound and fast forwarded all at once.

"You're the guilty ones . . ."

Casey whipped back around, every nerve in his body screaming, but the clearing stood empty. Light wind. His pulse roared in his ears. Maybe it had just been the rustling of the leaves, the scrape of branches twisting against each other.

"Benson. You copy?" Chief Hart's voice.

Casey panted to catch his breath, glancing around wildly.

"Yeah, I'm here," Casey breathed, clutching the radio. "I've got something."

Casey put a hand on his brow and tried to settle his nerves.

"Well, so do we," Hart said. "Get back to the station, over."

Whatever they had, it didn't sound good, if the Chief's tone was any indication.

"On my way."

He grabbed an evidence bag and gloves from the car, collected the Walkman, got in the driver's seat. He flipped on the siren, the red and blue lights spearing through the last shreds of morning fog as he sped down the dirt drive. The memory of Mrs. Potter's words echoed in his mind.

Red lights in the woods.

He shook the thought away and hit the gas.

Later, Casey would remember this moment. He would mark it as the moment everything in Westville changed.

He didn't know then that Millie was no longer the only one missing—or that they had a suspect.

RUMOR MILL

It was too dark to see.

The air, thick and humid.

There was a familiar sound she couldn't place, but mangled, distorted and oppressive.

Like a constant growling exhale, blowing warm fetid air against her cheeks.

Something was wrapped around her head, and she could barely move.

Caught somewhere between sleep and dreaming.

There was a pressure in her arm, stabbing into her skin.

A voice, resonating, and echoing, said, "Collect what you can. Then give her a break."

Something warm dripped on her leg, and she heard the tap, tap, tap of drips on the floor.

She wanted to go home. She wanted to wake up from this nightmare.

Something deep inside her said she wouldn't be doing either.

1

Casey slid the clear evidence bag containing the Discman across the counter to Larry, a part time retiree lab tech.

He watched it skid to a stop, scuffed and left out overnight in the cold.

Larry tagged it with a label, logged it in.

"Let's get some men over on the scene," Chief Frank Hart said to Gail, his voice gruff, low, steady. "Put a call into the county sheriff if need be."

Gail, already picking up a ringing phone, nodded.

"Johnson's there now," she said. "and DeYoung's on his way."

Hart wore remnants of his hunting gear—boots dusted with mud and a jacket reeking of wood. He had cut his weekend short, or rather off completely, when he got the call, showing up in his usual fashion: ready to drop everything for the town and the people in it.

Casey admired the longtime Westville police veteran but saw the cost of that kind of diligence—a mustache of far more salt than pepper, short, fading hair, and permanent bags of fatigue hanging beneath pale eyes.

He nodded at Casey as he strode out of the admin office and said, "You look like you've seen better days."

Ironic given how Casey was thinking the same about him.

"You could say it's been that kind of night. Or morning, I guess."

Chief Hart pulled him aside, his face tight as he relayed the latest.

"We got a call from First UMC. Howard Meyers never brought the church bus back. No one can get a hold of him or track him down. We're looking at two people missing now."

Casey's stomach sank like a stone.

"And," Hart continued, "someone at the Shell station reported seeing Millie talking with Howard last night. He was running his shuttle route for the game."

A muscle in Casey's neck tensed.

A missing girl. A missing bus driver.

Both last seen in the same place.

"We think he's a suspect?"

Hart's mouth flattened into a grim line. "I would have hoped to hell not, but based on those tracks by the cabin and the fact we've got a witness putting the two of them together . . ." He shook his head, a flicker of doubt in his eyes. "If things go that way we'll have a whole town of angry, scared parents wondering if they've had a wolf in sheep's clothing around for years." He sighed, rubbing his temple. "Couldn't be, though. Had his trouble with drinking back in the day, but . . ." Hart trailed off.

He was trying to convince himself.

"The guy wouldn't hurt a fly," Casey chimed in, more to break the tension, but also because he believed it. Howard was something of a gentle giant, and he had a hard time picturing him as anything but. Then, wasn't that what everyone said about the ones who ended up in the electric chair?

Casey started toward the interview room, footsteps echoing down the hall. Before he could reach the door, Sergeant Gordy Reynolds stepped out. His face was grim, lined with a kind of fatigue Casey recognized. He gave a brief nod and moved past.

Aly stepped out next. Her hand was steadying Olivia's shoulder. Olivia's fiery green eyes darted around the hallway, landing on Casey for only a split second before she looked away.

Not fear.

Something sharper. Irritation. Frustration.

A quiet exchange passed between Casey and Aly—a recognition of the worry pressing down on all of them.

Olivia crossed her arms.

Her face was puffy from crying, but her eyes burned with defiance, her red hair wild, unkempt, reflecting that same fire inside her. Casey cleared his throat, keeping his tone even.

"Thanks for coming in."

She huffed, glancing away. "Yeah, sure . . ." she muttered. "Just doing my civic duty."

Aly shot her a look, but Olivia's gaze flicked back to Casey, her frustration boiling over.

"So, what's the plan now?" Her voice was tight, edged with something dangerously close to anger. "Are we just going to sit here talking about it, or is someone actually out there looking for her?"

Aly's hand moved to calm her, but Olivia shook it off.

She stepped forward. "Millie's out there—scared, maybe hurt, or worse. And you're all in here, acting like this is just another case file to put in a drawer."

Reynolds spoke first, his tone measured.

"We're doing everything we can to find Emily."

"It's Millie," Olivia scoffed, crossing her arms tighter. "And everything you can? You can't get out of this building. I bet I could find more people willing to look for her than you have here."

She glared past Casey, daring him to argue. Casey let out a slow breath, forcing himself not to react. Because the truth was, if he were in her shoes, he'd be doing the same thing. A tense silence followed.

Casey met Olivia's eyes and cleared his throat in an effort to steady his voice. "You're right. We should be out there. There are other officers securing the scene now. We'll find her."

But as the words left his mouth, Casey saw disbelief lingering in her eyes.

Aly's hand hovered near Olivia's shoulder, uncertain. Olivia turned sharply, stalking toward the door. Aly lingered a moment longer, eyes meeting Casey's.

A quiet plea for patience.

"If she thinks of anything else, we'll call."

Casey gave a stiff nod, watching as Aly followed her sister out.

Casey exhaled, glancing toward the lobby.

Joe and Erin Thompson sat motionless, worn down, exhausted. Erin looked like she'd aged ten years overnight, a cup of coffee trembling in her hands as she stared blankly past the blinds.

Joe was pacing, tension etched into every movement. For a second, Casey wondered if he should say something. But what the hell was there to say? What comfort was there?

He turned away, his mind already racing ahead.

Millie was missing.

Howard Meyers was missing.

Whatever connection there was, it couldn't be good.

And the longer they stayed that way—the less likely they were to come back at all.

2

A half-hour later, the door opened and in came Jack and Mary Thompson.

Jack's big presence was commanding as he assessed the room, eyes settling on Joe.

Casey noted Joe's discomfort immediately; he seemed unable to look his father in the eye, his hands clenching and unclenching around the floral paper coffee cup until he crushed it and hit the rim of a wastebasket, falling to the floor.

Joe abruptly stalked over to his father. There were harsh whispers, and Casey averted his eyes for a moment, until from behind he saw Joe shove his father, turn and leave the room. Jack straightened his flannel with one hand, the other clenched tight.

A rustle of murmurs went up from the few department staff and others in the lobby as he stormed out, leaving Erin to watch him in silence.

Mary greeted Casey and made nervous small talk, asking how Dave and Deb were doing since the move. He said they were good and ignored the fact that Mary was prying about his mom's early stage dementia diagnosis. It hadn't gotten bad yet. Hardly noticeable.

Still, he didn't like to think about it.

Jack's eyes lingered on the door, his expression a mixture of disappointment and frustration. He turned to Casey, his tone formal but laced with a subtle edge.

"Good to see you, Case. Shame it's under these circumstances."

Casey nodded and shook his hand, his chest tightening. Jack had a certain way of making everyone feel on trial. He remembered it well from when they were kids, and though that judgement fell heaviest on Joe growing up, he had felt it too by proximity.

Jack's eyes drifted back to the doorway where Joe had disappeared, tucked something in his pocket that jangled against loose change.

"Sometimes I wonder if I taught that boy anything about handling responsibility," he muttered, just loud enough for Casey to hear. "And now this . . ." His voice trailed off, a mixture of anger and regret flashing across his face.

Casey's jaw tightened. "He's doing his best, Jack. We all are. It's his daughter that's missing."

Jack's mouth thinned into a hard line. "That's my granddaughter too. And if Joe had—" He stopped himself, glancing toward Mary, who was visibly uncomfortable with the tension.

Casey met Jack's eyes, feeling strange all of a sudden being in a position of proximal authority over a man whom Casey had worked under at PRINCE for multiple summers, his imposing stature seeming all the more so back then.

"Best we can do right now is stay calm. Chief is organizing a search party."

A flicker of faint recognition passed over Jack's face, but he didn't respond. Instead, he gave a stiff nod, acknowledging Casey's point—or at least letting it go for the moment.

The cold air bit through Casey's jacket as he stepped down the station's front steps to where Joe stood, staring off toward the Riverwalk and the glistening lights on the showboat, bright white reflecting on the pitch-dark Slate River.

Joe grabbed at his nose and adjusted his jacket. "I just . . . needed some air." His voice was strained, as if speaking at all took everything in him.

Casey placed a firm hand on his friend's shoulder.

"We'll find her, man. We will."

Joe's jaw tensed. Before he could respond, the station door creaked open behind them.

"Casey. A word," the Chief said.

Joe didn't wait. He just turned, walked toward his truck, climbed in, and revved the engine. Casey watched him go, headlights cutting through the thickening fog, tires grinding against the pavement as he peeled off into the night.

A prickle crawled up the back of Casey's neck.

He turned and saw Jack Thompson, standing in the doorway. Watching. Not after Joe—not entirely. More like looking out into the town, to the neighborhoods and searching the aether for anyone who knew anything about Millie or had anything to do with it.

It was the same look Casey remembered from high school basketball regionals, when Jack had stood at the edge of the court, eyes locked on Joe's every move.

Like he was memorizing it all—or watching something slip away.

Casey glanced down the street, toward the old high school. Where that very game had been played.

Then Hart cleared his throat, drawing Casey's attention back up the stairs.

"You need some rest, son."

Casey turned back to the Chief, shaking off the unease.

"I'll manage."

Though even now, his skull swelled with stored-up fatigue.

Hart studied him.

"I'm sure you would. But you're way over on hours."

Casey clenched, the protest rising in his throat.

"I've got this. I'm not going to sit on the sidelines."

Hart's expression didn't change. "Can't have you burning out on me, Benson. Go home."

Casey shook his head.

"Millie may as well be family."

Hart nodded. "Which is why I need you to step back. At least for the night."

"With all due respect, sir, I know how to parse the job."

Hart's eyes narrowed, something harder settling in them now. "I'm not sure you do."

Casey straightened, heat flaring in his chest and brow.

"What's that supposed to mean?"

Hart exhaled, slow. "I didn't ask too many questions about why you moved back from Chicago. Lord knows the job is tough as is, let alone in the damn homicide capital of the country."

Casey's breath hitched, but he didn't respond.

"There were some rough ones, sure. I got over it."

Not easily, though.

One of his first crime scenes in Chicago had been a murder-suicide. A father who botched the job—left his own son alive with a bullet wound through the eye, barely holding on by the time Casey arrived.

He remembered the kid's breathing.

The sound of sirens cutting through the night.

The weight of the bullet casings in his hands as he bagged them for evidence.

He got over it. But the nightmares stuck.

Hart didn't let up. "Maybe. But you haven't been the same since the wreck with the Hopkins kid."

Casey's fingers twitched. His shoulders pulled back.

"That was almost two years ago."

"Exactly."

The words hit deeper than Casey expected. Hart's voice softened, but his eyes didn't waver.

"I'll handle the family. You get some sleep. We'll talk tomorrow."

Casey nodded stiffly, knowing Hart was right—even if he didn't want to admit it.

He needed rest. But that didn't mean he was backing off. He had to help find Millie. Any way he could. As he turned toward the station, a shudder of unease crawled up his spine.

Tomorrow, Hart had said.

But as Casey stepped outside, starting the mile walk home as his breath curled in the cold air—he couldn't shake the deep-seated worry that tomorrow would be too late.

3

That night, patrol cars prowled the dim streets of Westville—county sheriff's and W.P.D. cruisers alike—creeping down back roads and dirt lanes. Foot patrols combed the state game land, sweeping along the North Country Trail, flashlights cutting jagged paths through the darkness.

Chief Hart had ordered Casey to stay away until dawn, to rest. But rest wasn't possible; he lay awake feeling the night press down like a wet blanket.

Olivia Fischer fared no better. She stewed in silence, simmering over the expectation that she should simply wait, play along, pretend everything was fine. When sleep did come, she dreamed of being somewhere hollow and cold, alone and afraid.

Somewhere where Millie might be.

Sometime after midnight, the Westville United Methodist Church bus rumbled away from the loading dock at PRINCE Milling. It rolled onto Main Street, but Ethan Crawley wasn't aiming for the church.

He guided it onto Riverside Drive, past darkened houses and into the looming pines, their shadows flickering over the windshield. He hummed along to Nirvana's *Lithium,* cranking the volume to drown out the stifled sobs from the bound and helpless man in the back. He preferred the new stuff over the likes of Hendrix and the Stones, which had blared in the helicopter speakers while he mowed down villagers and tasted the burnt flesh and chemical tang of napalm.

Years ago. But yesterday. He tried to forget.

Though the new part of him wished that he would remember—all of it.

Ethan nudged the bus up Burroughs Hill, veering it onto the shoulder and bringing it to a rough stop. He rolled his shoulders, trying to keep the boiling rage beneath his skin from spilling over. The red wanted out—wanted to tear, burn, break—but he kept it leashed, for now.

"Almost done," he muttered to himself, as if soothing a rabid dog. He snapped off the radio.

Turning, Ethan ripped the gag from the man's mouth and jammed a cheap bottle of liquor against his lips.

"Drink," he ordered.

Howard Meyers sputtered, whiskey spilling down his gray-white beard. "Francine . . . please . . . she needs to know where I am—"

"No one needs to know," Ethan said, his voice low and final.

Howard struggled, fear turning his movements jerky. He managed a clumsy punch that caught Ethan on the jaw.

Red.

Ethan's vision blurred, rage painting the world in shades of crimson. He inhaled sharply through his nose.

"Thank you for that."

With a quick, brutal twist, he snapped the fat man's neck, his head slumping forward, pressing the horn into a blaring wail that cut through the stillness.

The red purred, satisfied. Ethan's lips curled.

He whistled Cobain as he stepped off the bus, searching the area until he found a rock that would do the trick. He wedged it onto the gas pedal, revving the engine to a fevered roar. Then, with careful precision, he grabbed the shifter and slammed it into drive.

The bus lurched forward, wheels spinning wildly, and Ethan threw himself out the door. He tumbled down the hill, arm snapping at an unnatural angle with a sickening pop. Pain shot through him, but the red relished it.

Ethan gritted his teeth and forced his arm back into place, rising just in time to watch the bus barrel down the embankment, flip violently, and crash into the river. It rolled once, twice, before plunging in, disappearing beneath the water with a frothy churn.

He stood, shaking his head, the red inside him momentarily sated. But beneath that satisfaction, a sudden fear crept up—had he gone too far? That small, weak part of him, the one that still cared, clawed at the edges of his mind. But he couldn't afford to let it resurface. The red wouldn't allow it. It needed to consume, to tear apart anything that lingered of the old him.

His new employer had made that clear. This was the better way.

He wanted to *Seethe*.

The StarTAC phone in his pocket rang, and Ethan flexed his jaw, cracked it open and held it to his ear.

"Is it done?"

"Yes," he answered.

Ethan snapped the phone shut and slipped it into his pocket. He glanced once more at the dark, rippling water, red brake lights fading into blackness.

He turned and walked back up the hill, whistling Cobain as he went.

4

Casey stood by as the crane groaned, pulling the mud-slick minibus with *Westville First UMC* painted on its side from the Slate River's depths.

Its emergence displaced water in choppy waves that slapped against the banks. The Slate widened here into a lake at Burrough's Bend, where swirling eddies suddenly seemed tailor made for swallowing secrets and keeping them. There was something to be said for a kid's imagination, but the scene playing out now was one his wandering mind never conjured up while fishing in the summer here with his dad.

Casey had been roused by the wail of sirens cutting through the crisp dawn air. The cacophony shattered the stillness of his sleepless night, where fractured dreams twisted past regrets into new horrors.

Metal scorched orange. The Hopkins wreck. Only it was Millie in the wreckage of that twisted Camaro.

Careful not to lose his footing on the steep incline where the bus had carved a path, Casey approached the scene. Yellow police tape cordoned off the immediate area while Chief Hart, in his mud-streaked boots, surveyed the chaos. EMTs and divers worked in tandem, heaving a large bloated body onto a stretcher, plastic sheets crinkling with every move.

Johson, standing at the tape's edge, raised a hand. "You quit wearing the uniform or what, Benson?"

Casey lifted the arms of his heavy flannel coat and slapped them back down. "Not on today. Just here to support."

Johson sniffed with a grin, stepping aside. "Right. Well a fisherman spotted bubbles near the bank. Said he smelled fuel. Now here we are."

Casey nodded, scanning the crowd of Sunday morning onlookers attending some kind of gallows humor driven church service. Half the town had gathered on the ridge above, their murmurs growing louder.

In Westville, rumor spread faster than confirmation. Casey cast a wary glance at the spectators from the neighborhood across the street, many clutching mugs of coffee and whispering behind their hands. Casey's gut tightened as he came closer to where they'd set the body, though he already knew who it was.

Howard Meyers.

By now, near every soul in town knew Millie Thompson and Howard Meyers had vanished hours apart. Speculation filled the gaps law enforcement hadn't yet bridged.

Casey's boots squelched in the muck as he reached the water's edge. Chief Hart stood with arms crossed, rubbing his mustache in that telltale sign of nervous deliberation. The divers had secured the minibus, and techs snapped pictures. One placed numbered markers near fuel-slick patches on the bank.

"Thought I told you to get some rest," Hart said, his tone heavy and tired.

"Got some," Casey lied. "Anyone called the family yet?"

Hart shook his head. "Francine's in the nursing home. Not sure she'd understand. And his kids are out on the West Coast mostly, I think. Tried calling, no answer yet."

Casey nodded, recalling Francine Meyers' sharp wit when she worked the antique mall's ice cream parlor, now claimed by old age and mental withering.

Hart's eyes tracked the stretcher being carried up the incline. Then came the commotion.

The gurney slipped, and Howard Meyers' body tumbled onto the wet slope, rolling several feet before stopping. The crowd gasped, a few onlookers clutching their mouths in shock. Hart thundered out some good old fashioned blasphemy on the bright crisp Sunday morning as they both rushed to help, steadying the body while EMTs repositioned it.

Something slipped from the pocket of Howard's soaked overalls—a flash of pink catching Casey's eye. He picked it up, brushing mud away to reveal a W.W.J.D. bracelet. The clasp broken.

In his mind, he saw Millie waving with that same pink bracelet on her wrist the last time he saw her on Joe's porch.

Then a flash of red.

A high pitched screech—a distant scream.

Casey lost his balance for a moment but steadied himself, his left temple pulsing.

"What's that?" Hart asked, walking up alongside him.

"Fell out of his pocket," Casey murmured, shaking off—whatever that was.

The sky felt too blue, the sun too cheerful for this morning tableau, and for what he'd just seen. He didn't want to believe it was Millie's.

He glanced up at the road, where the tow truck strained and whined, pulling the crumpled water-logged church bus free of the forest slope.

But a gnawing instinct laced with creeping dread whispered otherwise.

5

The flickering red neon sign that spelled out *Westville Lanes* buzzed overhead, drawing a twitching cloud of moths and flies near the glow.

Olivia stalked under the yellow awning, pushed through the doors, and was greeted by the clatter of pins, the rolling crash of a ball. The air was thick with the smell of old popcorn, pizza grease, and shoe leather.

Her gaze cut through the dim arcade, past the battered booths and flickering game screens, until she found Austin and Kyle. They were glued to *House of the Dead*, fingers tight on the triggers, eyes locked on the screen as pixelated zombies lunged.

They flinched, fingers twitching on the trigger as another wave of undead shambled forward. Austin knocked into his friend as he veered the neon green plastic gun right.

He stood a head taller than Kyle, the gangly running type, and wore one of maybe two or three striped long sleeve polos he always wore (and she'd begun to realize wasn't just a preference), this one green and blue and a little big, his bowl cut black hair framing swarthy cheeks.

Kyle's wardrobe on the other hand consisted of overpriced American Eagle band branded t-shirts, a plethora of shoes and pants in more colors than Olivia would have wanted to deal with choosing between, and over-gelled hair that often developed a strange kind of crustiness.

"Take that, bitch!" Kyle yelled as a zombie head exploded in a mess of digital gore. His face twisted in concentration, mouth curled into something feral.

"Watch your mouth, Anderson!" Mrs. Rodgers barked, slapping a pair of rental shoes onto the counter. Her gray MSU sweatshirt was damp with sweat, her usual look of unmovable exasperation settling over her features.

Kyle barely glanced her way. "Yes, ma'am."

Austin barely looked up. "Hey, Liv."

Olivia's patience snapped.

She circled around them, boots squeaking on the sticky tile, and smacked each of them across the back of the head.

"Ow!" Kyle yelped, twisting to face her, one hand gripping the fake, oversized pistol.

Austin blinked, slow to surface.

"How can you two play games right now?" Olivia demanded. "Millie's missing, and you're here shooting zombies like it's just another Sunday."

Austin opened his mouth, but no words came.

Kyle dropped his gaze, shuffling his feet. "We've been asking around, just.... trying to keep busy."

Austin nodded, his voice small. "What else *can* we do?"

Olivia clenched her jaw. The anger was fading, leaving something heavier behind. Something thick and cold.

"I don't know," she admitted, softer now. "But it feels wrong. She's out there—scared, or worse—and we're just standing here."

Silence thickened between them, swallowed by the bowling alley's noise—the rhythmic crash of pins, the sound of zombie groans clashing jovially with the 'Macarena' thumping through the overhead lane speakers, like the shambling corpses wanted to dance.

"You think the cops are close to finding her?" Austin asked.

Olivia shook her head. "I doubt it."

The game's tinny speakers erupted in a high-pitched cackle as *CONTINUE?* flashed across the screen in blood-red letters, a thirty-second countdown beginning.

"Damn it," Kyle muttered, slamming the plastic gun onto the console.

"Last warning, Anderson!" Mrs. Rodgers yelled. "You want me calling your father?"

Kyle gave her a sheepish shake of his head, digging through his pockets.

"Got any more quarters?" he asked Austin.

Austin shook his head.

Olivia rolled her eyes and grabbed the thick black cables tethering the weapons of undead destruction, holstering them back on the arcade machine.

She sighed, dropping into a chair, eyes drifting toward the group of younger kids huddled by the *Street Fighter* machine.

"I keep thinking it's my fault," she murmured, more to herself than them. "Millie got mad at me Friday night and took off."

Kyle looked up. "Why? What happened?"

"Does it matter?"

Kyle frowned. "I guess not."

Austin cleared his throat. "It's not like we can just go wandering through the woods looking for her."

Olivia sat up straighter, a spark flaring in her chest. "Why not?"

Kyle scratched his head. "Uh, because there are, like, a hundred reasons."

Olivia's eyes flicked to the *House of the Dead* screen, where the zombies staggered forward, hungry for more quarters. The demon on screen let out another high-pitched cackle.

"Shut the hell up," Kyle snapped at it.

Mrs. Rodgers threw open the counter flap, storming toward them. The three of them scattered, beelining for the exit.

At the door, Olivia nearly collided with her sister.

Aly's expression was too much like their mother's—one part wrath, two parts worry.

"I've been looking everywhere for you," she snapped. "You can't just take off, not with what's going on."

"Quit acting like Mom," Olivia muttered.

Aly's eyes narrowed. "Mom's flying home tonight. I'll let her deal with you."

"I don't want to sit around doing nothing while Millie's out there."

Aly's face softened, but her stance didn't. "We're going. Now."

Olivia glanced back at Kyle and Austin, resignation settling in. Aly stormed out to the car.

"Your sister is so hot when she's mad," Kyle blurted.

Austin jabbed him in the ribs.

Olivia rolled her eyes. "I'll see you guys later."

Kyle lifted a hand in a halfhearted wave. Austin just watched her go, uncertain.

As she followed her sister outside, a hundred worries churned in her chest—mingling with fear, frustration and regret.

More than anything, she just wanted to know where her friend was.

6

A throng of reporters, from Westville's small-town *Ledger* to regional news stations, clung to the front steps of City Hall as Chief Hart took his place on the makeshift podium late Sunday afternoon.

They crowded along the narrow sidewalk—a space clearly never meant to withstand this much buzz and bluster. Their microphones jutted forward like spears, camera lenses capturing the Chief's every twitch and frown.

Casey hovered to one side, still out of uniform.

The Chief had continued to deter him from any more direct involvement for now. None of that cautioning did anything to lessen the pull, the way he felt grafted to finding Millie.

He owed it to Erin and Joe. He owed it to Millie.

Westville wasn't used to chaos—unless you counted debates over what to do with the decaying *Ulysses S. Grant* showboat, the first letter of the northern general's last name on the stern having worn away to read, appropriately, '*Rant*', which is what people loved to do about it.

But a missing kid in a town with nothing of the sort in its history had a way of unraveling things fast.

Holt Country Sheriff cars lined Main Street, a grim parade, an added presence Hart wouldn't typically welcome, but the scale of this was beyond typical.

Rumors were already spreading like the flu in February—some insisted Howard had fallen back into his old drinking habits, let loose some long-dormant darkness inside him. Others swore it was nothing more than a tragic accident. As for Millie, theories ranged from *she ran off* to *she fell in the river* to the kind of talk people didn't want to say out loud. The kind that made people keep their kids a little closer, check their locks twice.

The potential truth was hard to swallow, but it loomed all the same: the tire tread marks found near the Boy Scout cabin were consistent with the size and weight of the Ford E-350 Econoline Howard had driven into the river.

Not to mention that bracelet.

Had he run the bus off the road intentionally? Had he done it after doing the unimaginable to an innocent girl, because he couldn't live with himself? Or had it been a freak accident and the consequence of a twenty-year-delayed relapse? And if Howard had done something to Millie, where was she? Where was her—

No. She's out there still. We just need to find her. Worst case scenarios be damned.

Locals had gathered beyond the press, drawn by dread or morbid curiosity. Some had been at the river that morning. Others had only heard whispers. Drivers slowed to gawk, turning Main Street into a gallery of faces pressed against car windows. He felt a strange dissonance watching his town turn into this—as if a sordid Chicago headline followed him home, waiting in some dark corner these last two years.

A fissure in the dam spidering unseen in jagged shoots.

And now Westville's rural bubble was bursting. Casey wondered what might churn up to the surface when it did. Above him, the sky darkened, a quiet omen that quickened his pulse.

They were coming up on 48 hours fast.

Hart stepped up to the podium, shoulders squared, and cleared his throat.

"Good evening and thank you all for being here."

The murmurs ceased, replaced by the eerie stillness of a crowd holding its breath.

"Yesterday morning, Emily Grace Thompson, a girl we all know as Millie, was reported missing."

Hart's voice was steady, but Casey caught the weight beneath it—a quiet crack only those who knew him well might hear.

"Since that time, every available resource has been dedicated to locating her and bringing her home safely. We've mobilized search teams with the help of local volunteers, our department, and neighboring agencies."

A camera clicked. A reporter from Channel 7 raised a hand, but Hart pressed on.

Casey scanned the crowd. Familiar faces stared back—teachers, store clerks, retirees. Their faces full of the panicked kind of terror that came with realizing the world wasn't how you thought it was.

He looked away.

"The safety of our residents, especially our children, is our highest priority," Hart continued. "We are doing everything in our power to reunite Millie with her family."

Erin and Joe clutched each other's arms. Joe glanced over to Casey, a look that said he was glad he was there. For as much as Joe was the guy who had it together and had the looks to back it up, he was fragile too.

And it was Casey's turn to be there for him.

A reporter near the back shouted, "Do you have a suspect? Is this an abduction?"

Hart didn't flinch, though his grip on the podium tightened.

"At this time, I am limited in what I can share about the specifics of our investigation. However, I want to assure everyone that we are pursuing every lead with urgency and care."

"Chief!" A voice from the press pack broke through. A wiry man from Channel 7 thrust his microphone forward. "The body of one Howard Meyers was pulled from the Slate River this morning at the site of an accident. Are the cases connected?"

Casey didn't think Howard's name had been released yet. Neither did the Chief, from the look of it.

Hart paused, eyes narrowing slightly, keeping his composure. "As I said, I'm limited in what I can share. We are treating all leads and incidents with the seri-ousness they deserve, but at this time, our focus remains on bringing this girl home."

A worthy stretch of the truth. No need to feed the rumor mill—it was already churning fast enough.

The murmurs returned as Hart stepped back, signaling the end of his speech. Questions broke out, words blurring together in a cacophony of urgency.

Casey looked across the street, where a shiny, new, black Crown Victoria was pulling into a spot by the curb. An unfamiliar sight for Westville, especially with Illinois plates.

The doors opened.

A tall, older black man stepped out, followed by a woman with dark copper hair.

The sun caught the yellow flash of the three letters emblazoned on their jackets.

Casey's gut clenched.

Feds.

The reporters felt it too. Some invisible wire tugged them toward the federal agents, a ripple through the pack, microphones snapping up, voices rising in unison.

The county sheriff's deputies stiffened. Chief Hart's face darkened to a shade Casey knew well—the color of barely contained fury.

"Chief Hart," a reporter fired off, "are these cases now under federal jurisdiction?"

"And if so, why?" another piled on.

Hart didn't answer, though the sudden redness in his cheeks and seeming instantaneous deepening bags under his eyes said enough. "No more questions," he muttered, before shouldering through the double doors of City Hall. Reynolds ushered Joe and Erin inside after.

Casey hung back, watching. The agents flashed their badges, cutting through the press like a hot knife. When they disappeared inside, he slipped around the back, through the station's garage, and into the building. Casey made his way around the back entrance, avoiding the chaos.

Through the bullpen, past the cracked-open office door he heard Hart's voice, sharp-edged with irritation.

"You want to tell me why the hell I wasn't informed you were coming?"

A pause. "Let's get off on the right foot, shall we? There's only one side here—the side of the victims." A smooth, measured reply.

Casey stiffened. *Victims.* Plural.

A sharp sting, a catching burr on the skin. When the agent slapped multiple files onto Hart's desk, his gut twisted.

Hart stared at the folders like they held a bad poker hand.

"How about some names first?"

A hand extended across the desk, firm and unflinching. "Special Investigator Stephen Lochlear." His voice had a buttery sort of starkness to it, a strange combination of hardness and ease. "And this is Special Field Agent Dana Reeves."

Hart muttered something and shook their hands.

Casey lingered in the hallway, debating his next move. He wasn't technically supposed to be here, but whatever the feds were digging into, it wasn't going to make life in Westville any simpler. It never did.

The door swung open.

The male agent stepped out first—tall, crisp edges, polished demeanor. He filled the doorframe like it had been built for him. His gaze landed squarely on Casey.

"You must be Officer Benson."

Casey straightened. "That's right."

Lochlear extended a hand. "I like to know who I'm going to be working with."

Casey shook it.

Up close, the man smelled faintly of leather and paper. His suit was impeccable, but something about him set Casey's nerves jangling. Fastidious bureaucratism as its finest punctuated with a forced smile—the kind that said *I already have you figured out.*

Behind him the female agent, Reeves, observed with sharp, hazel eyes. Copper-red hair framed her face in deliberate, no-nonsense strands. A gray pantsuit, navy FBI jacket—professional but not rigid. There was a hardness to her brow, though. A wryness to her mouth, a mirror of the badge he saw hanging down, obscured a bit by her jacket. But he noticed bold letters next to 'Field Agent' that read 'PK'. Some kind of security clearance, maybe.

"Your name came up in the brief," she said, flipping through a folder. "Seems you've been close to this investigation." A pause. "And a hometown boy."

Casey's jaw tightened. "I'm off-duty today. Chief's orders."

"Yet here you are," Lochlear noted, tilting his head. "Interesting."

Casey simplified his first impression of Lochelar to *asshole.*

He glanced to Hart, whom he could tell was already flustered, and he didn't blame him. Casey looked back to Lochlear.

"You want to tell me what you're here for? Because from where I'm standing, it looks like you're about to step on a lot of toes."

Hart cleared his throat.

Lochlear didn't blink. "We're here to ensure this doesn't turn into something bigger than it already is. These situations have a way of spiraling if we're not careful."

Casey's gut twisted again. "What kind of situations might those be?"

Reeves flicked to another page. "The kind that involve multiple victims over a period. A pattern."

"So serial killings," Casey said flatly.

Reeves only nodded.

"Howard Meyers is our best suspect regarding Miss Thompson," Lochlear said. "And you recovered a bracelet at the scene."

"That's right," Casey said. "We're not sure if it's hers. He handed them out all the time."

Reeves was listening, but Casey could see it—she was working angles he couldn't.

"We'll need to set a time for a more formal interview and take a statement," Lochlear said.

"Sounds like a waste of time and manpower," Casey muttered.

Lochlear pocketed his glasses. "The cooperation of this department is paramount to ensuring the best outcome."

"And that sounds like a bureaucratic mouthful of nothing."

"Benson," Hart snapped.

Reeves stepped forward. "All it means is that we're here to help."

Lochlear nodded. "And if you're at all interested in finding Emily Thompson, I suggest you take that help."

"Millie."

Lochlear's brow arched. "Pardon?"

"She goes by Millie."

"So you know the victim personally?"

That word—*victim*—caught in Casey's ribs like a rusted nail.

"That's right."

Lochlear didn't blink. "Noted. But let me give you some advice, Officer. There may be more at play here than you realize. And the sooner everyone in Westville understands that the better off they'll be."

Before Casey could respond, Reeves snapped her folder shut. "We'll be in touch."

He turned back to Hart.

"Don't you think it's weird the feds showed up this fast?" Casey asked.

Hart exhaled hard. "Not if they think there's a link to other missing girls in the greater Iron Falls area."

Casey flipped open the file.

Brittany Renee Foster.

Stephanie Michelle Wright.

He vaguely remembered hearing about these over the past year and a half or so. They were the sort of unthinkable stories that were earth shattering and life ruining for the people they happened to, but for those removed were nothing more than a blip on the news cycle.

They were girls Millie's age. One bore a striking resemblance.

Hart sighed, grabbed a bottle of scotch from under his desk, and poured it into his W.P.D. mug. "Things are about to get a lot more complicated."

Casey pushed back from the desk.

"And Howard Meyers could be pinned for all of them."

Hart gave him a hard look. "No one's saying that. Yet. But you know how this goes. People need answers. They'll latch onto the first explanation that makes sense—even if it's the wrong one."

Casey nodded absently, his thoughts spiraling.

Why *had* the feds come down so fast?

As he stepped outside, cold air biting his skin, the Crown Vic was already pulling away.

He was walking to his car, the dull silver curves of the Monte Carlo's long hood glimmering faintly under the streetlamps, when across the street just beyond the flickering glow of a streetlamp, a figure shifted. And stood there.

Still. Watchful.

Casey blinked, heart quickening. He stepped forward.

The figure stepped back, vanishing into the dark.

Casey got into his car and started the coughing sputtering engine in fits and starts. He glanced in his rearview at the street corner by the mill. Casey was starting to feel something he had never felt living here.

The town—or something in it—was changing. And right now he wasn't so sure change was a good thing.

1

Westville seemed to hold its breath.

Olivia felt it in pulses of unspoken tension, a low, humming fear that things weren't safe anymore. Olivia saw it in the way people talked in hushed voices at the gas station, in the way parents clutched their kids' hands tighter at the grocery store.

News of Mr. Meyer's death in a wreck was all over the TV and radio, along with the ongoing missing minor alerts. Millie's face was everywhere—on the news, the Westville Ledger and the Iron Falls Tribune, and on flyers tacked to telephone poles.

Or . . . Emily was.

Emily Grace Thompson, age 13.

Everyone called her Millie though, so Olivia didn't know why they didn't just use that, and it pissed her off for some reason.

At school, it was worse.

When Olivia walked through the doors that Monday morning, the weight of a hundred stares pinned her in place. Some were sharp, like the red pupil tips of Judge Doom's dagger eyes at the end of *Roger Rabbit* that had once given her nightmares. Others softer, sad-eyed spotlights of pity, but both made her stomach turn. Not to mention the way people were talking about her friend, like a sick joke or a victim in a slasher movie. Already a goner.

Olivia kept her head down, but the week dragged.

Every time she passed the empty desk in algebra, something twisted inside her. By Wednesday, it was unbearable. She swapped her biology book for an advanced algebra one, her fingers tracing the worn cover, remembering how Millie had saved her from failing so many times.

The thought made her gut churn.

She veered down the hall for Mrs. Summers' classroom, dreading both the test and the empty seat waiting inside.

As she rounded the corner, she nearly plowed straight into Kyle and Austin. They were lurking by her locker, glancing over their shoulders as if they were waiting for someone to jump out at them.

Kyle's voice was unusually subdued. "Hey, Liv. You . . . doing okay?"

"Define *okay*," she muttered, shoving her book into her bag. "Millie's missing, the whole town's on edge, and people are treating me like I'm cursed. You?"

"Pretty much the same." Austin fidgeted with the strap of his backpack. "Everyone keeps asking about her. It's . . . weird."

"Annoying, is more like it," Kyle said, crossing his arms. "Especially when we don't know anything more than they do."

Austin gave him a sidelong look. "At least they're trying to care."

"Doesn't feel that way."

Olivia shut her locker harder than necessary, her jaw tight.

They started walking, their footsteps echoing down the hallway.

"It's messed up," Kyle muttered.

Silence settled between them, heavy and uncomfortable.

Then, just before they reached Mrs. Summers' room, a voice cut through the din.

"Fischer."

Olivia turned.

Brett Huizinga was pushing off the lockers across the hall, flanked by two of his usual lackeys. One of them was Kevin Davis—the same Kevin who'd been down by the river the night Millie disappeared. The other was named Matt, she thought.

Kyle and Austin tensed beside her.

"Guess that friend of yours should've stuck around the other night," Brett sneered.

Olivia's pulse spiked.

"Oh, right." Brett smirked. "Don't wanna upset you too much. You might throw up on someone else's shoes."

"No. I'd make sure to aim for yours again."

Brett's smirk widened.

"I'll bet that stuck-up nark got what was coming to her."

The hallway noise dulled, conversations pausing, a few heads turning toward them.

Kyle muttered, "Let it go, Liv."

Olivia stopped walking.

Kyle's hand brushed her arm, a silent warning, but she shook him off.

Millie would've walked away. But Millie wasn't here. And that was the problem.

Olivia clenched her fists, pressing the heavy algebra book tight to her side.

Brett took a step closer, his voice carrying. "Maybe she did us all a favor and ran away. One less spoiled Thompson in this town."

Kevin shifted uncomfortably. "Come on, man—"

Austin's eyes darted between them, nerves creeping into his voice. "Just ignore him."

She didn't. She took a slow step forward. "I'd listen to your goons if I were you, Brett."

Brett scoffed. "Why's that?"

Olivia gripped the book tighter. "Because. I hate math."

Brett frowned. "The hell is that supposed to mean?"

"This."

She reeled back and swung, slamming the rigid spine of the algebra book into Brett's nose.

The satisfying *crack* echoed down the hall.

Brett staggered, his hand flying to his face. Blood streamed between his fingers.

"Solve for *that*, prick," Olivia hissed.

His face contorted in pain and fury. "You crazy b—"

"What is happening here?"

Mrs. Summers' sharp voice cut through the tension. The teacher stormed toward them, her face a mask of fury.

"Miss Fischer," her gaze flicked to Brett and back to Olivia, "did you do this?"

Brett's mouth snapped shut, probably unwilling to admit he'd been beaten by a girl. So Olivia answered for him.

"Yeah. Because he's an asshole."

Kyle and Austin sucked in twin breaths beside her.

Mrs. Summers' lips thinned. "Come with me. Now."

As Olivia was marched toward the office, she shot a glance over her shoulder. Kyle gave her a nervous thumbs-up. Austin offered the faintest, uncertain smile. For all the trouble she was about to be in, Olivia felt a strange satisfaction settle in her chest. Maybe, if she were lucky, she'd get suspended—and that meant more time to go looking for Millie.

It felt good to do *something*. The cold, gnawing worry hadn't gone away.

But neither had her resolve.

After whatever reprimand awaited her, she was going to find her friend—no matter what it took.

8

"That was *awesome*," Kyle said, dramatically miming the way Brett had flopped when her algebra book connected with his face. He raised his Go-Gurt like a trophy, finishing the reenactment with a grand flourish. "End scene."

"Doesn't change anything," Olivia muttered, stabbing at her lunch without interest.

When she'd walked out of the principal's office, all she wanted was to bolt. To run straight out of school and start looking for Millie. But she knew full well that if she ditched, Kathy would ground her into oblivion, making everything harder. And she had not, in fact, been lucky enough to get suspended, which probably would have also been negated by grounding anyway.

So she forced herself to head to the cafeteria instead, trying to think.

"Yeah, but it had to feel good," Austin said, nudging her. "Brett had it coming, the way he was talking about Millie."

Olivia nodded absently, her fork twisting through the limp excuse for stir-fry, the cafeteria's Wednesday special.

"It's been five days." Her voice was barely above a whisper.

Austin and Kyle exchanged a look. The joking faded, replaced by something heavier. She knew they were just trying to lift her spirits. She appreciated it, even if it didn't help.

"Nothing from the cops?" Austin asked quietly.

Olivia shook her head. "I called Mrs. Thompson last night." *Again.* She bit down the frustration that clawed at her throat—she'd been calling every night, spending hours at their house, trying to be useful. But she wasn't sure if it helped or just made things worse. "The police think she ran into the woods near the old Scout cabin."

Austin swallowed. "I heard search parties were all over there through the weekend."

"And they didn't find—" Olivia stopped herself before finishing the thought. *A damn thing.*

"Burrough's Bend," Kyle said, shifting uncomfortably. "They didn't get any . . . evidence?"

"Millie didn't get murdered," Olivia snapped. "I know that."

She meant it too. Call it hope or whatever other delusion, but she did. Had to.

Kyle nodded slowly, eyeing her with a sort of boyish confusion. "I mean I don't think so either but they found that church guy's truck and . . ."

"It was a bus and it doesn't mean anything. Doesn't mean he killed her and doesn't mean she's dead, okay?" She caught her breath. "I just feel it."

Kyle raised both his hands in surrender. "Right. Fair. I . . . feel it too I guess."

"Very convincing," said Olivia.

Then Austin muttered, "Devil's Peak."

Olivia looked up sharply. A flicker of something unsettled ran through her chest.

"That's near where they think she went missing, right?" Austin said, taking a long sip of his chocolate milk, like it was something stronger. "The trail leads right up to it."

Olivia swallowed, a memory creeping in before she could shove it back down.

Her dad, sitting on the couch, the glow of the old TV flickering across the room. His stories—some he made up, others picked up along the way. Slate River Jim. A hermit who lived near Devil's Peak, some lost old man who'd show up just in time to help people find their way back to town before disappearing again.

She remembered how those stories always ended—with him grabbing her, tickling her sides until she squealed, both breathless with laughter.

She forced the thought down, stabbing at her food, and started to recount the legend of Slate River Jim, which she ultimately regretted.

"Sounds like a Cotton-Eye Joe ripoff," Kyle blurted.

Olivia gave him a flat look and continued. "In the stories, he helped people. If they got lost in the woods, he'd find them, lead them back."

Kyle shrugged. "Okay, but what about the *Banshee*? Big hairy bastard who screams so loud it stops your blood. Scouts still tell that one at campouts."

Olivia snorted. "Great bedtime story to tell a bunch of kids alone in the woods."

Kyle ignored her. "What if the banshee *is* Slate River Joe? But like really old and like a bigfoot or something now?"

"Yea probably not," Austin said, leaning in. "But my Grandpa says there was an Odawa shaman who lived up there too. Trickster type. Made people strike bad deals with dark spirits, that kind of thing."

Kyle wrinkled his nose. "What the hell kind of prank is that?"

"Not a prank," Austin said. "More like . . . persuasion. He tricked people into eating human flesh. Drinking blood."

Kyle recoiled. "Why? That's messed up. But isn't your gramps a little . . . you know?"

"Old and forgetting stuff? Yeah. But he knows a lot. He's an Odawa Lore Keeper, tells the traditional stories at powwows. It's kinda like the Wendigo story. Someone gets a taste for it, and they lose their mind. Endlessly hungry, never full."

Olivia's stomach turned, the unappetizing concoction of noodles and greasy chunks of meat suddenly more unappetizing. She pushed her tray aside.

Still, Olivia shook her head. She was long past believing in ghosts and curses.

"All I know," she said, her voice firm, "is that Millie is out there. And I *can't* sit around doing nothing."

"That's why they have search parties," Kyle said.

"I need to go, and I will one way or another."

Kyle made a face. "Whoa, whoa. You can't just wander into the woods without, like, gear and stuff. Flashlights, compasses, radios . . . a map wouldn't hurt either."

Austin and Olivia exchanged a look.

Kyle sighed. "What?"

Austin smirked. "Your uncle's the Scoutmaster."

Kyle's face darkened. "So?"

Austin gave him a knowing look. "He has the key to the shed by the cabin. All that stuff would be *in* there."

Kyle groaned. "I'm not gonna ask my uncle to help us sneak out past curfew—"

"I'm sure Eli would help."

Olivia frowned. "Who's Eli?"

"No way—" Kyle groaned louder.

Austin snorted. "He's not that bad."

"Yes," Kyle asserted, "he is."

"You just can't stand the fact that he's earned more badges than you, and he's a year younger."

"Whatever. He didn't get the Astronomy badge, and I passed that one with flying colors."

"Thanks to space nerd camp," Austin remarked.

"If you think Eli he could get us what we need," Olivia said, pushing between their back and forth, "we have to try."

Kyle let out a long-suffering sigh. "Fine."

Olivia had perked up by now, but it was short lived.

"What about curfew, though?" Austin asked.

That was a real problem. No one under sixteen was allowed out after dark unless they were with an adult. They'd never make it into the woods without someone noticing.

For a moment, that put a damper on things.

Then Olivia remembered what she and Millie were supposed to be doing tonight. Their annual Hocus Pocus viewing party.

"Halloween," she said. "That's when we go."

Kyle frowned. "What?"

Austin nodded. "It's tomorrow. And I haven't heard them cancel trick-or-treating."

Kyle jabbed a finger at him, chewing a mouthful of chips. "The curfew's so tight right now that I saw a cop car drive by our house, like, four times last night."

"Exactly," Austin said. "They're all watching for kids breaking curfew." He leaned forward. "But if everyone is out, dressed up, walking around, blending in?"

Olivia smiled. "They won't look twice at us."

Kyle exhaled, running a hand through his hair. "This is insane."

"Are you in?" Olivia asked.

Kyle hesitated.

Then he sighed again. "Fine. Tomorrow night."

Austin gave Olivia a look.

Hold on, Millie. We're coming.

9

The not so distant slam of a hammer reverberated through the floor of Casey's bedroom, startling him awake.

"*Son of a—!*" BANG. "*You better believe you're fixing your own damn dinner tonight, you miserable old—*"

BANG. BANG. BANG.

Mrs. Blythewood at it again.

He wiped the taste of sleep from his mouth and for a few minutes, he just lay there, staring at the ceiling. The dull ache behind his eyes told him he'd slept too long—or not enough. The hammering picked up again, sharp and insistent.

Casey groaned and sat up, rubbing his face.

Technically, what Casey rented was a house. Realistically, it was a box that someone had decided to slap doors and windows on. One bedroom, barely a kitchen, and a living room small enough that he could toss his remote at the TV without much effort. The front door faced the backyard—because of course it did.

Mrs. Blythewood owned the place and was in the process of renovating the unfinished basement beneath him, desperate to get a tenant in as soon as possible. Casey had a feeling she wanted someone to split the mortgage, given how often she muttered about "that useless, good-for-nothing S.O.B" between swings of her hammer.

He ran a hand through his matted hair, thinking he needed a shower, trying to shake off the lingering weight of sleep, and reached for his watch on the nightstand. 4:47 p.m. He still wasn't used to the rhythms of working nights again.

Pushing himself up, he shuffled into the living room, flipping on the TV as he passed.

Static. A flicker of the news about the aftermath of that freak tornado outbreak he'd heard about Saturday morning—before it all started. He'd been staying away from the news of purpose. He didn't need reminding that she was missing. He flicked the channel.

CLAP, CLAP, CLAP, CLAP.

The *Friends* theme song blasted through the speakers, the opening guitar riff too peppy for the dim sleep haze clinging to his brain.

CLAP, CLAP, CLAP, CLAP.

A sharp migraine bloomed, the kind that made his head seem to float.

He inhaled sharply, pressing his fingers to his temples. A flicker in his mind. Metal.

A room. Stark. Industrial. Wrong in the way dreams were.

A slow, steady drip hitting the floor.

Labored, scared breathing.

Casey exhaled the scatter of the afternoon's vague dreamscape. Bad sleep, no sleep, or irregular sleep being the primary triggers for the migraines flaring up, it wasn't exactly surprising. He'd learned to live with them, but now they were getting worse—his skull too tight around his own thoughts.

For a while in Chicago, he thought they stopped. But that didn't last long.

He forced himself up, shaking it off. A random leftover from some dream he didn't remember.

That was it.

The fridge's dim yellow light flickered as he opened it. Not much inside. A bottle of mustard. A Coke. Something in an old takeout box that had probably become its own ecosystem.

He threw that away, and grabbed the jerky from *Jerry's* and an apple, taking a bite as he leaned against the counter and closed the fridge.

He had a city council meeting to get to, and he needed a shower. He made it quick. Casey grabbed his coat, took one last glance at the TV before shutting it off. Then he noticed his magnetized W.P.D. calendar on the floor near the fridge. He walked over and replaced it, pulling the door shut behind him.

10

The city council was set to meet in the old middle school, now the administration building off Graham St. But when Casey got there, it looked like the last train out of London before the Blitzkrieg.

A lingering musk of pencil shavings clung to the pockmarked ceiling tiles under fluorescent lights, stirring something dusty in Casey's memory. Maybe that was why his brain kept filling the edges of his mind with grainy black-and-white footage of air raid sirens and firebombed streets from history classes gone by.

People clamored to get inside, pressing in wall to wall. By 5:55 p.m, it was obvious they'd need a bigger space, and the Chief suggested the upstairs of the current department, which had at one time been the community theater stage, now used by the department for a makeshift shooting range. Bullet holes peppered the concrete back wall, and Officer DeYoung along with Gail hastily went to work sweeping up the scatter of glass bottles and shreds of paper targets.

Travis remarked that they were cleaning up his best work, which DeYoung was not amused by, and offered him the broom instead, the tired old officer working out a crick in his back.

Westville was scrappy when it came to shared spaces. Plans for a new City Hall were up in the air, hinging on a millage proposal that had taken a decisive backseat the last few days.

Casey took it all in—people wiping the dust off the rows of seats that probably should have been removed long ago, the old musty theater chairs creaking under the weight of anxious bodies shifting nervously between questions and mostly unsatisfactory answers.

He recognized plenty of faces. Mark Estes and Laura Rogers—now Laura Estes—high school sweethearts who'd done the white picket fence thing. Looked solid from the outside, at least.

Abby Corliss, homecoming queen turned barfly. Brad Perry, burnout turned real estate mogul—if that term applied in small-town Michigan.

Others whose names had faded but whose faces were carved into the memory of ten years' worth of shared proximity.

After a forty-minute delay, things got off to a rocky start. The lionized Mayor, Scott Douglas tried to establish control over the raucous crowd.

"Let me make it clear from the outset," he said, gripping the edges of the podium. "We're not here to speculate. We're here to move forward as a community in the safest way possible while supporting the Thompson family."

Vicky Robertson, the new school superintendent, fielded a question about increasing background checks on school employees. Howard Meyers hadn't worked full-time for the schools, but people were panicking now, scrutinizing every adult with so much as a foot in the education system.

Casey learned early in law enforcement—*innocent until proven guilty* might be the mantra, but in an investigation you were better off assuming the worst and being wrong than the other way around.

Still, everything about Howard as the boogeyman didn't settle in his gut, like silt in the river bed where the bus sank into muck and mire.

Kevin DeGraff, John Baker, and Bill VanDorn sat on either side of Douglas, mostly silent. It wasn't just listening—it was calculated restraint. Deliberate. Heavy. Casey couldn't help but wonder what they weren't saying.

The floor opened to public comment, and the room became a funnel for every pent-up worry and wild-eyed theory in town.

Stan Blythewood—Westville's appliance repair and electrical guru whose wife was likely still hammering out her aggression—gave what was probably supposed to be a reassuring speech about community values but fell flat. Old man Klein started ranting about a UFO shining strange lights in the woods behind his property last week. It earned a few eye rolls, but Casey's stomach twisted.

He thought about Ruth Potter's complaint. About red lights in the woods. The flash of red in his own head.

He rubbed a hand over his left temple.

Bob Morgan stood at the far end of the panel.

"Things are tough right now. I get it. We're all on edge. That's why I'm pulling guys off the dairy to help with the search in any way they can. Chief and I have talked, and we're making plans to canvas and cover all the ground we can."

The door clicked open. Casey didn't bother to look at first—people had been filtering in and out all evening. Someone leaned against the wall next to him. He turned his head and met the sharp eyes of Agent Reeves.

"Couldn't miss the party?" he said dryly.

"Not exactly my scene," she answered, eyes flicking over the room. "Then again, I don't think anyone wants to be here."

"No, they don't."

The murmurs died down as Mayor Douglas cleared his throat.

"The curfew remains in place and minors must be indoors by 7 p.m. sharp. This includes Halloween and trick-or-treating. There is no reason to think anyone is in further immediate danger, but for caution's sake."

Reeves leaned closer. "On a scale of one to seven, how well do you think people in this town will obey that curfew?"

Casey shifted to face her. "Think you got people pegged already?"

"No," she answered quickly. "Just spent enough time wandering through *po-dunk-ville* U.S.A. to know a few things."

Casey wasn't exactly sure what she wanted him to say to that backhanded insult.

"Didn't realize the FBI made a habit of casing small towns."

"They don't, unless they have to," she replied, straightening. "Experience from a prior career."

"And what might that have been?"

"P.I."

"Ah. So you've made it a lifelong habit of getting paid to pry into people's business."

Reeves smirked. "Believe it or not there are more dishonest and despicable ways to make a living."

Casey shifted. "Westville is stubborn, not stupid. I'll give them an eight."

Her lips quirked, looking unconvinced.

"We'll see."

When the meeting adjourned, Casey made for the doors, but Reeves cleared her throat.

"You need something?"

"Thought now might be a good time for that interview."

"Actually, I'm about to head out for a patrol shift. Rain check."

Besides, the last thing he wanted was to waste his time regurgitating things for the feds.

"How about a ride-along? I could use someone to show me the lay of the land."

"Yeah, you know, I've actually already got that booked tonight."

Reeves followed his gaze. Joe Thompson stood across the room, towering over the mayor, who had clasped his hands in some gesture of reassurance.

Reeves nodded, lips pursed in irony. "Another time, then."

She turned to go, but Casey spoke up.

"Those letters on your badge. *PK*. Preacher's Kid?"

Reeves squinted at him, head tilted. "Not quite. Actually, far from it." Her gaze flicked back to Joe. "Word to the wise—don't make promises you won't be able to keep."

Casey frowned. "He just needs a friend right now. And if driving around makes him feel like he's doing something, what's the harm?"

"All I'm saying is, we don't know how this is going to play out. I've been on the wrong end of these things more times than I like to think about."

"You feds sure know how to bring the 'can-do' spirit."

"Being realistic is painful. But trust me, when it's all said and done and things go the wrong way—the bad way—you're better off."

Whatever trace of personality had been in her voice vanished as she said it. She stalked off, disappearing into the crowd.

Casey exhaled. He was about to follow Joe outside when a familiar voice stopped him.

"Hey."

He turned to see Aly walking toward him, weaving through the clattering sea of folding chairs.

"Didn't see you up there," he said.

Aly sighed, puffing her cheeks in that way he remembered—the same look of exasperation he'd been on the receiving end of more than once.

"Mom thought one of us ought to come hear what's happening."

"Good idea. How's Liv doing?"

"She's all right. Won't talk to either of us much." She glanced toward the exit. "Who was that?"

"One of the department's new *shadow helpers*. FBI."

Aly shook her head. "Feels like a movie."

"Doesn't seem real, I know."

They stood there, the momentum of conversation stalling. There was plenty to say. But maybe they were both too worn out—on words, on each other.

"See you around the café," Aly murmured, turning for the door.

Casey watched her go, metal chairs clattering in loud echoes behind him.

11

The quiet hum of the cruiser's engine filled the cab as Casey guided it down a rain-slick back road, the rhythmic thrum of the windshield wipers marking time. Darkness pressed close, broken only by the cruiser's headlights cutting through mist that clung to the trees.

Joe sat stiffly in the passenger seat, his hands clasped together so tightly that his knuckles were pale. He hadn't said much since climbing in—just a quiet nod when Casey asked if he was sure about riding along. Coming off of that city council meeting, he figured he could use the company. Casey hadn't bothered to tell the Chief, and he figured he wouldn't approve.

But it didn't matter. Not tonight.

Casey glanced over at his friend, the shadows on Joe's face making him look older, worn. "You doing okay?"

Joe didn't answer right away. Instead, he remained fixated on the rain streaking against the glass.

"Was this me, Case?" Joe's voice was low, almost a whisper, but there was no mistaking the weight in it.

"What do you mean?" Casey asked, guiding the cruiser around a bend.

"Erin's right. I've been distracted. Been—" Joe's voice cracked slightly, and he stopped short.

Casey wiped a hand down his mouth, one hand on the wheel. "Can I ask you something?"

"I haven't had a drink since the day she went missing, if that's what you're wondering."

Casey nodded, gripping the wheel a little tighter. "That's good. I know it's tough, man. All of this is. What you've been fighting and . . ." He hesitated, searching for the right words.

"The night before, when Millie was last seen."

"What about it?"

"Erin said she couldn't get a hold of you."

Joe shook his head. "I was at the cabin. Just needed some time to think. I—lost track of time. Erin and I, we got into it about things with the company—with the mill. Jack wants me to take over. Didn't have a drink that night, just . . . didn't sleep. Couldn't."

Casey knew the feeling.

Joe let out a sharp breath. "If I had just been there, maybe I could have—" He nodded as if acknowledging himself. "Maybe she would be here now."

Casey knew that feeling too. The same weight he'd carried after TJ Hopkins.

"To answer your question, no. This wasn't you. There's no use in blaming yourself," Casey said, feeling the tension of his own hypocrisy.

Joe turned to him, his eyes hollow, searching. "Then who?"

Casey didn't answer right away.

He thought about saying 'the bastard who took her', but he couldn't. Even if suspicion ran wild about Howard Meyers, Casey couldn't bring himself to believe it and neither could Joe, he could tell. Whenever Howard was brought up, instead of the fervor of a vengeful father, there was little to no outward response. Just a contemplative numbness.

The truth was, they didn't know anything for certain, and that was the worst part.

"Just have to keep pounding the pavement," Casey said instead, his voice quieter now.

Joe leaned back in his seat, his shoulders sagging. "Heard the Feds got involved," he said after a moment.

"Yep," Casey replied.

"Doesn't sound like a good thing."

"It's not," Casey admitted, his tone clipped.

"How's things with Aly, man?" Joe blurted out of nowhere. "Change of subject, I know."

Casey glanced over at him, realizing he probably just wanted a distraction. Someone else's life to ease his own.

The truth was Casey was just as shredded by the same things, but he'd play along. As much as he could. He explained the lukewarm feedback loop they were stuck in, and that he wondered if that's where they were meant to stay. They had gone out with Erin and Joe a few times well over a year ago and had some of the best nights Casey could remember, cackling over the stupid things a Westville kid resorted to for fun when they were in high school. Including but not limited to attempting a midnight joyride in Jack Thompson's brand new '81 F-150—two-tone cherry red and cream— through a freshly storm-drenched field of a known misanthropic farmer. They'd ended up with a nice smattering of buckshot in the truck bed door, a debt he'd made both of them work off.

"You guys seemed good together," Joe offered.

Casey was pulled back in from the bittersweet reverie.

"Yeah, maybe." Casey asked, "So things with your dad—"

"Are shit," said Joe, laughing bitterly and shaking his head. "Always have been, always will be."

Casey felt a pang of selfishness for dredging it up, but some compulsion told him to pry. "What's going on?"

Joe's eyes narrowed, his jaw working as he stared out the window. "All he cares about is the company. Doesn't matter what's going on with me, with Erin. Doesn't matter that his granddaughter's missing. It's all just business with him."

Casey hesitated, unsure if he should press. This tension between father and son was nothing new, but there was something sharper in his voice tonight—something raw.

"Look, Joe," Casey said, keeping his eyes on the road. "You're doing everything you can for Millie. Don't let your old man or anyone else make you think otherwise."

Casey pulled into Joe's driveway, the cruiser's tires crunching softly on the gravel. He shifted into park and turned to his friend.

"You can't change anything about what happened. But we'll find her, Joe. We will."

Joe didn't respond at first. His hand hovered near the door handle, and for a moment, Casey thought he might say something more.

Joe just muttered, "Thanks for the ride along."

Casey watched him trudge up the walkway to his house, shoulders hunched against the rain.

For a long moment, Casey didn't move, just sat there with the engine idling and the wipers sweeping back and forth. Joe was breaking under the weight of it all. Casey could see it. And a part of him feared that when they did find Millie—whatever the outcome—Joe might not come back from it.

Casey pulled out of the driveway, the rain drumming against the cruiser's roof.

12

One week.

One week since Millie Thompson first went missing.

In that time, Westville had been turned upside down and around at all angles—a snow globe in the hands of a hapless toddler.

Fervid platitudes about the days-away election had dwindled down to a dull roar, and taking its place were all the hushed murmurs about Howard

Meyers, his death, and, at the same time, his suspected connection to what happened to Millie.

Casey had attended the funeral himself. The pall of those rumors hung like smoke in the Methodist Church sanctuary and an awkward silence over the luncheon. Poor Francine Meyers in her wheelchair was subject to it all, the small blessing of her condition blotting out the worst of the talk about her late husband from registering:

"No wonder he liked driving that bus with all those kids around. Damn pervert."

"Sounds like he collected bits of their hair."

"Don't think he could have done the thing . . . but if he did, damn him straight to hell, the bastard."

Looking at the newly widowed woman in the throes of late-stage dementia, he tried to blot out the image of his own mother in the same position years from now.

All the while, Westville was locked in the same old small-town routine, and most everyone with it. The annual Slate River Antique Mall Expo went off without a hitch, and signs were already going up for the array of holiday events to come. It all seemed so out of touch and removed from the dark reality.

Then, that was life.

People murdered and kidnapped every day in every state and county. Most of them you didn't hear about, and when you did they were just a bit of uncomfortable information between fluff pieces on the news.

Whether as a way to cope or because a place like Westville knew no other way, life moved along regardless of tragedy or crisis.

Casey had his own way of coping.

He sat at his usual booth in Fischer's, leafing through the reports for what must have been the ten thousandth time, hoping he'd see something new. Wishing for some kind of bright, bold revelation—the kind that lead detectives on crime shows seemed to have in the last five minutes of an episode.

He sipped his now-tepid coffee, seated in his usual corner booth with his least favorite clown frowning down at him from the picture frame on the wall.

Though Westville felt different, on the surface, it looked the same. The town never really changed. But now, instead of the usual leisurely pace and complaints about the temperamental weather, or another pizza place or an auto parts store opening in a vacant building, people were talking about curfews and casting suspicious glares at any new and unusual faces.

One of those faces happened to be sitting in the other corner booth—a man Casey hadn't seen before. Older, probably late 50s, early 60s, wearing a heavy coat, thick rimmed glasses, and sporting a mustache and goatee. Between sips of coffee, Casey noticed the man glancing his way every now and then.

Probably he was curious about Casey's spread of papers and pictures, which by all rights Casey probably shouldn't have been looking through out in the open, but he often did his best thinking elsewhere, and at this mid-morning weekday hour the café was mostly dead.

Casey returned to reading the interviews with the last people who had seen Millie, including Olivia Fischer, a kid named Brett Huizinga, and a handful of other students at the game.

He looked at a photo of the bracelet that he himself had found. One on the scene caked in mud and the other with it cleaned up. They hadn't been able to get prints off it.

If it was Millie's, why did it look so new? She'd been wearing that thing for the past couple years, at least. Maybe she'd snagged a replacement. The clasp had been broken by force, either by getting caught on something or someone doing it intentionally. To make it align with the trail of assumptions they were on now.

Then the wreck itself.

The fact that there were no skid marks on the road to signal the sudden accidental (or intentional) veering off and down the embankment felt wrong. Sure, he could have pulled it up and hesitated. But that wasn't how most people did these things. Impulse. Emotionality. A pause would have allowed for the rational mind to kick in. He was no shrink, but he'd retained more than a couple things from his criminal psychology course.

He'd already mentioned it to the Chief, but between his caution of Casey's direct involvement and the feds already muddying things, it didn't go anywhere, other than the general 'noted' file.

He rubbed his brow and glared up at the clown picture on the wall.

"What're you looking at?" he muttered.

"Someone who needs some sleep."

Casey turned toward the familiar, weathered voice.

"Hey, Dad."

Dave Benson patted him on the shoulder, folded himself into the booth with a grunt and a sigh. In the past few years, the sides of his now-wispy hair had turned gray-white, with only a tinge of brown left on top, and what used to be a hearty beard was down to little more than stubble.

He smiled across the table—the same smile people used to say Casey inherited when he was a kid. Come to think of it, no one said that much lately, though Casey knew he was looking more and more like his father by the day, set apart only by the asymmetrical slant of his left eye. Julie came by with a steaming cup and offered to refill Casey's. He waved her off with a tired hand. Dave took a sip.

"How's Joe holding up?"

"Not great. Last thing he needed trying to kick the drinking was all this."

"Probably not. But we never get to choose what happens. All you can do is handle it."

Casey breathed out through his nostrils. "Easier said than done."

"I know it is," his dad said, looking out the window wistfully toward the white steeple of the Methodist Church across the street. They talked about the place up in Godwin—Casey's grandparents' old house, which his parents moved into. Casey asked how his mom was doing— how she was really doing.

The same dementia that had lulled his grandmother into catatonia seemed to be showing signs in his mom, albeit very early ones. It was something no one wanted to acknowledge or talk about, but someone would have to at some point.

"She's fine, Case. Nothing to worry about."

"Not yet," Casey said.

"You know, you've always been a worrier. Ever since you were little."

"Yeah?" Casey asked, half-expecting his dad to offer some magical explanation for why he was the way he was.

"I remember one night, snow blowing like hell had frozen over, you sat by the door looking down the road for your mom's headlights for two hours, waiting for her to get home from the office."

Casey remembered it too. His dad was right—he'd always worried. Carried weights of concern that weren't his to control.

His mind flashed to the burning Camaro.

"I stopped over to Mrs. Potter's the other day," Casey said, changing the subject. His dad asked how she was, and for a split second, Casey thought of saying something about his mom not driving anymore, having noted Ruth's car sitting idle on flat tires. But he thought better of it. His dad wouldn't hear it. Not yet.

His Dad shifted and stretched in the booth. "I'm headed back up to Godwin after I run to the hardware store for a few things."

"Tell mom hi for me."

"You coming for Christmas?"

"Probably. Dunno. Depends." Casey gestured down at the paperwork.

"I'm sorry, Case. It's a helluva thing. God, Howard Meyers?"

"Nothing is proven yet, Dad. Nothing for sure."

"I know, I know. Still . . ."

"What about Mel?" Casey asked, shifting back to the subject of holiday plans.

"Well, your mom was trying to convince her to come home this year. Would be good to see the grandkids. I guess Steve has a big caseload right now—some lawsuit between the Navajo Nation and the State of Arizona."

Casey nodded. He hadn't seen Melissa for a couple years now—or his litigator brother-in-law and his niece and nephew. She'd married several years older than herself, so the rush had been on to have kids.

They didn't talk much. Not like they should.

When they'd finished breakfast, Casey walked his dad up to the counter. As usual, they did the old song and dance of who would pay the bill, his dad winning out by sheer seniority. "We'll talk soon, give you a call."

"Sounds good, Dad."

"Take care of yourself, Case."

Casey spotted Aly on his way out, catching her eye, but she was busy, and he needed to get back to the station. After his dad stepped out the door, Casey went back to the booth for his paperwork and coat.

That was when he saw the business card. *JG Logistics*, written in black corporate font on white.

He flipped the card over and saw a red-and-black hexagonal logo, two of the sides broken before meeting the others, and two small circles near those breaks.

Casey looked around the busy café, spotting a couple of old regulars sitting where the stranger had been. He thought about throwing it in the trash and chalking it up to somebody seeing him going over official looking documents and figuring him for an entrepreneurial type who might have need for the services of a logistics company. A shameless plug and nudge.

But throwing on his coat, he tucked the card in his pocket and gathered the reports under his arm. He wasn't sure why. Just a twinge and pull in his mind that said keep it. The faint tugging on the corner of his mind that he wished so many times he'd listened to the night when he'd pulled over TJ Hopkins.

He started at the chintzy warble of a motion-sensing ghost hanging by the door as he made his way out.

Halloween.

That's right. Curfew or not, missing kid or not, kids would be hitting the streets tonight. For a couple tightly watched hours anyway.

He got in his car and cranked the heat. He pulled that card back out again, set it on the dash, wondering who the hell had left it, with a hunch it had been that man in the corner booth. Casey just knew he hadn't seen him around before, and now wasn't exactly the best time to be a stranger in Westville.

Who was he?

And who—or what—was *JG Logistics*?

DEVIL'S PEAK

Surveyor-5 Radio

Transcript Date: *[REDACTED]*

HQ: Surveyor-5, confirm status. You're at Grid Reference 73-A. Proceed with geological readings.

Surveyor-5: Copy, HQ. Initial scans show . . . uh, anomalies. Surface disruptions. *[REDACTED]* deposits aren't matching projections. Hold on . . . There's . . . some kind of disturbance here.

HQ: Clarify. What kind of disturbance?

Surveyor-5: Wildlife remains. Recent. But . . . not scavenger activity. Patterns are . . . off. Blood's fresh, but something's . . . weird.

HQ: Acknowledged. Proceed with caution. Confirm status.

Surveyor-5: *(static)* I can't breathe... the air is too thin. *(Pause)* Something's watching. I see *[REDACTED]* *(muffled static)*

HQ: Surveyor-5, fall back immediately. Await retrieval. Do you copy?

Surveyor-5: *(unintelligible)* It's here . . . *(distorted static)*

HQ: Surveyor-5, respond! Do you copy?!

HQ: *(silence)* Get me the Director. Now.

1

"I can't believe I'm doing this," Kyle grumbled.

He fidgeted with his neatly pressed Boy Scout uniform. His sash was weighed down with badges gleaming under the dim glow of the porch light.

"Would you just knock already?" Olivia said, crossing her arms.

The white plastic of her *Scream* mask dangled loosely from her fingers, its hollow eyes staring back at her in some cheap, unspoken dare. Same costume as last year. Same cheap vinyl cloak. She could've picked something new, something different. But everything else had changed, and it was something familiar, despite the reek of plastic, chemicals, and sweat.

A sharp wind tugged at her hood, carrying the distant echoes of kids laughing and sneakers slapping against pavement. Up and down the block, jack-o-lanterns flickered, faces grinning in dimming light.

Meanwhile, Kyle had been stalling for a good two minutes, his knuckles hovering just shy of the door.

Austin, already impatient, shoved him forward. His half-assed zombie costume—a collection of mismatched, tattered clothes—did little to hide his irritation. "Come on, man. We don't have all night."

Kyle groaned but finally knocked. "Happy now?" he muttered.

The door swung open, revealing a man with a thick mustache, a shiny bald patch surrounded by a ring of gray hair, and a flannel shirt that strained slightly over his belly.

He squinted at them before his expression softened with recognition.

"Hey, Uncle Roger," Kyle mumbled. "Is Eli ready?"

"What, no trick-or-treat?"

"Ah, I'm kidding," Roger said, rubbing the back of his neck before calling inside. "Eli! Your friends are here!"

A few seconds later, a gangly boy with pale blond hair and oversized glasses bounded onto the porch, throwing back a mini-package of purple and neon pink Nerds, his Boy Scout uniform nearly identical to Kyle's but twice as weighed down with merit badges.

"Hey, guys!" Eli chirped, practically vibrating with enthusiasm as he crunched on the candy.

"You kids be careful out there," Roger said, his tone pointed. "Things are . . . you know."

"We will," Olivia replied coolly. "I'll keep them in line."

Roger grunted, clearly unconvinced, but shut the door behind them.

As they stepped off the porch, Eli beamed. "Man, I'm so jazzed for this. Isn't this great, Kyle? We get to put our Scout skills to *real* use. Oh, man."

"How many times have I told you that no one says '*jazzed*'?" Kyle let out a long-suffering groan, dragging a hand down his face. "Remind me to not let him have anymore sugar."

Eli wheezed, took a quick puff from his inhaler, and extended a hand to Olivia. "Eli Lancaster, troop leader in training. Nice to *officially* meet you."

Olivia shook his hand, hiding a smirk as Kyle groaned again. "Olivia Fischer, future Westville restaurateur and heiress," she quipped, because she couldn't think of anything else. "Thanks for helping us," she added.

"Helping? Are you *kidding*? This is the most exciting night of my *life*!"

Olivia tried to steer him back on track. "Did you get the key to the shed?"

Eli grinned mischievously. "No need. Dad keeps it hidden under a barrel around the side."

Kyle threw up his hands. "You *could* have told us that earlier."

Eli shrugged. "Where's the fun in that?"

Austin sighed. "We should hit a few houses first."

It was part of the plan—stick to the river-adjacent houses for a while, trick-or-treating just enough to look convincing. Later, they'd loop down toward the cemetery and Harrison Street, where they'd ditch the candy run and slip toward the Scout cabin. If anyone saw them, they'd just be another group of kids pushing curfew.

Eli nodded, hefting his pillowcase like a soldier preparing for battle. "Excellent idea. Plus, I could really go for a Snickers or two."

Olivia laughed despite herself, the sound foreign in her throat after days of tension.

"Let's do that," she said, her voice softening. "Once it's darker, we head to the cabin."

"Yes, ma'am!" Eli snapped a salute before marching down the leaf-strewn sidewalk.

Kyle moaned. "See what I mean? Why'd I even bring him?"

"You know why. And at least someone has a good attitude," Olivia replied, brushing past him.

"Whatever. You can thank me later. *He* made me promise to wear this stupid uniform. Lamest costume ever."

They moved down the street, the night deepening around them.

Kids in costumes darted between porches, plastic pumpkins bouncing at their sides. Olivia's gaze snagged on a pair of girls dressed as princesses, their sequined skirts glimmering in the glow of a nearby porch light.

Last year, she and Millie had been out here, too.

They'd gone home afterward, dumped their candy onto Millie's bedroom floor, and argued over trades. Millie offered up her Almond Joys first, pretending she wasn't secretly hoarding all the Kit-Kats. Eating too much and watching *Hocus Pocus*, reciting most of the movie until sugar induced delirium drew them into laughing fits.

That was last year.

Now, the streets felt wrong. Like a place she didn't belong anymore.

Her grip tightened on the mask in her hand.

Ahead, the street curved toward the woods, where branches clawed at the gathering clouds. The wind whispered through them, rattling dead leaves.

A cold determination settled deep in Olivia's chest, sharp and unyielding.

Tonight, they would find Millie.

They had to.

2

Darkness swallowed Westville before 7 p.m. and a light spit of rain began misting down in a steady hush, softening the edges of the world. The last traces of the sun faded behind thick clouds, turning the world to a shrouded blur.

Olivia hoisted her pack higher, the straps digging into her shoulders as she led the way down the winding dirt road toward the Boy Scout cabin. Her flashlight cut through the night, its narrow beam bouncing off slick mud and scattered leaves.

They'd spent the last hour maintaining the ruse—hitting a few houses along the way, keeping up appearances.

Old Mrs. Potter, predictably, had been the most suspicious.

"Now, just what are you kids supposed to be?" she'd asked, peering at Austin over her thick glasses.

Austin hesitated. "Uh . . . zombie."

"An *Indian* zombie," Kyle quipped, grinning.

Austin shot him a look, flicking long, dark hair from his brow. "Sure. Undead Indian."

Mrs. Potter didn't look convinced. Her papery fingers hovered over the candy bowl a second longer before handing them each a handful of sticky, old-fashioned sweets wrapped in red-and-white stripes or crinkled gold foil.

"You kids stay outta trouble tonight," she warned.

A slight edge in her voice. A knowing one.

Now, the house was far behind them, and Olivia pushed forward, setting the pace. She felt better here, away from the prying stares and suffocating concern.

Out here, they could *do* something.

They came to a dirt turn around, and walked up wooden stairs to the cabin.

Eli jogged ahead, already searching along the side of the building. "Barrel ... barrel ... there." He dropped to a crouch, feeling along the ground until his fingers closed around something small and metallic. He shot back up, holding the key triumphantly.

"Got it."

Kyle exhaled hard, shifting on his feet. "Alright. Let's get this over with."

The inside of the cabin smelled of old wood and damp earth, the air thick with dust and time.

Olivia moved toward a shelf lined with gear, running her fingers over the cold metal casings of the flashlights before grabbing a few and checking their batteries. She tossed one to each of them, the dim beams casting eerie, shifting shadows against the walls.

Eli stuffed a walkie-talkie into his pocket, gave the other to Kyle, and tucked another flashlight under his arm. "Alright, here's the plan," he said, adjusting his pack. "To get to Devil's Peak, we follow the trail until we hit the power lines. We follow those the rest of the way."

"How many miles?" Kyle asked, frowning.

Eli shrugged. "Dunno."

Austin smirked. "You can handle a few, right?"

Kyle rolled his eyes.

As they turned for the door, the silence shattered.

A violent crash split the room, followed by the sharp clatter of falling metal.

Olivia jolted, her flashlight trembling in her grip. Kyle let out a strangled yelp.

Austin snapped his head toward the noise, his whole body tensed. "Something moved back there."

No one breathed.

The corner of the cabin seemed darker than it had a second ago.

From the pile of toppled supplies, something small and furred scrambled out, glaring at them with beady black eyes.

Eli exhaled sharply. "Oh, come on."

The possum hissed, pale teeth flashing, before scurrying across the floor and disappearing through a gap in the wall.

Kyle groaned, pressing a hand to his chest. "Alright, that's it," he said, producing a bottle of strawberry passion Fruitopia from his bag and cracking it open.

Olivia was joined by the others in staring at him.

"What? Everything a growing boy needs."

"You do know there's not any real fruit in that, right?" Eli offered cheerfully.

Kyle glared at his cousin downing a hearty swig, smacking his lips.

"Here," he said, offering the bottle around. Austin shrugged, and took a swig. Olivia, despite the inevitable boy backwash, did the same. She tried to pass it over to Eli, but Kyle snatched it away.

"You've had enough sugar already."

Olivia zipped up her pack and threw it on. "Let's go. Before the rain gets worse."

She shouldered open the door, stepping back into the night, the weight of what lay ahead pressing against her ribs.

Outside, the silence stretched wide, broken only by the rustling of brittle leaves and the occasional plunk of rain against the thinning canopy. The cabin shrank into the dark behind them, swallowed whole by the night. Olivia kept her flashlight trained on the narrow path winding alongside the riverbank.

Sparse fat drops splattered against her hood. The wind picked up, whispering through the trees.

Then—a sharp crack of underbrush. A low, mocking chuckle.

Olivia whipped around, the beam of her flashlight slicing through the darkness.

Brett Huizinga and his cronies—Kevin and Matt—emerged from the trees, grins curdled with malice. And, probably a cocktail of stolen halloween candy, sugar, and liquor, judging by the pillowcases slung over Kevin's shoulder and the mostly empty peppermint schnapps bottle that Matt juggled playfully.

"What are you doing out here with these freaks, Fischer?" Brett sneered.

Kevin snorted. "Probably looking for that snitch."

Olivia clenched her fists. They didn't have time for this.

"None of your damn business, Brett."

"What she said," Kyle barked, flipping him off with both hands.

"Just cool it," Austin muttered, stepping forward.

Brett's face darkened, a slow flush creeping up his neck.

"Someone needs to teach you some respect."

Behind Olivia, Eli took a deep, wheezing hit from his inhaler. She could feel the younger boy trembling.

"It's okay," she muttered under her breath. "They're all talk."

Brett wrenched the schnapps bottle from Matt, slammed it against a tree in a shatter of glass, jagged points glinting in his grip now.

Austin swore.

Olivia's gut lurched.

Brett grinned, raising the crude instrument of pain. "Let's see about that."

"Run!" Olivia grabbed Eli's arm and yanked him back.

The flashlight swung wildly as they bolted into the woods, branches slapping at their arms and legs. Behind them, Brett's voice erupted in a furious shout, followed by the chaotic thrash of bodies crashing through the brush.

"FREAKING RUN!" Kyle yelped, his voice cracking.

The woods blurred into a twisting maze, the narrow path slick with mud, roots, and stones jutting out.

Austin sprinted ahead, Olivia right behind him, her breath ragged. She stole a glance back—Eli's pale face shone in the beam of her flashlight, Kyle just behind, his uneven gait jerky with panic.

She didn't hear Brett anymore.

Didn't mean he wasn't there.

"I think we lost them!" she gasped, slowing, her pulse thundering.

The shadows thickened, trees closing in, swallowing what little moonlight filtered through the cloud-scattered sky. Olivia's flashlight flickered, the bulb buzzing, and steadied.

A deep, sour feeling twisted in her stomach.

Eli skidded to a halt, gripping her arm. "Wait!" He doubled over, gulping for breath, his fingers clenched tight around his compass.

Austin bent over, hands on his knees. "What?"

Eli's head snapped up, his glasses slipping down his nose. "We're off the trail."

A cold fist closed around Olivia's ribs.

"We're fine," Austin said, though his voice wasn't nearly as confident as he wanted it to be. "Just have to—find our way back."

"Right," Olivia said. "Could be worse."

Kyle straightened. "It so happens that this astronomy badge of mine allows me to navigate by starlight. Just need the clouds to clear out a little and—"

And then, because fate had a cruel sense of humor, the sky cracked open.

Rain pelted them in sheets, cold and needling.

"Son of a bitch," Kyle yelled, kicking the ground.

The trail pitched upward, winding into steep switchbacks, leading toward the ridge overlooking Westville. Every step was a fight—boots slipping, hands scraping against wet bark.

Olivia checked over her shoulder, making sure they were together.

Eli, soaked and shivering but focused on his compass.

Austin, steady but tense, his eyes darting through the dark.

Kyle, muttering curses under his breath, tripping over roots.

The rain roared, drowning out everything. Until somewhere behind them, the trees shifted. Something moved. Olivia wasn't sure if it was just the wind and wasn't sure she wanted to know.

"Stay together," Olivia reminded them, her voice barely carrying over the steady patter of rain and the low murmur of the river. Her grip tightened on the flashlight, her knuckles white. The ground was turning slick beneath their feet, mud sucking at their boots, the path ahead vanishing into the shifting darkness.

The climb grew steeper. Roots shot up—broken bones through the earth—and slick rocks waited for a careless footfall. The trees pressed in around them, their jutting limbs tangling into a dense canopy that swallowed what little moonlight managed to slip through the storm. The deeper they went, the more Westville and its streetlights and houses felt like something imagined, a place that had never really existed.

Austin pulled up beside her, his breathing a little heavier now. "Not gonna lie, the trails are just a little creepier at night. In the rain. On Halloween," he muttered, casting his flashlight toward the trees, his beam catching nothing but black trunks and restless shadows.

She couldn't help but agree, times a novemdecillion. That weird-ass, useless number sailed into her head from nowhere, from a time she'd jabbed at Millie for knowing more about numbers than she would ever need to. All as Millie helped her—for the novemdecillionth time—to not completely flunk math class.

A warm plume of regret flared in her throat. But at least it reminded her why they were out here.

They pressed on, the river fading behind them as the trail wound into the thicker woods, the switchbacks climbing higher. Olivia's legs burned, but she didn't slow down. She kept the flashlight trained ahead, trying not to focus on the way the darkness seemed to shift at the edges of its glow.

Austin's light bobbed beside her. "Think we're almost there?"

She nodded. "Almost."

Ahead, the trees thinned, revealing a break in the canopy where the ridge opened onto a clearing. Relief flickered through her. They were close now.

Then Austin stopped short. "Wait."

"What?" Olivia turned toward him. She froze.

The silence pressed in all at once.

Not the usual quiet of the woods, full of hidden rustlings and distant night sounds. This was something else—something *wrong.* The wind had stopped. The trees no longer swayed. The rain too, seemed muffled.

She heard Eli take another hit from his inhaler. "Didn't think Devil's Peak went that high . . . anyone else having trouble breathing?"

"No, because no one else is asthmatic," Kyle snapped.

Olivia slapped Kyle's arm. "No," she said, drawing in a slow breath that ended up not enough of one. "He's right."

The air felt thin.

Olivia's stomach clenched. Her flashlight beam trembled as she swept it over the trees.

Then she saw it.

A red glow, faint at first, pulsing through the black. Hovering. Watching.

"What is that?" Kyle whispered.

Olivia's breath hitched as it seared through the trees, moving closer. The temperature dropped so quickly she could see her next breath come out in a cloud, misting the beam of her flashlight. The red light flickered and danced, its edges rippling as it took on the shape of an orb, the air around it blurring in iridescent swirls.

The glow shifted—moved.

It shunted forward so fast she barely had time to register it, a flickering red streak tearing through the trees. A deep thrumming filled the air, vibrating through her chest.

Then came the hissing.

It sliced through the silence, sharp and menacing. A shadow began to take form within the orb, its jagged, spindly limbs flickering out. Two glowing red eyes appeared in the darkness, locking onto them.

"Come on!" Olivia's voice cracked as she yanked Eli's arm, her grip iron-tight. They bolted, her flashlight beam slicing wildly through the rain-streaked dark.

The orb followed, its crimson light warping the forest, casting shadows that bent and twisted in ways that shouldn't be possible. They *moved*—elongating, retreating, snapping forward like grasping hands.

The hiss rose, folding in on itself, layering with whispers that clawed at the edges of Olivia's mind. The words weren't spoken so much as imprinted in her mind:

"You . . . are the guilty ones . . ."

Olivia's pulse pounded in her ears, drowning out the rain. Her lungs burned, her legs ached, but she pushed forward.

A scream to her right.

Olivia skidded to a halt, her flashlight swinging wildly as she scanned the slope. Her heart dropped as she spotted him, crumpled on the ground, holding his leg. "Eli!"

Panic ignited in Olivia's chest. She barely registered her own movements as she slid down the slick hillside, catching only flashes of wet leaves and jagged rock before she hit the ground beside him.

"Can you stand?" she asked breathlessly, her words barely audible over the pounding rain.

His ankle was bent wrong.

"I think it's broken or . . . ah . . . dislocated," he choked out, his breath shuddering. "I can't—"

Olivia felt it before she saw it. A weight pressing down, like the world had folded in on itself. The red light pulsed, stretching into something more—something solid.

A shape bled out of the darkness.

Limbs, too long and jagged, shattered antlers and twisted roots and broken bones fused into one. Claws curling, trembling, flexing. A head, featureless save for the two burning pits of red boring into her skull. A blurry and wrong shadow.

The hiss coiled around her bones.

You are the guilty ones . . . You are the guilty ones . . .

Something in Olivia fractured.

Her mind split between now and then, between Millie's last look of frustration before storming off and her father's fading laughter, a life that had slipped through her fingers, leaving only ghosts in its wake.

Her foot slid back. Her hand brushed something solid.

A flashlight. Eli's.

Her fingers closed around it. Without thinking, without knowing why, maybe because it was the only thing she could do, she flicked it on.

The air shattered with a sound like splintering glass. Static and whispers in reverse. Rippling shards creased the air as the shadow recoiled, its form stuttering, flickering, distorting.

Smoke rose—iridescent colors, shifting in unnatural patterns.

The shadows jerked back. The red glow fractured.

Olivia didn't wait to understand what she was seeing.

"Come on," she gasped, ducking down, pulling Eli's arm over her shoulders. Every muscle in her body screamed as she forced them both forward, the weight of him nearly taking them both down.

"Olivia! Eli!"

Kyle and Austin's voices cut through the rain, distant but closing in.

She stumbled forward, heart hammering, her flashlight swinging wildly. Every few steps, she dared a glance behind.

It was gone, but the feeling wasn't.

By the time they reached the field behind the Scout cabin, Austin's flashlight bobbed toward them. Relief was instant and crippling. Her limbs were a mushed blob of jello fallen to the floor.

Kyle's face was twisted into something between horror and exhaustion. "Your dad is gonna kill me," he muttered, eyes locked on Eli's ankle.

"If he does . . ." Eli muttered, "can I have your Playstation?"

"How about we focus on the fact that we're alive after being chased by—" Olivia stopped, breath hitching.

By what?

She didn't know. Didn't want to. But she knew, then and there, she *had* to.

Blue and red lights flashed, accompanied by the quick alarming wail of a police siren; a door opened and shut as a flashlight speared toward them.

Kyle gulped. "Or the fact that we're in deep shit."

Broken curfew. A broken ankle. Teenagers wandering the woods the week after a girl went missing. Probably, they were in deep shit.

But it didn't matter. Not after what they'd seen.

Olivia's hands shook. She swallowed, looked at Kyle and Austin in turn, her own breath still ragged.

Whatever that thing was, she could still feel it.

She could still hear the whispers.

And the worst part was—

She knew somewhere deep down, it had Millie.

3

When Casey pulled into the station late Halloween night, he didn't expect to see Aly's lime-green Beetle parked in the lot.

A prickle of unease crawled up his spine. He killed the engine of the Monty, but for a moment, just sat there.

Whatever this was, it wasn't good.

Inside, he spotted Aly, her mother Kathy, and Olivia Fischer in the interview room, seated across from Travis Johnson.

Reynolds met him in the hall, looking as tired as Casey felt.

"What happened?"

Reynolds sighed, rubbing a hand over his face. "Seems like that girl just can't stay outta trouble. She and a few other kids went off into the woods earlier tonight. Said they were looking for the Thompson girl."

Casey swore under his breath. It was something he probably would have done as a kid—hell, he and Joe both—if one of their friends had gone missing. Now, as an adult, knowing what he knew about the things that lurked in the dark, it wasn't so easy to shrug off.

Especially not right now.

"Roger Lancaster called it in when his boy didn't come home on time," Reynolds continued. "Kid broke his damn ankle falling down a ravine. They told Johnson some story about running from something."

"Running from what?"

Reynolds snorted. "Benson, we're talking about a bunch of kids out on Halloween night. You think they needed much more than a twig snapping to send 'em running scared?"

Casey frowned. "Except they went out there knowing one of their friends had just gone missing. Had enough guts for that."

"Fine line between courage and stupidity."

Casey nodded, but as he looked through the window at Olivia—pale, tired, her arms wrapped around herself bracing against something more than just the cold—he knew there was more to it.

She wasn't just scared.

She was *haunted*.

A muffled voice rose through the door, sharp and clipped.

Kathy Fischer shot up from her seat, bracing her hands on the table as she snapped at Johnson. Casey didn't catch the words, but he caught the tone. He was at the door in two strides, throwing it open just as Reynolds stepped up beside him.

"She broke curfew, and believe me, I'll deal with her." Kathy's voice was taut with restrained fury. "But my daughter doesn't need to be interrogated like this."

Travis kept his eyes locked on Olivia.

"You're going to stop lying and tell me what you were really doing out there," he said.

"We didn't do anything wrong," Olivia shot back, her tone defensive but frayed at the edges. "We just wanted to find Millie."

"Apart from breaking curfew and trespassing on private property."

"Eli had a key. We didn't break into anything."

Travis slid something across the table. A dime bag of weed.

Olivia barely looked at it. "That isn't mine."

"That's what your friends all said too. So whose is it?"

She exhaled a sharp, humorless laugh. "Talk to Brett Huizinga. Him and his goons were out there too." Her lip curled. "Went after us with a broken bottle of booze."

Kathy jerked toward her. "Why didn't you say that before?"

"That's a big accusation," Johnson said, folding his arms. "You better be sure."

"So find him and ask," Olivia snapped.

Casey stepped forward. "And that's who you were running from?"

Olivia glanced at him, then looked away. "Yeah."

Johnson stiffened. "Stay out of this, Benson."

Casey felt a flare of heat crawl up his throat, but before he could respond, Reynolds cleared his throat.

"Alright," he said, opening the door wider, "I think we're good here."

Johnson's hand slammed on the table.

"I'm getting tired of being jerked around."

"Johnson!" Reynolds barked. "You're done."

Travis leered at him, breathing hard, as if just realizing the Sergeant was there. His gaze flicked briefly to Casey, then Olivia.

"I—I'm sorry, Sarge . . ."

"Take a breather, son."

Casey watched him go, his movements stiff. Travis had always been a hothead.

Reynolds exhaled, looking back at Kathy. "I apologize for that."

She sighed, the fight draining out of her. "I appreciate the stress you're all under. And I'm very sorry my daughter's actions have added to that." She placed a hand on Olivia's back, who flinched, jerking forward, then bolted for the door.

Aly stepped into the hall just as Olivia pushed past her. "What happened? I heard yelling."

"It's fine," Kathy muttered, pinching the bridge of her nose.

Casey caught up to Olivia before she reached the lobby.

"Can I have a word?"

Kathy nodded. Olivia sighed, but followed him as he stepped to the edge of the hall.

"Heard you said you were being chased tonight," he said. "Want to tell me about that?"

She was silent.

"Why? So you can tell me I'm making shit up too?"

"Try me."

Her throat bobbed. Her fingers twitched at her sides.

"...Someone—*something*—was after us."

Casey's pulse ticked up. "Not just Brett?"

She shook her head. "They chased us, yeah, but there was something else. It was like a shadow."

Casey frowned. "You mean couldn't make out who it was?"

Olivia's brows furrowed, her head jerking. "No. Not just that. There was this red light too. Shooting between the trees. Until it caught up to us and—this thing, this *thing* came out of it."

His stomach twisted.

Olivia uncrossed her arms, her voice unsteady. "And there was this hissing sound . . ."

The words hit him like a hammer to the chest.

His mind flashed back to the clearing, the whispers curling at the edge of his thoughts, the sensation of something watching.

"You're the guilty ones," Olivia said.

His breath caught.

"What did you say?"

"That's what I heard," Olivia murmured. "Like a whisper."

A chill prickled the back of Casey's neck. He swallowed, forcing himself steady.

"Let me guess. You don't believe me."

"Didn't say that, did I?"

Olivia chewed at her lip for a moment, glancing at the floor. "I guess while we're at it, there was this guy at the mill."

"When?"

"Saturday morning. A truck driver, I think maybe. Ethan."

"What about him?"

Olivia hesitated. "He just . . . looked at me weird. And he was dirty. Muddy boots, muddy pants. Like he'd been walking in the woods or by the river."

Casey exhaled through his nose. "Could be nothing."

"Maybe," Olivia muttered.

"You told all this to Reynolds when he interviewed you Saturday morning?"

She shook her head. "I told him about Friday night, but I couldn't think straight and before I knew it we were leaving the interview room."

Her eyes flicked toward the breakroom just as Travis stalked past, his movements taut, like a coiled wire.

She frowned. "Who shit in his Count Chocula?"

Casey let out a dry chuckle despite himself, and despite all the threads looming through his mind.

"Maybe Aly *should* go out with him," Olivia mused, smirking. "Might make him less of a buzzkill."

She started toward the door.

Casey hesitated. "She said no?"

Olivia turned, lifting a brow. "Why do you care?"

Casey sniffed. "Your ride's waiting."

"Snooze you lose. If you want to date her just ask. She won't bite." She gagged melodramatically. "That I know of."

"Duly noted," Casey said, scratching the back of his neck and straining to be sure Aly didn't hear from the lobby.

Olivia studied him for a second longer. "Thanks for listening."

Casey nodded as she walked off.

He checked in with Reynolds, who was already in the process of reaching out to the Huizingas about Brett. If the kid really had pulled a weapon of some kind, Reynolds would handle it.

Casey's mind was elsewhere.

'Ethan' was worth looking into. And more than that—he *believed* Olivia.

How could he not, when they'd heard the same thing?

"You're the guilty ones . . ."

The shift was going to be hell with all this rattling around in his brain. Might as well put the time to use.

He picked up the phone and dialed Joe.

Joe answered, his voice rough.

"Hey, man," Casey exhaled. "Wish I had more to tell you. Nothing new yet."

A pause. "So why are you calling?" Joe's voice was edged with barely restrained frustration.

"Listen, is there an 'Ethan' that works for PRINCE?"

A beat of silence. "Yeah, Crawley. Hired him not too long ago to replace a guy we had to let go. Decent guy, hard worker."

"Got it."

"Why?"

"His name just came up."

Joe went silent. A weighty, unspoken static between them.

"Something to do with Millie?"

"No," Casey lied. "Nothing like that."

There wasn't proof this Crawley was involved. Not yet. But no good would come from getting Joe worked up over a false lead.

Casey could feel the shift on the other end of the line. The clipped, careful silence.

Joe exhaled sharply. "Alright."

Casey hated the way it landed because he knew what Joe was thinking.

If Casey—his best friend—was already onto other things, other cases, what did that say about the rest of the department? The investigation as a whole? Feds or not, it probably seemed everyone was already letting off the gas.

The opposite was true.

For Casey, at least.

Before heading out, he ran a search on the NCIC terminal.

Ethan Crawley, 43. A veteran. A possession charge from years back, plus a couple misdemeanors, public intoxication. Nothing major, but enough to keep him on Casey's radar.

Casey rubbed at his neck as he walked out to the garage trying to shake off the conversation with Joe. Right now, what mattered was taking the next best action—not fixing whatever his friend thought about him.

There'd be time for that—after Millie was found.

He climbed into the patrol car, started it, and pulled out into the night.

4

Casey cruised down Main Street, veering into the gas station and cutting the engine.

He sat there for a while, staring past the rain-streaked windshield at the looming silhouette of PRINCE Milling. The grain silos edged with a metallic red glint, bleeding out from the sign on the far rooftop.

Just before 3 a.m. a PRINCE tractor-trailer, having snaked off the highway three miles south of town, would rumble into downtown Westville. Casey had watched the pattern enough times to bet on it. At 3:05, the distant whine of semi-truck brakes cut through the rain.

There it was. Right on time.

The truck slowed at the blinking red light before pulling into the warehouse lot. PRINCE trailer 042.

Casey sat up straighter, locking onto the driver's side window. He couldn't make out every detail, but the semi-gaunt face and stringy hair matched what he'd seen in the database.

Ethan Crawley.

As Crawley cracked open the door of the black Kenworth tractor and onto the step, he paused.

Crawley stared—not just at the road, not just toward the patrol car, but straight at Casey.

His breath slowed, the way it did when someone cornered you, the static hum of unease curling in his ribs.

Crawley's posture wasn't tense, wasn't challenging.

He just stood there. Watching.

Then, in the quiet, Casey heard it.

A faint, curling hiss, a sibilant slithering between the raindrops.

Crawley disappeared into the warehouse, and the garage door rumbled down behind him.

Casey tapped the steering wheel, exhaling through his nose as the wipers slashed in rhythm, fluorescent blooms of gas station lights made thick by the mist and light rain.

He had nothing solid on Crawley. Except for the way he'd leered at the patrol car just now and Olivia's account of her interaction with him. But something pulled at the corners of Casey's mind, tugging them right up and over his frontal cortex—or at least that's the term he thought he remembered from his biology and anatomy courses.

His temple throbbed thinking about Sunday when the feds came to town, and whoever he'd seen standing near the road, right on the corner of the PRINCE front offices beneath the wrought iron street lamps of Main Street.

Could it have been Crawley?

He popped a Tylenol and swallowed it with a swig from a crunching water bottle.

Olivia was right. There was something about him.

And right now, Casey needed something—anything—to go on.

5

When Casey knocked on the front door of the PRINCE Milling offices early Friday morning after his shift, none other than Jack Thompson himself answered.

"Casey," he said, pulling off reading glasses and holding a packet of papers in his hand. "Come in."

The scent of fresh drywall and money calcified into real estate hit him as he walked in. The offices had just been renovated, coinciding with the company's recent expansion and the unprecedented growth two years in a row. He and Joe had celebrated several months prior, which was also about the time Casey became aware of Joe's excessive drinking problem.

Casey followed Jack up the stairs to his office.

Jack walked over to his desk, grabbed something dull and metallic with a scrape and set in a drawer that he closed. He slapped the paperwork down. "So," he started, expression hardening as if bracing himself, "anything new?"

"No, sir," Casey said. "Not exactly."

"I see."

"I'm sorry. The feds are on it too now."

"So I've heard. Can't be a good sign."

Casey paused, weighing his words. "I'd say the more manpower, the better our odds." Which also meant Lochlear and Reeves breathing down their necks at every turn.

Casey glanced down at a framed picture on Jack's desk of the whole Thompson clan, including Joe's older brother who had moved out of state. Millie was young in the picture, standing between Erin and Joe, her arms clasped tight around her dad's leg.

"First Thompson girl in a couple generations. We're proud of her. She became our little cheerleader around the mill, and 'Millie' just stuck."

"She's a smart kid," Casey offered. "And tough."

Jack sniffed and nodded. "That she is. Well, what can I do for you?"

"I wanted to ask you about Ethan Crawley. He's a more recent hire of yours."

Jack straightened, picking up a thick black mug with PRINCE emblazoned in red across the side. "Sure. One of Joe's." He took a few long strides over to the coffee machine and poured himself a cup, offering some with a tip of the pot. Casey waved him off.

"Olivia Fischer, one of Millie's friends," Casey said, "She had a . . . strange interaction with Ethan last Saturday morning."

"What sort of interaction?" Jack pressed.

"Jittery and allegedly a little aggressive toward her."

"Okay," Jack said, taking a couple of steps toward Casey and sipping the steaming liquid. "And where was this?"

Casey drew in a breath. "Just here outside the loading dock."

"So she was trespassing?"

"I suppose so, yes."

"Well, from what I hear, Ethan can be a little prickly, but I'm sure he was just doing his job. Didn't want a kid being a liability."

That had been Casey's first thought too.

"Could be," Casey said, thinking of the way Crawley had stared *him* down.

Jack narrowed his pale eyes. "You think he might know something about Millie?"

"I'm not sure about that, sir."

"If that's the case, you just say the word. I'm all about standing up for my employees, but if there's a whiff that he had anything to do with—" Jack stopped himself and drew a deep breath. "You tell me, son."

"It couldn't hurt," Casey said.

Jack gave him Ethan's information. Apparently, Ethan was renting one of the dingy apartments across from Wahl's Softee Cream. Not far.

"Anything you need, you don't hesitate," Jack said.

Casey started to head toward the door but turned.

"Actually, there is something. More of a question really."

Jack raised an eyebrow. "What's on your mind?"

"Is there anyone you can think of," Casey began carefully, "anyone at all, who might have a grudge against you or PRINCE Milling? Something from years ago? I know it's a long shot, but . . ."

"You think this is about me? About the mill?" Jack's face darkened, and for a moment, he looked insulted.

"I'm just covering all the bases," Casey said, holding up his hands.

Jack set his coffee cup down hard enough that it made a dull thud on the desk.

"Casey, I've spent my life keeping this company above water and this town on its feet. Sure, there are people who resent success. But none of them have the guts or brains to pull something like this."

Casey nodded, sensing the conversation was close to souring. "Fair enough. But a list of more recent hires wouldn't hurt. Just to rule out anything. Could be someone wanted to get close enough to hurt you or the company."

Jack frowned and just looked at Casey for a moment but eventually parted his lips and drew a breath.

"Sure. Whatever you need." He picked up the phone and called down to his secretary, asking for a printout of the document, and outside the door Casey heard the whir and grate of the dot matrix printer.

"Thanks Jack. Just trying to turn over every rock we can."

Jack nodded, and stepped toward the window, gesturing his mug to the old antique clock on the wall, the second hand ticking.

"My great grandfather salvaged this clock after the Wooden Row fire. Used to be on a post at the corner of Main and Harrison." He took a sip, his lips tight. He turned to look straight at Casey, the classic Jack Thompson size-up-stare. "Vetting some of my people is one thing. I just don't know what kind of answers you're hoping to find by dredging up some ancient history. This town's moved forward from all that. And time is one thing we can't afford to waste right now."

"I agree," Casey said. "And I'm giving her every second I can."

"And I'm—" Jack paused and looked down at the family photo on the ledge. "We're grateful, Casey."

Casey nodded and walked out the door. Jack's long-time secretary, a stout woman named Becky, handed him the employee list fresh off the printer. He thanked her absently as he read down through the list and walked back to the patrol car.

Jack had been quick to dismiss the notion of anyone within his own company or in the town sinking so low and doing something as heinous as kidnapping or harming his granddaughter. Casey would have wanted to deny that too were he in Jack's shoes.

Matter of fact. Point blank.

The reality was that enemies are made when you gain influence and power. It was the way the world worked, and as a cop you had to look at who had the most to gain or to lose, and follow the money trail.

He heard one Hart in his mind:

"Partiality isn't part of the equation. It can't be."

Everyone could be a suspect. Capable of anything.

Crawley was a better fit in Casey's mind. The evidence found with Howard Meyers had been circumstantial, and there was nothing conclusive about it.

If Jack knew anything—suspected anyone could have it out for him enough to do something to his granddaughter—he would have spoken up immediately and with all the fury and bluster big Jack was known for. Casey knew that for sure.

Then, grief and guilt made people do strange things. Casey of all people knew that well enough from the way his own compunctions had a habit of torpedoing his life. At least he wasn't oblivious. Just blissfully accustomed to it.

By the time he got back to the station, clocked out and changed out of uniform, his curiosity got the better of him.

He started walking.

He knew he shouldn't be doing it, but the old house Crawley was renting a room in was just a few blocks away. The cracked sidewalk across the road from Wahl's Softee Cream, which was shuddered up and closed for the season, led up to a barely hinged screen door. Casey opened it, and knocked on the cheap, thin wooden one behind.

He heard a muffled stereo blaring within. An old man, who immediately reeked of cigarettes and cats, opened the door. The guitar and vocal tandem snarl of Alice In Chains' *'Man In The Box'* spilled outside, bleeding into relative morning quiet as a couple cars hissed by at a trundle.

"Hell do you want?"

"Ethan around?" Casey asked.

The old man snorted and spat on the porch, close to Casey's shoe.

"He stiffed me on rent. You a friend of his?"

"Something like that."

"Well, get better friends. Haven't seen hide nor hair of him for two months."

There was a hitch in Casey's chest. "Any idea where he is?"

"Shit if I know. You tell him to pay what he owes."

The door slammed in Casey's face.

Casey started the walk back and wondered whether Joe, Jack, or anyone at PRINCE knew of Ethan's change in address—or maybe lack of address altogether. He was a truck driver mostly. Maybe living a vagabond lifestyle. The kind of guy who, if he was wandering Westville, might find his eyes wandering and lingering on people too.

Girls like Millie Thompson.

Casey knew that was a whole lot of assumptions. Maybe dangerous ones. Didn't change the fact that Olivia's account of Ethan—and now the fact that he wasn't living where his employer thought he was—didn't sit well.

When he got to the station, he unraveled said dangerous assumptions about Ethan couched as cautious suspicions to the Chief.

"Not much to bring him in on," Hart said, shuffling a small portion of the mountain of paperwork levied on him by the federal investigation. "Even for simple questioning."

"It's worth looking into, though. Right?"

"Maybe. But not by you."

"Why not?"

"I think the days are numbered with us as lead on this case. Those feds are becoming a pain-in-the-ass staple around here."

Casey glanced out the hall and down toward the radio room where Lochlear, Reeves, and now an assortment of other agents who'd come into town had set up shop.

"Running a check wouldn't hurt though," he added, holding up the PRINCE Milling employee list.

Hart sighed. "Do it. Just don't come to me unless there's something solid."

"Chief Hart," Lochlear said from the hall, pulling off his glasses and holding a document. "A moment?"

Hart nodded and walked out, seeming to visibly brace himself as he did. He headed for the briefing room, which meant the radio room would be vacant. What was that phrase from *Dead Poets Society*?

Carpe diem.

The faint green glow of the bulky CRT monitor illuminated the now dim empty room—Lochlear's conservative fastidiousness having single handedly tightened the department's neatness and house rules in the span of a few days—including turning out every light he could. The hum of the equipment was a familiar comfort, as tension buzzed in the back of his mind. He had the list of PRINCE Milling's recent hires laid out beside him, a crisp print-out with names, addresses, and hire dates. He had already underlined Ethan Crawley's name in red ink.

Casey started typing in the others. One by one, the names on the list turned into files on the screen. As he worked, a pattern began to emerge— DUIs, public intoxication, possession charges, domestic disturbances. Men with broken pasts, scraping together second chances under Jack Thompson's banner of redemption that he wasn't exactly shy about.

Casey's jaw tightened. He wanted this to be the thread that unraveled something bigger, something solid. But the more he thought about it, the more he realized these weren't criminals—they were screw-ups. A common denominator didn't mean guilt, no matter how much his gut twisted over Crawley.

The door creaked open behind him. Casey didn't need to look up to know who it was; the quiet click of deliberate footsteps gave it away. Agent Reeves.

"You always work this hard off the clock?" she asked, her tone casual but sharp enough to carve through the silence.

"Call it a bad habit," Casey bristled, his fingers pausing mid-typing. "Something I can help you with?"

Reeves stepped closer, her arms crossed, a faint smirk tugging at the corner of her mouth. "Just curious what's got you digging through PRINCE Milling employee records. Thought you were off this case."

"Funny. I didn't think I needed to run my tasks past you," Casey replied, turning back to the screen.

"Who pissed in your Froot Loops this morning?"

Casey exhaled through his nose, thinking suddenly that in a strange way Olivia Fischer and Reeves might have got on just fine for being at least twenty years apart. Casey figured Reeves had a few years on him, maybe 36 or 37. But he wasn't about to prod for a woman federal agent's age.

He resumed typing in each name and navigating the green and black interface as he relayed Olivia Fischer's run in with Ethan Crawley—mostly an attempt to be left alone.

But she leaned against the desk, a power move, her gaze flicking to the monitor, shining hazel eyes narrowing slightly. "So, you're running background checks on the whole roster."

"Just covering the bases," Casey said, his tone clipped. "And not everyone, no. PRINCE made a batch of new hires just recently. Focusing on those, for now."

She leaned in slightly, scanning the list beside him. A sharp scent of dark perfume smelling of smoke and mirrors gave him pause, and the screen gave her skin a kind of radioactive glow.

"DUIs, drug charges, public intoxication. Thompson's got a type, doesn't he?"

Casey turned to her, his frustration simmering. "You think this is funny?"

Her smirk faded, replaced by something more serious. "No, I don't. These are people who fall through the cracks, trying to start over. Sometimes they're just trying to keep their heads above water. Sometimes . . ." She trailed off, shrugging.

"Sometimes, what?" Casey pressed.

"They've got nothing left to lose," she said simply.

Or they're the kind of people the police and the feds wouldn't trust if they did speak up, Casey thought.

He turned back to the monitor, pulling up Ethan's file again.

"Crawley's got a few marks against him, nothing major. But he hasn't been living where he's supposed to. His landlord says he hasn't seen him in two months."

Reeves nodded slowly, thoughtful. "Not a good look but not much to go on."

Casey clenched his jaw, the edges of his irritation sharpening. "You don't think it's worth looking into?"

"Didn't say that," Reeves replied, her voice calm but firm. "I'm just saying it's thin. And in my experience, you don't want to stake your claim on thin ice."

Casey turned to her fully now, his frustration bubbling over. "And the alternative is sitting back and waiting for the perfect lead to fall in your lap. Meanwhile, Millie's out there, and we're running out of time."

Reeves didn't flinch. If anything, her eyes hardened. "You think we're not trying? I know what's at stake here. I do what I do for a reason, and I'm damn good at my job. So let us work."

The room fell silent, the tension between them taut as barbed wire.

After a beat Reeves stepped back, her expression cooling. "Look, you've got good instincts, but instincts don't close. Action does, with the evidence to back it up."

His eye caught on her badge again—'PK' below her name.

"Professional Killer?" he asked.

She cocked her head for the briefest moment then glanced down at her lanyard.

"If I told you, I'd have to kill you."

Casey snorted and shook his head as she turned and strode out of the room. The soft click of the door closing behind her echoing in the quiet. He turned back to the screen, his thoughts churning.

Reeves was right about one thing—he didn't have enough. But she was wrong if she thought he was going to let this go. The right thread was hanging loose somewhere.

And when he found it, Casey was going to pull it until the whole thing unraveled.

The green cursor blinked on the screen—like the ticking of a clock.

6

Olivia was grounded. Again.

This time, she didn't argue. What was the point? Sneaking out was one thing. Getting caught past curfew, when the whole town was on edge? Getting picked up by the police?

There was no talking her way out of this one.

Not that she had the energy for it. Not after what they'd seen in the woods on Halloween night.

Kathy stood in the doorway, arms crossed, trying to sound motherly again.

"I know you're going through a lot right now," she said, voice softer than usual. "But you can't keep doing this, Liv."

"Fine. I get it."

"I want to be here for you."

A sudden white hot plume ignited in Olivia. "Oh, like when you were there for me when dad was turning into a different person?"

"Liv, I know that it wasn't easy. And I could have handled things differently. But it was hard on all of—"

"I know it was hardest on you because you had to deal with everything. The restaurant, me, him. Whatever."

Kathy sighed, pressing her fingers to her temple. Defeated already. Good.

"You talk to her," she told Aly before walking out.

Aly lingered, arms folded across her chest.

"Are you going to lecture me too?" Olivia asked.

"I'm not telling her about the drinking last Friday," Aly said. "Or the pot."

Olivia stilled. She hadn't expected that.

"Why not?" she asked, voice quiet, wary.

Aly sighed. "Just stay put and out of trouble. For a few days, okay? Casey and the police are handling things."

Olivia swallowed the sharp response at the back of her throat. Handling things. Yeah. Sure.

"Alright," she muttered. "Thanks."

Aly nodded, heading for the stairs.

"You gonna date him again or what?" Olivia called after her.

Aly stopped mid-step, turned just enough to shoot an exasperated look over her shoulder. "I've gotta get to the restaurant."

She was gone.

The rest of the day, Olivia's mind spun in circles.

The woods. That thing.

She could see it—the way the red light had pulsed and fractured the air, thinning the world itself.

Her stomach twisted.

She'd heard stories before. About people who vanished—some in the woods, some in national parks. Stories where they were never found. She just never thought anything like that would happen here.

And Millie—dead or alive, wherever she was—was all she could think about.

It made her sick. Made her head pound, a dull, twisting ache right behind her eyes.

And the worst part?

She'd felt that same pain the second the red glow appeared, only amplified five times over.

A whisper in her bones. A sickness in her stomach said it had already marked her.

All shadow and claw.

7

Saturday dragged, the hours thick and heavy.

She wandered downstairs, poured herself another bowl of Cinnamon Toast Crunch—her third of the morning. These were the sort of eating habits that Kathy was on her about all the time—to the ends of asking Dr. Langdon at her last appointment a year ago whether Olivia could have a tapeworm, to which he said probably not, and it was teenage metabolism, to which he added that 'It must be nice'.

Right now, those habits, bad or neutral or neither until they caught up with her in ten years, were exacerbated by the fact that she was cooped up and stuck replaying the impossibility of what she'd witnessed Halloween night, and moreover the dread about what it meant for her friend.

She paced the kitchen, slurping the last from the bowl, and walked toward the sink, her eye catching on the stovetop. Which for some reason shot her mind right to the kitchen at Fischer's, and the commercial not-so-stainless steel stovetop her dad used to cook on.

To the summer night over a year ago when she'd been relegated to helping him clean the kitchen again, and he cranked up her grandma's old silvertone radio playing the reggae version of dad's favorite Peter Frampton song, *Baby I Love Your Way*. He'd called it her song—the only one that would turn her colicky cries into giggles as a baby—and he'd dance with her and rock her while she laughed until she fell asleep.

And that summer night in the greasy restaurant kitchen he'd taken her hand with his thick sweaty one, and they danced to the island groove as the key brightened and changed. Kathy walked in, started wiping down counters, smiled and laughed.

That was the last time she could remember when they were all happy.

A phrase threatened to intrude then, one she'd fought hard to keep out.

That she wished her dad was here.

She scowled at the stove and threw the bowl into the sink with a sharp clatter, went upstairs and showered.

The whole time knowing it wouldn't wash away her carouseling worries and sinking dread, and she wondered how, only a week ago, she'd been biking over to Millie's to apologize for some stupid fight they'd had. All of that seemed a lifetime away now.

As she finished drying off, a sudden rapping on her window startled her.

She tightened her towel, glancing around for something to defend herself with. Her hair dryer was closest.

She snatched it, unplugging it from the wall, and crept closer to the window, heart hammering. The light blue curtain stirred in the chilly November breeze as the window edged open.

With a quick breath, she whipped the curtain back and swung in a wild arc and made contact eliciting a painful yelp and hiss.

"Austin?" she gasped, dropping the hair dryer. "What the hell?"

He rubbed at his head, wincing. "Maybe don't try to concuss me next time."

"Maybe don't break in through my window!" she shot back, trying to steady her breath.

"I wasn't breaking in! I just—" Austin trailed off, his words stumbling to a halt as his eyes darted to the floor. He quickly looked away, his face flushing.

Olivia frowned, confused for a moment, then realized she was in nothing but a towel.

"Just . . . give me a second," she muttered, her cheeks burning as she grabbed some clothes from her dresser and darted into the bathroom.

A minute later, she returned in a worn gray sweatshirt and matching joggers, her damp hair pulled back into a messy ponytail. Austin stood awkwardly near the window, inspecting a scuff on his shoe.

"Okay," she said, crossing her arms. "What's so important you decided to play Spider-Man up the side of my house?"

He held up a worn leather notebook and set it carefully on her dresser. "This belongs to my grandfather. Passed down by the tribal elders. Found it in the old trunk in our . . . storage unit."

His voice tapered off, reminding Olivia of when he and his mom had to move out of their already quaint rental house into something even more quaint at Key Vista trailer park outside of town, about a year ago.

Flipping through the brittle pages, he stopped at a black-and-white image that sent a chill through her—a figure with tangled hair and hollow eyes, staring out from the page to pull her into whatever darkness it came from.

"Skadegamutc," he said, his voice low.

"Bless you," she said.

"That's what it's called. Or, the ghost-witch."

Olivia's mouth went dry. Austin glanced at her, then back at the book.

"The Skadegamutc," he started, "said to be what happens when a sorcerer—a really evil one—refuses to stay dead. At night, it comes back to life, turns into this . . . this ball of light. It floats, stalking the woods. It has to . . . eat people. To stay alive. To keep itself immortal. That's what it does—hunts, waits for anyone who's unlucky enough to cross its path."

She stared at the illustration, the empty eyes of the ghost-witch searing into her.

"You really think that's what it was?"

He shrugged. "I know it sounds insane."

"No more insane than what I saw." Olivia swallowed. "If this thing got Millie—" She faltered. "Do you think she's—"

"I don't know," Austin hurried.

Then Olivia thought about what she'd felt that night.

"I saw it. It was like a shadow. Bigger than a man, but not quite there."

"What do you mean?"

She breathed out her frustration. "It felt like it wanted to hurt us. But it couldn't. Maybe it's more of a ghost than anything else." She thought, in a surreal and somehow blurry memory, how it had shattered and screeched when she'd shone her flashlight. Something out of damn *Ghostbusters*.

"Could be." Austin stared down at the book. "And there's this."

"According to my grandpa, shamans were supposed to be healers of the tribe. But some ended up dealing with bad spirits and tricked people. The one that used to live up there, the one I told you guys about, was named Migizi, and the name was written on the page right before the Skadegamutc."

"Then maybe we should talk to him."

"Uh, pretty sure he's dead."

Olivia felt a flare of annoyance. "I mean your grandpa. He might be able to tell us more."

"I don't know. Maybe. He forgets things a lot. Some days, he doesn't know me when I go in there."

Olivia felt a barb of something all too familiar as she recalled how foggy and strange her dad had acted in that last month before he died. The way he looked at her—or more like straight through her. Like he was seeing someone or somewhere completely different. It was why she hadn't wanted to step into the room anymore toward the end. She swallowed and shook the memories away, like blood-hungry mosquitoes eating at her.

"And anyway," said Austin, "aren't you grounded?"

"Tomorrow is Sunday, the busiest morning at the restaurant. Kathy and Aly will be swamped and won't know any better."

"Who's Kathy?"

"My mom."

"Oh, right."

The door creaked open and shut downstairs. Someone was home.

"You should go," Olivia whispered.

Austin nodded. "Right." He left the book. "Visiting hours start at 10am," he said, rifling through his jacket pocket. He pulled out a zebra cake, a little squished. "They were . . . all out of the Oatmeal Creme things," he said, rushing back toward the window.

She felt a smile tugging at the corner of her lips.

It stopped when she sat on her bed, opened the book, and stared at that gaunt, ink-dark face on the dog-eared page. And it stared right back.

8

The automatic doors of Silver Pines Assisted Living slid open with a faint hiss, releasing a burst of warm, disinfectant-laced air into the chilly mid-morning.

Olivia pulled on her hoodie and glanced over at Austin, whose hands were jammed deep into the pockets of his faded denim jacket. His usual air of calm was absent, replaced by a nervous energy that made him seem smaller, more uncertain.

"You think he's okay to talk?" Olivia asked as they stepped inside.

Austin shrugged, his dark hair falling into his eyes. "Depends on the day."

137

A heavy silence fell as they approached the front desk. In the staff room just beyond, a nurse in scrubs decorated with cartoon turkeys bent over picking up several magnets near a fridge. She glanced over, rose, and greeted them with a polite smile. "Good morning. How can I help?"

"I'm here to see to Mr. Wasegijig. My grandfather."

"That's a mouthful," Olivia breathed, faster than she could filter her thoughts. Then again, she was talking to someone who regularly took racist native jabs from his best friend and who dealt them back in dueling jest to his yankee counterpart, which had gotten both of them a reprove during history class and had Mrs. Russell sweating bullets and yelling for them to stop.

Austin snorted. "Yeah. That's why I took a note from grandma and started using Williams. Telling people how to spell that gets old fast."

The nurse checked a clipboard and motioned them toward the east wing. "He's in the sunroom today. It's usually his best time of day. Just keep your visit brief—he gets tired quickly."

Austin uttered a quiet thanks, leading Olivia down the corridor. The soft murmur of television sets and muffled conversations drifted from the open doors they passed. Olivia hugged herself, her stomach twisting with unease.

"How long's it been since you last saw him?" she asked, trying to fill the silence.

"A while," Austin admitted. "I don't come as often as I should. It's just . . . hard."

Olivia understood that.

Way more than Austin knew.

When they reached the sunroom, a flood of golden light spilled through the wide windows, casting long shadows across the room.

Elderly residents sat in wheelchairs, some napping, others staring out at the fading tree colors beyond the glass. At the far end of the room, a frail man with a wrinkled, tan face and wispy white hair sat in a recliner, a blanket draped over his lap.

"Ah, Fred," he rasped. "You're still here."

Austin had told her he called him by his dad's name most of the time. "It's Austin, grandpa. I'm back."

"And you've brought a friend," he said, shifting to Olivia. His voice was cracked but steady, soft yet deliberate.

"Uh—yeah," Olivia said, stepping forward awkwardly. He seemed plenty sharp so far to her. "I'm Olivia."

His eyes narrowed. "You have a heavy look for someone so young," he said after a pause, voice low. She read the flushing on Austin's tan skin. She was a hundred pounds soaking wet, so it didn't bother her.

"Maybe I've been going a little too hard on the cereal."

"Guilt," he said quickly. "It is a heavy burden. But it is not yours to carry."

Olivia froze, her breath catching in her throat.

Was he talking about dad? How did he . . .

Austin shot her a look, but she couldn't speak.

"I . . . we've been looking into some things," Austin said, "about Devil's Peak. About the shaman who lived there once. Migizi Waa-Ngwaam."

At the mention of the name, the old man stiffened, his eyes widening. He gripped the arms of his chair, his gnarled fingers trembling.

"You should not speak the name of a Skadegamutc," he whispered, his voice tight with fear, his pronunciation much sharper than Austin's, a long *mooch* at the end.

Ghost-witch, Olivia recalled.

Austin leaned forward, his voice urgent. "Grandpa, we need to know. A girl—our friend Millie—she's gone missing."

At those words, the old man's breath hitched, and he began to mutter rapidly in Odawa, the words tumbling out like a chant. His hands fumbled with the blanket, clutching it tightly as if to anchor himself.

His eyes snapped back to Austin's, his voice sharp and clear.

"The *miskwa*. It is not a thing. It is many things. A hunger that never ends. The wendigo spirit our ancestors warned of. Those who dabble in blood ritual. A fire that consumes but never warms. It feeds on the weak and greedy, those who fall prey to lust and vengeance and languish in grief and guilt. It grows stronger with every drop of innocent blood."

"What does 'miskwa' mean?" Olivia asked in a whisper.

Austin swallowed. "Red."

Olivia felt a chill crawl down her spine.

"This shaman—what happened to him?"

The old man's gaze turned distant, his voice dropping to a whisper. "Migizi Waa-Ngwaam was a healer, once. Wise and kind. But he made a pact with a bad spirit from the spirit world, and it changed him. Twisted him. He began to see hunger as a gift, the fire as a blessing. He lured others to it, promising them power, wealth, vengeance."

He turned his cloudy eyes to Olivia, his voice trembling. "And it seems the hunger may have found its way back. It will not stop until it has what it needs."

"What does it need?" Austin asked.

The old man shuddered. "Blood."

Olivia felt her stomach drop, her breath coming in shallow gasps. She wanted to ask what he meant, to press him for more answers, but he suddenly slumped back in his chair.

A nurse appeared at their side, her expression kind but firm. "I think that's enough for today," she said gently. "He needs his rest."

Austin nodded, his shoulders sagging. "Thanks, Grandpa," he said softly. "I'll come back soon."

As they walked back down the hall, Olivia's mind raced, and when they stepped outside, the cold air slapped her.

"We need to go back. To Devil's Peak," she said, her voice firm despite the tremor in her hands.

Austin hesitated; his eyes troubled. "You heard what he said. Whatever it is—it's dangerous."

"That's exactly why we can't wait," Olivia said, her voice rising with determination. "If we don't stop it, who will? And who will help Millie?"

Austin stared at her for a long moment, and Olivia knew what he must be thinking. That Millie was already a victim of whatever they'd seen that night. This thing that the Odawa believed in and thought was real enough.

A bloodthirsty sorcerer, or the burning red spirit that was left behind by one.

"Hey," she said, a sudden question rising as fast as the dread that threatened when she thought of the red light. "That night, did you hear anything?"

Austin hesitated. "Like . . . what?"

"Whispers."

"I heard Kyle screaming, Eli crying, and myself hyperventilating. But no whispers." He looked at her, a ripple of concern on his brow. "Why?"

"I just thought I—heard it say something."

For a beat it seemed like he was waiting for her to say what that something had been, but she didn't want to say it out loud, and when she started walking he didn't press.

She eyed the treeline across the road. Olivia couldn't shake the feeling it was out there watching them.

Waiting.

And hungry.

9

Travis Johnson stood at the edge of the woods, wind howling through the trees, cold gnawing at his bones.

His cruiser idled behind him, engine humming, headlights cutting pale beams into the dark. He couldn't remember turning it on, or getting out.

He did not know why he was here—but he was.

Fists clenched. Heart pounding. Jaw tight.

He hadn't felt this way since he was using.

That electric, thrumming energy—the kind that sharpened the world to a needlepoint and made him feel godlike—except now, it wasn't from blow, wasn't something he could grind his teeth through until it passed.

Travis licked his dry lips.

When he applied to the department, he'd known his background check would come back clean. He'd been careful. Kept his record tidy. No arrests. No DUIs.

But the character references? They had to go and ask his ex. He wasn't sure how he got hired after that. By now though Jane had picked up the habit he'd kicked, and then some. She was on to crystal now, and probably she was involved in the meth lab fire forty minutes down the road in Pendell he'd heard come through on the County Sheriff dispatch. Served her right.

A sharp snap in the underbrush pulled him back to the moment. Travis stiffened, hand hovering near his holster.

A figure stepped out from the trees. Plaid jacket. Mud-soaked boots. Heavy-browed and tired-eyed.

"Officer."

The voice was calm. Flat. Like they already knew each other.

Travis's fingers twitched. "Who are you?"

"A like-minded individual."

"I said, who are you?" His voice cracked, and something primal in him rose—a fight response, sudden and sharp.

The man stepped closer.

"Name's Ethan," he said, "Not that it matters."

Travis swallowed against the thick lump in his throat. "Why am I here?"

Ethan tilted his head. "I think you know."

And then it hit.

A violent rupture behind his eyes. A flash of red. A hiss that was less sound but a feeling, a weight, a knowing.

They're the guilty ones, Travis. They must be punished.

His stomach twisted. His hands trembled. He hadn't felt this kind of certainty since the worst nights with Jane. When he convinced himself she deserved it.

"I—I can't," he stammered.

Ethan stepped forward. The wind died. The woods held their breath.

"We just have to clear the way," Ethan said, voice low. "The Red will do the rest."

A sharp clank against the hood of Travis's car. Ethan placed something there. A gold pocket watch. Old, weathered and stained.

A pulse of red shimmered against the metal in the dark.

Ethan nodded toward it. "Go on."

Travis felt it—the pull. His own heartbeat crashed against his ribs. His veins ran too hot. The air around him seemed to warp, crackling embers at the edge of a dying fire. He reached out, fingers brushing metal. And then—

He saw it. Felt it. Heard it.

Seethe . . ...

A shudder rolled through him. A tear burned hot down his cheek. He trembled. Then, he smiled.

"You understand, don't you?" asked Ethan.

Travis exhaled—ragged, reverent. "Yes."

Ethan's lips curled in approval. "Say it."

The words rose from somewhere inside him. From the Red.

"Skin of the hunted. Bones of the guilty."

Travis stopped, hearing the surreal sound of his own voice. Words not his, but spoken like a prayer.

Ethan finished. "Blood of the innocent."

Travis nodded. He let go of the watch. Handed it back.

It no longer mattered why he was here. But he knew.

Ethan tucked the watch into his pocket. "See you on the road, Officer."

Travis nodded, shaking.

Not from the cold.

From the terrible, beautiful weight of the Red inside him.

BURIED

D.C.B. Interview Transcript

Incident Report Interview Series 3:

The Westville Incursion

Lochlear: Now for this next portion we'll need to be very thorough, Mr. Benson.

Benson: Ah, so I must have been hallucinating all the anal-retentiveness earlier?

Lochlear: You were not as a matter of fact. And I can assure you we'll talk about each classified issue in turn. For now, enlighten me as to exactly how you retrieved your information.

Benson: Retrieved is a stretch. More like it fell in my lap.

Lochlear: As in, presented to you?

Benson: Sure.

Lochlear: For purposes of the record: presented to you by whom?

1

A windstorm stripped the leaves overnight, leaving skeletal branches to grasp at a roiling gray November 4th sky.

Casey eyed the warring Dole and Clinton campaign signs planted in neighboring lawns like political headstones. Two in particular blew in the breeze, waving at one another as if in mocking display of their human owners, who could not be bothered for these last tense weeks to give more than a passing awkward glare to each other as they hastily slid into warming vehicles and off to their daily tasks.

Come tomorrow people would be filing in and out of city hall, and that would be that. They'd move on.

Meanwhile, Casey took yet another detour down whatever side road pulled him along, thinking maybe, one of these days, a hunch would lead him to something pointing toward Millie.

When he'd impossibly happen upon her stumbling along the side of the road having escaped from whatever hell she'd been trapped in.

He mostly did it to make himself feel anything besides the hopeless ache of days gone by with no decent leads.

When he stepped into his cubicle, the faint hum of the precinct surrounded him. He dropped his coat on the back of his chair and glanced at the paperwork on his desk. He'd started in on filling out his expense report when he noticed the folder.

Bloated and sealed with a rubber band, it sat precariously on top of a stack of case files.

Casey frowned.

"Gail," he called, holding it up as she walked by. "You drop this off?"

She squinted at the folder and shook her head.

"Innocent," she said, raising her coffee cup in a toast.

Casey removed the band and opened it. At first, he wasn't sure what he was looking at. The top paper was a grid, the second, a map of familiar streets. A map of Westville.

Unfolding the page, he read the heading at the top: *Sanborn Fire Insurance Map,* dated *April 1892.*

Buildings were drawn by their shape and mostly colored a pale yellow, denoting each one's zoning, and businesses were labeled in slanted pen—Barber, Carriages, Meat. Along what was now Main Street—labeled as *Wooden Row*—crossing the Slate River, was the PRINCE Mill Yard. Certain buildings were marked in red and fewer in green. Flipping through more pages, he found it an interesting snapshot of old Westville but seemingly irrelevant.

A small slip of paper fluttered to the floor.

Casey unfolded it. The handwriting was neat, the words brief:

Red marks the spot.

— H

Casey paused, glanced back down at the maps. He noticed a star symbol near the northern part of town, close to the river and down Harrison Street, scrawled in dark red ink, the color of copper, reminding him of dried blood.

Just about where he'd found Millie's things. Near Devil's Peak.

Casey stared at the star marking, his pen hovering over the map.

He stood back for a moment, wondering what in the hell he was doing. Looking for answers, but in random century-old maps that had inexplicably ended up on his desk? If this was a desperate time, this was a half-measure at best. Something to placate his own compunction and give him a phantom feeling of progress.

That was when he spotted another marking—this time near the fairgrounds. He found another as his eyes scanned, his pulse quickening and a flush of heat on his brow.

Casey cleared off his desk and laid out the maps. He traced his finger down streets, through residential areas and school zones, looking for more stars. When he found one on the east side of town, he circled it—at the intersection of Main and Water, the same block Fischer's and the Methodist Church were on. Another to the northeast, near Arrowhead Road. On the west side, he found a star near the river, not far from the old high school. North of that, another one inland near the Allwell Factory, which the old map had labeled as *Graham Lumber*.

He placed the first map next to the second, creating a larger picture of old Westville. He circled the star near Devil's Peak and the one at PRINCE Milling.

Casey sat back, staring. He found himself reaching for the police handbook on his desk and using its spine as a straightedge to connect the stars—ironically very much aware he was *not* doing things 'by the book' at present—and when he drew lines from Devil's Peak to Main and Water, to PRINCE Milling, to the riverbank and north to the old factory and connected the others, he wiped a hand over his eyes and down his mouth.

He'd drawn a perfect hexagon that loomed over Westville.

His mind flashed to the business card left on his table at Fischer's two days earlier. He fumbled in his coat pocket.

JG Logistics.

Flipping it over, his stomach turned. The hexagon logo.

Stylistically broken on the top right and bottom left with two circles near the openings.

And below it, the slogan in small font he hadn't really bothered to read before: *Opening doors to better futures.*

Casey swallowed. What was the connection? The better question being whether there was a connection at all. The map was dated 1892. He didn't figure a modern logistics company had been around for over a hundred years, but maybe. And here he was in 1996—a girl missing, presumed dead; their main suspect a water-bloated corpse; a terrified town clawing for answers—picking through century-old municipal maps that had mysteriously landed on his desk. A laughable waste of time.

Only this wasn't random. It couldn't have been.

And that bothered him.

The dull hum of the station pressed in as Casey slapped the business card next to the hexagon he'd drawn over Westville. The folder held nothing else. He exhaled sharply, rubbing the bridge of his nose. That familiar faint, buzzing ache crawled behind his eyes, making his head float. Pressure building, like static.

He needed coffee.

Casey shoved the maps and notes back into the folder and stalked toward Reynolds' office, pouring out the last remains of a lukewarm pot into a flowery paper cup on the way.

He poked his head in and rapped on the doorframe.

"Hey Benson." Reynolds wiped a hand down his mustache and slapped his pen down on his paperwork. "That time of the month," he said, glancing down at the financials spread out on the desk. "My wife says I get EMS."

Casey sniffed, humoring him. "Those figures do a number on your heart or what?"

"No more than the McDonald's," he said, eyeing the yellow and red streaked brown bag in the wastebasket. "Expense Menstrual Syndrome. She's got hers, I got mine."

Normally Gordy's laughter at his own jokes was endearing and contagious, but right now Casey's mind was stuck in one gear.

"Who's been in this morning?"

Reynolds, looking up from a coffee-stained report, barely blinked. "Just the usual suspects. Johnson clocked off night shift a while ago, and Frank stepped out to meet with the feds. DeYoung's due in soon."

"No one stopped by to file a report or anything?"

Reynolds arched a brow. "Not so far as I know. Why?"

Casey hesitated. The headache flared again. "Nothing, I'll figure it out," he muttered. "Just some stray paperwork."

Walking back toward his cubicle, a flicker of movement outside caught his eye. A car idled across the street, exhaust billowing thick in the cold morning air.

A man sat behind the wheel. Watching.

Casey grabbed his coat and stormed outside.

The window rolled down before he could knock. Thick-rimmed glasses, a fading goatee.

The man from the corner booth.

"Good morning, Mr. Benson." His voice was calm, deliberate. "Heat's on if you'd like."

Casey held up the business card. "Who the hell are you?"

The man glanced at the card, then back at him. "A concerned citizen."

"Who deals in fire insurance maps?"

"I dabble in a few areas."

"You know it's illegal to tamper with police files, right?"

"I simply left a message."

"We've got a kid missing," Casey snapped. "I don't have time for riddles."

The man's fingers drummed the steering wheel. "I want to help you find her. I'd say to find the others as well, but . . ." He exhaled. "I fear it's too late for them."

Casey's pulse kicked. Others. How the hell did this guy know about the feds' theory on the other missing girls?

"You'll make more connections soon." The man's voice dropped. "But this is all I can give you for now." He glanced across the road, "There are . . . interested parties watching."

He reached for the gear shift as Casey followed his gaze to where the shiny black Crown Vic was parked by Westville Granite Company. Lochlear and Reeves.

"If you really want to go down this road, you know where to find me."

Casey stepped forward. "Hey, you can't just—"

Turned out, he could do just that. The tires spat up gravel. The car tore off, leaving Casey standing in a fog of exhaust.

His fists clenched. The note. The hexagon. This wasn't how leads were supposed to come together. But it *was* a lead. Now he just had to see if it bled when he prodded.

And vague as the bastard had been, he did in fact know where to find him.

Fischer's.

Casey looked across the road as he stalked back to the station entrance, tempted to flip the feds a one finger salute before he thought better of it.

Casey got back to his desk and stared at the maps. Despite his general frustration, a flicker of hope came to life inside him. What if, in some backward, roundabout way, this led to something about Millie—to finding her. What did he have to lose? The Holt County Clerk's office was only about twenty-five minutes outside of town in Iron Falls. He didn't have much to go on, but could easily get the information he needed—his mom had been something of a legend in that office through a long career—and Casey could probably pull some strings to get historical muniments and records pulled fast, on the properties and buildings marked with stars on those maps.

Maybe he'd figure out what, or who, connected them.

Probably, that was exactly what the man in the corner booth wanted him to do.

Casey collected the maps and stowed them in the folder, tucking it under his arm.

But when he stepped out of his cubicle, his eyes caught on a gaunt face and a gray PRINCE Milling shirt and the red name tag: *Ethan C.*

Casey tensed.

He was stepping out of the Chief's office. Ethan turned and nodded toward Casey with the faintest hint of a grin.

Casey stepped forward as Travis Johnson guided Ethan out of the bullpen, down the hall and toward the exit.

"Well, you were right about one thing," Hart said.

Casey stopped, staring off after Crawley. "What's that?"

"He's been living out of his truck."

"Did Johnson bring him in?"

"Nope. Came right down to the station of his own volition, about fifteen minutes ago."

And Casey had been preoccupied with maps, notes, and strangers speeding away in cars.

"He wanted to let us know he'd seen the Thompson girl the night she disappeared."

"Okay, and what else?"

"That was about it. Mentioned seeing Olivia Fischer too the morning after. Said she was trespassing."

Casey snorted. "Just like you said."

"Guess so. So that's that."

"Don't you think it's a little strange he waits to come in until after I ask a few questions?"

"Life is strange, Benson. All this is. Just leave it be and do your job."

Hart stepped back into his office, and Casey walked back down the hall to his car.

As he pulled out, he saw Ethan getting into his rusted-out army green Toyota truck. Johnson, who stood nearby, nodded at Casey before walking back into the station.

As Casey pulled out of the precinct lot, Crawley leered at him out the window, locking eyes with him for a long, uncomfortable moment before driving away.

Casey exhaled, gripping the steering wheel tighter. His eyes flickered to the folder on the passenger seat, the maps spilling slightly from its edges.

If Crawley was a dead end, he could only hope this wasn't.

For Millie's sake, it couldn't be.

2

"The good doctor is in play," Reeves said, lowering her binoculars as Casey Benson's car disappeared down the main drag of town.

The engine's soft hum filled the silence, the clean chemical scent of treated upholstery so strong it made her eyes water as she narrowed them and lowered the binocs, tracking a fading plume of exhaust.

"Of course he is," Lochlear replied from the driver's seat, not looking up from his notebook. "You're not surprised, are you?"

"No," she said, matter of fact, turning to face her partner. He seemed to have aged about twelve years since they'd met five years earlier. "But I am surprised that the Director—or any number of his superiors—never rein him in." Her voice sharpened. "Why is it we're having to babysit and clean up his breach of NDA?"

Her partner sighed inwardly, and remained silent, patting his pen on a piece of paper he'd been looking at for ten minutes. Thinking. "Any *brilliant* insight to dissuade my malcontent?" she asked.

Lochlear closed his notebook, his expression neutral. "No."

Somehow, wonder of all wonders, that didn't surprise her. Reeves raised an eyebrow and nodded toward the road. "Still need to get that interview with Benson."

"When the time is right," Lochlear said, his tone firm. "For now we focus on containment. HQ got back with the latest readings, and to his credit and my chagrin, Heiser was onto something after all. There's been a low-level incursion already, with negative magnetic anomalies pointing toward a widening of the morphic curve."

Reeves paused, tapping her binoculars against her thigh as she mulled over his words. "And if we can't contain it? What if this does turn into an incursion event?"

Then Heiser would be right, she thought, answering her own question. And it would be the third one in a year. In her relatively short time with the Bureau, she knew enough to know it wasn't a good sign. Not to mention her *hunches* she'd been getting again lately—and they were coming on strong. Her mental passenger was a persistent bastard.

Now is not the time.

Lochlear's jaw tightened. "What happened in Iowa was an isolated incident."

Reeves smirked faintly. "So far as Director Wren wants everyone to know. And are we just going to pretend that massive tornado outbreak out west is completely unrelated to the geomagnetic spikes here in farm-ville, Michigan?"

Lochlear's glare could have cut through steel. "I know I shouldn't be surprised so long as I've known you, Reeves. But you know that protocol comes *first*. We have to play this smart. We might have a real shot at the Company for the first time in a long time. I'd think you of all people would appreciate that."

Her hands clenched on the binocs hard enough that a nail scratched the black metal surface. She did appreciate that, but what she would really appreciate is if once in a while Lochlear would crawl out of the Director's ass long enough to see things in the clear light of day.

"For now, we hold course. And we make sure Heiser doesn't start playing scientist—or detective—with Benson."

Reeves tilted her head, studying Lochlear for a beat too long. "You're not worried about Benson. You're worried about Heiser."

Lochlear said nothing, his silence louder than any answer.

Reeves leaned back in her seat, staring at the dark outline of hilly woods in the distance. She felt the pressure in her mind, a dull imprint.

"It's already spreading, you know," she said. "Site 73's breach isn't contained. It hasn't been for days."

Lochlear's hand gripped the wheel tighter. "Containment is possible. If we act decisively and with discretion."

"And Heiser?" Reeves asked, her voice low.

Lochlear exhaled sharply, his eyes fixed ahead. "If he really steps out of line, I'll deal with him personally."

The radio crackled, a burst of static interrupting the tense silence. Reeves glanced at it, her fingers twitching slightly.

"Don't get jumpy on me now, Reeves," Lochlear said, his tone flat.

"I'm fine."

"Good. Site 73 isn't going to care about Heiser, Benson, or any of our plans. Not yours, not mine, and sure as hell not the Director's hesitance."

Reeves let out a long breath. "I'm well aware of that." She hesitated as a swell of regret welled to the back of her mouth, making her mildly nauseous. "What about the kid?"

"There's nothing we can do for her."

Reeves turned to him, her eyes sharp. "You really going to feed me that line? We're supposed to be partners."

The weight of unspoken truths filled the van like a third passenger.

"Until we know exactly what we're dealing with," Lochlear said, breaking the silence, "we don't move."

Reeves bit her lip, her gaze drifting out the window to the dark sky.

Static on the radio hissed.

3

The slam of Kyle's locker echoed down the hall, sharp and metallic, making Olivia flinch.

"There's no way we're going back there."

"After what we saw?" Olivia shot back. "After what we heard?"

"Especially after that!" Kyle's voice spiked, loud enough to draw a few lingering glances from students trickling toward class.

Austin approached, his usual easy stride gone, replaced with something heavier. His eyes flicked between them. "What's going on?"

"Kyle doesn't want to go back."

Kyle turned to Austin, eyes wild. "Can you blame me? You were there. You saw that thing. You want to walk right back into that? After what happened to Eli?"

She took a slow breath. "I think I know why it left us alone."

Kyle scoffed. "This should be rich."

Olivia ignored him. "When I was down there with Eli—I shined my flashlight at it. And it . . . recoiled. Maybe even hurt it somehow."

She didn't bother mentioning the shatter of screams and whispers in reverse because apparently, she was the only one who had heard them.

Kyle blinked. "Are you serious?"

"I know what I saw."

Kyle gave a sharp, humorless laugh. "Great. Let's just blind it to death. Problem solved."

"It worked." Her voice hardened. "That's probably the only reason Eli and I are standing here."

Kyle's jaw clenched.

"How is Eli, anyway?" she asked, softer this time.

Kyle crossed his arms. "Broken ankle means he just gets to lay around and play N64, or read or whatever he likes to do. He's fine, considering. Could've been worse. But I'm not going back."

"That red light, whatever it is," Olivia pressed. "It took Millie."

Kyle's expression darkened. He looked away. "You don't know that."

A sick weight settled in Olivia's chest. "What I know is if we don't do something, no one else will."

Austin shifted beside her. "We just have to figure out how. And what it really wants."

Kyle exhaled sharply. "And your grandpa didn't happen to mention that part, did he?"

Austin hesitated, shook his head. "Not exactly. But he said . . . it's not just one thing."

Olivia frowned. "What does that mean?"

Austin's voice dropped lower. "It's . . . a lot of things. An evil spirit merged with a restless soul. A hunger that doesn't stop. And it feeds on blood."

Kyle rolled his eyes, but Olivia felt her stomach twist.

Austin glanced down the hall, as if checking for eavesdroppers. "My grandpa said it's tied to the land. That it started with a shaman who lost his way. Migizi Waa-Ngwaam."

A sharp chill crawled up Olivia's spine.

"The Skadegamutc," she whispered.

Kyle glared at her. "Did you just have a small stroke?"

Austin sighed. "Scah-day-gah-mooch," he pronounced. "The ghost-witch. A sorcerer who refused to stay dead."

"Awesome," Kyle said through a tight humorless laugh. "So a homicidal zombie sorcerer ghost-witch. Totally manageable."

The bell rang, but Olivia barely heard it.

Her mind was spinning. Pieces clicking into place, terrifying in their clarity.

She squared her shoulders. "Library. After school."

Kyle groaned. "You're not gonna let this go, are you?"

"Not when we're this close."

Mrs. Summers' voice cut through the hallway. "Let's move it along."

They scattered.

The rest of the school day crawled, every lesson blurring together. Olivia's thoughts stayed fixed on Millie.

And on the Red.

4

Casey slapped down a bloated folder of documents tied with a rubber band onto the cheap faux wood corner booth table of Fischer's.

The man with the goatee and glasses, '*H*', so far as Casey knew, looked up and smiled glibly.

"Ah, Mr. Benson. Please take a seat." He stirred a steaming mug of tea and examined the local business ads plastered on the sides of said mug with a strange delight.

"I get it," Casey said, sliding into the booth and tugging at the collar of his jacket. "You wanted me to pull these. Because you couldn't."

"You catch on quickly," he said, taking a sip, and glancing around the restaurant.

"What I don't get is why all the cloak and dagger, how you came by those fire insurance maps, or who the hell you are."

"I apologize for not being straightforward," he said, leaning in and glancing to the front door as the shrill bell rang out. From the skittish look that flickered behind the man's glasses Casey thought maybe one of those porcelain clowns had decided to jump to life at the suggestion of his own perpetual nightmares.

"On the first count, I'm in the unfortunate position of being a man with too much knowledge and information having been demoted to civilian status. As for the second, a good friend of mine who works for the Library of Congress did me a favor. They're all public record, but it took some legwork to track down those originals."

'*H*' extended his hand awkwardly across the table.

"Gregory Heiser."

Casey hesitated but extended a hand. "I'd say something, but I figure you've already done your research on me."

"How's that?"

"Enough to know my name and know that I'd probably bite if given a little bait. Something vaguely in the shape of a lead. Well, there you go," Casey said, glancing down at the fat folder.

"Know thyself," Heiser said. "A powerful truth internalized by many great thinking men. Seems you might be among them."

Casey scoffed. "Flattered. But I'm not interested in much except what you think that map or any of this has to do with Millie, what happened to her and who's involved."

"Fair enough. Why don't you start by telling me your findings so far."

Casey felt a prickle of annoyance run up his neck and flush his cheeks. What was this, a dissertation?

"Well, 'JG Logistics' is apparently a subsidiary for a much bigger conglomerate. Janus Global."

Heiser raised his glass. "Indeed they are. An industrious bunch with an ambitious board of directors." Casey noted his darkened tone as the wry wit left his voice, and the shadow of something in the past flickered over his face.

"From what I could tell they have their hands in a little of everything," Casey continued.

And they did. Their holdings in Michigan and the Midwest alone were diverse enough. Some usual stuff for a logistics company—railcars, freight, shipping containers. But agriculture too, and a whole chain of storage units under different names. Casey started to open the folder, but Heiser slapped a hand down on top of it.

"No need to rush into it," he said. He picked up the menu and eyed it. "Do you have a favorite here?"

A flare of annoyance bubbled up in Casey along with a growling pang of hunger, followed by a sudden drop of his stomach as Aly came by the table with a steaming pot of coffee, and he remembered that he'd neglected to call her after Halloween like he'd said he would, both of them probably knowing better.

"Morning," she said, eyeing Casey and Heiser in turn. "Didn't know you two were acquainted."

Casey swallowed. "We weren't."

"The usual my dear," Heiser said cheerfully, glancing up and handing Aly the menu.

"Famous waffles and a side of bacon coming right up," she said, flashing a smile. One that seemed to fade as she looked to Casey. "Anything for you?" Her words sounded overly cold as she poured coffee in his mug, but it was probably his imagination.

"I'm not too hungry," he lied.

She gave a weaker smile as she turned, that—despite the oppressive all-consuming pall of Millie's disappearance—still managed to put a stranglehold on him.

"Well never mind," Heiser said. "I think I found your favorite," he commented wryly.

"That's not—" Casey stammered. "Are you some kind of shrink or something?"

"Not quite. A minor in Psychology, but my focus was Quantum Physics, followed by World Religions. My biggest field of interest."

"Right. And you're in Westville looking into small town history during a federal missing persons and possible homicide case, why exactly?"

For the first time in earnest Heiser's whole demeanor tightened, his slight smirk fading away. "I'm here because there's more under the surface of this little town than anyone truly realizes. Including my own peers."

"And who might those be?" Casey pried.

Heiser breathed out his nose and folded his hands in front of himself, prim and proper at the table's edge. "Best you didn't know. Plausible deniability and such."

Heiser glanced around the restaurant, and Casey couldn't help but follow his searching gaze. Right now, there were no feds and no suits here. Just old, retired men at a round table complaining boisterously about their wives followed by wheezing chortles.

Heiser took a slow luxurious sip of his tea, then raised his mug toward Casey. "Ah . . . Small town charm."

Casey sniffed and shook his head. "So did you invite me here just to eat and shoot the shit, or are you going to fill me on your own *'findings?'*"

Heiser smacked his lips and slid his mug gently aside. "I've devoted my career, most of my life in fact, to naming the unnamable. Bringing to light the dark unknowns at the reaches of human understanding. Sometimes, logic as the common population understands it fails to get to the heart of the matter. And this is one of those times."

"Unless you're trying to tell me I'm living in some kind of *Twilight Zone* episode, I don't follow." Which, Casey thought, wasn't a stretch just now.

Heiser's smirk returned. "Have you ever heard of ley lines, Mr. Benson?"

"Call me Casey. And no."

Heiser didn't skip a beat. "An archeologist by the name of Alfred Watkins once proposed a theory. Energy lines across the globe, running between certain landmarks, historical structures of great cultural and religious importance. Often, they form uncanny geometric patterns when transposed on top of one another. You might have heard of the Bermuda Triangle, or perhaps the lesser known Alaskan one."

Casey glanced down at the shut folder and thought of the hexagon he'd drawn between those markings, outlining most of Westville.

"It just so happens that your little town falls on the intersection of a few very powerful ley lines. A confluence of streams. What we at the Bureau would call a Location of Power. LoP for short."

"Bureau. As in the FBI?"

Heiser drew in a breath, then his face went pale, his eyes on the door.

Casey turned to see none other than the dynamic duo of Lochlear and Reeves walking into the restaurant, being guided to the smoking section by Julie.

"Let's . . . pick things up this evening," Heiser said, face falling slack, putting on his coat, slipping a ten out of his wallet, and setting it on the table. "I have your address."

Casey flared out his hands. "Of course you do."

"It's just best if we talk further somewhere more—discreet. Enjoy the waffles," he said, clapping a hand on Casey's shoulder, glancing toward the front and darting out the back entrance.

The hell was that about?

If he *was* FBI then what beef did he have with Lochlear and Reeves? Was Heiser even with the Bureau?

Were they?

A plate clanked down in front of him as he rapped his fingers on the folder.

"Hey," he said, "Sorry I didn't call the other—"

He turned to see Julie, a flat smirk across sun-wrinkled skin. "Apology accepted," she quipped.

He didn't see Aly the rest of the time.

Casey stabbed into the sugar coated liège waffle mindlessly and after a few bites snagged a piece of bacon then headed home to make some more sense of the records he'd pulled. If he wanted answers from Heiser, the kind that led to finding Millie or whoever knew where she was, he had to be ready—with the right questions.

Problem was, he had no idea what the hell those were.

5

The Pray Memorial Library was situated in an old yellow brick historic home and was about as claustrophobic as it could get before reading a book required a contortionist's agility to open it between shelves, book carts, and chairs.

For as much as she had teased Millie for her over-assiduous study habits, which she secretly admired, she wished that her friend could see her here now.

Olivia had never been the kind of kid to make a beeline for the books immediately after school let out, but today she was indistinguishable from an advanced placement junkie. As she pored through pages of Holt County historical accounts though, her mind drifted to the grim reality that maybe all of this was in vain.

Maybe Millie was dead and gone. Killed that night and left somewhere to rot.

She pinched at the skin of her forearm—a habit when she was stressed, leaving little white nail marks—almost to punish those thoughts as she read something about the fires of 1902 in old Westville.

A loud clap and shake of the table made her jump back and take the good Lord's name in vain.

"The legend of the Ottawa Treasure," Kyle announced, having dropped a timeworn book onto the table.

Austin exhaled, already unimpressed. "My grandpa said that might've been exaggerated."

Kyle shrugged. "So are all legends. Doesn't mean they aren't based on something real." He flipped through the brittle pages, his finger skimming across faded print. "Says here when the settlers bought the land from the Odawa people . . ."

His eyes rolled up at Austin, a smirk tugging at his lips.

Austin returned a flat stare, followed by a swift middle finger.

Olivia sighed. "Just keep reading."

"Alright, alright. The chief worried his tribe would squander the money, so he hid it away. They tortured him to death trying to find it."

"Solid plan," Olivia muttered.

"Then they realized the error of their ways and buried him sitting upright, so he'd always look out for them even in death. When they were digging things out for the new sewer systems in town back in the '30s, they found the skeleton. Upright."

Olivia frowned. "Was the treasure ever found?"

Austin leaned back in his chair. "Probably in the records if someone got stupid rich."

Kyle tapped the book. "Depends. Maybe they just didn't want anyone to know. Or maybe the tribe did eventually find it. Thoughts?"

Austin exhaled sharply, shaking his head. "Let me guess—because I'm half Indian, I should know about that?"

Kyle threw up his hands. "No, because your grandpa is, like, Jedi-level with all this weird local history."

Austin waved his hand. "Kyle, I swear to God—"

"Alright," Olivia interrupted before they could launch into another verbal war. "Let's focus."

They hauled over stacks of books, flipping through crinkled pages and faded type. Olivia pored over one thick volume, tracing the lines of an old town charter.

"Westville was originally named *Dansville*—after a Daniel Thompson." Her stomach twisted. "Think this guy is related to Millie?"

Kyle barely looked up. "Probably."

Austin furrowed his brow. "Maybe he started the mill?"

Olivia shook her head. "No. That was someone else." She turned the book, pointing. "Thomas Prince."

Austin nodded. "I wondered why it was named PRINCE Milling."

"Says here that Arthur Thompson, Daniel's son, bought the mill from Prince in 1903. Prince had been his father's business partner." Olivia's throat felt tight. "He bought it right after a huge fire burned the original mill to the ground."

"And half the town with it," said a voice behind them.

Olivia heard a shuffling behind her and whipped around to see a thin boy hobbling over, grinning despite the crutches tucked under his arms. Eli.

"Hey guys," he said cheerily.

Kyle scowled. "What are you doing here?"

"Returning books and getting new ones," Eli said. "That *is* what people do at a library."

Kyle bristled. "Yeah, but—"

Eli waved him off. "Turns out it's just a sprain. Guess I'm tougher than I look. After the woods—" His face went paler, and his lips quivered.

Olivia glanced at the others and saw the memory of Halloween cast a darker pall over them as well, one she felt deep in her bones.

"Anyway," Eli said, "it gives me a good excuse to read more."

Kyle groaned. "Of course it does."

Eli ignored him, peering at their pile of books. "Oh, good ones! I've read them a few times."

Austin cocked his head. "You've read *all* of these more than once?"

"Sure. Good to know about where you live, right?"

Olivia's interest sharpened. "So you know a lot about Westville's history?"

"I guess you could say that." Eli grinned, then glanced down at the book Kyle had brought over. "What do you want to know?"

"The Ottawa Treasure," Olivia said. "We've been trying to—"

"Ah, classic," Eli said, rocking back on his crutches. "Well for starters—"

"Let me just stop you right there, big guy," Kyle said, slapping his cousin on his frail back so that he toppled a little. "We already know about the chief hiding the money and getting killed and stuff."

"Oh. So I take it you already know they also murdered an exiled shaman?"

Kyle stammered, and Olivia stepped in front of him.

"No . . . We didn't."

"Well it's a crazy story, the kind of thing you'd never think of a little town like ours. But I guess things were different back in those days. The tribe had exiled their shaman because they blamed his vision for tricking them into killing their chief. When no one could find the treasure—they figured maybe the shaman had taken it for himself—so a group of people from the town and some of the Odawa tribesmen beat him to death too, and buried him under a foundation of some building in Westville. No one knows where for sure, but . . . yeah. Fun story."

"Fun is one way of putting it," Olivia breathed.

"What's with all these people buried in sewers and under buildings?"

"They believed the chief would watch over them," Austin said, "buried somewhere undisturbed and upright. As for the shaman under a foundation, they probably didn't want him—coming back."

"What, like a damn zombie?"

Austin shook his head. "I mean, kind of. That's sort of the legend of the Skadegamutc."

"Alright," Kyle started, "so who found the treasure?"

Eli flipped a few pages forward in the book, and pointed. "According to Nicholas Graham—the first mayor of Westville—he did. And already being from a wealthy family, he used it to invest back into the town." His voice lowered slightly. "But hard to say for sure. A lot of accounts say he's just a blowhard who took credit for it. Others say Arthur Thompson made some kind of deal with the shaman before he was killed, and others that no one ever—"

"Wait, Arthur Thompson?" Olivia blurted.

"Made a deal . . ." said Austin, a heavy silence settling over them as he looked to her.

Olivia swallowed and felt a cold knot tighten in his chest. "Skadegamutc."

The grandfather clock chimed from across the library and rattled through Olivia's ribs like a heartbeat—sharp, hollow. The Thompsons. The Ottawa Treasure. The fire. It was all connected. They just had to figure out how.

Eli adjusted his grip on his crutches. "You know if you really want to dig deeper, you could check the microfilm."

6

The dim light of the reader cast a pale glow over Olivia's face as she leaned in, fingers poised on the crank, scanning each faded page and trying to get the stupid thing to focus already.

Kyle slumped beside her, flipping through a battered notebook, while Austin perched on the edge of a chair, arms crossed, looking between the reader and stacks of film reels.

"Are we sure it actually works?" Kyle muttered, fiddling with the machine's knobs.

Olivia slapped at his hands. "I've almost got it."

"Of course it works." Eli beamed from across the table, carefully threading another spool into place. "This is my favorite part of coming to the library."

Kyle snorted. "And me with my dumb PlayStation at home."

Olivia ignored them, turning the crank slowly. "October 17, 1902," she read. "*Great Fire Devastates Westville: PRINCE Mill Reduced to Ashes.*"

Austin straightened. "Anything about how it started?"

Olivia continued, eyes narrowing as she traced the article's delicate script and continued to read: "Westville awoke in terror as flames swept through the town's core in the early morning hours. PRINCE Milling Company bore the brunt of the destruction . . . two men killed, several others injured. The origins of the fire remain shrouded in suspicion."

She hesitated. "No accelerants found. No evidence of arson. But some people believed it wasn't an accident. Something about *Sanborn Fire Insurance Maps.*"

Kyle tapped his pen against his notebook. "Alright. So the mill burns down. What next?"

Eli perked up, pulling a new spool from the pile. "Maybe not next . . . but before. Here. Swap this in."

Olivia slid the reel into place, turning the crank with quickened precision. Headlines blurred past until—

'*Gambling Ring Busted at Dawkin's Tavern.*' Just two doors down from the library.

Austin leaned in. "What is it?"

"Arthur Thompson, once a respected figure in Westville's burgeoning mill industry and son the town's original founder, has been named among several individuals involved in an illicit gambling ring . . . accrued significant debts.'"

Kyle let out a low whistle. "Yeah. That'd do it."

"There's more." Olivia scrolled further, her pulse quickening.

"Auction to be Held for Thompson Family Estate, December 1898. Following financial troubles, the Thompson family announced an auction of their remaining assets . . . Arthur Thompson has not been seen in public since."

Austin exhaled slowly, shaking his head. "That explains how things fell apart."

Eli, already anticipating the next step, swapped in another reel.

Olivia turned the crank again, her stomach twisting as the next headline surfaced.

"September 1902. '*Arthur Thompson Acquires PRINCE Milling Company.*'" The article showed a picture of Arthur Thompson shaking hands with Thomas Prince, the latter looking less than enthused but both looking oddly solemn in the way people often did in turn of the century photos. In his other hand, he clutched a golden pocket watch.

Kyle frowned. "Hold on—wasn't he broke? How the hell did he afford to buy back the whole mill?"

Olivia shook her head, scanning the article. "Despite the significant financial burden, Thompson has pledged to rebuild the mill. When questioned about his sudden wealth, he attributed foresight and frugality."

Kyle gave a loud scoff. "Guess the foresight didn't apply to placing bets."

Silence settled between them.

Olivia read more, her voice low. "Rumors swirl in Westville following Arthur Thompson's acquisition of PRINCE Milling. Once destitute, Thompson has risen seemingly overnight to reclaim his family's lost prestige."

Kyle sat back. "The Ottawa Treasure."

Austin nodded grimly. "Maybe he did find it. Maybe because of whatever deal he made with that shaman."

The overhead lights flickered off for a moment, and the microfilm reader powered off and on again.

"What was that?" Olivia said, startled.

"My dad worked on the electrical in this building," Kyle said. "Said it was a mess."

The grandfather clock in the corner struck five-thirty, each chime sharp and hollow, rattling through Olivia's chest.

She stared at the screen, her thoughts spinning.

If Arthur Thompson had made a deal to restore his family's fortune—if he'd bound himself to whatever 'bad spirits' Austin's grandpa mentioned—that *hunger*—maybe it lurked somewhere in Westville. Maybe Millie's disappearance wasn't random.

It was part of something much older. Something that was still feeding.

A wave of unease crawled through her. She checked the clock again. 5:35. Kathy would kill her if she wasn't home before her shift ended, but she couldn't walk away from this.

She'd already let too much time slip by.

Millie had been gone for over a week now.

That fresh realization struck Olivia like a punch to the ribs, sharp and breath-stealing. In the frantic momentum of their research, she'd let it blur into a problem to be solved, a puzzle with missing pieces. But in the stillness of the library, it crashed back into focus—

Millie was still out there.

Maybe alive. Maybe not.

But someone or some *thing* had taken her.

And in her worst nightmares, Olivia saw it: red light and bone-thin shadows, some amorphous jaw stretched wide, and harsh, slicing whispers:

You're the guilty ones . . ..

Her chair scraped against the floor as she shot to her feet.

"I'll see you at school," she said, ignoring their protests and questions.

She needed to talk to someone who could actually *do* something about this.

Someone who might believe her.

The payphone by the vestibule was old, the buttons stiff beneath her fingers with something sticky she didn't want to know about. She flipped through the directory, skimming quickly past rows of names until she—didn't find it.

Benson, Casey wasn't listed. She couldn't call Aly for his number or his address—who would have been working the restaurant right now—because Kathy could answer the phone instead and also her sister would be likely to raise the alarm given Olivia was *technically* grounded. Technically, because she hadn't been locked and chained down in her room like some princess in a fairy tale, which was messed up now that she thought about it.

Focus, Liv.

Thinking of the restaurant, she remembered one Sunday morning last year when they'd been having breakfast with the Thompsons at the restaurant after a church service, which Olivia had very much not wanted to go to being only a few weeks removed from dad dying, knowing full well the well-intended sympathies that would be doled out upon her. And it was, and she wanted to climb down into the gaping sewer grate by the cement stairs up to the sanctuary, right about where they'd found that Indian chief's bones.

Eyes on the prize, she reminded herself.

She recalled Casey leaving Fischer's that morning, and not getting in a car. He just walked down the sidewalk, passed the old '*Roll-Time*' skating rink and turned on the street a block past. And she knew he drove the rusty silver boat of a car (a Monaco something?). If she could just find it, she'd find him.

Olivia closed the fat phonebook, and when looked up she noticed a golden placard above the payphone.

'In memory of Gerald H. Pray, who believed in a brighter future.'

She'd read enough about rich old guys to last her a while.

She turned and walked straight into the cold November dusk, striding beneath the marquee of the old Smith Theater—which probably would have been the place to go chasing ghosts given all the superstition around it—whose sign presently was plastered with STAY STRONG WESTVILLE.

Olivia didn't think some worn out blocky letters were going to do anyone any good, and as she passed Dawkin's Saloon and glanced through the windows at the crowd, she thought maybe most people were just finding their own little ways forget it all.

But Olivia wasn't going to forget about it. She hoped Casey wouldn't either.

Because she had *a lot* to explain.

1

Janus Global Logistics.

The name kept appearing, in all its variants. Janus, other times JG Logistics. Casey stared at the documents littering his kitchen table—property deeds, business filings, purchase agreements. Robinson's Gravel. The Allwell factory. And now, talk of buying the riverfront, including the old high school.

And then there was PRINCE Milling.

On paper, it looked clean—Jack Thompson owned it outright through PRINCE Inc. But it was marked on the Sanborn maps. Just like the others. Three of those spots belonged to Janus.

He flipped through pages, scanning for patterns. Janus Global was big—high-end logistics, government contracts, elite clientele. Yet their only small-town holdings were here—in Westville.

A barely-profitable factory. A gravel pit in nowhere, Michigan. A condemned high school.

There were two other marked locations: The intersection of Water and Main. Right where Fischer's Café sat across from the old Methodist Church. A shadowed stretch of woods along the North Country Trail. Where he'd found Millie's things.

He traced the hexagon's lines again, an unshakable chill working into his bones. Something was wrong.

A knock at the back door.

Casey pulled the blinds back. Thick glasses. Pale eyes. A fading goatee framing a tense smile.

Heiser.

He cracked the door. "So you know where I live, just like that?"

"Perks of a small town. Just had to ask."

"Uh-huh." Casey folded his arms. "So from the way you darted out of Fischer's when Lochlear and Reeves came in, I take it you're *Ex*-FBI?"

"Not exactly." Heiser adjusted his glasses. "It's more complicated than that."

Casey sighed. "Then uncomplicate it."

"How about a proper *reintroduction*? Dr. Gregory Heiser, Dimensional Containment Bureau. Head of Phenomenological Studies. At least, I was. Until my . . . leave of absence."

Casey stared. "Containment of—what exactly?"

Heiser glanced over Casey's shoulder at the maps and documents spread across the kitchen table, pushing past him and notably past his question. "I see you've been busy."

Casey exhaled sharply and stepped aside with an exasperated swing of his hand. God he was tired. But if Heiser could tell him anything that would help get to the bottom of what happened to Millie, what did he have to lose?

His sanity, maybe.

Heiser studied the papers. The drawn-on hexagon. The crisscrossing lines.

"Interesting, aren't they?" he murmured. "The old fire maps were designed to maximize detail—structures, hazards, water sources."

"Yeah, sure. But how about filling me in on why they matter."

Heiser tapped the table. "I think you're already figuring that out."

Casey folded his arms. "Did you mark these maps?"

"No." Heiser shook his head. "Those are the originals, marked over a century ago."

"Then who did?"

"Another good question." Heiser smiled faintly.

Casey exhaled through his nose. And of course, no good answers.

He tapped one of the hexagon's angles. "What I know so far is most of these properties are owned by Janus Global. PRINCE Milling. A warehouse. A storage facility south of town. Two spots in the woods."

"Go on."

Casey narrowed his eyes. "Sorry to disappoint, but that's about all I've got."

Heiser nodded. "Well it's a start. As I alluded to before, there's something unique about your little town."

"Because of those energy lines or whatever?"

"Ley lines. An intersection of them." Heiser corrected.

"Right," Casey muttered. Persnickety bastard.

"Making Westville a Location of Power."

"And what kind of power are we talking about?"

Heiser leaned forward, hands on the table. "Ley lines are like streams of raw geomagnetic energy. They run beneath the earth, forming a kind of grid. Usually self-regulating—but every so often, they . . . surge."

Casey huffed. "So Janus is in the energy sector, too."

Heiser's lips twitched. "They tend to stick to their 'logistics' brand—focused on a certain kind of transportation."

A pause. "Not sure I follow."

"In Roman mythology, Janus was the two-faced god of beginnings and endings. And of doorways. Imagine a door that could take you—or many people and many things—across the globe in a near instant. Or even—elsewhere."

Casey sat back, memories of the first and only movie date he and Aly had gone on to see *Stargate* in an empty theater, which he'd fallen asleep halfway through, only to be woken by Aly leaning to kiss him. He was awake then, but he didn't see much of the movie. Still, the image of a sci-fi metallic ring radiant with blue energy was conjured in this mind.

"You mean like some kind of portal?"

Heiser smiling and apparently enthused. "Precisely."

Casey ran a hand down his face. "Okay, got it. Great. You know, this all sounds—what's the word . . ." He snapped his fingers in the air. "Ah, right. Insane."

"I've come to expect that reaction from people. Granted, I'm new to disclosing classified information."

Casey was suddenly aware he might be privy to government secrets he wasn't supposed to know. Granted so far, it all seemed about as credible as the lunacy scrawled on cardboard signs by the many homeless men wearing tin foil hats back in Chicago.

"You think I should be signing something first so I don't end up in a federal penitentiary? Or Roswell."

Heiser laughed at that, hard. The kind of overactive laugh of a guy who probably didn't get out much. "All of this *is* rooted in science, I assure you. Though science and technology to an advanced degree are indistinguishable from the supernormal, to paraphrase Asimov."

"Uh-huh."

"It all has to do with the polarities and magnetism of the earth's core, but in short—a doorway, or perhaps more a bridge, to a different plane of existence, when astronomical and geological conditions are right. At first brush, a little hard to comprehend, granted."

"You think?" Casey exhaled sharply. "Alright, let me just humor you here. Your 'Bureau'—you what, shut these doors?"

"Yes," Heiser said. "Well, we try to not let them open at all."

"And Janus?"

"They open them."

"Great," Casey muttered. "So you're the locksmiths, and they're the vandals."

Heiser didn't disagree.

Casey pushed back from the table, shaking his head. "Unbelievable."

Heiser stood. Met Casey's gaze.

"Haven't you ever seen or heard something, Mr. Benson—something you couldn't explain?"

Casey stiffened.

Heiser's voice lowered. "Something you wrote off as a trick of the mind? A sound that wasn't right? A shape in the dark?"

A cold knot formed in Casey's stomach.

The Scout cabin. Those whispers in the thick fog. The flash of red. His aching head.

You're the guilty ones . . .

Casey didn't answer. But Heiser knew. The way he looked at Casey, somehow he knew.

A frantic knock shattered the silence.

Casey and Heiser both turned. "Friends of yours?"

Heiser frowned. "No, I—" He hesitated. "Well. Possibly."

Casey sighed. He gestured for Heiser to get out of sight. Casey crept to the door and peeled back the blinds just enough.

Olivia Fischer.

Standing on his porch. Wide-eyed and breathless.

He cursed under his breath—then threw the door open.

8

Olivia didn't wait before shoving past Casey and into the house, heart racing.

"I need to talk to you."

She stopped abruptly in the kitchen, an explosion of maps and papers sprawled across the table. The sight made her pause but only for a moment.

"Liv, what—"

"It's about Millie. And the Skade—Skadega . . . Skadda . . ."

Casey raised an eyebrow as he shut the door behind her. "The what?"

"Ah screw it." She spun to face him, gesturing wildly. "The ghost-witch! I just came from the library. And there's something else—Arthur Thompson."

"Olivia—" Casey started, his tone already laced with exasperation.

"Just listen!" she snapped, stepping closer. "Arthur Thompson, Millie's great, great, something grandpa. He made a deal with the ghost-witch. The thing you're looking for—it's tied to him! There's an old book in the library—or there was—it had records from when he—"

"Enough," Casey said, cutting her off.

Olivia froze, her frustration boiling. She was about to fire back when a man's voice, calm and measured, interrupted from behind her.

"That's quite an accusation."

Olivia spun, startled, to see a stranger, his thick glasses catching the light as he watched her with quiet interest. "And perhaps not without its merits," he added.

"Who the hell is this?" she demanded, taking a step back.

"One. None of your business. Two. Watch your mouth," Casey snapped, grabbing the phone off the counter and dialing.

Olivia's face flushed. "What are you doing?"

"I'm calling Aly to come pick you up."

"What? No! I'm not leaving!" Olivia shot back, her voice rising. "This is important!"

Casey's sharp glare stopped her cold. "You *are* leaving. And this isn't the time."

She clenched her fists, pulse pounding in her ears. "You're seriously just ignoring me?"

"That's the plan."

Olivia glared at him then turned her attention to the man near the table, who had been silently watching their exchange.

"So who are you?" she demanded.

The man adjusted his glasses, looking amused. "My name is Dr. Heiser," he said evenly, then looked at Casey. "You can call me Greg."

Olivia shifted, and thought she'd rather stick with Dr. Heiser instead of *Greg*. He didn't look like a 'Greg', and the name reminded her of Reggie Gregerson, one of the longtime cooks at Fischer's who smelled of onions all the time and probably not just because of working the grill.

"Miss Fischer's claims are intriguing," Heiser said. "You may want to hear her out."

"Don't encourage her."

"There's something weird going on, Casey," Olivia insisted, her frustration boiling over. "You know it too. I saw the look on your face when I told you about what happened in the woods." She held out a finger to accentuate the point. "*You* believe me."

Dr. Heiser cleared his throat, and gave Casey a knowing look. Casey's jaw tightened, and he hesitated before answering.

"I may have thought I heard . . . something. That first morning. But it was just the stress."

The fact that Casey had just admitted that he had *heard* something, unlike the others, made her feel less alone. Even if he was trying to dismiss it.

"First instincts are often the most accurate," Heiser interjected, his calm voice cutting through the tension. "Following mine brought me to Westville—and also got me fired."

"How's that?" Casey asked.

Heiser stood and paced past Olivia, walking aimlessly around the kitchen mumbling for a moment in which she caught Casey's eye and wondered if he was thinking this guy was a little or a lot 'off', too. He came back to the table, and looked at the maps and documents, and pointed a finger down at the one with the hexagon drawn on it.

"It started with a series of ley line spikes and spatial distortion activity. We've seen it before. First signs of an incursion. Electromagnetic disruptions. Anomalous weather patterns, often separated by a long distance. Not connected by basic logic, but when you consider our mapping of ley lines . . . well."

Olivia thought of the power flicker at the library. Of the magnets at the nursing home.

"Most often these spikes resolve on their own, the earth's geomagnetism rebalancing itself," Heiser continued. "But, when there's something pulling from the other side . . ."

"The other side of what?" Olivia asked.

Heiser looked to the ceiling, as if considering his response, then back to Olivia.

"There are many dimensions to our universe—at least ten according to String Theory, but probably more including the astral plane. We only occupy three of them. Between the others there exists a sort of liminal space. We call it the Seethe. Because often, it does just that—seethes through a 'thin spot.'"

"And you think it's doing that here? In Westville?" Olivia asked.

"Where the rivers meet," Heiser said smiling, looking between her and Casey to see whether his pun using Westville's town slogan had landed. It didn't. He cleared his throat. "Or, where ley lines converge. My research of a particular phenomena brought me here, and its connection with Janus Global's most recent activities."

Olivia didn't like the way he said that last word, and what it could mean.

"Correct me if I'm wrong," Casey said, "but you worked for a top secret branch of the U.S. government, so why the hell hasn't some alleged secret cult company like this been shut down?"

A fair point, Olivia thought, and checked off a mental point for Casey.

"For one, they have roots much deeper than our great country, Mr. Benson. I believe they are and have been here in the area for many years now. Playing a long game of sorts. And, as Mrs. Fischer here astutely alluded to, may be tied to the oldest families. Even the Thompsons."

Score one for me, she thought.

"How?" Casey demanded. "What evidence do you possibly have to back that up?"

"Nothing, yet." Heiser made a strange, breathless noise, causing both Casey and Olivia to look at him. He stood and started pacing. "But it seems things are further along than I thought."

"Alright," Casey said, clapping his hands together, his lips stretched in a strained expression. "Let's recap. You're saying that some shadowy global organization has deep roots in Westville, is working with PRINCE Milling, and has abducted multiple young girls, including the CEO of PRINCE Milling's own granddaughter. All to use them to somehow open a door to some other worlds or realms or whatever."

"Dimensions," Heiser interrupted. "More precisely, a bridge between here and the astral plane."

"Great, thanks for the clarification. Are we going to talk about E.T. next?"

Heiser sat back in his chair. "Now that would definitely violate my NDA. Not that most of this doesn't . . . but for the record I prefer the terms ultra or crypto-terrestrial."

Olivia watched as Casey stood with a look of disbelief on his face, trying to wipe it away with a hand that stretched the bottom lids of his eyes and drooped his one brow even more.

Her throat tightened. It *did* all sound crazy, and she knew what she wanted to ask next sounded just as crazy. But all of this did. Their 'research' into a cursed town treasure and deals with bad spirits.

A shadow. A monster. Wherever it had come from.

"Is it possible that's where Millie is?" she blurted. "In that other place? The . . . 'in-between'."

Heiser looked at her, lowering his glasses and nodded slowly. "The 'in-between' is perhaps the most precise way to put it, and it's certainly a possibility. But I fear if she is there would be no getting her back. The Seethe, from all we've gleaned, is an endless ocean, consuming most minds who venture there."

Olivia caught his wording of *most* and wondered about what that could mean for a beat before he pressed on.

"As for the astral plane itself, we've only just begun to comprehend . . ." Heiser trailed off. "Well there is a lot we don't know."

"Devil's Peak," she blurted, as soon as it shot to her mind.

Heiser looked at her curiously.

Casey glowered. "What about it?" he asked.

"I told you what we saw," she said. "And when that thing was chasing us, the air was—thinner somehow. "

Casey's face went pale, but Heiser's went paler, and his eyes wider. "RE-728." There was concern there, but also a strange intrigue. "You've seen it."

The red orb. The jagged, jerking, wrong looking shadow. And that shatter of reverse hissing whispers when the flashlight beam hit it.

Heiser wanted to press more, she could tell, but Casey interrupted.

"So if I believed a shred of this, what do I do? What sort of police work would you recommend to find some evidence of . . . whatever the hell we're talking about."

"Trans-dimensional spatial distortions?" Heiser offered.

Olivia's nerves were electric within her, and her heartbeat faster, so there was no stopping the quip coming across her lips. "What he said. Keep up."

Casey shook his head and pointed at her, while staring at Heiser.

"If nothing else, congratulations on leading an impressionable teenager along with your little song and dance."

"I'm not sure I need to lead her anywhere," Heiser said. He walked toward the table and held up one of the sheets denoting PRINCE's dealings.

"The disturbances do align closely with the historical footprint of the Thompson family," Heiser said. "The mill itself, the location where Miss Thompson went missing, and there's the family history itself. The original mill owner, Arthur Thompson. And these dealings you mentioned with this local medicine man. Compelling."

Olivia shook her head. "My friend's grandpa—he mentioned some kind of sorcerer who lived up in the woods, right near Devil's Peak."

"Oh, a *sorcerer*," Casey exclaimed. "Good."

"More accurately to native culture, a shaman," said Heiser. "Many incursion scenarios involve ritualistic and religious rites, burial mounds and the like, because they perpetuate belief. Not to mention hallucinogens like peyote and other stimulants trigger neural responses conducive to dimensional insights."

"So getting high as a kite lets you see this stuff?" Olivia asked without thinking.

"Or, you just hallucinate," said Casey.

Heiser smirked. "Maybe. But it is well documented that people in heightened or lowered states of awareness have had uncanny experiences. Consistent with many religious and mythological belief systems."

Casey was looking over the papers Olivia had brought, a look of frustration coating his face.

"The Ottawa Treasure. I read about this once. The local chief buried the money from the sale of their lands."

"And his tribe buried him," Olivia finished.

Casey nodded. "And the treasure was never found."

"That's what we thought too." Olivia picked up one of the newspaper articles, a headline reading *Arthur Thompson Acquires PRINCE Milling Company*. "Austin's grandpa mentioned people would make . . . deals in blood with this shaman."

Heiser nodded. "Often there is an item of importance at the center of the rituals like these. A family heirloom perhaps," said Heiser, eyes gleaming with intensity. "Legends often carry a grain of truth."

Casey leaned against the table and stared flatly at Heiser. "So now we're talking about some Indiana Jones curse?"

"More like an imprint," Heiser corrected. "Bound by belief, ritual, and blood. It's likely to be disrupting the natural geomagnetic energies of leylines, allowing for an entry point."

Casey's eyes narrowed. "Want to try that in English?"

"Something has been feeding on this town, syphoning." Heiser said. "And now it's waking up."

"And ready to tear Westville a new one," Olivia muttered, thinking about the rage and violence she'd felt emanating off that thing in the woods.

Heiser nodded. "In a manner of speech, yes. A tuning fork, reverberating and creating a feedback loop. Some converged objects are known to act of their own volition and cause strange phenomena as well. I've got plenty of examples I can—"

"No thanks," Casey said.

"Whatever it is," Heiser continued, unfettered, "it would attract attention. From both sides."

Olivia felt the question coiling in her gut before she spouted it off.

"Attention from what?"

"There are things which are drawn to the Seethe, like moths to a flame. Often presenting in phenomena which people hold belief in, in the given area." Heiser glanced knowingly, sympathetically, at her. "One of which being RE-728."

She swallowed. "So, what should we do now?"

Heiser's expression darkened. "That's the question isn't it. I do know that once to a critical resonance point, there will be an incursion the likes of which hasn't been seen for some time. A dimensional bleed of sorts."

Before Olivia could respond, the sound of tires crunching on the gravel outside broke the silence.

Casey glanced out the window. "This is over. Your sister's here. Let's go."

"I'm not done—"

"Yes. You are." Casey opened the door and gestured for her to leave, his expression making it clear the discussion was over.

"Are you even hearing any of this?" she protested.

"Yep."

Fuming, Olivia stomped outside, brushing past Aly as she stepped out of her car.

She wasn't done, and this wasn't over. Not by a long shot.

9

"Well," Heiser said, giving Casey a thin smile. "I'll leave you to handle . . . this." He glanced toward Aly and Olivia. "Keep pulling on strings. See what comes loose. I'll be in touch."

As Heiser walked off Casey stood in disbelief, wondering just what kind of asylum circus he had just joined. The part that confused him the most was that some part of him had almost believed it.

As Heiser stepped past Aly, she furrowed her brow, smiled and said hello, calling him by his first name.

He stopped, nodded politely, and climbed into his car.

Aly stepped forward. "He's been coming into the café for a couple months now. Said he's in town on business. Nice guy."

"Yeah. Consultant for the feds," Casey lied, trying to figure out just what the hell he was himself.

"What was he doing here?" she asked, concern feathering her jaw.

He watched as Heiser's taillights disappeared down the street.

"Just stopped by asking for directions."

Aly didn't buy his thin sorry excuse for a sidestep. Why didn't he just tell her? Oh right, because all this was straight out of a jump-the-shark episode of *The X-Files*.

"Another thing you can't tell me?"

"It's not worth talking about."

"Right," Aly snapped. "Sorry about Liv."

"It's fine. She's a kid. Aly—"

But she was already walking briskly to the car. Casey sighed and swore under his breath, shutting the door. He stalked back up the stairs to the kitchen table and put his hands on the mess of papers, his mind whirring.

Pull on some strings, he thought, replaying Heiser's words.

He got in the shower, thinking about just which ones he could pull on, and put on his uniform and grabbed his keys.

He paused, and despite himself dashed back to the table, rolled up some of the maps and documents, and walked out the door.

10

A cup of coffee later, Casey started his patrol car, the maps in his passenger seat.

Casey veered right out of the station garage. Straight for the Allwell factory. It was a place to start. A thread to pull on and see whether it held, being one of the marked locations he couldn't draw a clear connection to. Everything that Heiser had been going on about, his theories on dimensionality, was completely inactionable for Casey. He only knew his job and how to do it. And he had to do something.

Semi-trucks came down this way regularly, making deliveries. The factory specialized in the distribution and manufacturing of marine parts, so they came and went from all over. It wouldn't be the biggest stretch to assume there was some kind of illicit operation, equipment, or kidnapped people being trafficked through here as Heiser made it seem Janus was in the business of doing. Certainly not any more of a stretch than the rest of the psychobabble he'd been spouting off.

Presently, a few cars were coming and going, the automated barrier rising and falling as workers changed over. Casey didn't know what he was looking for, exactly. He just knew he couldn't barge in and start asking questions—not when he was already on thin ice with the feds, and starting to get there with Hart as well.

He pulled off to the side of the road, cutting his engine and lights. From here, he could see the quiet orange glow of the factory's parking lot below, the still, ridged cement walls of the sprawling building, and steam rising from rooftop vents. Back downriver, PRINCE Milling glowed red, a watchful eye in the night.

To his left, movement caught his attention. Headlights floated onto the thin cement drive winding through the middle of the cemetery. Casey frowned. Midnight graveside visits weren't exactly common in Westville—or anywhere, for that matter. He doubted whoever it was had seen him, his car partially obscured by the pines that lined the edges of the lot.

For a while, Casey just watched.

The driver killed the truck's headlights and climbed out, moving toward a cluster of headstones, a shovel glinting faintly in the moonlight.

The sharp shing of metal meeting earth broke the quiet.

Casey rolled down his window, the cold air biting at his skin.

Sliding out of the car, Casey crept along the edge of the path, staying near the trees. He dipped behind the taller headstones, his breath fogging in the cold air. His fingers brushed the flashlight clipped to his belt.

He steadied himself, flicking it on.

The beam slashed through the dark, landing on a figure mid-dig. And revealing the dark green and deep rust of a Toyota truck.

Ethan Crawley.

"Westville Police," Casey barked, his voice cutting through the night. His other hand hovered near his holster. "Drop the shovel and put your hands up."

The man froze, straightening slowly. A wool mask obscured his face, and he raised an arm to shield his eyes from the light.

Casey took a cautious step forward. "I said, drop the shovel—"

The crack came out of nowhere.

Blinding pain shot through Casey's skull as something hard and metal slammed into the side of his head.

He hit the ground, ears ringing, vision swimming. Gravel bit into his palms as he tried to steady himself, his flashlight rolling uselessly away.

When his vision cleared, he saw a second man standing over him, another shovel in hand.

Casey blinked up at him, disoriented.

The man peeled off his wool mask, revealing Crawley's gaunt, sneering face. "Evenin', officer."

A boot came down hard on his face, and his world went black.

THE GIRL IN THE RIVER

D.C.B. Interview Transcript

Incident Report

Interview Series 3: The Westville Incursion

Lochlear: Walk me through Monday November 11th.

Benson: You know what happened that day.

Lochlear: The purpose of this interview is to get your own account of things, Mr. Benson.

Benson: I want to hear you say it.

Lochlear: I don't follow.

Benson: You know what happened. Why don't you say it? Say her name.

Lochlear: Emily Grace Thompson. Age 13.

Benson: How'd that feel?

Lochlear: I'm not inhuman, Mr. Benson. I'm no monster.

Benson: But you left her with one.

Lochlear: You mean Ethan Crawley?

Benson: Him. And whatever was inside of him.

Lochlear: Speculation, Mr. Benson.

Benson: Speculate this.

Lochlear: Perhaps it's time for a break.

Benson: You know what, no. I'll tell you what happened. You just let every word sink in nice and deep. Then we'll see who the monster is.

Lochlear: Alright. I'll bite. Go ahead.

1

Casey's lungs burned, fresh damp earth and diesel lingering in the frigid air.

His head pounded as shadowy branches of pines against a dark sky came clear out of the blur. Casey rolled over with a groan and stumbled to his feet, remembering where he was.

Elmwood Cemetery.

Crawley's truck that had been pulled up along the center path was gone, and so was he. But who was the second man?

He took a couple steps then seized in pain. His ribs were bruised—best case scenario. Casey pressed forward in the dark, looking back toward his cruiser. He had to call it in, get an APB out for Crawley and his accomplice.

He started down the paved pathway and saw his flashlight laying there. He picked it up, and it flickered. It shined where they had been digging, right in front of a plot of dark granite gravestones, uniform in size and shape.

Daniel Thompson. Arthur Thompson. Jack Thompson Sr.

He stepped closer to the holes. They'd made a lot of progress however long he'd been out. Enough to reach the caskets.

All of which were open—and emptied.

2

A swarm of police and federal vehicles gathered around Erin and Joe Thompson's place that night, their flashing lights carving through the dark.

The official assumption following the exhumation of the Thompson family graves was that someone was now targeting the entire family—and that the same parties had also taken Millie.

For Casey, it seemed open-and-shut. He'd seen Ethan Crawley. Crawley had knocked him out cold. Crawley had been at the graveyard. It should have been the simplest arrest of his career.

Problem was, Crawley had an alibi—an airtight one. He'd been on the night shift at the mill, and none other than Jack Thompson Sr. was able to corroborate.

"I was working late myself, just trying to keep busy," Jack said, sitting stiffly in the interview room, his silver hair catching the fluorescent light. He wore a look of grim control, but Casey caught the subtle twitch of his fingers, the smallest sign of strain.

Maybe now at least he was ready to concede that there was someone who had a beef with him and PRINCE personally that was behind all of this.

Casey's mind flashed back to the surreal conversation he'd had with Heiser just before his shift, the doctor and Olivia both spouting off things straight from a bad B-movie. There was a strange comfort in having witnessed what he had in the graveyard. Flesh and blood people, suspects. Not red orbs and voices and some paranormal academic researcher wanting to make his big breakthrough. Casey felt a fear bubble up in then, the kind that told him he was hiding from a truth he'd probably sensed through the past week and a half.

Something *wasn't* right about all this. Something *wasn't* normal.

He just wasn't sure how outside of normal it was, or how far he was willing to let himself go.

Chief Hart had been collecting a few more paltry details. He leaned back in his chair. "And you're sure Ethan was there from 9 p.m. to 5 a.m?"

"That's right. My shift manager confirmed it as well."

"Thank you, Jack. I think that's all we need from you for now."

Jack rose with a nod, but as he passed Casey, he stopped. "You put yourself in harm's way for us," he said softly. "For my family. I won't forget that."

Casey didn't respond. He couldn't. His eyes were glued to the holding room door, where Crawley was being released. Crawley's pristine boots shuffled as he stepped out, his face unreadable under the harsh lights—bastard must have changed them. He didn't look at Casey as he left.

Casey turned to the Chief. "You're just letting him go?"

Hart sighed, rubbing his temples. "Casey—"

"I know what I saw," Casey snapped. "Crawley was there. He knocked me out. He was digging up those graves. And he wasn't alone."

Hart raised a hand to calm him. "You got clocked in the head pretty hard. And when you woke up, maybe your mind filled in the gaps. You've been under a lot of stress, son—"

"That's not what this is," Casey snapped. "I'm not imagining things."

"Maybe you're seeing what you need to see," Hart said evenly. "You're chasing answers because you can't stand not having them. I get it. But we have to go where the evidence leads. Right now—and I need you to hear me here—none of it is leading to Crawley."

Casey opened his mouth to argue but closed it again, his fists clenching at his sides. back

Casey followed the Chief into the lobby, his head spinning. He didn't notice Lochlear and Reeves until they stepped into his path.

"Benson," Lochlear said, his expression colder than usual.

"Not now," Casey muttered, trying to push past.

"Exactly now," Lochlear said, firm and leaving no room for argument. He held his arm out, gesturing toward the interview room. Casey shook his head, a cold resignation settling over him mingling with an indignant fire in his belly.

A moment later, he sat at the table, glaring up at Lochlear. Reeves slid in as he closed the door behind them.

"This will only take a moment," Reeves said, holding up a folder, the twinge of a consolatory look quavering across her lips. She unrolled a set of maps, the ones Casey had pored over feverishly the day before.

"We found these in your cruiser," Lochlear said. "We know where they came from. Stay away from Heiser."

Casey's stomach tightened. "Why? Because he's interfering with your cover-up?"

Reeves' jaw tightened, and Lochlear stepped closer.

"Because he's a liability," Lochlear said. "And you're shaping up to be one yourself."

Casey stood, his voice sharp. "You're not looking for Millie, are you? You're just here to sweep this under the rug."

"Watch your tone," he hissed.

Reeves' eyes darted to the ground.

Casey let out a bitter laugh. "*Dimensional Containment*, right? Heiser told me all about it."

Reeves froze, glancing up, and Lochlear's face darkened.

"You're way out of line, Benson," he growled.

"Am I?" Casey shot back. "Because it seems to me you're more worried about your secrets than finding that girl."

"You've been dodging our request for an interview, and now I see why. You're unstable. At this point, I have to question trusting your judgment—and your credibility."

"Trust. That's rich!" he yelled. "You want to talk about—"

"Enough," Reeves spat, her hard hazel eyes piercing. "Quit while you're ahead."

The door flung open. Chief Hart stepped inside, glancing at the agents.

"I need a word."

"We're not done here," said Lochlear, storming out into the hall.

Reeves leaned against the wall, but after a moment she joined her partner, the hushed voices in the hallway betraying nothing good. Casey shot up from his chair, his ribs aching, and stepped into the doorway.

Gail was sniffling and red faced as she brushed past, walking back toward reception at a hurried clip. Hart cradled his face in one hand. Lochlear and Reeves were jetting out toward the back entrance to the parking lot.

Casey knew. Somehow, he did.

"Where?"

Hart nodded and turned his head up toward a flickering fluorescent light.

"In the river."

3

The sky had shifted to bright blue as the morning cleared, but the air snapped with bitterness, as if no matter how bright the sun shone, there would be no warmth to be had here in Westville.

No warmth, no comfort, no hope.

A runner had seen her first, stopped, stared, and thought maybe it was just a wrong looking collection of sticks and debris from the windstorm.

She screamed and ran further, toward the police station, when she realized what it was.

A frail, young gray body rolling in the frothing churn of the dam.

Olivia heard the sirens early.

She had been tired. Tired of everything. She wanted to dream of finding Millie in that in-between place. Instead, she slept deep, but not soundly. And when the sirens wailed through her window—the sound of someone else's soon-to-be-known sorrow—she regretted every wasted second.

She felt it then. The fear of the end.

She swallowed it and marched right downstairs, straight past Kathy and Aly in the kitchen, both glancing out the window toward the sound.

Olivia didn't pay any mind to her mother's protests and her sister calling after her. She threw on her shoes and got on her bike, following the sound.

It was coming from the river.

4

By the time she got there, emergency vehicles choked the street and the memorial parking lot by the dam. A firetruck, three police vehicles, an unmarked black car with a blue siren on top.

And an ambulance.

Olivia's chest clenched, her breath coming in tempered heaves as she thought about what that meant. It meant they had found someone. An ambulance meant they found someone alive and that they needed help.

Millie was okay. She had to be.

Olivia laid down her bike along the sidewalk over the bridge and pushed through the crowd.

Then she heard it. A wail.

Not a siren but the kind that stilled the air and was all pain, shock, and awe.

Olivia felt her limbs grow heavy and numb, and with fearful eyes she scanned the area, looking for the source. Mrs. Thompson was crumpled to her knees on the pavement, near a stretcher, upon which Olivia could make out a flash of gray skin and tattered clothes.

Mrs. Thompson's face was twisted in a silent scream, body trembling. Mr. Thompson paced in circles, hands above his head, gritting his teeth and averting his eyes from his wife and from—

Whoever that was.

Olivia sprinted forward, breaking through the crowd, but came to a line of yellow tape. A woman in an official looking jacket with copper hair and intense hazel eyes met her there.

"You need to stay back."

"Who is it? Who did they find?"

She frowned, then looked over Olivia's shoulder to someone approaching. Olivia turned to see Casey.

"I've got her," he said.

Olivia was taken aback at his blackened eye and a bandage around his head. She noted he was walking with a limp.

"What happened to you?"

Casey winced and knelt down. "It's nothing. Olivia—"

"I know. They found her," Olivia said, her mind changing course. That was *her*, she decided. She just needed help. "She's going to be okay."

Casey shook his head.

"She's going to be alright. There's an ambulance. They'll take her and—"

"She's gone," Casey said.

"No," Olivia said, throat tight and burning. "She's right there. She's—"

She clung to the idea that the ambulance meant hope—that the gray figure on the stretcher *wasn't* Millie. She needed to. But then Mrs. Thompson's cry cut through the roar of the dam, belief shattering like brittle ice.

Olivia knew. Of course she did.

Hot tears welled up in her eyes, making the whole world bleary as the cold sun shimmered.

A pair of hands clasped her shoulders, and Olivia cried and fell into them. Aly held her for a long time right there by the river's edge, long enough for the ambulance to drive off and for the police to begin dispersing the crowd.

As Olivia walked to the car with her mom and sister, she saw Kyle and Austin across the road on their bikes. Their eyes met for a moment.

And in that moment she felt the cold crystalline sky shatter, and she wished for a portentous covering of cloud to shelter her from the falling shards. She didn't want them to slice into her skin. She didn't want to admit what the look she exchanged with her friends meant.

It was over.

5

She never had a chance.

The thought coursed through Casey's mind like debris on the river. He stared out at the dark waters of the Slate through the windshield of his idling car parked in the funeral home lot.

Four days ago, they'd found her.

Casey stepped out of the car and joined the queue that snaked along the sidewalk. A cool breeze blew, rattling the early Christmas display on a house across the street. Another house flaunted macabre Halloween leftovers and fake tombstones.

Inside, the dim lighting of the funeral home did nothing to soften the grim mood. Casey's eyes found Joe and Erin Thompson at the end of the receiving line, standing beside the gleaming cherry wood casket. A photo of Millie rested on a stand: her winning smile, inherited from Joe, and blonde waves, courtesy of Erin. Her blue eyes sparkled in the image, so alive it hurt.

Casey clenched his jaw and remembered the last time they'd talked.

"You keep calling me nutcase, and I just might start to believe it," Casey had said, sitting down next to her on the deck.

Millie fiddled with her CD player. "I call 'em like I see 'em."

"Sure you do." Joe had gone inside to grab burgers for the grill. Casey noticed three empty Corona bottles and glanced at his watch—4:30 p.m.

"How's everything been?"

She shrugged. "I don't know. A little better, I guess. Mom's picking up more shifts at the nursing home, so she's not around as much. Which means they're not fighting as much."

Casey nodded. "Things will work out. Okay?"

Millie took her headphones off her neck. "Here, listen to this."

Casey hesitated but obliged, slipping them over his ears.

She pressed play. The yodeling grit of Alanis spilled into his ears in front of phased guitars and a muted drum groove.

"Good song," Casey said. "Sounds like she's talking about you. Short but healthy."

Millie laughed. "Why are you yelling?"

Casey pulled off the headphones. "Because I'm a nutcase, I guess."

"Anyway," she said, "a friend let me borrow the album. It helps. Everything's gonna be alright. You know?"

Casey snapped back to the present, his chest tightening with red-hot anger. Whoever did this to Millie was out there. He hadn't given up on the idea that Ethan Crawley was their man. But the court of public opinion had already settled on a story, aided by the Feds: Millie's body had simply been caught downstream and freed during the storm, either Howard Meyers, some other unknown assailant, or just a freak accident as she walked along the North Country Trail and fell.

Just plausible enough. Tragic. The kind of story people would believe.

He moved closer to the end of the receiving line, his eyes scanning the room. The funeral home had a frozen-in-time feel, its creamy white walls accented with ornate crown molding. The mold-yellow carpet and gloomy lighting made the place seem more lifeless than comforting.

"Casey," Erin said, stepping forward to hug him.

"How are you holding up?"

She nodded vigorously. "I'm still standing."

Casey glanced around. "Joe?"

"He needed a break."

Casey gave her a rueful nod, and after a moment a halfhearted 'hang in there' hand on her arm and drifted toward a table laden with silver carafes and water pitchers. A figure near the green, ornate couches to the right caught his attention.

Heiser.

Casey stalked over to him, the man's sharp eyes scanning the room.

"What are you doing here?" Casey demanded, his voice low but brimming with anger.

Heiser looked at Casey, unfazed. "Paying my respects."

"Don't give me that," Casey snapped. "You don't belong here."

Heiser sighed, glancing toward the closed casket. "Maybe not. But I have an obligation."

Casey's eyes narrowed. "What the hell is that supposed to mean?"

"It means," Heiser said, his voice calm but deliberate, "if certain people get what they're after, this town will be mourning more than this."

Casey's chest tightened. "You're talking about Janus."

Heiser's lips quirked. "They don't make moves that come into the public eye unless they're after something big."

Casey took a step closer, his fists clenched. "What are they after? What did Millie have to do with it?"

Heiser hesitated, glancing back toward the casket as if weighing his words carefully. "Let's just say, I believe they needed someone specific and alive to pull this off. That they still do."

Casey froze, the word *alive* reverberating in his mind like a struck bell. His pulse quickened.

"You don't think she's dead."

"And you do?"

Casey paused. Of course he hadn't wanted to believe it—no one did. But she'd been identified. Dental records confirmed it. He'd even seen the body, and though whatever had been done to her combined with time spent in the river made her near unrecognizable—forensics had filled in the gaps.

Heiser's gaze was steady but distant, as though he were staring through Casey. A cold certainty settled in his gut, mingling now with indignant rage.

"If that girl wasn't Millie, then who was it?"

Heiser turned and looked him in the eyes this time. "You're a good cop from what I've observed, Casey. I think you already know the answer to that."

The other missing girls from the greater Iron Falls area flashed through his mind. He could see some of their faces on the missing persons posters and the local news. Both had been similar in age and appearance to Millie.

"They need her alive to finish what they're doing," Heiser said. "Do you understand?"

Casey's breath hitched, rearing back and feeling his own brow contort to the point he was aware of his own expression. "No. What are they trying to do?"

Heiser leaned in slightly, lowering his voice. "Open a doorway. One that should never be opened."

Casey's stomach churned, the image of the red light in the woods flashing in his mind. The Thompson family history. Olivia's account of Halloween night. Heat rose in Casey's chest. Reeves, Lochlear, and now Heiser, who were nothing but conspiratorial bureaucratic sidetalkers in equal and opposite measure.

"Bullshit," Casey spat. "You're just here to stir the pot while this town falls apart."

Heiser straightened, his expression unreadable. "You're not wrong about one thing. There's a crack in the foundation of this place. A deep one. If you don't want it to split wide open, I suggest you keep digging."

Heiser turned and walked outside, leaving Casey standing frozen in the gloom of the parlor, his thoughts racing. Could Millie be alive? It was crazy.

Wasn't it? But then, the feds would have been well within their power or at least their ability with whatever government clearance they had, to make things read how they wanted them to read. Lochlear himself had made the statement to the media.

Casey's mind swam. He wasn't in the funeral home anymore. He was replaying that morning and the flurry of everything that had happened.

"Hey," said Aly, walking up behind him. He turned. She was in a well-fitted black dress, her blonde hair down and loose.

Casey struggled to come to the moment and cleared his throat.

"You okay?" Aly asked.

"I—yeah. You come alone?" Casey asked.

"Mom's here. Liv wasn't up for it."

"Can't be easy for her."

"She doesn't believe Millie's dead. I know denial is part of this. I felt it with Dad too. But Liv keeps saying Millie's out there. That the body wasn't her."

Casey only nodded, but Aly could read him like a book.

"She keeps talking about you. And mentioned some . . . maps?"

Casey frowned. "Heiser, or . . . Greg, I guess," he said, remembering he'd been a regular of Aly's, "he came to me with some theories. Just left, actually."

Aly furrowed her brow. "What is going on, Casey?"

He shook his head. "I don't know. Look, I can talk to Liv if you want."

"No," Aly said quickly. "I mean, it's probably best if she has space."

When the silence got heavier, unspoken questions of past and present hanging in the air between them, Casey offered a quick goodbye and left Aly by the coffee.

When he reached the parking lot, he heard hard voices cutting through the cold air. He crept across the street and pressed against the wall of the funeral home.

Before he knew it, he was eavesdropping on a conversation between father and son.

"You knew this was coming," Jack Thompson said.

"No." Joe's voice, low and dangerous. "This is your fault. You and your damn legacy."

"Our legacy, Joe. I can't afford not to deliver. Just a little longer."

"What does it matter? How am I supposed to move on from this? How is Erin supposed to—"

"She will. In time."

"Go to hell."

"Joe—"

"I'm done. I don't care who comes knocking. Let them. I'll tear them apart."

"Don't do this, son."

Joe stormed inside.

Casey leaned back against the wall, his mind racing.

What had he just heard?

Jack Thompson tore off in his red and cream Ford truck, leaving Casey with one haunting phrase: *I can't afford not to deliver.*

He needed to talk to Joe. But pulling him away from the visitation in the state he was in wouldn't do any good. It also couldn't wait long.

Casey drove home, got the maps out again, the copies he'd made when Reeves and Lochlear hadn't been hovering around.

He traced faint lines with his finger, his mind replaying the words. What did Jack need to deliver, and who was he so afraid of? Janus Global was Casey's best guess. But they were about as well defined as the Dimensional Containment Bureau, and half the time he felt convinced all of this was some elaborate ruse he was caught in the middle of. A nightmarish prank.

None of that changed the fact that it was all too real. And, if he was going to confront Joe tomorrow, he needed to be ready for answers he might not want to hear.

He left a message on Heiser's motel phone, his voice low but firm.

"If you're serious about stopping whatever the hell is going on here, I'm listening. Just come ready to explain everything."

Casey leaned back in his chair, the maps spread before him. His eyes fell on a faint red line he hadn't noticed before, branching off the main pipeline and marked with a single word: *'CHASM'*, annotated with a question mark. When had Heiser written that?

The phone line clicked as his message ended. Casey paused, unsure if it had been disconnected—or whether someone had been listening.

6

Olivia sat in the living room, staring at a blank TV screen when Kathy and Aly came home.

She'd tried to find the remote in time to make it look like she was watching something—anything—but hadn't managed. Instead, the forensics book she'd borrowed from the library was shoved under the couch, its pages open to the section on dental records.

Kathy didn't miss a beat. She glanced at the TV. "Nothing good on?"

"Just relaxing," Olivia muttered, sharper than she'd intended.

"Everyone asked where you were," Kathy said, setting her purse down. "I'm sure they will tomorrow too."

"Did you tell them I wasn't going to a fake funeral?"

Kathy's face tightened. Her cheeks flushed as she lowered herself onto the couch next to Olivia.

"I didn't want to believe it either, you know. When your father got his diagnosis."

"I don't—"

"I'm going to tell you," Kathy said, her voice strained and final. "Because you need to hear it."

From the corner of her eye, Olivia saw Aly slipping out of the room, clearly not wanting to be caught in the crossfire.

"I wanted it to be a dream," Kathy said. "Then I told myself maybe the doctors got it wrong. Maybe they mixed up the scans. But it wasn't either of those things."

"I know that," Olivia shot back. "Cancer sucks. What else is new?"

"Here's one thing," Kathy said, her voice softening. "I can't remember the last time you called me Mom."

Olivia looked down, refusing to meet her eyes.

"You're scared. You're hurting. Just like I was. Just like I am now, only for you."

"I don't want to talk about this."

"Which is exactly why we need to."

Olivia shook her head, fighting the hot sting of tears. "All I think about when I think about Dad is the way he looked in that bed. I just thought he wasn't there anymore. His mouth hanging open. Those damn eye twitches—"

"It wasn't easy to see him like that," Kathy said, her voice quivering now. "But I believe he could hear us. He wanted his girls with him, right until the end."

"Don't!" Olivia shot to her feet, trembling with anger and grief. "Don't tell me that."

Kathy's voice broke. "He wouldn't have blamed you for not wanting to be in the room, sweetheart. I know that's what this is about."

Olivia's chest heaved. "I wanted to, Mom. I wanted to be there, but I didn't want him to be that way." The words spilled out between sobs. "I didn't want him to."

"I know, I know," Kathy said, standing and pulling her into a tight embrace. She guided Olivia back down to the couch as she cried uncontrollably into her shoulder.

Aly reentered the room, quietly sitting on Olivia's other side and rubbing her back.

"I miss him," Olivia choked out. "I want to tell him I'm sorry."

"We all miss him," Aly said softly. "And there's nothing to be sorry about."

Olivia didn't believe that.

They stayed there for what seemed like a long time.

"It's your choice whether or not you come tomorrow," Kathy said. "I just don't want you to regret it."

Olivia sat there for a moment, and for a few more moments until Kathy and Aly had both gone up to get ready for bed. She didn't want to regret anything.

They were right about that.

The luncheon was at Millie's grandparents' house on River's Edge Drive. One of the most recognizable houses in the whole town, known simply as Thompson House, and people talked about like it was some kind of palace. Westville royalty.

Olivia wondered what kind of person it made her that, as she went to her room to pick out what clothes she was going to wear to her best friend's funeral, she also grabbed the camcorder she'd been borrowing semi-permanently from

Aly—who never used it—from under her bed. If she brought a purse with her, it was small enough that she could fit it.

What she *would* regret is not taking this chance to find out the truth. To suspect a family member of having anything to do with what happened to Millie was a horrible thing, and she was more certain now it made her a horrible person for thinking it.

But Olivia didn't care. She wanted answers. She wanted to believe that somehow, the police had been wrong about that body.

She had to make sense of this. No matter what.

1

A grim hush filled the sanctuary of the old Methodist church, tinctured with murmurs of the gathered, their eyes averted from the terrible truth.

The truth was undeniable: Westville had been scarred, changed irreversibly. How could it not be?

Emily Grace Thompson, Casey read on the white bulletin, with a flowery design around the edge. As though there was supposed to be beauty somewhere in all of this. This was only ugly.

He'd pored over the maps and county documents until Heiser left at 2 a.m., and sleep slowly overtook Casey, just as the doctor was going off on a tangent about his CHASM theory. Supposed entry points to these doorways, or the *'in-between'* as Olivia had called it.

Most of what Heiser pitched seemed like impossible crackpot theory. But other aspects were more plausible—like Janus Global having deep roots in Westville. In fact, they'd seemingly had a hand in shaping the town's prosperity since the early 20th century, investing in infrastructure and businesses that had made the town thrive.

Only back then, the Company, as Heiser referred to them, weren't called Janus. They'd operated under various other names, presenting themselves as seemingly disconnected investors. But every one of those entities shared a common thread: they were all tied to the same families—families who now held major stakes in Janus Global Logistics.

Casey could buy into that. The shadowy corporate history you might uncover in investigative journalism or cold-case work. At least it had a paper trail.

What he couldn't buy into were 'dimensional anomalies'—cracks in the window, as Heiser called them—created and exploited by forces beyond human understanding. Burial mounds, spirits, and monsters from campfire stories.

It was the kind of talk that belonged in pulp novels or late-night conspiracy shows, not a funeral parlor and certainly not in a real investigation. And yet for reasons he couldn't yet name it was becoming harder for Casey to dismiss outright.

Sitting there in the sanctuary as the funeral began, Casey tried to push it all to the back of his mind. He had to. If he didn't keep a clear head, if he let himself get sucked into Heiser's world of unprovable theories and ancient horror stories, he'd lose his grip on what was real—and that was dangerous.

But what if Heiser's theories weren't so far-fetched? What if this town wasn't just grieving a senseless tragedy but was standing on the edge of something far worse? The thought lingered despite his best efforts, like a storm on the horizon, impossible to ignore.

The one bright spot was that the feds had left town, according to Chief Hart. Though Lochlear made a point to say he'd 'be circling around', whatever the hell that meant.

Pastor Rick Garrett stepped up to the pulpit and began to recite Psalm 23:

> *'Even though I walk through the valley of the shadow of death,*
> *I will fear no evil, for you are with me; your rod and your staff,*
> *they comfort me.'*

That shadow loomed large over Westville now, over everyone in it. And maybe—just maybe—it wasn't a metaphor.

After the service, Casey found Joe shaking the hand of Mayor Douglas in the Fellowship Hall, bathed in surreal syrupy light filtering through yellow-paned and black iron webbed windows.

Casey approached cautiously.

"Hey man," he said, giving his friend a hug. "Sorry I missed you at the visitation yesterday."

"I had to step out for a while," Joe replied. "It's just a lot, you know."

Casey glanced around to ensure no one was listening. "I heard you and Jack. Outside the funeral home. It didn't sound like just family stuff."

Joe's jaw clenched, and he looked away. "That's between me and my dad."

"Maybe, but this isn't just about you, Joe. It's about Millie. What's going on?"

Joe's head snapped back toward him, his voice low but sharp. "Don't do this here. Not now."

"I know what I heard," Casey pressed. "You said you were 'done' with something—some kind of legacy. 'We can't afford not to deliver.' What the hell does that mean?"

Joe's face flushed, and he stepped closer, his voice a harsh whisper. "It means nothing. Just my old man rambling on about the family business. You know how he gets."

"This isn't about the mill," Casey said firmly. "And you know it. You've been different, even before Millie went missing. You've been distracted, angry. The drinking. And now she's gone, and—"

Joe's hand shot up, silencing him. His voice cracked with barely restrained anger. "Stop."

Casey hesitated but didn't back down. "I know this isn't just grief. There's something you're not telling me. If it has anything to do with what happened to Millie, you have to—"

Joe shoved him hard, his voice rising. "You don't know what you're talking about!"

Casey stumbled as a stark stab of pain radiated from his ribs, making his eyes water. He caught himself against a support beam. Several heads turned toward the commotion, and the room fell silent.

Joe pointed a trembling finger at him, his voice breaking. "You think you can just come in here and throw around accusations? You think you know what it's like to lose her?"

Casey steadied himself, aching, and took a deep breath. "Joe, I'm not accusing you of anything. I'm trying to help."

"Help?" The word was venom from his mouth. "You're not helping anyone, least of all me. Just stay out of it, Casey. Stay the hell out of it."

Before Casey could respond, Joe turned and stormed out of the room, leaving a stunned silence in his wake. Casey stood frozen, the weight of Joe's words sinking in. From the corner of his eye, he saw Jack Thompson watching him intently from across the room. Casey pulled himself upright. Aly stood and moved toward him. He saw Olivia step away from her friends.

He figured he should leave before this went any further.

Casey walked out the door, down the stairs, and onto the pavement of the church lot. He couldn't get the scared, angry look in Joe's eyes out of his head. But then, of course, Joe would be both of those things. Casey would have been too, if it were his daughter. No idea where she was for weeks, with a fading chance of her being alive.

And one day, there she is.

A girl in the river. Lonely, cold, and faded to gray.

Casey's arms shook, chills running through him and making him shake as he made his way out of the church and into the parking lot.

Aly called out behind him, but he didn't turn around.

He had to reckon with what he'd become. What he'd gotten sucked into.

Hart had been right. This was the Hopkins kid all over again. Casey searching for reasons, excuses, a way things could have gone differently. Instead of accepting it for what it was.

A failure. A loss.

But this was worse. He thought back to TJ Hopkins, that cocky smirk as Casey let him off with a warning. The weight of the report he'd written later, describing how the Camaro had wrapped around that oak tree, killing him on impact in a blaze. The same feeling crept in now, settling lead in his chest. They'd buried their son, but they never knew what Casey did. Or didn't do.

That he could have stopped it.

And now Joe, confronted by his supposed best friend spouting conspiracy theories about his daughter being out there somewhere and the killer at large, despite having seen her body. Despite the knowledge that the killer had been found in the river weeks earlier, with plenty of evidence to corroborate. Howard Meyers. Casey just hadn't wanted to see it.

A blinding jolt shot to the front of his skull, making his eyes water.

He thought of that whisper, and knew it was right.

As Casey walked down the sidewalk under the gray November sky, the first frozen particulates of snow fell. He shook his head as if to ward off the thoughts from invading again. He didn't want to think about it, not anymore.

It was over. That girl in the river he had wanted to believe so badly wasn't Millie Thompson. He realized that he had to believe.

For the sake of everyone around him who was already moving on.

He couldn't do this again.

When he got home, he called Heiser, hands shaking as he hung up the phone. Moments later his car pulled in the drive. Casey grit his teeth, grabbed all the maps and documents after throwing on his coat, then walked straight to his driver's side window.

"Casey. I thought I ought to update you on—"

"Go to hell," Casey said. He let the pile of papers drop to the damp ground outside Heiser's vehicle. "Take your shit and get out of my town. If I see you again, I'm giving Reeves a call." He turned and looked straight at him before getting in his own car. "She might be interested to know what you've been pulling."

"You're making a mistake, Casey. You think walking away will make this easier?" Heiser yelled. "It won't!"

Casey sped off.

8

The Thompson house loomed over River Edge Drive like something out of a gothic novel—a majestic brick Victorian, wrapped in iron fencing, with a turret that stretched toward the sky. Its signature parapet sported a circular attic window, the kind Olivia thought looked like an unblinking eye. Watching.

The air smelled of fresh-pressed linen and something faintly floral, old-money refinement that made Olivia think she was tracking mud across the floors just by existing.

Inside, the luncheon unfolded in a low murmur of voices, silverware clinking against fine china. She sat stiffly at the long mahogany table, pushing food around her plate while her mother chatted politely with someone she didn't recognize.

Some she did recognize. Kids from school. Jimmy Morgan, a junior and star running back on the football team glanced over at her, attempting what she guessed to be a sympathetic smile that just made him look constipated. One person she hadn't recognized herself when she looked in the mirror on the way out of the house, in an old violet dress of Aly's. Kyle and Austin both wore button downs and khaki's of different shades, thought Austin's seemed too short.

Across the table, Kyle poked at his plate with a fork. "Food church people make weirds me out. This Jell-O looks like it has mayonnaise in it."

Austin, sitting beside him, muttered, "That's because it does."

Kyle let the neon red mash slip out of his mouth, back onto the plate, and then into the trash.

But Olivia was barely hearing them. Her focus was elsewhere.

Jack Thompson's study. The attic with the circular window.

Somewhere in this house—there were answers.

She glanced to the winding wooden staircase with a glossy sheen.

"Time to move."

"Bad idea," Kyle hissed, grabbing her wrist before she could take another step. "You want to get caught snooping around in the Thompson crypt?"

Olivia pulled free. "Just keep watch. If I'm not back in ten . . . cause a distraction or something."

"Or *something*?" Kyle exhaled sharply, exchanging a wary glance with Austin. But neither of them tried to stop her again. She slipped through the hallway, past the guests, past the closed doors of studies and sitting rooms, past a gallery of Thompson family portraits staring down at her with their frozen expressions.

She reached Jack's office first. Locked.

Her pulse spiked. She glanced down the hall and, heart hammering, turned toward the attic stairs. The air changed the moment Olivia stepped onto the attic landing.

Colder. Stiller.

Dust motes swirled in the faint light filtering through the circular window. The space smelled of old paper, varnished wood, and something faintly metallic.

Rows of wooden storage crates lined the walls, stacked haphazardly beneath sagging shelves of books and ledgers. She swept the light of the camcorder over them, her breath catching when she saw a name burned into one of the crates—A. Thompson.

She crouched, pried the lid open.

Inside, wrapped in aging linen, were stacks of yellowed pages. Handwritten notes. Dates. Numbers. Strange symbols she didn't recognize.

A cold prickle crawled up her neck.

She reached into her purse, pulled out the small camcorder, and flicked it on.

Beep. Red light. Recording.

She turned toward the shelves, sweeping the lens slowly, capturing everything.

Then—a creak behind her.

Olivia's stomach plummeted. She whipped around. Mary Thompson stood in the doorway. For a long second, neither of them moved.

Then, slowly, Mary stepped forward. Her hands trembled slightly as she smoothed down her skirt, but her expression was unreadable.

"You shouldn't be up here," she said softly.

Olivia's grip tightened around the camera. Mary's eyes darted to the open crate at Olivia's feet. For a moment, Olivia thought she was going to storm over, yelling and cursing at her the way her face quivered and twitched.

Instead—she walked over slowly, reached forward, and, with careful fingers, closed the crate.

Olivia's breath came sharp and fast. "I—"

"Just, go," Mary said. Her voice straining for calm, wavering. "Please." She meant it.

And that—more than anything—made Olivia's stomach sink.

She stepped backward, slipping the camera into her purse as she turned toward the attic door. She stepped into the hallway.

Jack Thompson was there. Waiting. His expression dark and cold, his eyes locked onto hers. And then—he smiled. Not a friendly smile. Not even close.

He reached out, clamping a firm hand on her shoulder.

A squeeze. Not hard. But enough. Enough to tell her: I see you. Enough to send a chill all the way down to her bones.

"Olivia!"

Her mother's voice.

Kathy appeared at the base of the stairs, breathless, her expression shifting between concern and quiet embarrassment.

"I'm so sorry," Kathy said, looking between Jack and Mary. "She shouldn't have—Olivia, we're leaving. Now."

Before Olivia could argue, her mother reached for the camcorder and pulled it from her pocket. Olivia let her take it. Because the tape was already gone.

Kyle had said this was a bad idea.

But Olivia was beginning to think it had been worth it.

She felt leering eyes on her from the windows of the Thompson home as they drove away.

9

When Olivia got home from the funeral, she took out the forensics book to re-confirm her theory about how dental records could be faked.

Or better yet, for the authorities to just lie about them entirely.

Then, she examined the tape she'd taken out of the camcorder. Kathy would have locked it down tight now, since she'd been the silent kind of mad.

Maybe that was the worst kind.

What little she'd seen in that journal, she hadn't liked the look of. And yet that told her something. She wasn't all wrong about this. Millie's grandmother had looked so pale Olivia thought all the blood had run out of her. Millie's grandfather on the other hand looked at her like—

Almost like Ethan Crawley had . . .

She clutched the tape and put it on her bed stand. In the morning, she could go to the Family Affair, and they could transfer the tape to a VHS. She knew that Austin didn't own a camcorder and if Kyle did, Mr. Anderson was so anal about things the odds weren't good.

That night she lay in bed and didn't dream. The last thought in her mind was of the girl in the river. Of Millie being alive, in that in-between space.

And how long they had before Millie really did end up the same way.

She had to talk to someone who could point her in the right direction. And just then, only one person came to mind.

10

Fat gray clouds pregnant with rain or snow or something in between loomed over Westville, and it was quieter than usual for a Saturday when Olivia got on her bike.

Between half the town out to the *Redhawks* state semifinals game two hours away and opening weekend for gun season, it was right back to football and assassinating Bambi after burying a murdered girl.

Back to reality.

But for Olivia, this was reality. Finding her friend. Or finding out what really happened to her. Whatever came first.

She parked her bike outside the *Family Affair* and headed for the photo center. Olivia needed the footage like yesterday, but according to the hook-nosed lady clerk chewing gum with wet rhythmic clicks, that wouldn't be happening.

"Not until tomorrow," she said. "On second thought, that's Sunday. So not until after the weekend."

"Seriously? Don't you just stick it in and let it play or something?"

She spat her gum in the trash and walked away dismissively.

Olivia stormed out, swearing and mumbling about how that lady should have just shoved her gum up one of her gaping nose holes, and rode her bike down the sidewalk then paced up to the dingy white Westville Motel on the corner of Nash and M-12. She heard Dr. Heiser was staying here, but didn't know what room. She approached the front desk and rang the bell.

A fat man who smelled of cabbage and old cheese came trundling out of the back room where a TV blared, looking at her like she'd just run over his pet squirrel on her bike. When she asked what room Heiser was in he droned that he couldn't give out that information, and Olivia pretended to leave, but glanced back at the wall to where the keys to each room hung against a cheap lined wooden wall on crooked hooks with white numbered key tags. Only two were missing. 3 and 7.

Olivia tried 3 and heard only faint stirring and a hacking cough after knocking. She moved on to 7. No answer.

"Miss Fischer," said a voice from behind her.

Dr. Heiser walked up the sidewalk and passed her bike, holding a donut from the bakery down the road and a copy of the Westville Ledger in the other. "If I'd have known to expect company I would have brought more."

"I'm not hungry," Olivia said quickly. "Listen, if Millie were lost in that other place . . ."

"The Seethe," Heiser offered, the word making her neck tingle. "Or the *in-between*, to use your term."

"Right. That," said Olivia. "How would—someone else get there?"

Heiser stopped chewing his bite of donut for a moment, swallowed it with a grimace and drew a breath.

"There is little we truly understand about these doorways, let alone how to enter them with any kind of safety. The Bureau exists solely to contain breaches. When I left we'd only just begun to explore—well, that's neither here nor there."

Olivia's chest tightened, whatever faint hope she had being squeezed through the pores of her skin.

"But," Heiser admitted, "the marked locations on the Sanborn maps would likely be thin spaces. I believe them to have been made by an early operative or predecessor to Janus, personally. These points wouldn't allow anyone through necessarily, but they at least would be a one-way door, from the other side. Though from the most recent readings I've seen, things have calmed down."

Olivia ran through the list of locations she could remember. Of course there was Devil's Peak. They'd been there and done that. She thought of the spot she'd seen Heiser make a note the night she had gone to Casey's.

"What about the river? By the dam?" she asked.

"I had my suspicions about that location, but readings have shown—"

"Thanks," Olivia said. It was good enough. It was something.

He called after, but her gut told her what she needed to know. There was something about that spot by the river. It was where Millie had been just before she had gone missing, and where the not-Millie's-corpse had washed up.

She stopped off at a payphone, called the boys, and headed for the river.

11

Half an hour later, Olivia paced around pooling water dripping from the drainage pipe at the edge of the woods.

"Liv, the police said it was her," Austin said.

"And those weren't just cops," Kyle said as he sent another rock skipping and clanging down the fathomless pipe. "Those were feds. My dad said so."

"I don't care who they were. Millie's alive."

Pushing down a grimace of doubt, Olivia told them about her theory involving the falsification of dental records. She told them about Dr. Heiser and the maps, and how he thought maybe there was something by the river.

"So what exactly are we looking for here?" Kyle asked.

"I don't know . . . some kind of door. To the in-between place."

Neither of her friends were very convinced, on any count.

It couldn't have been her.

Or was it that she didn't want to believe it? She regretted the one look she'd gotten at the corpse—bloated, mangled, and stripped of flesh in places that showed bone and tattered remains of gray skin.

She swallowed against the threat of nausea.

"It's all just so messed up." Despite her best efforts, when she drew in a shaky breath, she started crying—again. Man, she hated this.

She turned away from Kyle and Austin and walked to the river's edge, nostrils burning and eyes bleary. She wasn't sure how long she'd been standing there, the constant drone of the rushing water off the dam roiling beneath the train trestles, blissfully blocking out the rest of the world.

A hand tentatively landed on her shoulder. She turned sharply, and Austin pulled his hand away.

"Sorry," he said, turning, his black hair glinting in the gray light.

Before she was aware of what she was doing, she grabbed his wrist. "It's okay."

He stepped up alongside her, and for a moment, she wanted to lean right into him. She thought better of it—*not the time*—and sniffed, wiping her eyes instead.

They stood together for a moment before either of them said anything. A couple of sharp pings echoed as Kyle continued to pelt the corrugated metal of the drainage pipe with rocks.

"His way of dealing, I guess," Austin said. "Everyone's got one."

"Yeah," she said. "What's yours?"

"I remember when my dad died—choked on his own vomit. But they still held a traditional warrior's burial up at the reservation. I didn't want to go. I didn't want to watch him burn."

Olivia looked at him, his eyes on the river. "How old were you?"

"Six," he said, and Olivia tried to imagine being that young and watching her father cremated right before her eyes. Instead, she'd watched him get sicker and sicker day by day in the downstairs bedroom of their house. She didn't know which was worse.

"What'd you do?" she asked.

"I don't remember. I just know I didn't cry. That bundle of cloth didn't feel like Dad to me. But the other day—"

"That *wasn't* Millie," she said.

Austin swallowed. "Not anymore."

"But I'm saying that wasn't her. She's alive, and I know it."

"Liv, come on—"

"If you want to give up on her, fine—go home and just stop thinking about it." Olivia stalked up the rocky slope toward the parking lot. "I'm not giving up."

"What about Millie's parents? They don't want to believe it either. But they have to. Just like you do."

Olivia turned, feeling the rage, the hurt contort her face. "Screw you, Austin."

"Guys," Kyle said.

"Shut up, Kyle," Olivia snapped. "I don't want to hear it from you, too."

"You don't have to take it out on us," Austin said. "She was our friend too."

Heat boiled up in Olivia's chest. "Well, you're not acting that way."

"Guys!" Kyle yelled again. "We've got company."

The thump of a boombox blossomed and then grew closer, blasting out a song she recognized by *Sublime* as the high end came clear.

She glanced up to the parking lot and saw none other than Brett Huizinga along with Kevin and Matt in tow. Probably making their all too obvious way down to the riverbank to smoke and drink. Apparently too stupid to change things up, which didn't surprise her in the least.

They spotted them and made their way down to the riverbank.

"What's this? A second memorial?" Brett spat.

"You need to shut the hell up and leave," Olivia said, not wasting any time.

"Got some mouth on you, bitch," he snarled back.

Austin stepped forward. "Leave her alone."

"Or what? Gonna tomahawk me to death?"

A rock flew out of nowhere and hit Brett square on the forehead, another arcing stone smacking Kevin right on his fat neck. Kyle.

Olivia felt a rush of satisfaction and the urge to laugh followed by panic as the boys swore and ran forward. Austin scuffled with Matt and Kevin in turn, as Brett shoved Olivia to the ground. He stormed off toward Kyle, who stood on the drainage pipe making his stand with another rock in hand, which he threw and missed horribly in his panic.

Olivia scrambled to her feet and saw Brett wrench Kyle off the pipe and punch him in the mouth, busting her friend's lip in a spurt of bright red blood.

"Get off of him!" she yelled.

Kyle got up, Brett looming over him.

"Alright let's play, tough guy," Brett sneered.

He reared back for another blow, grabbing Kyle by his polo shirt collar, and froze. Olivia had just gotten up behind him. He stood motionless, started shaking and released Kyle, who fell ass first onto the wet lip of the pipe.

Brett ran off toward the others. "No—don't tell me that," he said, clasping his head like a bee had flown into his ear canal and was stinging repeatedly. "Stop it!"

He ran off, voice breaking and cracking. The others looked bewildered. "What the hell man?", Kevin called. They let Austin go and both ran after Brett.

"That's right," Kyle said proudly. "You better run!"

Austin wiped his long sleeve red and white striped shirt off and straightened his jacket. "What happened?"

Olivia stared after the stoners, wondering the same thing. She walked over and peered into the pipe. Nothing but a stream of dirty water and corrugated metal until all of that disappeared into the black.

Her stomach did a somersault as an eerie red glow lit up far down the pipe, pulsing brighter and dimmer several times in a row, fading over time until it was gone again. A stabbing hiss shot out of the pipe and into ear—or her mind. Garbled whispers, indiscernible until the last fading phrase:

. . . guilty ones . . .

"What is it?" Austin asked.

Olivia pointed. "Just wait." A moment passed, until there was another pulse of red. "There!"

Kyle and Austin were both standing behind her now, and reacted with a combination of loud swears. She knew it was the same thing from Devil's Peak. It had whispered to Brett—he'd heard it too. No time to think about what that meant. She only knew that somehow, that red orb and this red light and that dark presence, it was all connected to Millie.

She put one foot on the edge of the pipe and heaved herself up, just barely ducking to walk in.

"Whoa, what are you doing?" Kyle said.

"It's the red light from the woods. Ghost-witch, Skadegamutc, whatever. It could lead us to Millie."

Kyle shook his head wildly. "How?"

"Not sure. But I'm gonna find out."

"I'm coming with you," said Austin. He stepped up into the pipe and nodded at Olivia. The cold resolve she felt pooling in her unsettled gut warmed a bit as he offered a forced smile.

Kyle gulped audibly.

"First rule of any horror movie—never go into a creepy tunnel. Second rule, don't keep going down a creepy tunnel if you see some weird-ass lights glowing down it."

"How about don't split up?" Austin said.

Kyle stammered at that. "Tch. I'm staying out here. Where I can *see*."

"Suit yourself," said Olivia.

"You guys can't just—damn it. Damn it, damn it."

He climbed up into the pipe, his Boy Scout cursing echoing in the tunnel as they started forward.

"How long do you think it goes for?" asked Olivia.

"I think it spits out somewhere by PRINCE Milling, so it can't be too long," Austin said.

The moment they were deep enough for the muted overcast daylight from the entrance to disappear, the air thickened. A sour, electric stench coiled around them—ozone and decay, like something burnt and rotting at the same time.

Then came the sound.

A sizzling pulse.

Now that they were closer, a harsh sizzling joined it, and the back of her neck prickled with gooseflesh.

"Anyone else hear that?" Austin said.

"Yep," Olivia murmured.

"Og, God, this is dumb," stammered Kyle. "This is so gay, you guys. Why—"

Olivia stopped in her tracks once they got closer, and the pulse of red light faded. Darkness again. They were at a cross-section.

She really wished they had a flashlight.

A low basso rumble rattled Olivia's skull, vibrating through her teeth. The others felt it too—she could tell.

Ahead, the tunnel split. To the right, a thin, pulsing red glow bled through the darkness. If they kept going straight, they would probably get to the place Austin mentioned where it spit out at PRINCE Milling. And with it, heat. It wasn't natural warmth—it was fevered, oppressive, pressing against her skin as the pulse came closer.

Not a sound. Something beyond sound. A raw, piercing static that curled inside her skull like a hooked wire. Olivia stumbled back instinctively, her stomach twisting, her fingers clenching into fists.

It made her angry for some reason and terribly afraid. The way she'd felt all these last two weeks, only multiplied by ten. It whooshed by them, and that sinking dread came to a staggering low point and rose as the light faded down the left of the tunnel.

"Man, you guys. I think I'm gonna be sick."

Austin was clutching his forehead. "What *is* that?"

Olivia looked down to the right. "We have to go this way."

"We need to turn back," said Kyle.

"He might be right, Liv." Austin cleared his throat. "As much as I hate to say it."

Everything in her told her not to come that close to the red light again. She thought if she did, she might not be able to contain her rage—that she might never have a good feeling again.

Then she thought of Millie. She thought of the time she'd broken her arm on her bike, and Millie had run two miles as fast as she could for help and spent the next three nights with her, missing out on summer camp just to be with her while she recovered.

Another wave of the light came down the tunnel, and they all braced. Olivia covered her ears out of reflex, and the others did the same. It seemed to help, and as it got closer, she yelled, "Close your eyes!"

The fleshy blackness of the back of her eyelids flared only slightly brighter as it passed again, and the sick, sinking feeling wasn't nearly as bad as before.

"We just have to close our eyes as we go down. We can make it."

"All to take us who knows where," said Kyle.

Austin stood at the edge of the cross section of the pipes, bouncing on his toes and blowing out a breath. He took off running down the pipe.

Olivia jolted and followed.

"Dammit!" Kyle yelled, and she heard him running after as well.

Red light swelled ahead, and Olivia slowed and closed her eyes. Her head ached and legs quaked. But she kept moving. Suddenly, the ground wasn't clanking metal as they jogged down the pipe but dirt and rock. There was a steady hum and whine and a slight tinge of orange red light emanating from the walls of the tunnel itself.

"What is this?" Olivia said.

"My grandpa told me the Odawa had some underground burial sites but nothing like this."

"You guys do know we're underground, and no one knows where we are, right? If something collapses—"

"Then you'll use your Scout skills to get us out," Olivia offered.

"I missed the badge for subterranean survival, I guess."

Olivia looked ahead. It just kept going. She traced Austin's gaze somewhere behind her. His face grew pale in the crimson pulsing light.

Olivia turned, and, worse, those waves of red rolled through her, making her stomach drop like an elevator in freefall. A wall of dirt and stone blocked where the metal pipe should have been.

Kyle ran back and slammed his fists against it, kicking and swearing.

Olivia swallowed hard. "Can't go back. Just have to see where it leads."

Austin walked ahead, and Olivia reached back for Kyle's hand. "Come on."

He didn't take it, but gave her a faintly appreciative look as he walked around her. They pressed on amid the strange dull red glow the tunnel gave off, pulsing and undulating.

Then, there was a brighter light up ahead.

Olivia saw it and started moving faster, wanting more than anything to be out of here. Kyle and Austin fell into step with her, their eyes fixed on the end.

"Wherever this leads, just be ready," said Olivia.

"Ready for what?" Austin asked.

"To kick some ass," Kyle replied.

Olivia and Austin stopped and looked over at him.

"Sorry . . . sounded cooler in my head."

When they got closer to the opening, the blinding light ahead swallowed the tunnel, forcing Olivia to shield her eyes with her arm. The hum grew louder, evolving into an oppressive vibration that seemed to come from everywhere at once. As they stepped in, her gut lurched, a sudden migraine assailed her head.

She caught herself on something solid and metal next to her, regaining her bearings. She glanced over and saw the others doing the same, groaning and clutching their heads like they'd just gotten off of an out-of-control tilt-a-whirl 4-H fair ride.

"I don't feel so great," Austin breathed.

They had stepped into a new cavernous space beyond the tunnel. All three of them froze and quieted. The world had changed—again. A dark metallic hallway stretched endlessly in front of them.

Red shuttered doors lined the walls, their surfaces gleaming faintly in the dim light coming from indeterminate fixtures in the ceiling of the impossibly tall space. Strange symbols were etched onto the center of each door in black angular lines, some forming a near complete hexagon and others only one or two sides in varying lengths. Some with an outlying circle.

She thought of the maps at Casey's house. The logo on the back of that business card.

As she drew in a breath, her nostrils were assailed with harsh sterility and something acrid lingering just underneath it all.

"What the hell is this place?" Kyle asked, voice cracking.

Olivia's hands trembled as she stepped forward. "I don't know, but we're not leaving."

"Not leaving? Liv, we're underground in some kind of nightmare maze. What if—"

A vacuous whirring followed by a deep thud cut off his words. All three of them spun around. The tunnel they'd emerged from was gone, the air blurring and rippling like disturbed water until it settled, revealing another identical and endless hallway.

"No way," Kyle muttered, his face pale. "No freakin' way!"

A sudden, guttural thrum tore through the air. Olivia turned her head, catching movement at the edge of her vision. Two of the doors in front of them on either side had shuttered open, bright, white light emanating from within.

Three men stepped out, their faces hidden by smooth, black featureless masks, matching uniforms blending into the oppressive metallic walls, and gloved hands.

Like shadows.

Olivia's heart raced. Around their belts were strange looking dark batons that glowed on the ends with a blurry sort of crimson.

"We need to go!" Austin shouted.

The masked figures moved too fast. Gloved hands snatched Olivia from behind, yanking her off her feet. Her scream choked in her throat as she was dragged, boots scraping against the floor, toward the yawning red door.

"Let her go!" she heard Kyle yell and saw him launch at one of the figures. He managed to land a hit before another grabbed him, pinning him to the floor.

Austin swung his fists, connecting once, but the figures moved as though they really were shadows. They overwhelmed him in seconds, locking his arms behind his back. One jabbed him in the chest with his baton. A pulse of distorted air and a dull thrum. Austin went limp.

She thrashed and writhed against the grip of her captor, calling him every four, five and twelve letter word that flushed her mind. A flurry of rage and panic.

The red door across shunted open with a deafening screech. They dragged Austin in, his terrified face vanishing into a void of white, as Olivia was swallowed by the same.

THE PIPE

D.C.B. Interview Transcript

Incident Report

Interview Series 3: The Westville Incursion

Lochlear: Let's go back to Saturday November 16th.

Benson: You know, not all of us are walking calendars.

Lochlear: The Pipe incident.

Benson: What about it?

Lochlear: The more you fight it, the longer we're stuck here, Mr. Benson. You were placed on administrative leave that morning following the events of that day, correct?

Benson: That's right.

Lochlear: And yet, you didn't stay away.

Benson: Would you?

Lochlear: What exactly did you think you were going to accomplish?

Benson: I was trying to stop what was coming.

Lochlear: And what was that?

Benson: You already know. You knew before I did. Before any of us did.

Lochlear: Humor me.

Benson: No. You don't get to sit there and pretend you didn't see what I saw. That you don't already have it all typed up in one of your little classified reports.

Lochlear: Then help me clarify the record.

Benson: You want to know what happened?

Lochlear: Yes.

Benson: We lost control.

Lochlear: You lost control.

Benson: . . . Call it what you want.

Lochlear: So then, what did bring you back?

1

The freight elevator groaned as it descended into the depths beneath PRINCE Milling.

Ethan Crawley watched the two unconscious teenagers sprawled on the floor, their faces illuminated by the red emergency light that pulsed overhead. He thought he ought to dispose of the Fischer girl right now, given her interference these past weeks.

He could do so more humanely than he'd disposed of the children hiding unbeknownst to him in that thatched roof hovel in the jungle. It had gone up like a Christmas tree in March the first time he'd been permitted to use the flamethrower. He was given a playful commendation from his commanding officer, who was a sick bastard.

He pictured what remained of the curled up charred bodies, and the Red flared.

No . . . Not yet.

This wasn't how his employer did things.

The girl twitched in her chemical sleep. As if the presence of that ancient hunger stirring inside him had invaded her dreams. He smirked involuntarily at the thought, while his gut roiled in fear of himself. Such was his existence now.

A man or a thing. He could no longer tell. He only knew he had to *Seethe.*

Ethan rolled out a knot in his neck as the elevator shuddered to a stop, iron gates rattling as they opened onto a concrete corridor that stretched into darkness. The walls here were older than the mill above, marked with symbols that predated the town itself. Their edges seemed to writhe in the crimson light, hungry for something only they could see.

Two of the corporate officers in black tactical gear stepped forward to help move the kids. Crawley held up his hand, stopping them.

They looked at each other. One wore that stupid, thin, black mask over his face. The other had a squared off jaw and a hard look.

"Look man, I've told you before, protocol states—"

"Protocol?" Crawley smiled, though it didn't reach his eyes. A tear rolled down his cheek—they did that now, when the Red spoke through him. "We're well past that."

The men exchanged glances but stepped back. They'd learned not to question him, not after what happened to the last team that tried.

Crawley knelt beside Olivia, brushing a strand of red hair from her face. She flinched at his touch, even unconscious. Smart girl. But not smart enough to stay away.

"Some doors you shouldn't open," he whispered, then he reached into his pocket and withdrew the jagged bone knife, its surface stained with something dark and flaking. "And others must be."

She groaned, starting to stir. The chloroform was wearing off faster than expected. That wouldn't do.

Crawley stood, tucking the knife away.

"Take them to holding," he told the men, pointing to the Fischer girl and the smaller boy. "I'll track down the one that got away."

As they moved to comply, Crawley felt it again—that familiar pressure building behind his eyes, the whispers growing louder.

The Red was getting stronger. Soon it wouldn't need him anymore.

But for now, there was work to be done, and no one could interfere.

The door had to be opened.

2

Rain came down in sheets, drumming against the forest green awning of Fischer's Cafe as Casey stood under it, already soaked to the bone. And cold. More than just the damp biting chill—a numbness that sank down to the marrow.

He'd spent the evening before just driving. Past the orange-yellow sodium lights along the highway through Iron Falls, through the gloaming onto M-23, until he reached a small town on Lake Michigan. He hadn't been there since he was a kid. He grabbed a motel room. Thought about Millie. About Joe and Erin.

He regretted ever getting involved with Heiser's crazy conspiracy theories and getting his hands in things with the feds, where he didn't belong. And inevitably, tumbling into the repressed spiral of what happened to TJ Hopkins.

He thought about the wreck he'd become, because he didn't know how to deal.

Then he thought about Aly.

And here he was.

In the window, Christmas lights strung up cast kaleidoscope colors across the wet sidewalk—the mid-November weekend marking the kickoff of the holiday season in Westville.

The neon 'OPEN' sign flickered once and died.

Before he could knock, the door flung open.

"Casey," Aly said, surprise evident in her voice. "What are you doing here?"

He didn't say anything. She let him in, closing the door against the wind and rain. The café felt too quiet, too still—like a confessional after hours.

"I'm closing down."

"Anyone else here?" Casey asked, scanning the empty dining room, eyes moving to the kitchen through the order window.

"Reggie just left a few minutes ago. Why?"

Casey just shook his head, trying to gather his thoughts, trying to talk himself out of what he was about to say. Aly had the small stereo on in the kitchen, playing *'Strong Enough'* by Sheryl Crow. Everything felt wrong since Millie had gone missing—since they'd found her body in the river. But being here, with Aly, it was all he could think to do.

"Casey, what's wrong?" Aly asked, taking a cautious step toward him. In the dim light, her green eyes searched his face.

"Nothing. That's the thing." He exhaled slowly. "At least until all this."

Aly nodded, looking down as she wrung the cleaning rag in her hands. "Millie."

"But before, there wasn't anything wrong. There wasn't anything wrong with you, Aly. You know that, right?"

She looked up at him, that familiar quirk at the corner of her mouth—the one that led to a dimple when she smiled or grimaced. Just then, he couldn't tell which she was doing.

"How was I supposed to know that?"

"I'm not saying you were, I just—"

"I know how hard it was after the accident," she cut in. "You blame yourself for what happened, but it wasn't your fault."

"I made the call to let him go home."

"You didn't want to ruin his life."

"Sure. So, I ended it instead."

Her green eyes narrowed, pale pink lips parting. "You can't actually believe that."

"I knew when Millie went missing," Casey started, his voice thick. He cleared his throat. "I knew it would end this way."

"No one could have known, Casey. God knows everyone hoped it wouldn't."

Casey sighed, running a hand through his damp hair. "This isn't why I came here."

"So you came to tell me it wasn't my fault, the way we ended?"

Casey shook his head. "I—that's only part of it."

"Because it sounds to me like you can't stop blaming yourself for everything. But you're just pushing everyone away. Like you pushed me away."

"And I'm sorry, Aly. I didn't mean—"

"You didn't mean to what?" she demanded with that emerald fire in her eyes, a strand of blonde hair falling loose from her bun. "You didn't mean to shut me out? Because I told you—every damn day—I'd be there. You wanted space. Time. I gave it. But it was never enough. And it hurt, Casey. It really hurt."

Casey swallowed against the jagged rock in his throat. "You didn't deserve that. Any of it. What you got from me and sure as hell things with your dad, and the rest of it."

Her slender neck feathered, and she nodded fervently.

"I've forgiven you," Aly said quietly. "What you need to do is forgive yourself."

Casey looked away, out the window where rain continued to pelt the glass. Fat rivulets ran down the pane, catching the colored lights and transforming them into bleeding watercolors.

"But you won't hear it," Aly said, turning away toward the kitchen. The rag hit the counter with a wet slap.

Casey swallowed again, tasting the bitter pill of his own pride, his own stupidity and selfishness. Hell, maybe what he was about to do was just as selfish. He didn't know. He just knew he was done living this way.

Aly stacked dirty dishes, facing the stainless-steel pass-through window. Casey walked up beside her, and that quirk pulled at her lips again. He reached out, tucking the loose strand of blonde behind her ear. She stilled, glancing at him.

"What are you doing?"

"I don't know," Casey said, holding her gaze.

She turned toward him. Casey put a hand on her arm and drew her in, the familiar smell of her clementine perfume mingling with the permeance of kitchen grease, lips parting and meeting. Hands pressing and soft rhythmic breath through her nose, warm on his cheek, and the unmistakable heat and tightness of chest that came with it all.

Casey pulled away.

"I'm sorry."

"I'm not."

The urgent screech and wet hissing of tires on soaked pavement drew both of their attention toward the window. A black sedan pulled up.

Casey walked around the counter and toward the front door, the unwelcome tension of the past two weeks returning in force. A rapping on the door.

He opened it.

Standing there under an umbrella wearing her jacket declaring the faux 'FBI' moniker over a gray sweater was Agent Reeves.

"Benson," she said.

"What is it?" Aly asked, stepping behind him.

Reeves stepped forward, lowering the umbrella as she moved further under the awning.

Casey shifted. "Heard Lochlear left town. Figured that meant you'd be out of here too."

Reeves, smacked her lips. "Sorry to disappoint," she said over the rain. "He was called away on another assignment."

Casey thought about pressing more but knew he'd be met with 'need-to-know' or whatever hand-wavy classified term Reeves would choose to toss around.

"So what is this about?"

She shifted and glanced at Aly. "I have reason to believe your sister may be in danger."

The words hit like a fist to the ribs.

"What reasons?" Aly asked.

"Right now, what's important is finding her. When was the last time you saw your sister?"

Aly's face had gone pale beneath the multicolored light strands. "Last night, at home. After the funeral."

Reeves nodded quickly. "Anywhere you could think of she would be? Where she would go. Trying to rule things out. This investigation doesn't need another abducted girl."

Casey didn't give a damn about their investigation, how it looked for her. He did however feel the all too familiar surging tightness in his throat and had some ideas.

Devil's Peak. Looking for answers that weren't there.

"I'd advise calling around anywhere you think she'd be," said Reeves. She turned away and strode back toward her car. Casey realized Aly had already rushed back inside, and he heard the old rotary phone clicking off the stand.

Before the car sailed off into the rain, Casey noticed the faint silhouette of someone else in the back behind tinted windows.

He closed the door and walked up to Aly, who was hanging up the phone.

"Barb Rodgers says he hasn't been at the Lanes. God. I have to call mom," Aly said, dialing.

Casey put a hand to his brow where a pulsing ache spiked to a sharp migraine. His mind jutted to the marking Heiser had made on the map.

His theory about something called a CHASM. By the river.

"The dam," he blurted.

Aly had her ear to the phone and cocked an eyebrow.

"Maybe she'd go there. Where—the body was found."

Casey grabbed his wet coat and bolted for the door. "You stay and call who you need to. See what you can find out."

But when he turned Aly was already behind the counter grabbing her own coat off the rack.

"I'm coming. You going to stop me?"

Casey shook his head. "Nope."

Rain lashed against the pavement as they bolted for the car.

3

As they sped down Main Street, the wipers slashed back and forth in vain.

The glow of the black iron street lamps and Christmas lights attached to tinsel trees and Santa heads mounted on them reflected off the rain slick road, and the faint smell of Aly's clementine perfume lingered in the car.

The memorial parking lot by the dam came into view, and the headlights of the running black sedan.

What a coincidence.

Casey nosed the long front of the Monte in, parking near the edge where the woods crept close to the river. He killed the engine, and they sat in silence for a moment, the sound of rain hammering against the roof filling the space between them. Aly opened her door first, stepping out into the downpour and pulling her coat tight around her. Casey followed, his boots splashing in deepening puddles that had already formed.

Reeves handed her umbrella to someone in an oversized raincoat and hood as she pulled out a flashlight and shined it into the drainage pipe further down the bank at the edge of the woods. As they approached, Aly stayed close to Casey, her hand brushing against his arm.

"They think she went in there?" she asked, her voice barely audible over the sound of the rain and rushing water. "Why?"

"Because they know more than they've been letting on," Casey muttered.

He stepped down the wet jagged mud-caked stone to the bank by the dam and down toward the woods where the drainage pipe hung over the river's edge. The hooded figure turned.

Heiser.

"Got a lead already?" Casey yelled over toward Reeves, glancing at Heiser knowingly. The doctor averted his eyes.

"Miss Fischer came to me asking some questions," he said over the rain falling in wet, angry drops on the thin canopy of trees above them. "I'm afraid the answers I gave could have led her here. Or at least her conclusions."

Aly immediately reacted, stepping forward, and though she was even in height with the doctor the outrage in her voice and posture made it look like she loomed over him. "What did you tell her?"

Heiser cleared his throat and stammered. "Nothing specific, mostly what she already knew."

"But it was something crazy enough to get her to crawl into some drainage pipe looking for her dead best friend?"

Heiser looked to Casey, as if for some kind of help. He let him squirm.

"Possibly, yes."

Aly cupped her face with her hands.

"We need to go in after her," Casey said.

Reeves didn't say anything right away. Instead, she looked into the drainage pipe, and back to Casey. "This is out of your jurisdiction. You shouldn't be involved."

"I am now," Casey shot back.

Casey walked to the lip of the pipe, and he saw it. Faint but there. A flare of red light. He looked at Reeves, a tacit understanding between them. They both saw it.

Casey shook his head. "I'm going in."

Reeves stepped forward, blocking his path. "No, you're not."

"If Olivia's in there I'm not standing around waiting."

"As acting senior agent it's well within my scope to arrest you," said Reeves.

Casey stepped up into the pipe. "Then do it."

Reeves stared at him with diamond edged eyes for a long moment, hand on her holster, then shook her head. "Just follow my lead."

Aly stepped closer to the pipe. "I'm going to look anywhere else she could have gone."

"I'll go with you," Heiser said. "I can't help feeling somewhat responsible."

"You had better."

Casey threw her the keys. "Be careful," he said.

Aly nodded. "You too."

They walked up to the parking lot and got into the Monte.

Casey turned and started walking into the drainage pipe.

"I get bucking authority once in a while, believe me. Even applaud it," Reeves said. "But how you haven't been booted off the force by now is beyond me."

"I'm a man of mystery."

Reeves shoved past him. "Just so you know: You have no idea what we're dealing with."

With every step the pulsing red light grew stronger, and to the right a path opened up, the jagged walls of stone and dirt seething beneath the surface. The sibilant hiss was all-encompassing and so strong Casey had to stop and cradle his head.

Reeves adjusted something on her earpiece and glanced back at him, and reached into her jacket pocket. From it, she produced an identical black earpiece to her own, triangular with the same rounded clip over her ear. She clicked a tiny switch on it.

"Here," she said, throwing it to him.

Casey caught it and heard a slight whirring. "What's this?"

"Put it on your ear. It helps mitigate the bio-dissonance."

Casey hesitated only for the slightest moment, not knowing what bio-dissonance was but at the same time knowing it probably had a lot to do with the strange hissing static he'd first heard the morning Millie went missing by the Scout cabin. And the whispers. But that felt from a darker, deeper place. More personal.

Casey put it over his ear, and Reeves walked up to him and flipped a switch. There was a sudden dullness to his hearing, then it faded back to normal.

That growing, piercing, dread-inducing hiss was gone.

"Thanks," he said.

"Let's keep moving."

Reeves led the way with her flashlight and her Smith and Wesson .357 drawn. Casey felt a flare of envy. He shot better with a revolver, his Grandpa Judd having taught him on his .38 special.

"Nice piece."

She stopped and glanced over her shoulder with an appraising look, sharp hazel eyes narrowing. "Thanks, but not interested."

Casey flushed. "I meant the magnum." He gripped his Glock with both hands, palms sweaty.

"I've got a hang up about walking with guys through dark tunnels. Long story." She started moving again. "Anyway, seems like you've got a good thing going with Fischer."

"Don't really know what that thing is, but yeah, it's something." He wanted a change of subject badly.

"So what *should* I expect, here?"

"Some bad actors and some potential heavy hostility."

"Great."

What he did know was that all of this was very *wrong*. Where the hell were they? Judging from the direction they'd turned, they should have been beneath the Slate. But that would be impossible. A tunnel under the river?

"Up ahead," said Reeves. Casey looked and saw a white light as the pulsing crimson walls narrowed.

"Is this all just normal to you?"

Reeves hissed at him and put her index finger to her mouth.

Casey looked ahead, where a figure clad in a black uniform emerged from the opening. Reeves threw herself flat against the wall of the tunnel and pulled Casey's shirt, urging him to do the same. The sudden motion sent a flare of pain from his bruised ribs, and he suppressed his reaction.

A beam from a powerful flashlight shone down, scraping the edges of Casey's boots. He clasped his pistol and thumbed the safety. Reeves shook her head.

There was a crack of static down the tunnel.

"Janus Unit Alpha reporting," the voice reverberated. "Passage B3 is clean, over."

Reeves peeled herself from against the wall and gave Casey the all-clear.

"Come on, let's move," she whispered.

"Who are these guys, really?" Casey hissed, louder than he or Reeves would have liked. He lowered his voice and added, "First your Dimensional Bureau comes in masquerading as feds, and now there's some kind of deep-ground special ops military unit disguised as a logistics company in my hometown."

"It's a lot to take in," said Reeves, her voice steady. "But if your small-town mind can just calm itself, let's find those kids and save the disclosures for later, yeah?"

Casey knew Reeves was right. Still, his head swam with the seeming reality of the situation.

He nodded silently. "After this is over, you owe me answers."

Reeves gave him a grave look. "I might work for the Bureau, Benson, but believe me, there's plenty I'm in the dark on."

She led the way to the opening ahead, seemingly unguarded. The sentry in black had moved on.

Casey followed Reeves into harsh white light.

4

Travis Johnson sat in his cruiser, fingers flexing against the wheel. The engine hummed beneath him, steady and low, but inside, he was anything but.

Through the windshield, he watched them.

Aly and that doctor—Heiser—climbing into Benson's car. Their faces were drawn, their words clipped as they spoke, neither of them noticing the Crown Vic idling in the lot across from them.

They wouldn't notice.

Not until it was too late.

The Red burned, seeping into the cracks of his mind, filling every hollow place inside him with something hot and bright and unbearable. Travis swallowed hard. His grip on the steering wheel tightened until the leather creaked beneath his hands and his skin pulled taut.

Travis exhaled through his teeth, his jaw aching.

He wanted to *Seethe*.

He let the thought roll through him, a muddy syrup over raw nerve endings. He wanted to feel it crackle beneath his skin. Wanted to feel the world peel away, piece by piece, until only the truth remained. He didn't want to hurt Aly, just like he hadn't wanted to hurt Jane. But what choice had either of them left him with?

It was that truth the Red had shown him. They were the guilty ones. They had to be punished.

He watched Aly shift the car into reverse, headlights slicing through the cold November dark.

Travis flexed his fingers one last time, slipped his cruiser into gear, and followed.

5

Olivia's consciousness dripped back in slow streams.

Acrid chemicals. They coated her tongue, searing the back of her throat. Her fingers pressed against cool, packed dirt. The air held a dampness, but not like fresh earth—something stale, artificial. A constant, low drone. Machinery, humming through the walls, punctuated by a steady hiss of vented air.

It hit her in a wave, thick and cloying—a musty, organic rot. Not just dust, not just mold. Something sharper, heavier.

Food left to sour. Her stomach lurched.

She jerked upright, coughing. Her breath came shallow, her lungs filling with the same thick scent that clung to the walls.

Where am I?

The drainage pipe. The Red. Hands grabbing them. Something pressed over her face. Then—nothing. A rustling nearby.

"Hey," she rasped. Her throat burned. "You okay?"

Kyle's voice, rough in the dark. "Define okay."

She heard him shift, probably trying to get his bearings too. Then—realization slammed into her.

Austin wasn't there.

She twisted, scanning the dim space. The room—if it could be called that— was narrow, walls made of something between stone and metal, slick with condensation. A single vent near the ceiling pumped stale air into the space.

Her stomach clenched. A sound outside—voices.

Olivia froze, inching toward a small slit opening in the heavy door.

Through it, she saw them.

Two men in black uniforms and some kind of black masks. Mean looking military rifles strapped to their shoulders.

They carried something else—batons, but wrong. The ends pulsing with dim, curling red light.

The same Red they'd seen in the woods. Her heartbeat thundered in her ears.

Kyle edged closer, his breath quickening. "What do we do?"

Olivia didn't hesitate.

"When I say go," she whispered, "we run."

6

They emerged into what could only be described as impossible space.

Casey stared up at black concrete pillars stretching up into darkness, where catwalks and platforms seemed to defy gravity. The metallic floor extended in all directions, yet somehow felt contained, a cube folded through extra dimensions.

He took in row after row of red metal doors lining the walls, each marked with variations of the broken hexagon. Some doors seemed to vibrate in place. Others rippled like oil in a dirty pothole.

"The Company has been busy," Reeves said, checking readings on a device that resembled a modified Geiger counter.

"They built this?" Casey asked, his voice low.

"Not exactly."

Casey glanced sidelong at Reeves, giving her a flat stare. "Don't make me ask."

"They're using leyline resonance to bend space. Basically creating shortcuts between places that should never connect."

Casey glanced around, his boots echoing faintly on the cement floor. The air carried a metallic tang, undercut by the acrid scent of burning fuel and sulfur. The red shutters seemed to stretch on forever. Some kind of twisted funhouse storage facility.

He noted the symbols painted in silver on the bright red doors. Each was a partial version of the Janus Global hexagon logo, some with single lines and others nearly complete but marred by gaps. He traced the line of doors with his flashlight.

"Alright," Casey breathed. "I know we agreed to save the disclosures for later, but where the hell are we right now?"

Reeves turned back toward him. "You wouldn't believe me if I told you."

"Try me."

"This is a trans-dimensional intersection," she said evenly. "They've been honing this facility for a long time, using ley line convergence points."

"One of which happens to be Westville," Casey said, his disbelief thick in his tone.

Reeves nodded. "Yes. But right now, we're not anywhere near Westville."

"Where the hell are we then?"

"Not sure. Somewhere remote, likely northern Canada where we've seen spikes in activity. Ultimately, this is a liminal space. Somewhere between dimensions."

"And above my paygrade, apparently," Casey muttered, mind reeling. "How do I know you're not just screwing with me and we're under the Slate right now somewhere?"

"One: I don't have the time or energy to screw with you," Reeves snapped. "Two: a portal or an underground tunnel beneath a river in a small town having been constructed without anyone noticing. You tell me which is more plausible."

"Fair point," Casey breathed.

He turned toward one of the doors. Its hexagon was fractured with a large, jagged gap in the bottom left corner. Something about it felt . . . wrong. And familiar in a way he couldn't shake.

"These doors," Casey said, holding up the bracelet he'd found earlier. "Where do they lead?"

Reeves stepped closer, studying the door and the symbol etched into its surface. "I doubt Janus knows where most of them lead—yet. The marked doors are the ones they've mapped out so far."

His mind flashed to the maps he and Heiser had pored over.

That bottom-left corner—the missing piece. It was PRINCE Milling.

1

Olivia waited hand in hand with Kyle, ears tuned to the approaching footsteps. They had to stay together. If one fell behind, the other wouldn't stand a chance.

Warm air blew in from above, carrying the faint scent of chemicals. The lock clicked.

"Go!" Olivia hissed.

They barreled through the gap, shoving past the startled men in dark uniforms.

One gave a strangled yell as they sprinted away, the corridor's dim circular lights blurring as they ran. The walls were the same corrugated metal, curving endlessly.

"We have to find Austin," Olivia panted.

They turned a corner, coming face-to-face with one of the red metal doors. The symbol etched onto it was a broken hexagon, segmented in three places. Olivia glanced behind them, the shouts of pursuit growing louder.

"Screw it," Kyle growled, grabbing the shutter-style door and yanking it up.

A blinding white light poured through the opening, forcing them to squint. Without hesitation, Olivia stepped through with Kyle.

They were back in that strange and unreal warehouse, the oppressive white, fluorescent lights above making them blink and stumble. Endless red doors stretched in every direction, the faint hum of machinery filling the air.

"They'll be on us any second," Kyle gasped.

They turned right and ran, their footsteps echoing in the cavernous space. The corridors twisted into a maze, each intersection splitting left and right, lined with more doors. At the next fork, they slammed straight into two figures, sending Olivia sprawling to the ground.

Kyle swung wildly, yelling incoherently, but a woman in a suit wrestled his arms down, her sharp voice commanding him to calm. A hand reached out toward Olivia. She recoiled, pulse pounding.

"Olivia," a familiar voice said softly.

She froze. Her head tilted up, her eyes locking onto the face of the man crouching in front of her.

8

Casey helped her to her feet. "You okay?"

She shook her head, her voice trembling. "Yeah. But Austin—they took him somewhere else."

"Get off me, lady!" Kyle snapped, jerking his arm away.

"You need to calm down," Reeves said firmly. "We're here to help. Were you being followed?"

Olivia nodded.

"Officer!"

The voice, haggard and dripping with venom, echoed down the hallway, reverberating through the cold, dark metal corridors and the endless stream of red doors.

Casey turned slowly, stomach tightening as he recognized the smarmy vitriol in the voice.

Crawley.

He stood about forty yards down the hall, gripping Austin with an arm around his neck, his lanky frame struggling, sweat matted black hair against his face. In Crawley's free hand, an ivory knife gleamed under a faint red glow coming—his eyes. Casey's throat went dry.

A blur of iridescence and pale light spilled from a door beside him—the one he'd presumably just stepped through.

Casey stepped forward, Glock raised. Reeves moved into a ready stance beside him.

"Let the boy go," Casey said, his voice steady. "He's not involved in this."

Crawley sneered, tightening his grip on the boy. "He is now."

"Just stop this, Crawley! I don't know what they've got on you, but we can end it now. Together."

"There's no stopping anything, Benson. I want to *Seethe*. *We* need to *Seethe*."

The words sent a shiver down Casey's spine. Deep down, he understood. The hissing, the red lights, "*the guilty ones*"—it was all connected.

"Stand down!" Reeves barked. "Federal agent!"

But Crawley just smirked. "Come and find me. Where it started."

In a flash, he yanked Austin through the glowing doorway, vanishing into the light.

"Shit," Casey hissed, his pulse pounding. "I'm going after him. You take them."

"Benson, stop!" Reeves shouted, but Casey was already sprinting down the hall.

Ahead, a door to his right slid open in a blur. Two men in black uniforms stepped out, assault rifles raised. Casey spun back, seeing Reeves usher Olivia and Kyle through another door.

The crackle of gunfire erupted, sharp and relentless. Something caught on his arm almost like he'd been grabbed and pulled, and he panicked as he was flung by the unseen force to the side of the hall—just out of the way of three sharp bursts from the rifles.

He glanced around, frantically regaining his equilibrium from whatever that was, and fired four quick shots in a shaky two point stance, forcing the men back.

He looked back at Reeves, who frowned but gave him a reluctant nod.

Casey dove through the door Crawley had entered into white light, feeling the space thin and contract around him, until it widened again, and he was tumbling down a muddy slope, rolling through wet leaves and thick underbrush.

The sharp scent of damp earth and decay filled his nose. The forest was alive with the sound of rain hammering against the canopy above. Casey pushed himself upright, recognizing the slope of the hill, the winding trail toward the river.

Devil's Peak.

Through the trees, he spotted the Boy Scout cabin. Its windows pulsed with a sickly red glow, stark against the rain-soaked darkness.

He sprinted toward it, heart racing. The back door creaked open under his hand, the sound swallowed by the rain. Inside, the red glow poured from a room down the hall. The oppressive hissing sound grew louder, pressing against his skull like a living thing.

Casey moved in cautiously, pistol raised, his breath shallow. His mind raced with fears of what he might find—the boy dead at Crawley's hands, or evidence of whatever had been done to Millie before she was dumped in the river. He reached the door at the end of the hall. The red light pooled beneath it, casting jagged shadows. Casey clasped the doorknob, bracing himself, and shoved it open.

Austin stood in the main room of the cabin, looking terrified. Casey looked left and right stepping into the room, looking for any sign of Crawley.

He moved toward the boy.

That was his mistake.

A body careened into him. He was pinned down. A hot stabbing pressure seared and Casey glanced down to see the knife sinking into his shoulder. He screamed and swung the pistol, hitting Crawley on the side of his head.

Crawley toppled off and stumbled backward up against the wall.

"Drop the knife!" Casey yelled, restraining himself from firing, stumbling to his feet and holding the gun on him. "You're done."

But Crawley only smiled—a twisted, unnatural expression that made Casey's skin crawl. A single tear rolled down Crawley's cheek as his eyes flickered, unsteady and strange. Austin stood against the back wall, shaking.

"Just stay back," Casey told him, as warm blood pooled and trickled down his left sleeve which he tried to ignore.

Crawley growled as he pulled himself to his feet, his forehead bleeding. Something strange in his eyes. Deranged.

"You need to *seethe*, officer."

"You're insane."

His eyes were glowing, Casey realized, burning crimson.

"You see Red . . . Red sees you."

"Shut up!"

"You see Red . . . Red sees you."

"I said shut the hell up, Crawley!" His heart pounded in his chest. Voices whispered and hissed; his head seared. He winced against it all. "Drop the knife!"

"You see Red . . . RED. SEES. YOU!!!"

Casey clutched at his ear, realizing the earpiece Reeves had given him was gone—lost in his tumble down the hill. The noise grew unbearable, splitting his skull, blurring his vision.

You're the guilty ones . . . You're the guilty ones . . . You're the guilty ones . . .

"Get out of my head!" Casey roared, shaking it off.

When he looked up, Crawley was gone—along with the knife.

Casey's breath came in shallow gasps. He turned to Austin, whose wide eyes were filled with fear.

"Get to the road. Head back toward town. Don't stop."

Austin nodded and ran.

Casey jumped through the cabin window, his boots hitting the muddy ground. A tearing pain in his shoulder and his sleeve sticky wet from the bleeding. Rain lashed against him as he ran through the woods, the pounding in his head relentless.

Then he saw it.

By the river, a figure stood, pulsing with red light.

And in front him, facing the river—it was Aly.

9

The woods swallowed them.

Travis Johnson followed.

The rain had started slow—a whisper against the fallen leaves, a damp chill curling around his collar. Now, it was heavier, soaking into his uniform, beading along the brim of his hat, running in thin rivulets down the side of his face. He didn't care.

He kept to the trees, moving where the light didn't touch.

Aly and the doctor were up ahead, flashlights cutting narrow tunnels through the dark, sweeping over trunks and underbrush. They spoke in hushed tones, their words drowned beneath the steady hiss of rain.

They thought they were alone.

They weren't.

Travis clenched his jaw, feeling the heat crawl up his spine. The Red was here, humming beneath his skin, pulsing behind his ribs like a second heart.

Aly was just Jane all over again. She'd chosen this, and there was nothing anyone could do about the way things would end now.

It sees you. It wants you.

He let her slip ahead, let Heiser take the lead, the doctor muttering something about about residual signatures.

His throat felt tight, raw, like something inside him had been rubbed down to exposed nerve endings. Travis's hand flexed at his side, twitching toward the holster.

He let it drift instead to the baton.

Slow. Controlled. Measured.

Up ahead, Aly stopped. Close now. So close.

He stepped forward, silent as the dead, the rain masking his approach.

And then—she stilled.

Somewhere inside her, she must have felt it. The weight of him in the dark.

Her breath hitched. Travis smiled. She knew. And this time—

She wouldn't walk away.

10

The figure raised a hand behind her.

Casey didn't think. Didn't hesitate. He aimed and fired his last two rounds.

The figure crumpled.

"Aly!" Casey shouted, running to her. She was screaming, her hands trembling as she pointed at the ground.

Casey's breath caught. Rain pooled around the crumpled body, dark red spreading from its chest, spurt of struggling breath and the confusion rendered by a gunshot.

Travis Johnson.

The Glock slipped from Casey's hand, his knees buckling. There was no knife. No weapon drawn.

Aly's voice was a distant echo, screaming his name, but he couldn't move. He'd acted without thinking, and now—

"No, no . . ." Casey whispered, his voice breaking. Out of reflex he knelt and put a hand on the wound. "Go for help," he heard himself say to Aly.

She did, and he was alone, keeping Travis's head elevated.

What had he done?

11

The hum of the place felt alive somehow, pulsing through the soles of Olivia's shoes as they moved cautiously through the endless corridor of red doors. Each one urging something she couldn't hear, their silver-marked symbols catching the pale overhead lights like jagged scars.

"You two keep moving," Agent Reeves said.

Those men in black uniforms were coming for them. They raised their rifles.

"I said go!"

Olivia grabbed Kyle's hand and they ran on. She heard the loud pops and cracks of automatic fire behind them as they continued down the dark corridor and followed the curve of it. There was a strange building whooshing sound, and the gunfire behind them stopped.

So did they.

"Do you think she's—" Kyle started.

"Dead?" Reeves said, coming around the corner at a jog; hair mussed and hands shaking, Olivia noticed. "Not yet."

Reeves pressed forward, her flashlight scanning the strange symbols etched into the nearest door. "Stay close," she ordered, her tone clipped. Her hand hovered near the handgun on her hip, as if she expected one of the doors to swing open and unleash something terrible.

Kyle trailed behind, muttering under his breath. "This is a movie. We're in a freaking movie. This can't be real . . ."

"Calm down," Olivia breathed, though she moved faster now, her breath quickening, wondering if and how Reeves had killed those men.

The idea of getting out of this claustrophobic maze pushed her forward, though her legs ached from running. Kyle grumbled but kept up, and Reeves stayed close, her movements deliberate and precise.

The door ahead of them flickered—not opened, just . . . shifted. The symbol on it glowed faintly, an incomplete hexagon with jagged edges that seemed to burn into her memory. Before anyone could say anything, it swung inward with a low groan, revealing a hollow blackness that surged with crimson light.

"We don't have much of a choice," Reeves said, stepping forward.

Kyle shook his head. "We definitely have a choice."

Olivia didn't wait. She lunged forward, stepping through, feeling a sharp jolt in her chest as the world shifted and twisted around her. For a moment, she wasn't anywhere—just a formless space filled with that same red glow. Her feet hit metal, the hard clang echoing around her, and she slipped and fell onto muddy ground.

Rain lashed her face, sharp and cold, the sound of it thundering all around. Her heart raced as she realized where they were—back at the drainage pipe near the dam. She could hear the river roaring behind her, the heavy churn of water spilling from the dam.

Kyle appeared next, swearing as he slipped on the wet metal, and Reeves emerged, pistol drawn.

The neon PRINCE Milling sign loomed above them in the downpour, its red light smeared through the rain. The glow felt wrong now, too close to the color of the doors they'd just left behind.

Then Olivia saw it.

A figure on the train tracks just past the dam, silhouetted by the glow of the PRINCE sign and by the headlights of police vehicles screeching into the memorial lot above.

Slender, small, and familiar.

She froze, her breath catching in her throat.

"Millie!" she screamed, already running.

"Liv, wait!" Kyle shouted behind her, but she didn't stop. She tore across the slick ground, her feet slipping on the wet rails as she climbed onto the tracks. The rain blurred everything, but she didn't care.

Millie Thompson, wearing nothing but a dark, stained, whisper-thin medical gown in the cold autumn rain, turned toward Olivia.

It was her.

Olivia's chest tightened. Her legs shook beneath her, and her throat burned as tears mingled with the rain on her cheeks. She stopped just a few feet away, staring at her best friend's pale face, her wide, unblinking eyes.

"Millie," Olivia whispered, her voice breaking.

Millie's lips moved, but no sound came out. She swayed slightly, her frame unnaturally thin, her skin ashen under the red light. Blonde hair matted down thick and her normally brilliant blue eyes duller somehow.

Olivia reached out a trembling hand. "It's me. I'm here."

For a moment, Millie just stared, her expression blank. Then, as if something inside her broke free, she collapsed forward into Olivia's arms.

"I've got you," Olivia whispered fiercely, holding her tightly despite the rain soaking them both. "I've got you, Mil. You're safe now."

Behind her, Kyle and Reeves caught up, their flashlights cutting through the gloom. Reeves stepped forward, her eyes scanning the tracks for any sign of danger, while Kyle stood frozen, his mouth slightly open.

But Olivia didn't notice. All she could feel was Millie's frail body trembling in her arms, and the overwhelming relief that, for the first time in weeks, she wasn't looking at a memory or a dream.

Millie was here.

She was *alive*.

12

"You shot an officer, Casey. One of our own."

Chief Hart's voice was heavy, his usual gruffness tempered by something closer to grief. "There's nothing I can do, son."

Casey stood in the doorway of Hart's office. "I know, Frank."

Hart's eyes flicked up from the stack of paperwork littering his desk. The incident had spawned reports, statements, and inquiries, each one heavier than the last. Casey was being put on mandatory leave, effective immediately, his eventual return pending an initial investigation and psychological screening. Nothing about it looked good.

Millie Thompson found alive, Travis Johnson shot, that tunnel or whatever it was beneath PRINCE Milling seemingly erased as if it had never existed—as though it were some shared fever dream.

Both were in the same hospital—Mary's Heart in Iron Falls. Millie had been close to dehydration, starvation, and low on blood. Syringe marks on her arms and jagged cuts. She hadn't said much yet.

"Good news is," Hart started, "Johnson looks like he'll pull through. Lost a lot of blood, and he's not awake yet. But he'll live."

"I thought it was Crawley. Thought that he—"

"That he had a knife. One you described as carved from 'some kind of stone'. That he was going after Allison Fischer. I've read the reports, Benson."

"Then you know that Crawley was there. He had the Williams boy. He can confirm that too. I'm not making this up. What reason would I have to—"

"The kid was knocked out, Casey. His memory is blurry at best, same as the rest."

"They found Crawley's blood at the scene."

"He's in the wind. And he's a suspect in all of this now. That doesn't change the fact that you shot Travis."

Casey scoffed. "So we're just going to let Reeves and the feds cover up everything?"

"Wherever you claim you were, Casey, we didn't find anything in that pipe and neither did the feds."

"Of course not."

"It's crazy talk, son. Some kind of underground operation, a mammoth storage facility guarded by black ops? Have you been hearing yourself?"

"Look, I don't know how it's possible, but it's what happened. Somewhere beneath the mill, maybe."

"Casey—"

"She said she had called in backup, and did any of them ever show? Don't you think it's strange that just like that Reeves is gone, nowhere to be found? And Lochlear was out of here before Millie's funeral."

Frank slammed his hand down on the table. "Dammit, son! All I care about is keeping this town and the people in it safe. All you care about is proving these crazy theories and suspicions of yours because you can't deal with that weight. I don't know what you need, Casey, but it isn't to be found here right now. And, no, I have no idea what federal agents far beyond my jurisdiction and line of questioning are up to. Because it's not my place. My place is here."

Casey felt hollowed out, more than he already was and more than he thought possible. He swallowed that truth. Hart was right. His place wasn't here. Not anymore. He had to get out of here.

Hart's pale eyes, lined with age and wear, softened briefly. "You had a future here, Benson. Hell, I wanted better for you than this."

The words cut deeper than Casey expected, but he didn't flinch. He stood there, numb, as though the weight of the last two days had dulled his ability to feel anything except shame.

His gaze drifted to the desk where his badge and sidearm sat.

"Take care of yourself, Frank," Casey said, his voice quieter than he intended.

Hart looked up at him, his jaw working like he wanted to say something—anger, forgiveness, maybe both—but in the end, he just nodded.

As Casey turned to leave, he felt the weight of Hart's silence pressing against his back. It wasn't forgiveness, not really. But it wasn't condemnation either.

It was just another ending that felt like the wrong one.

13

Casey pulled up outside Fischer's Café. The neon sign buzzed faintly, casting a warm glow against the wet pavement.

Aly opened the door before he could knock. "You're leaving," she said. Her eyes searched him.

Casey nodded. "I need . . . I don't know what I need."

She crossed her arms, leaning against the doorframe. "So, that's it? You're running again?"

"I'm not running," he said, though as the words left his mouth, they tasted like a lie.

Aly shook her head.

He stepped closer, rain dripping from his jacket. "I just keep screwing everything up. I shot Travis. I almost . . . I can't keep making things worse."

"Then stop," she said, her voice breaking. "Stop running and face it. Face us. Face yourself."

For a moment, he thought about staying. About trying. But the weight of everything—Millie, Travis, The Red—pressed down on him.

"If you leave now . . ." She stopped herself, swallowing whatever she was about to say.

Silence hung. He turned, and got back in his car.

14

The sun was setting by the time Casey finished packing.

He'd thrown what he could into boxes, leaving behind his sparse furniture. Maybe he'd be back. Maybe he wouldn't.

The image of Travis's body haunted him—crumpled in the mud by the river, blood pooling around him.

You're the guilty ones . . .

Casey rubbed his temples, trying to ward off the memories of that hissing voice. He'd heard it first by the Scout cabin the morning Millie disappeared.

He grabbed the last box and headed for the door when someone knocked. Through the window, he saw Dr. Heiser standing on his porch, hands clasped behind his back.

Casey pushed past him.

"I know what you saw, Mr. Benson," he said quietly. "In their eyes. It takes hold slowly at first. Makes them paranoid. Angry."

Casey's jaw tightened. "I don't want to hear this."

"But you need to. Because it's not over. Janus Global didn't just choose Westville by accident. The ley lines here, the convergence points—they're trying to open something. And they're using people to do it. People like Travis. Like Crawley."

"And Millie? What was she to them?"

Heiser's expression darkened. "A key. They tried with others but it had to be her. This was only the first step."

Casey dropped the box in the maroon carpeted trunk of the Monte.

"I don't know when," Heiser blurted, "but I believe something is coming. Janus isn't finished yet."

"I can't help you anymore. I can't help anyone," Casey said, slamming the trunk. "I'm done."

Heiser nodded slowly. "You can leave Westville, Mr. Benson. But it won't leave you. Not after what you've seen."

Casey got in the Monte and closed the heavy driver's side door. He watched Heiser go in the rear view, his sedan coasting away. He just sat there for a moment, grabbed his keys, started the engine.

"Something is coming."

As he pulled away from the house and out of town, he couldn't shake the feeling that Heiser was right. Whispers that would not be put to bed so easily.

And those whispers only got louder the further away he drove.

15

Olivia sat beside Millie's hospital bed, watching her friend's chest rise and fall in shallow, uneven breaths.

The rhythmic beeping of monitors provided a sterile counterpoint to the silence. Millie hadn't spoken since they found her. The doctors called it trauma-induced catatonia. Olivia called it bullshit.

They didn't know what she'd seen down there. What they'd all seen—even if for each of them the memories had already begun to fade in a strange way. Like it all had been a dream. Almost as if wherever they had been—the 'in-between' place—wouldn't let them remember, or didn't want them to.

"You should eat something," Mrs. Thompson said, touching Olivia's shoulder gently. She held out a paper bag from Fischer's Café. The scent of grilled cheese—Millie's favorite—wafted from it, but it only made Olivia's stomach turn.

"I'm okay," Olivia said softly. "Thanks, Mrs. Thompson."

Millie's dad paced by the window, his reflection ghosting across the glass like a restless spirit. He hadn't sat down once in the three hours Olivia had been there. His hands kept clenching and unclenching, but every so often he'd flash a smile at Olivia, so forced that it felt . . . wrong.

"They want to talk to her again," Mrs. Thompson said, voice tight.

"She's not ready," Mr. Thompson snapped, tone sharp. The dark circles under his eyes seemed to hollow his face. "Those agents can wait."

Olivia reached for Millie's hand, gently cradling it on her own. It felt cold, lifeless. Something left too long in the dark. She swallowed hard.

The girl lying in that bed looked like Millie, breathed like Millie—but something was missing. Something vital had been stripped away in that place. Wherever it had been.

The door opened softly, and Aly stepped in, her presence a quiet disruption. "Hey," she said gently. "Time to go, Liv."

"Five more minutes?" Olivia asked, glancing back at Millie.

Aly shook her head, her expression kind but firm. "Mom's waiting. You need rest too."

Reluctantly, Olivia stood, her legs stiff from sitting so long.

She squeezed Millie's hand one last time, willing her friend to squeeze back. But there was nothing. Only stillness.

"I'll be back tomorrow," she promised, her voice catching in her throat.

Out in the hallway, she paused outside Travis Johnson's room. The door was closed, but through the small window, she could see him lying there, tubes running everywhere, machines breathing for him. Casey had shot him. But why?

Aly glanced uncomfortably toward the room. She'd told Olivia that Travis had been dispatched to go help with the search.

But Olivia knew her sister, and the look in her eyes said something else entirely.

16

The night nurse made her rounds at 2 a.m. checking vitals and adjusting IVs with mechanical efficiency. She noted nothing unusual in Millie Thompson's room—just another sleeping patient in the quiet dark, the girl's mother curled up on the couch on the other side of the room.

The nurse didn't see the figure standing in the corner.

It emerged from the shadows once she left, moving to Millie's bedside with unnatural grace. Moonlight caught the golden surface of an old pocket watch in its hand, the soft ticking echoing in the air.

Red light began to pulse around the figure, casting strange shadows on the walls. They twisted and writhed, taking on shapes that shouldn't exist—antlers and claws and hungry, reaching things.

The figure held the watch over Millie's chest. The ticking grew louder, more insistent, falling into rhythm with her heartbeat. Their merged cadence seemed to make the air itself vibrate.

"Soon," the figure whispered in a voice that was grinding metal. "The door is almost open."

Millie's eyes fluttered beneath closed lids, tears leaking from the corners. The monitors showed her heart rate climbing.

The figure tucked the watch away and reached out with long, pale fingers. They hovered over Millie's forehead, trembling slightly, as if held back by some invisible barrier.

The shadows on the walls grew larger, more grotesque. The red light pulsed faster, brighter, until it seemed to fill the whole room with its bloody glow.

Then, as suddenly as it appeared, the figure was gone. Only the lingering scent of ozone and the sound of Millie's sleeping whimpers filled the room.

17

Miles away, Westville slept.

In a silent, empty house, Joe Thompson shot awake from his own fitful slumber. He thought of his daughter, lying in that hospital bed, and guilt racked him. But it was the ticking pulse that had awakened him—the counting of seconds, minutes, and hours. A debt piling up that no one could ever repay.

He eyed the black gun safe in the corner of the room with disdain and dread before walking over to it. The pulse grew louder. He entered the combination: 10, 13, 18, 98. The safe clicked open. He pulled out his shotgun from the rack, then his hunting rifle. Sliding a secret panel loose, he saw it. The dull golden pocket watch, tarnished with streaks of dark copper in an unnatural way. It ticked endlessly—but the hands did not move.

He heard it again. The truth. The terrible, looming truth.

"It's time to Seethe."

SILOED

The hospital room was too bright, the nights there too cold.
When she dreamt, it was of her tearing skin and her seeping blood
Of hollow sockets and red pools of light within
Whispering and seething and burning
She still hadn't woken from the nightmare
She felt it as though she were still in the dark place
But freedom was a far cry away, and she still couldn't scream
She still felt that if she did, no one could hear her.

1

Barren trees swayed in the wind, the last stubborn maple leaves clinging to life after death. The breeze had a different way of howling up here in Godwin, an hour and a half north of Westville. Not "up north" by Michigan standards, but far enough removed that you could forget yourself, forget where you came from.

As it happened, that was just what Casey wanted.

Five weeks since Millie Thompson was found—for the second time, alive. Five weeks since he'd ventured into that pipe with Reeves, since they'd found Liv and her friends in that impossible place. Five weeks since he'd stepped through one of those red doors and ended up in the woods pursuing Ethan Crawley, only to put two bullets in Travis.

He thought about it every morning, let it get out of his system, and did his level best to let the quiet mundanity and remoteness of his grandparents' old house do its work. The place still smelled like them—pine and coffee and wood smoke.

Casey kept busy by chopping wood, building fires, taking the four-wheeler out through the back trails. December had been cold and brown so far, but word was a system blowing down from the northwest would bring the first proper shot of winter.

That morning, Casey sat on the edge of the guest room bed, staring at the bright clash of quilts against the persistent gray-brown gloom outside the window. The smell of coffee drew him out to the living room, where he found his parents sitting in their usual spots on the four-seasons porch. Their morning ritual, which he'd joined these past weeks.

He poured himself a cup of steaming black and walked out.

"Sleep good?" his dad asked.

"Better than I have."

Slowly but surely though, the frustration and shame faded in and bled to life in technicolor, acute and sharp. The more time went on the shorter the dulling effects of sleep staved it all off.

Two weeks ago, the Chief called to update him on the investigation and set up a touch base meeting for after the New Year. He hadn't heard much yet regarding the shooting, and part of him wondered if they would hear anything at all—if out of thoroughness and wanting to not leave any loose ends, the F.B.I. or D.C.B. or whoever would want it all swept under the rug.

Casey figured he wasn't that lucky. And wasn't exactly sure he would want to be that beholden to the feds. Either way, the Chief advised him to stay away from Westville for the time being.

Casey didn't argue.

"I'm glad you're still here, Case," his mother said. Deb Benson was wrapped in a shawl she'd gotten on her trip to Arizona and New Mexico where she'd visited his sister. Another for her collection. "You should get out for a walk, nice morning. Think I might head out myself."

"You feel up for that?" Casey asked.

He was met with the usual 'of course I am' stare. She'd had invasive surgery mid-summer, and recovery hadn't been easy. But really it was her forgetfulness he was more concerned with. Dave eyed him.

"Alright, alright," Casey said, throwing one hand up in surrender.

"I've learned the hard way, son. Don't get in her way."

Deb scoffed and playfully slapped her husband's shoulder as she stood and walked back into the kitchen.

"Plans today?" Dave asked.

"You're looking at 'em."

"Well, come on then. Let's get a fire going."

They walked out to the fire pit. Probably mid-thirties, warm for the third week of December in the morning, and would climb higher in the afternoon. Good bonfire weather once you'd warmed up and been cutting wood for a while.

They split in silence, the cracks of their axes slapping against the tree line and echoing back. Casey had to fight off the memory of his pistol's report in the woods that night, clawing its way back into his head. But after a few good splits, he blocked it out. Or tried to.

The longer he was up here, the harder it was getting.

Dave Benson seemed to have something similar on his mind.

"So how much longer you thinking you'll stay?" he asked.

"Dunno. Figured might as well stay through Christmas at least."

Dave nodded and split another piece. "Hear from Aly?"

"No," Casey lied. She'd sent a letter a couple weeks back, filling him in on how Millie and Liv were doing, how the town was coping with the roller coaster of events. The girl in the river had been identified retroactively as Jill Davis, fifteen, another missing girl from somewhere near the border of Indiana. There had been no real explanation for the misidentification, which didn't surprise him. Not with how they'd all been railroaded into silence about what happened beneath Westville—or wherever those red doors had led them.

"Well, it's a shame about you two," Dave said. "Thought you were good together."

"There was a time we were, maybe. Things got complicated."

"Listen son," Dave said, setting down his ax and grabbing pieces to build the fire. "I've always tried to let you figure things out. Never wanted to be overbearing. But you can't keep running."

"I'm not running, Dad. I'm just taking a break."

"Sounds like what you said two years ago."

"I needed some time."

"That wreck was never your fault. You made a judgment call."

"A bad one."

"It's called a mistake. I've made my share."

"Nothing like getting a kid killed."

Dave sighed, kneeling to arrange kindling beneath the logs.

Casey shook his head, regret uncoiling in his gut. "Look, I know you're just trying to help. It's just right now I don't want to think about it. Not now."

"Sure," Dave said, standing. "I get that. Trouble is, when that time comes, you'll be no further along in dealing with the past than you are now."

Casey stiffened. "If you think I'm running, why invite me up here in the first place?"

"Your mother and I wanted to see you. Spend some time."

"And dredge up the past."

"To be here for you, Casey. To tell you what you might not want to hear but need to."

"And what's that?"

His father looked him in the eye then, smoke from the starting fire swirling between them in the cold air.

"You need to let go if you want to move on."

2

They sat by the fire until about noon, when Dave went in to make his usual lunch—either bologna or grilled cheese. Casey stayed out and walked the back of the property, edging along the creek that ran through and eventually connected with a larger inlet that fed into the Slate River miles downstream.

He watched the current carry a freshly fallen maple leaf, rigid and crisp, until it disappeared where the stream dipped and deepened. Swallowed by dark waters.

Casey could barely believe Millie was alive. Ever since they'd found Howard Meyers in that church bus, with a bracelet identical to Millie's in his pocket, he'd dreaded the inevitable. Fears that came true, if only for those few surreal days of the visitation and funeral.

Until she'd wandered onto the train tracks—alive.

She barely spoke, according to Aly's letter. She was breathing, but Casey wondered how much of that bright-eyed girl remained after what she'd seen. His one hospital visit on the way up north, she'd been locked in catatonic sleep, Erin standing vigil like a mournful statue. Joe hadn't been there. Joe wouldn't speak to him since she'd been found—just caught his eye at the station, before leaving without a word.

But there was the irony.

Casey didn't deserve gratitude. He hadn't found Millie. He'd just chased conspiracy theories with Heiser. Granted, they'd turned out to be true, even if that truth was buried now, locked away in whatever vault the D.C.B. used for things the world wasn't ready to know.

He turned back toward the house. His dad was napping, and his mother had run to the grocery store. The quiet pressed in, broken only by the wind in the pines.

Then came the knock.

Casey moved to the front door, opened it to find a plain cardboard box on the step. No return address. Just his name.

He knelt to pick it up when the crunch of tires on dirt caught his attention. An unmarked sedan pulling away—not a delivery vehicle. For a moment, he fought the urge to chase it down, catch a plate number.

Instead, he took the box to the guest bedroom, cut it open with his pocket knife. Inside lay a stack of familiar documents and manila folders. On top, a handwritten letter.

It was from Heiser.

And once he read it, Casey knew. He had to go back.

3

The last week of school before Christmas break was pointless.

Teachers and students were checked out, ready to be done, which was why Olivia couldn't understand why her mother thought it was so crazy that she wanted to ditch.

"You've been distracted enough these past couple of months," Kathy said. "And you need to give them time to be with her too."

"They don't mind having me there, Mom."

"I know, I know. I just don't want you to overdo it, that's all."

Olivia begrudgingly agreed to attend the last three days of school before break. It was Wednesday, the 21st—just two more days. That didn't stop her from pleading with Aly to take her to the hospital after school. Surprisingly, her sister agreed with little protest.

They drove down M-12, cold, wet December days leaving the road with a permanent glistening sheen under gray sky, listening to the cassette tape of *Jagged Little Pill* along the way.

"Is it weird for you being there?" Olivia asked, recalling how Aly had glanced toward the room where Travis Johnson was being treated.

"Why would it be?"

"Usually, you're the one calling me out for being withholding."

Aly sniffed. "Fair enough. Look, I don't know what happened. Casey thought Travis was going to—" She stopped short. "I don't know."

"So, where is Casey now?"

"Went up north. To his parents' place."

"You guys talk?"

"Not really."

Olivia glanced out the window, drumming her fingers on the door as the heat blew her hair through the vents. They came over the hill and down toward a stretch of streetlights, the humble skyline of Iron Falls plastered against stony clouds. The highest building displayed majuscule gold letters on the top that spelled out Vangard, but was otherwise all glass windows, refracting and reflecting the world around it. For a moment Olivia's stomach knotted, as she pictured that strange iridescent blur in the air on Halloween—around red light and shadow—and the same folding in and out of those red doors.

As they banked left onto Lion Street toward the hospital, her nerves tensed even more. In part, she'd asked Aly if she felt uncomfortable being there because, well, *she* did.

Something about it all didn't feel right—least of all the fact that no one had been able to figure out where Millie had come from.

Olivia had some idea about that. The tunnels they'd followed beneath Westville, to that place. It all felt so fuzzy, like a nightmare she was forgetting hour by hour as the days passed. Only this nightmare she wanted to remember. She wanted to understand.

Reeves, the woman they'd escaped through the pipe with, asserted that she and Casey had gone in after them and that a chemical leak had caused hallucinations.

Olivia knew it was complete and total bullshit.

"How are you doing with everything?" Aly asked as they pulled into the five-story parking garage, beginning to wind their way through the concrete spiral.

"Fine, I guess. Just trying to . . . figure it all out."

Aly nodded and turned into an open spot. "You can talk to me, you know."

"I know. It's just . . . most of it, you wouldn't believe."

"Try me."

Olivia glanced at her sister, saw that she meant it. For once, after all of this, maybe Aly wasn't just trying to control her or judge her.

So she told her everything: the pipe that led to the tunnel, the facility, the red doors, the red light in the woods. Their research about the Skadegamutc, and Arthur Thompson's pact or curse or whatever it had been.

"The night I came to pick you up at Casey's," Aly said, "that's what you were talking about."

Olivia nodded. "And that Greg guy who was coming to your café—he's some kind of scientist, I guess. He works for the feds."

"The Dimensional Containment Bureau," Aly breathed.

Olivia looked at her, puzzled.

"I saw Greg in the café the day after Casey left town. I asked him what had really been going on. He wasn't shy about it."

"Why would he tell you?"

"I don't know," Aly said, and Olivia could tell that bothered her. "But this is crazy," she added. "Millie's here. It's over. Let's just leave it at that."

Aly got out of the car. Olivia followed and didn't argue further.

4

The elevator dinged open on the third floor, and they made their way down the familiar hallway to Room 312.

Olivia entered the hospital room, her breath catching in her chest. The bed was empty. The faint indentation of Millie's slight frame in the mattress was the only proof she'd ever been there. The heart monitor stood silent, its wires neatly coiled, and the IV pole stripped bare.

"Millie?" Olivia whispered, her voice thin against the sterile quiet. She glanced around the room, her pulse quickening. Her heart thudded heavily as she stepped closer to the bed, her eyes scanning for some clue—anything to tell her Millie hadn't vanished again.

She spun toward the hallway, her sneakers squeaking on the freshly waxed floor. A nurse breezed past, balancing a tray of medications. "Excuse me!" Olivia called after her, but the woman was already into the next room.

Olivia turned the other way, craning her neck to see down the corridor. Her mind raced with possibilities, none of them good. What if Millie had wandered off? What if something worse had happened?

Then she saw them.

Millie, pale and frail, shuffled slowly down the hall, her arm looped through her mother's for support. Mrs. Thompson's face was drawn tight, her movements deliberate, as though she were walking on a sheet of cracking glass. Relief surged through Olivia, and her feet moved before she could stop them.

"Mil!" she called, her voice cracking. She jogged toward them, her shoes barely making a sound against the linoleum.

Millie turned her head slowly, her sunken eyes catching the overhead light. She managed the ghost of a smile. Mrs. Thompson stopped walking and adjusted her grip on Millie's arm, her eyes softening.

"You're awake," Olivia said, her voice trembling with relief. "I didn't—when I saw the bed—" She swallowed hard, forcing her words into coherence. "You're okay."

Mrs. Thompson offered a small smile, though it seemed brittle. "She's better. Weak, but the doctors said she can go home soon."

"Home?" Olivia asked, her eyes darting between them.

Mrs. Thompson nodded. "She'll need rest. But after Christmas we'll bring her home." Her voice wavered, and she quickly turned her attention back to Millie, smoothing her daughter's blonde hair with a trembling hand.

"You'll come see me and keep me sane, right?" Millie's question carried on a breath than spoken.

"Of course," Olivia said, stepping closer. She reached for Millie's hand, feeling how cold and frail it was, and offered a smile. "Whenever you want. OCPs and Nintendo."

"When she's rested," Mrs. Thompson cut in, her tone sharper than she likely intended.

"Is daddy still here?" Millie said quietly, her voice barely above a whisper.

Her mom swallowed and nodded.

Olivia glanced down the hallway, where Mr. Thompson leaned against the nurses' station, voice muted as he talked with the staff. Aly offered to walk with Millie some more, and Mrs. Thompson agreed, dispensing some coffee from the Folger's machine into a styrofoam cup.

The questions clogged Olivia's throat. She'd only been told in the most vague sense what happened. That Millie had in fact been abducted by someone, that there were suspects, but the reasons for said abduction were unknown, as were the motives behind her blood being drawn leaving track marks all over her arms. But if anyone knew, surely her parents would.

"Mrs. Thompson," she asked, "what really happened to her? Has she remembered anything else?"

She swallowed a sip from the steaming cup, her throat quavering as she wet her lips. "Not much more. The police are following up on a few leads but—" She stopped short. "We don't know."

Olivia glanced down the hall toward Millie and her sister, and heard the shuffle of steps behind her.

She turned to see Mr. Thompson, and she couldn't help the memory of Millie's grandfather standing over her the same way after the funeral. Calloused hands clamping down on her shoulders and looking straight into her brain like he'd known what she'd been doing.

But now, her dad seemed to look right past Olivia, though he acknowledged her with a passing, "Thanks for being here, Liv." His voice, hollow.

"Let's move back to the room," Mr. Thompson said. Not a suggestion.

Once they'd filed in and gotten settled, Millie's parents explained to her that she needed to wait a few more days before coming home. Aly and Olivia stood just outside the door. Millie said that she hated it here and didn't feel comfortable, especially at night. That she just wanted to go home. Mr. Thompson said they would get her home soon. He promised.

They were invited back in, and Olivia sat by her friend's bedside while Aly and Mrs. Thompson talked, and Mr. Thompson looked out the window.

Olivia kept her voice low.

"I know it must have been a lot for you. Being alone, scared, not knowing where you were."

Millie nodded, lips stretching like she was trying to stave off sobs. Her blue eyes seemed so much paler now.

"You really don't remember anything about where you were, or who—"

"She doesn't need to talk about this right now," Mr. Thompson said, now near the foot of the bed, voice low and dangerous.

Just like his dad's.

The air seemed to shift, a faint hissing sound reaching Olivia's ears. She froze, her heart racing as the sound grew louder, more insistent. It wasn't just air escaping from a vent or the breathing of the IV drip machine.

"The police have already put her through enough. She doesn't need friends digging it back up. Not now."

Mrs. Thompson stood. "Joe—"

"I think it's best for Millie to rest."

"Dad, I'm fine. I can—"

"You're not fine. Not yet."

He turned sharply toward Olivia, his eyes unblinking.

"It's okay," Aly said. "It's a lot right now. Liv, let's go. We'll come by this weekend."

Mrs. Thompson stared at her husband. "Yes, that'd be great."

Millie smiled weakly, and Olivia stood up with her stomach twisting. She walked with Aly out into the hall. Something was wrong. She felt it on a level that was hard to explain.

Mr. Thompson watched them leave for a moment, then went back into the room.

As the elevator dinged, a faint pressure in Olivia's ears returned, followed by a whispering hiss that sent a shiver down her spine. She glanced at Aly, who didn't seem to notice.

"What was that about?" she asked.

"I don't know," Aly said, her eyes fixed on Mr. Thompson as he disappeared behind the elevator doors. "I mean it's just—stress does things to people."

Olivia shook her head. "At the funeral . . . Casey thought something was going on with him."

Aly nodded and sniffed. "You mean more than just the drinking?"

"I'm not blind. I can smell, and I spent a lot of time over at Millie's place the past couple of years. So, yeah, more than that."

Aly offered a not-so-reassuring smile. "I'm going to talk to Erin. See if there's anything I can do to help."

Olivia looked up at the red digital letters of the elevator, ticking down one by one.

Millie was here. Alive, and now awake. Olivia had thought maybe this night-mare was over. But as she watched those red numbers drop lower, counting down to the ground below, she couldn't shake the feeling that something was very wrong.

And that was when she remembered.

In the flurry of everything, what happened in the pipe—that in-between place—Millie being found and all that had followed, she'd forgotten all about it:

There was a VHS tape waiting for her at the Family Affair.

5

As luck, fate, or Michigan's delayed winter wrath would have it, Olivia got out of the last two days before break thanks to a snowstorm.

Overnight, a few good inches had fallen, covering the entire town in tufts of white that melded into pale gray then brown on the streets, where the scraping plow that woke her from a fitful sleep had carved its way through the slushy mire, dumping salt as it went.

Olivia had convinced Aly to stop off at the Family Affair on the way back from the hospital, and through several layers of snark regarding her initial urgency to get the tape and not coming back until over a month later, her favorite hook-nosed clerk handed it over.

She couldn't get the way Millie's dad had looked—how he talked—out of her head.

Olivia desperately wanted—more than anything, really—to believe all this was over. But she could tell Aly felt something too. She might not have heard what Olivia had—the awful screeching, static hiss from the woods and the facility at the end of the pipe—but she sensed it.

Olivia wondered if talking to Mrs. Thompson would do any good. She hoped so. She wanted to see her friend, be there for her through all of this. Millie looked so different now—skinny, pale, her arms all marked up.

Olivia walked into the living room and flipped on the TV to the local news on Channel 17. Westville Public was closed. Which meant tomorrow— Friday—marked the start of break.

Good. She had plans.

She popped the VHS into her all-in-one VCR TV she'd commandeered for her Nintendo a while ago.

Her footage was shaky, and only lingered on the journal page for a few staticky seconds, but after several attempts at pausing it in the right spot she was able to make out enough of the writing to start copying it down, in a mostly empty Lisa Frank notebook that looked like a unicorn threw up on the cover..

Once she'd copied the words down from the paused frame, a deep dark feeling came over her. Her limbs felt heavier and lighter at once. She started to get up, but her eyes caught on the photo of Arthur Thompson standing in front of PRINCE Milling, the same one she'd seen in the microfilm weeks ago. Standing proudly in a suit and bowler hat on old Main Street, a golden pocket watch chain and the watch itself in his hand. A mark of his newfound and maybe blood and fire bought wealth, she thought.

Olivia dialed Austin's home phone first. Turned out Kyle had slept over, anticipating the snow day.

Austin's mom went to his bedroom to rouse him from sleep and hand him the phone.

"Liv?" Austin's groggy voice crackled through the receiver.

"Hey. Fischer's this morning. 9 a.m."

"Isn't the whole point of a snow day to sleep in?"

"Don't care. Get Kyle up. And have him call Eli."

"What's this about?"

"All of this—it's not over. I'll explain. Just meet me there, okay?"

Austin grumbled in agreement. Olivia heard Kyle groan in the background as the phone clicked off.

She gathered the now far-overdue forensics books, Westville history volumes, and Native American lore texts she'd checked out from the library. Stuffing them into her backpack, she threw on layers—a long-sleeve Green Day sweatshirt, a coat, and jeans.

Heading downstairs, she caught her sister just as she was about to leave. Aly was slipping on her gloves.

"I'm not on this morning, but I can drop you off," Aly offered.

"Where are you going?" Olivia asked, curiosity piqued.

"Have to run a few errands, and meet someone later," Aly said. "Hop in."

6

The four of them commandeered a corner booth table at Fischer's, every inch covered in the remnants of breakfast carnage scattered among stacks of books—plates of waffles, bacon and sausage and Eli's dog-eared notebooks filled with his cramped, precise handwriting.

Olivia glanced out the frost-rimmed window, watching the snow-covered world outside while the café hummed around them—a low backdrop of murmured conversation, clinking dishes, the bubble and glug of coffee being brewed and poured.

Austin leaned back against the booth, arms crossed, his dark, snow damp hair hanging over his brow. Kyle sat next to him, drumming his fingers against an open book, looking like he wanted to be anywhere else. Across from them, Eli flipped through the notes Olivia had copied down from the footage on her camcorder—the journal entries from the attic.

He read aloud:

"The price of success and prosperity are threefold: the skin of the hunted, the bones of the guilty, and the blood of the innocent. And time. Always time."

The words hung in the air.

Kyle shifted uncomfortably. "Okay, that's creepy as hell, but what does it mean?"

Olivia's mind jumped to one of the many times she'd been dragged along by Millie to youth group at the Methodist church, where they'd talked about the proverbs of some rich guy with a lot of wives—words meant to guide, and to warn. This felt different. Darker. She glanced over her shoulder at the snow-covered steeple atop orange brick across the street. Behind them, a man in a hooded winter coat sat alone in the next booth.

She forced herself to focus.

Eli tapped his pen against the table. "Think about it. That skinned, decapitated deer found in the woods a couple months back. That's the skin of the hunted. The Thompson graves being dug up—those are the bones of the guilty." His voice dropped lower. "And the blood of the innocent . . ."

Olivia's chest tightened. "Millie," she whispered. "It's her blood."

Eli nodded grimly.

Olivia's mind raced, piecing together fragments of memory: Millie's pale skin, the marks on her arms, the vacant look in her eyes when she'd woken up in the hospital.

"So if it's the shaman's curse," Austin said, breaking the silence. "How do we stop it? Or break it?"

Eli hesitated, flipping through his notes.

"We're not letting anything else happen to Millie," Olivia said firmly. "We need to figure out who's really behind this. What about this Janus company?"

Eli pulled out another page. "I'm glad you asked," he said, scanning his notes. "I found an old article in the library archives. JG Incorporated came to Westville in the '70s, but maybe earlier. Supposedly, they were just here to build infrastructure for PRINCE Milling."

Kyle leaned back, rubbing his temples. "This is insane. We're supposed to fight off some ancient curse and take on a secret cult corporation?"

"We start by protecting Millie," Olivia said. "Whatever it takes."

The determination in her voice silenced the table. She didn't have all the answers—none of them did—but she wasn't about to let Millie become another victim. Not while they still had a chance.

Outside, snow fell steadily, piling in thick drifts against the windows. Inside, the air felt too still. "We can't let them have her," Olivia emphasized.

A shadow passed over their booth.

Olivia looked up—and met the hooded man's gaze. Dr. Heiser stood beside their table, his dark overcoat dusted with melting snowflakes. His sharp eyes scanned the mess of notes, books, and the leftover breakfasts before settling on Eli.

"Couldn't help overhearing," Heiser said, his voice calm, hushed, and tinged with admiration. "It seems you've connected plenty of dots, without my help."

Olivia recoiled. Could they really trust Heiser? He had to have known more than he let on all along. What was different now?

Kyle cleared his throat awkwardly after a beat. "Uh, sorry sir, table's a little full, and we're having a secret meeting."

"Commendable effort, but I'm afraid I heard loud and clear. From across the room actually." He gestured toward the corner booth at the far side of the restaurant. "I've been something of a regular these past months." He turned his attention back to Olivia, meeting her eyes, a sudden solemn look coming over him, unlike the usual air of thoughtful humor he had about him.

"I am sorry, Miss Fischer. For what happened to you, your friends, and Miss Thompson."

"And Casey," she blurted.

"Yes," he said, a fleeting smile flickering as he rubbed his goatee. "Benson as well. May I sit?"

"Who are you, exactly?" Austin asked, sitting up straighter next to Olivia from the inside of the booth, readying to leap up if needed.

"Dr. Heiser," Olivia filled in. "The guy I tried to tell you two about before the pipe."

Heiser grabbed a chair from one of the nearby tables, snatching up a piece of bacon off a plate as he sat, much to Kyle's chagrin. Eli frowned, stammering until his curiosity apparently won out.

"What's with the hood?" he asked.

Heiser raised his eyebrows and nodded. "Ah yes." He lowered it. "I suppose I won't be needing it. No use hiding. They'll be coming shortly."

Olivia leaned forward and clasped the edge of the table. "Who?"

"No one to be concerned about. My former employer isn't too pleased."

Heiser chewed on the borrowed bacon and then a piece of toast. "But perhaps now—by a happy accident or fate—I can impart what I can. Because like you, I don't believe this is over."

Olivia exchanged glances with the others. "Okay. We're listening."

"Until recently I was with the Dimensional Containment Bureau. I've been in Westville—what we refer to as Site 73—to observe and hopefully help mitigate the worst of things. You've all uncovered some critical truths. It's no small feat to untangle history, myth, and corporate deception into something coherent. Well done." He looked to Eli as he said, a brain apparently recognizing a brain.

Eli flushed. "Uh . . . thanks," he said with a gulp.

As Heiser began skimming the notes, the storm outside grew heavier, pressing against the café windows.

"Three keys," Heiser muttered, glancing at Eli's notes.

"Keys to what?" Olivia asked.

"To an unopened door. Or perhaps many doors."

Kyle slammed his fist on the table. "Like the red ones in that warehouse."

Heiser tilted his head, intrigued. "Ah, yes. The Janus facility you stumbled upon. I suspected they had expanded their operations, but it seems they've gone further than I feared."

Austin leaned forward. "What's behind those doors?"

Heiser's expression darkened. "Before I explain, I want you to understand something. What I'm about to tell you may sound absurd. It might scare you. But it's the truth. And whether you believe me or not, you need to know."

The group exchanged uneasy glances. Olivia gave him a small nod. "So spill it."

Heiser pulled a notebook toward him and began sketching.

"There are pathways, through other planes of existence. Janus has been using the geomagnetic and resonant energies of the ley lines which converge here in Westville to force these pathways open to the astral, and in so doing—opening the way for other things to seep through. Things that come from the space between our world and the astral. In this case, an entity known as RE-728. Or, colloquially, the Red."

Olivia felt herself go lightheaded, her blood running cold as flashes of the pipe and place with the endless doors, the metal cell bathed in red light they'd been taken to, and the twisted portrait of the Skadegamutc's shadowy form emerging from the red orb that night at Devil's Peak.

It was all connected.

Olivia drew a breath, forcing herself to ask the question she'd been too afraid to ask out loud since Halloween night, or really to let it fully form in her mind for fear of the Red, because she had heard it whisper right to *her*, unlike the others. And she'd thought maybe it would know, somehow, that she was trying to figure it out. But right now she couldn't afford to be afraid.

"So, what does it want? Or what does Janus want with *it*?"

Heiser rubbed at his goatee, eyes focusing on her. "Those are the very questions that brought me to your little town, Miss Fischer." He glanced over at Kyle, who had slowly been sliding his plate away from Heiser, who continued to pick at it. "As my colleagues and I began to study instances of the Red, its frequencies were unfocused and meandering. Similar to most resonant entities we've detected. But, in the past several years and our observance of things here in Site 73, it seems to have taken on an anti-zoetic shift."

Kyle spat out waffle. "Like we're dealing with a Nazi-ghost-witch now?"

"That's anti-semitic, dufus," Austin said.

Eli cleared his throat. "I had that word in the spelling bee two years ago. Zoetic comes from the Greek word that means life."

Heiser sighed. "Indeed it does."

Anti-life, Olivia thought. And the realization slipped through her, a sheet of ghostly ice.

"It just wants to kill, but it can't," she breathed. "Because it's not really here."

"At least not yet," Heiser said gravely. "RE-728 isn't like anything else I or anyone at the Bureau has encountered before. So much so that it's drawn us to ask whether there might be something on the other side influencing the shift in resonance."

Eli leaned in. "Resonance—as in sound?"

"More than sound," Heiser said, sketching a jagged line on a napkin. "Morphic resonance—emotional, mental, and spiritual energies that shape reality. The Bureau calls it 'the Seethe'—a layer connecting the temporal and astral."

Olivia felt a sharp stab in her heart then. She thought of her dad. She'd been so caught up in her own guilt over not saying goodbye, and so angry at everyone around her. Had she made it stronger too? Could it be a part of the reason Millie had been taken in the first place, in more ways than just dragging her to the river that night and getting into that argument?

No. She was already spiraling down the cycle again. That was its trick.

"In any case," Heiser continued, "Miss Thomson's blood is now a potent catalyst for the manifestation, because of the generations of belief. If the ritual completes, this 'Skadegamutc' will fully manifest. And when it does, it could release enough geomagnetic energy to open every door Janus has been trying to force for decades."

Heiser cleared away a plate in the center of the table, and slid the napkin to the center. A perfect hexagon, with a circle on the top right and the bottom left.

He pointed his finger at the circle on the bottom and traced it to the other. "A door will be opened. It's just a matter of when."

"That's the symbol we saw in that place," Austin said.

A chill skittered down Olivia's spine. "The hexagon from the maps."

"Holy shit," Kyle blurted, loud enough to cause a scoff from a mother of two young kids nearby innocently eating their breakfast and coloring. "I think I know."

"Know what?" asked Austin.

Kyle looked to Eli. "You aren't going to jump in before me?"

Eli shook his head, looking around as if he'd done something wrong. "I mean it's just a hexagon."

"The Winter Hexagon," Kyle said. "It's at its apex tonight."

Olivia thought for a moment that Kyle was just screwing with Eli again, but when she saw Heiser sit back in the booth and his eyes go wide, she knew that wasn't the case.

"An asterism," Heiser said. "Of course."

Kyle jumped in with fervor like he was answering a question on the Steps of Knowledge as a contestant on *Legends of the Hidden Temple*. "It's a group of stars that form a shape when they're connected—but usually smaller than a constellation—and this one forms a hexagon."

He looked around at the others, his brown eyes wide with surprise and glee that Eli was apparently at a loss. "I guess that nerdy space camp paid off after all."

"Wow," Eli said. "I should probably get on that Astronomy badge."

Heiser rubbed a hand through his already mottled head of salt and pepper hair. "Astrological rhythms like these have a massive effect upon the energy flow within ley lines. If this asterism really is at its peak then—tonight may indeed be the night."

The table fell silent, the weight of his words pressing down on them as the snow piled up outside, any glee Kyle had emanated dissipating to a sudden dirge and weight of realization.

And it was Kyle who broke the silence. "But what are we supposed to do about it? We're just kids. How are we supposed to stop this?"

Heiser sighed, rubbing his temples. "I'll do what I can. But my hands are about to be tied in more ways than one." He leaned forward, his voice steady and urgent. "When it comes to rituals like these and generational belief in them, there are items used in the process with some special meaning. These are key to completing the ritual. It will be something important to the Thompson family, an heirloom, and perhaps connected to the Odawa as well. If Janus finishes what they started, the consequences won't just affect Westville. It could—"

The bell at the front of the café chimed, and Heiser glanced over his shoulder. Two men in navy-blue coats with FBI emblazoned on the sleeves strode in, beginning to search the restaurant.

Heiser stood, pulling a twenty-dollar bill from his wallet and placing it on the table. "I have to go. Can't let them see me speaking with you." He glanced at Olivia one last time.

"Good luck."

Then, he walked straight toward the approaching agents from behind, and turning one of them clasped a hand around Heiser's arm, and together they walked out, leaving the group in stunned silence.

Kyle slowly turned his head away from the door.

"What. The. Hell."

"Millie's safe now though," Eli said. "Right? She's at the hospital."

"But that doesn't mean someone won't come for her," Olivia said, "Crawley is still out there somewhere."

"So maybe . . . we get to him first," Austin said, a fire in his eyes and a trembling in his voice.

Olivia nodded, wanting to put her hand on his, but she dissuaded herself.

"So . . . what *do* we do?" Eli asked.

"You all heard him," Olivia said resolutely. "We need to find those—things."

"We don't know what we're looking for," said Kyle.

For a moment time stood still, and she glanced at the clown clock on the far wall.

A memory careened into Olivia's mind, like a rock crashing through a window.

It was the first time she'd ever hung out with Millie after school. They'd taken turns snapping Polaroids of each other, mostly striking poses on the train trestles singing very bad acapella karaoke of *'Stupid Girl'* by Garbage. When they were going through them later, a few more from the day before had fallen out of Millie's bag. In one of them she was making a duck lipped face and wearing a golden pocket watch around her neck. Olivia had laughed at Millie's bad white girl attempt to mimic Flava Flav. But Millie went quiet, saying her dad had cussed her out for messing with it, and not to touch it again.

Why, in the name of holy hell, hadn't Olivia thought of it before?

She explained.

"So we go and raid PRINCE Milling," Kyle said, "to look for a watch."

"And to make sure Crawley doesn't try anything," Austin added.

Or anyone else, Olivia thought.

Eli picked up the bill, turning it over. On the back, written in Heiser's neat handwriting, was a single word: PRINCE, followed by the numbers: 1-8-9-8.

"What does it mean?" Austin asked.

Olivia's eyes narrowed as the memory of a keypad near the loading dock elevator at the mill flashed in her mind. "I think it's a password. And we're going to need it."

7

The drive back was slow going, and that was being generous, even with his dad's Chevy Silverado and winter tires.

The lake-effect-fueled storm system was making good on its promise to dump days' worth of snow in a single night. Casey gripped the wheel tight, the road ahead swallowed by a churning white abyss. The wind howled, rocking the truck slightly. *Found Out About You* by the Gin Blossoms played on the crackling radio, something to keep him focused and distracted at the same time.

The main highways would be packed with holiday travelers crawling along, so he'd opted for back roads. Probably a mistake, but it was too late to turn back now.

Everything Heiser had sent him flew through his mind like the iced powder whipping against his windshield. It had all been there—laid out in black and white—the connection between Janus Global and PRINCE Milling that Casey had suspected. Accounting sheets, contracts, statements, all painting the picture he'd feared but hadn't been able to prove.

Jack Thompson had known too. Had known all along, his name plastered all over the signed contracts with *'JG Logistics'*.

And then there was Heiser's letter.

'I know that I wasn't up front with you, Casey. But for a man in my position I had to walk a delicate line, and I tried to bring you into the fold as much as I could, with what I knew for certain at the time. I don't know when, but Janus is going to make a move, and Millie has a part to play. She will suffer. Others will suffer. I need someone who believes me to do something about it.'

He clenched his jaw and drove in silence for the first hour, his mind a relentless storm of its own. He tuned the radio—old Christmas music, sounding detached and surreal through the blown out old speakers in the cab, then a weatherman's voice soon cut in, warning of worsening conditions, urging people to stay home, to travel only if necessary.

Casey needed to figure out what the hell was happening in Westville.

He had to confront Joe and Jack. The evidence was too damning to ignore. The real question was—had they actually sanctioned Millie's capture? Had they played a role in what happened to her, in Howard Meyers' convenient death and framing?

And Ethan Crawley.

He was wrapped up in all this. Were they protecting him? Why? Every new answer only unraveled more questions, twisting together like a tightening noose.

Then, out of nowhere, the radio feed cut and another voice broke through.

"We bring you a breaking story from Iron Falls, where an attack at Mary's Heart Memorial Hospital has left two staff wounded. The assailant was a patient—Westville police officer Travis Johnson, who was recovering from wounds sustained in a friendly fire incident in Westville last month that put another officer on mandatory leave. Police say the suspect is armed, dangerous, and unstable. He should not be approached. Contact local authorities with any information. A second patient—"

The radio sputtered into a hiss of static. Casey stared at the radio as if it had sprouted a mouth of fangs and evil eyes. His breath caught in his chest.

Travis.

A deep, sickening realization unfurled in Casey's gut. He knew Travis had been trying to hurt Aly that night. And now he was on the run.

The Seethe—the Red—whatever it was had gotten to him. Just like it had with Crawley.

As he passed through Iron Falls, he could just make out Mary's Heart Memorial through the thick snowfall—an eerie, glowing beacon in the dark. The radio towers atop the hospital blinked red through the storm, sending their silent warnings into the night.

Casey's pulse pounded. Travis was heading back to Westville. He felt it in his gut.

A piece clicked into place.

Travis had been the second man in the graveyard that night.

The exhumed Thompson bodies. The ritual.

Travis had been there when the graves were disturbed. And now he was unhinged, and armed.

Casey pictured the moment in the woods, the way Travis had come up behind Aly. What if he was going to try and finish what he started?

His knuckles whitened on the wheel. He wasn't letting that happen.

Gunning the accelerator, Casey tore through the blizzard, heading straight for Westville.

8

Aly should have known something was wrong the moment Erin Thompson didn't show up for lunch.

At first, she told herself it was nothing—the weather, maybe. The roads were bad. But still, the sour feeling in her gut wouldn't settle. She checked her watch, called the house. No answer.

Maybe she'd forgotten, or lost track of time at the hospital.

Aly tried to dismiss the unease, swinging by the restaurant to take care of a few things before heading home. Kathy was closing early, said Olivia had gone to stay with a friend for the night.

Still, the wrongness sat heavy in her chest.

Back at her apartment, she tried calling again. The line rang and rang—nothing. The unease turned sharp. No one answered at Joe's place either.

Snow swirled in the 5 p.m. darkness when she stepped outside. The wind had picked up again, tearing through Westville's side streets, sending drifts curling up against porches and driveways.

By the time she reached the Thompson house, the snow was coming down thick. She stepped onto the front porch, shoulders hunched against the cold, and knocked.

Nothing.

The house was dark. No Christmas lights, no warm glow in the windows, and she noted the same about the houses all around, save for a few. She listened and heard the hum of generators.

The power must be out.

She knocked harder. Still no answer.

That was when she tried the doorknob.

It clicked open.

Aly hesitated, breath fogging in the cold air, before stepping inside. The dark swallowed her.

"Erin?" she called, voice sharp in the silence. "Joe?"

Nothing.

Aly stepped further inside, boots creaking against the hardwood. A gust of frigid air followed her in before the door swung shut with a dull *clack.*

She moved through the house carefully, eyes adjusting to the dimness. The Christmas tree in the living room stood dark, the ornaments glinting dead eyes.

Something was wrong.

She made her way toward the hallway, glancing into the bedroom—where she saw a figure slumped in the corner.

Her stomach dropped. Erin.

Aly rushed forward, hands shaking as she crouched beside her. Erin's head lolled to the side, breath coming shallow. A syringe lay on the floor beside her, next to a near empty vial of pink liquid.

Morphine.

"Erin?" Aly whispered, pressing her fingers to her throat. A pulse. Weak, but steady.

A surge of relief mixed with fresh panic. She noted the gun safe in the corner, wide open. Where was Joe? Had he done this?

Aly stumbled to her feet and ran for the kitchen phone. She snatched it up and pressed it to her ear.

Dead.

She swore.

There was no time to waste. She grabbed her coat and sprinted back into the snow.

The drive to the police station was a blur, her tires skidding on the icy road. She barely registered the streets as they whipped by, her mind racing.

Then she saw it. Joe Thompson's pristine new F-150. Parked haphazardly in the abandoned high school lot. Aly slammed on the brakes. Her Beetle fishtailed before coming to a stop. The front doors of the school stood cracked open.

Her pulse pounded in her ears.

She got out slowly, her boots crunching in the fresh snow. Her breath curled in the freezing air as she reached for the door.

The hairs on her neck rose.

Then—hands seized her from behind.

A sharp prick at the back of her neck.

Aly gasped, struggling, but her limbs instantly felt leaden. Her vision swam. She was shoved forward through the doorway, stumbling into the dim, rubble-strewn entry hall. Her knees buckled, body sluggish and unresponsive.

A shadow loomed above her.

Travis Johnson.

Haggard, pale, and eyes burning red.

Blood stained the front of his t-shirt. His hands shook as he held the syringe, his breath coming in short, fevered bursts.

A voice echoed from the hall. Joe Thompson.

"Make sure she doesn't leave."

Aly tried to move, to run—but the world tilted and faded.

Travis, stared down at her with those glowing eyes, his lips curled into something between a grimace and a grin.

Then darkness took her.

9

The storm intensified as night fell, snow whipping through the streets and blanketing Westville in suffocating silence.

Olivia sat cross-legged on the worn carpet of Kyle's living room floor, her backpack by her side. The Anderson's were out at a company Christmas party in Iron Falls, and Kyle's kid sister was at his grandparents.

The others were scattered around the room: Austin flipping a switchblade nervously between his fingers, Eli thumbing through one of his notebooks, and Kyle sprawled across the couch, looking like he regretted every choice that had brought him there.

"We good on alibis?" Olivia asked, breaking the silence.

"Mom thinks I'm at Eli's," Kyle said with a shrug.

"Dad thinks I'm at Kyle's," Eli added.

Austin smirked. "My mom never cares as long as I'm back before sunrise."

Olivia pulled her sleeves down over her hands. "Alright. We wait until the roads are dead, then we go."

By 7 p.m, the snow had swallowed the town whole. The roads were deserted, the only sounds the howl of the wind and the crunch of their boots on the snow-covered sidewalks. Main Street stretched before them, streetlights casting eerie white halos through the swirling flakes, accented by the warm yellow of Christmas lights entwined in the red and green tinsel decorations, blowing in the wind.

"This is insane," Kyle muttered, his voice muffled by the scarf wrapped around his face.

"No arguments here," Eli said, limping here and there as he struggled to keep up.

Olivia led the way, head down against the biting wind. The towering silhouette of PRINCE Milling loomed ahead, the sign's red glow illuminating snow in bloodied air.

The group huddled at the edge of the parking lot, staring up at the mill's concrete facade.

"Last chance to turn back," Olivia said, not really meaning it.

Kyle snorted. "Yeah, because you'd let us hear the end of it."

They approached the loading dock cautiously, which at present was open, their footsteps echoing off the metal steps. She saw the freight elevator at the top of the small staircase, where nearly two months ago she'd first seen Ethan Crawley step through it. Crawley could be down there, and protecting the watch. She could feel it.

The keypad beside the elevator door was coated in frost, but Olivia brushed it clean with her sleeve and punched in the numbers: 1-8-9-8.

For a moment, nothing happened. Then with a shrill beep, the elevator doors shunted open.

"Everyone in," she whispered, stepping inside.

The freight elevator groaned as it descended. Olivia glanced at the others—nervous, but determined.

The elevator shuddered to a stop. The doors opened to a long, dimly lit hallway. Pipes snaked along the walls and ceiling, and the faint scent of something metallic lingered in the air.

Olivia nodded. "Let's move."

The group stepped out of the elevator, their flashlights cutting thin beams through the dim hallway. The hum of machinery was faint but ever-present, vibrating through the metal walls and floors like a pulse. Pipes crisscrossed overhead, condensation dripping occasionally and echoing softly against the floor.

"This place gives me the creeps," Kyle muttered, clutching his backpack tighter.

"Creepy or not, let's focus," Olivia shot back, keeping her voice low.

They moved cautiously, their footsteps muffled by the hum of the facility. The red emergency lights flickered intermittently, casting strange shadows that danced along the walls. Olivia led them around a corner, her breath fogging in the cold air.

Ahead, a door stood slightly ajar, faint light spilling through the crack. Olivia gestured for the others to follow as she pushed it open slowly. The room inside was small and sterile, dominated by a single hospital bed. Tubes and wires dangled from IV stands, their clear plastic catching the crimson glow. A monitor blinked faintly in the corner, its screen cracked and unreadable.

Olivia froze, her stomach tightening. She didn't need anyone to say it—she already knew.

"This is where they must have kept her," she whispered.

Austin stepped forward, his face pale. "Are you sure?"

"That's messed up," Kyle said, "right under the nose of her own dad."

And her loving grandfather, Olivia thought.

"She told me about the IVs, the needles." Olivia's voice shook as she pointed to the equipment. "This is it."

The room smelled faintly of antiseptic, and the sheets on the bed were rumpled as if someone had only recently left. Olivia ran her fingers over the bed's edge, her mind flashing back to Millie's pale face in the hospital. And there was a strange machine, something situated over the head of the bed, a halo of wires and metal bars connected to a metal box with multiple knobs and a black screen showing a static green blob.

A faint scuff of boots on metal cut through her words. The group froze, their eyes darting to the door. Another step, heavier this time, echoed down the hallway.

"Someone's coming," Kyle hissed, backing away.

Olivia motioned for them to turn off their flashlights. The emergency lights painted the room in shifting shadows as they pressed themselves into corners, barely daring to breathe.

The footsteps grew louder. Then, the door creaked open.

Ethan Crawley stepped inside, his eyes glowing an unnatural red. His face was slack, his lips slightly parted, breath fogging in slow, rhythmic bursts. His movements were eerily smooth—like something else was pulling the strings.

Behind him, three other men entered, one wearing a flannel and the others gray PRINCE Milling uniforms. Their eyes glowed the same vivid crimson.

Olivia's heart sank. She glanced at the others, their faces pale and terrified. Crawley turned to the other men, his lips curling into a grim smile.

Ethan raised a radio from his belt and pressed the button.

"Found them."

HOLLY AND FIRE

D.C.B. Interview Transcript

Westville Incursion Event

Interview Series 3

Benson: The whole time you were in Westville, you weren't even trying to stop it, were you?

Lochlear: We were trying to stop the source.

Benson: Janus. You were holding out to get at them no matter how people suffered.

Lochlear: I don't have the luxury of playing a short game, Benson. Neither does anyone here at the Bureau. We've been waiting for an opportunity.

Benson: Was it worth it?

Lochlear: We shut it down. So yes, it was worth it.

Benson: Glad you can rest easy then.

Lochlear: Let's get back to the interview proper, shall we?

Benson: Be my guest.

Lochlear: The incident at PRINCE Milling, and your subsequent encounter. Describe your account if you would, please.

Fat flakes blew wild in the winter dark, covering the streets of Westville in icy froth.

A warm glow came from the windows of shops all along Main Street, and the night was quiet. Families put the finishing touches on Christmas trees, trimming them with tinsel and holly. Bubble ornaments churning in translucent orange and red. Near the river, multi-color light strands adorned the stout pine tree near the Westville showboat.

Weeks removed now from when a girl had gone missing. Millie Thompson had been found, and the people of Westville could relax.

They did not know what had already begun.

Joe Thompson watched the glitter of Christmas lights with reddened eyes, through the slats of a boarded-up window in the old abandoned high school office. He stepped back into the hall utility closet, flung open a breaker on the circuit and another. A weak undulating buzz followed the clank, followed by the sizzle and click of the school's old intercom system, which was stuck on a local radio station, Sinatra's *Jingle Bells* echoing through the quiet empty halls.

His breath rose in plumes, illuminated by the glowing crimson EXIT sign.

Debris from demolition and intermittent vandalism crunched beneath Joe's feet, broken glass clinking as he gritted his teeth.

He was trying to resist the pull. The call. The command of the Red inside him.

That was useless. It had been this whole time. He stepped into the gymnasium, the basketball court where he'd played once, him and Casey both.

The jangling tune resounded all the more in here like a feverish nightmare. He thought briefly of brighter days, when there was a hope and a future. For him and for his family. He stepped up to where he'd left her. Still asleep. Still peaceful.

Millie was sedated. More morphine. He eyed the syringes he'd used with disdain—stolen from Erin's hospice nursing kit. A real family affair this has become. Revulsion rose in his gut, toward himself and his father and his damned dead grandfathers.

"It's time," said the Red. He heard the *tick, tick, tick.* He pictured his father.

Now, Joe had his own tree to trim.

He stepped toward the other end of the gymnasium, ignoring the unconscious body of Aly Fischer, toward the tarp that hung down, a curtain over the monstrosity nailed to the wall. He tore it off, revealing the macabre jigsaw puzzle he'd been assembling for months. Amalgam bones of his grandfathers. Antlers, ribs from multiple bucks, and their skins strung taut, torn, and rotting over the vague shape resembling something that might have been capable of standing.

He climbed the stepladder and straightened one of three skulls and cocked his head.

"Yes," said the Red inside, a low purring growl. *"Skin of the hunted . . . Bones of the guilty . . ."*

He stepped down off the ladder, and walked toward his beautiful daughter, peaceful in her chemical sleep.

"Blood of the innocent," Joe recited, as warm tears slid down both his cheeks.

2

Casey tore through the snarl of swirling white, careening into Aly's driveway outside of town.

The house was dark. Door was locked. No answer as he rang the doorbell and knocked.

He ran back to the truck and tore down the empty snow-swept streets. The Friday before Christmas Eve and one of the worst snowstorms in recent memory meant empty roads. He passed the *Family Affair* parking lot—the stakeout spot where it had all been about to start on a fog-laden silent Saturday morning two months before.

Everything was different now. Everything had changed.

And he had to make it right. To put an end to all the wrongs. Tonight.

He careened into the Shell gas station lot, just across from the PRINCE Milling offices, and killed the engine.

Casey saw the lights on in Jack's office on the second floor. The man was entrenched in something—maybe something they couldn't get out of—with Janus Global.

None of that changed the fact that all this time, as Westville feared for and mourned an innocent girl, terror gripping the heart of the town Casey called home, Jack had been right at the black heart of it all. Joe too. The bitter roots they themselves had grown. Crocodile tears doled out like grain in the wind.

Casey stepped out of the Chevy, shouldering the door shut, all the while his eyes caught on the crimson glow of the PRINCE sign looming above. He ran over to the office door and rapped on it hard. No answer. Again. Nothing. He climbed the window nearby and managed to jimmy it open. He dropped down and climbed up the stairs to the offices.

There at his desk, looming over papers as though it were just another work-day—was Jack Thompson. He looked up with a curious, confused expression that, with a sigh, shifted to his face falling slack.

"Casey. Thought you were up North."

"I was. Came down when I heard some news."

Jack stood. "And what news might that be?"

"Cut the crap, Jack." Casey stormed forward. "You're going to tell me everything. What you've been hiding. The truth about Millie and what was done to her and why."

"You don't know what you're talking about—or what you're dealing with," Jack growled and stood. He was never a man to back down. But neither was Casey. Not anymore.

Jack's eyes narrowed as he stepped closer, his presence filling the room like a storm about to break. He grabbed something small off the desk. Between his large fingers.

"You know what this is, Benson?" Jack asked, voice low and reverent. He held up the kernel between his thumb and forefinger, turning it in the dim light. "A single seed of wheat. Small. Insignificant. But you know what happens to it?"

"I'll pass on the agricultural lesson. How about the truth?"

Jack's lips twitched.

"This seed—it's buried in the dirt, forgotten. It dies there. But it grows stronger than before. From that death comes life. We harvest it, grind it to dust, destroy it again. And from that dust something new. Something vital."

Jack stepped closer to the window, gazing out at the storm battering the silos, their shadows stretching across the snow.

"My family founded this town. It was stolen from us, but we got it back."

"Through a convenient fire," Casey said.

Jack nodded, as if in silent concession. "My grandfather did his best. He dealt with someone he maybe shouldn't have. That's true. But you can't change the past. Just have to make a better future."

"If your idea of a better future includes what you've done to innocent people, I don't know what to say, Jack. But this isn't the way."

"You have no idea what it is to carry the weight of a town, looking to your family through generations, depending on you. We were given a new chance, and along the way Janus helped us sustain that. Wealth. Power. The chance to make this town into something more than just a backwoods dump. But none of that comes without a price. No harvest without the death of the seed. No bread without the mill."

He turned back to Casey, his voice growing sharper, heavier.

"Our family owes a debt, Benson. A blood debt. One that's been passed down for generations. Millie . . . she was always going to be part of it. The first girl born into the Thompson line in two generations. The debt was hers to pay."

Casey's stomach twisted, his voice rising. "She's your granddaughter, Jack. *Your granddaughter.* And you let them do this to her?"

Jack's face tightened, a flicker of pain crossing his features. "Do you think I wanted this? Do you think I don't lie awake at night seeing her face? Hearing her laugh? But this . . . this was bigger than her. Bigger than me. Bigger than all of us. And it has to be finished tonight."

"What are you talking about?"

"It's Joe's turn now," said Jack.

Casey felt a flare of panic seize his chest. "Where is he? Where's Millie?"

Jack paused, his knuckles whitening as he clenched the kernel. "Joe . . . he couldn't do it at first. He was too weak to take her blood. And Janus—they don't wait. They don't care about your doubts or your hesitations. It was time. Our family's debt was due, and there's no walking away from that."

Casey shook his head, his voice trembling with rage. "You had a choice, Jack. Don't stand there and pretend you're some victim."

"This seed doesn't get to choose its fate, Benson. Millie's blood . . . it was part of the cycle. The cost of what we've built. And if I hadn't done it, Janus would have taken her anyway. At least this way it's kept within the family."

That was when Jack pulled a gun from behind his back. A Ruger revolver trained on Casey's head from five feet away.

The storm outside howled, the snow lashing against the window as the two men stared each other down. Jack's face was a mask of resolve, but the cracks were there—regret and grief etched into every line. Casey's heart pounded in his chest, his breath coming fast, but he held his ground.

Then, a radio squelched. Casey reacted out of reflex, clasping for the spot on his shoulder where his police radio would have been. Jack reached backward to the desk and picked up a walkie talkie, keeping the gun locked on Casey.

"What is it?"

"We've got some visitors."

Through the thin static of the radio, Casey recognized the voice he'd come to loathe. It was Crawley.

"You've been protecting that creep all along too," Casey yelled. "You're pathetic, Jack."

A sharp blast thundered in the office.

Jack fired the gun to the right of Casey's head. He flinched, arms and legs shaking, ears ringing.

"I've got one too," Jack responded.

"Group of kids came down the elevator."

Kids. It had to be Liv and the others. Dread pooled in his stomach.

Jack frowned. "Dispose of them however you see fit."

Casey was done hesitating.

Indignant rage impelled him toward Jack, tackling him as the Ruger went off again. Sparks flew from the ceiling light it struck, showering down glass shards.

Jack growled and grabbed Casey's face, shoving him off with unhinged ferocity. Casey rolled over, grabbed a shard of the glass as Jack scrambled for the pistol. Casey stabbed down on Jack's hand, feeling the scrape on bone. Jack's enraged scream filled the room in harmony with the howl of the storm outside. His other fist met Casey's jaw with blinding force, white flashing in Casey's vision.

He was dazed as he saw Jack getting up and kicked at Jack's knee. He stumbled, dropping the gun. This time Casey was the one scrambling after it, and he grabbed hold of the gun, turned to train it on Jack.

But he was gone, the door to the stairwell swinging.

Casey picked up the radio that Jack had dropped and it squelched again, Crawley's voice on the other end.

"Silo 3."

Casey's gut sank, but he didn't hesitate. There wasn't time.

3

A crackle of static answered before a voice came through, gravelly and familiar.

"Dispose of them however you see fit," Jack Thompson said.

"Take them up," Crawley snapped.

The kids were herded down the hallway, their attempts to resist met with rough shoves. Crawley said something about a silo on the radio. His glowing eyes drilled into Olivia whenever she dared glance back.

They emerged into the tall and open factory floor, automated machine whirring and clanking, some shaking and undulating. It was deafening, until they were shoved into another elevator, the doors shutting out all sound as it ascended.

Olivia could hear the rigid labored breathing of Crawley and the other three men. She wondered who they were or once had been behind those burning red eyes, which she could not bring herself to look directly at. Neither could the others. Eli whimpered, clutching nervously at his dimmed flashlight, and Kyle tried to put a hand on his cousin's shoulder but was rebuked sharply by the fatter of the four red-eyes. Flannel carried a crowbar. The fat one looked like a troll out of some Grimm fairy tale, and the lankier man had a toolbelt, from which a rusty wrench hung.

Austin stood rigid, fists clenched, and Olivia remembered that he had brought his jackknife, which so far had not been taken from him. They exchanged a sidelong glance, quickly broken up by the lurch of the elevator as it reached the top, and the door opened to the whipping icy wind of the storm.

"Out," Crawley said, and to the other men: "Keep them moving."

Olivia saw Crawley stay behind, and click the radio. Trying to reach Jack maybe. But he wasn't answering. Something was wrong . . . and maybe that was good for them.

She tried not to get her hopes as high as they were now above the town—ten stories up and probably one bad move away from being shoved off by their red-eyed captors. Olivia couldn't decide whether splatting down on the concrete or being shoved in the icy waters of the roaring dam to very likely drown would be worse.

One instant and fatal, the other slow and a small chance of survival.

As the men corralled them across a catwalk to the inmost of four towering silos, she got the sudden sick feeling that it would be neither of those options. Something much worse.

A narrow staircase spiraled to its top, the steel glinting faintly in the red light from the PRINCE sign. Olivia kept searching for an opening, a chance to escape, but the men behind them stayed close, their glowing eyes unblinking.

At the top of the silo the wind tore and whipped. Kyle stopped, peering over the edge at the swirling snow below. "So what, you're just gonna throw us off ?" he yelled, voice trembling.

Ethan Crawley appeared behind them, smirking. "Not exactly."

Flannel stepped forward, setting down his crowbar, and grabbed a large metal lever. With a grunt, he pulled it, and a hatch on the silo's top slid open. The faint sound of shifting grain echoed ominously from within. Looking in she could barely see the bottom, the roiling grain far below illuminated by the red emergency light that came on when the hatch was opened.

"Oh no," Eli whispered, realization dawning on his face.

Crawley grabbed Olivia by the arm, yanking her toward the open hatch. She struggled, kicking and twisting, but his grip was iron-tight.

"Let's see how long you last," Crawley said coldly.

Olivia's heart pounded. Inside the silo, the grain churned, a living thing, a slow suffocating tide of golden kernels. She remembered Millie's second hand cautionary tales, and so did Austin and Kyle from the terrified looks on their faces. Eli probably just knew all about the auger waiting below because he was smart, and the fact that the grain below would be sinking sand.

The faint rustling sound was hypnotic, a sinister promise of suffocation.

Without warning Austin shouted, lunging at one of the men. He managed to land a punch before being shoved hard against the railing.

"Stop!" Olivia yelled. "You don't have to do this!"

Crawley ignored her, motioning for the other men to grab the boys. They all struggled, thrashing against their captors, but the men were stronger, dragging them toward the hatch too. Eli had slipped and fallen and managed a hobble-run across the catwalk.

"After him," he said to one of the men, leaving the bigger, fatter one with a hand clamped down on both Kyle's and Austin's arms. The lankier red-eye with the tool belt lumbered after Eli.

Olivia's mind raced. She needed to think of something—anything—to stall them. But before she could form a plan, Crawley leaned in, his glowing eyes mere inches from hers.

"Say goodbye," he whispered.

Olivia felt herself being pulled backward, the wind roaring in her ears.

Then she was falling.

4

Casey crested the top of the emergency ladder just in time to see the limping Lancaster boy being chased by a tall red-eyed man in a gray PRINCE shirt.

He pulled himself upright, slipping on the snow slick surface, and righted himself into a two point firing stance, gripping the Ruger.

"Get down!" he yelled, and fired twice. A strangled yell, and the man crumpled to the side. A gale kicked up just after, blinding white making it difficult to see anything more. Casey stepped in front of Eli.

"Where are the others?"

"The silo! They threw Olivia in!"

Casey's heart flew into his throat, and he turned, only to be met with the blood spattered face of the red-eyed worker he'd shot.

He swung at Casey, connecting with his jaw. Despite the blur of white across his vision he tackled forward. They rolled around to the edge of the roof and he felt the Ruger slip from his grasp. How was he still coming after taking a shot like that? Casey managed to pin him down and land a solid punch. That stunned him just long enough for Casey to lean back around and reach for the gun.

A boot came down hard on the back of his leg. Casey cried out in pain, and looked behind to see the man remove a wrench from his toolbelt and raise it overhead.

"Over here!" Eli yelled.

The worker glanced over as a beam of light met his red eyes, a sizzling hiss and iridescent smoke rising. Eli held his flashlight steady as the worker cried out in a multi-pitched scream, and Casey heard whispering in reverse. He shook himself out of the shock and awe, grabbed the Ruger, and fired up. The man finally slumped to the ground.

"The hell was that?" Casey asked.

"Olivia said it worked on that thing in the woods," Eli replied with a shrug.

"Olivia," Casey breathed, and ran across the catwalk.

He reached the silo platform just as Austin was slammed into the railing by a rotund man with the same red eyes. Casey raised his pistol but there was no clear shot. He saw Kyle yelling down into the silo after Olivia.

"You're all dead!" the fat red-eye growled, his voice low and guttural, running toward him.

Casey ducked a wild swing and delivered a sharp jab to his enormous gut, but he barely flinched. Red light flared in his eyes as he lunged again, catching Casey by the throat and slamming him into the metal platform.

His vision swam as the fat man grunted, more annoyance than pain, as he clasped at his back. Casey tore himself free to see Austin standing nearby, having sunk a small pocket knife into the fat man's shoulder.

His red eyes glowed as he stood to turn on Austin, but Casey summoned a surge of strength and awkwardly rammed his shoulder into the back of his knees, toppling him over.

"Help Olivia!" he yelled. "I'll keep him busy."

Casey drew heaving breaths as Austin nodded and ran over to the silo's opening with Eli.

The fat man was struggling to his feet. That was when he spotted Crawley the next silo over—with a shotgun in his hands.

A blast went off, striking the fat man and sending him reeling on top of a fourth man in flannel who had appeared around the corner wielding a crowbar.

The chaotic flurry made Casey hesitate, but not long. He had to buy them time. He fired a shot half blind in Crawley's direction, and ran for cover.

5

Her leg hit the edge of the open hatch with a crack of sharp pain. The world spun, and for a terrifying second she was weightless.

She was falling through it, the pungent musty smell of grain suffocating her as a sea of kernels closed around her, gripping her legs and dragging her down.

"Help!" Olivia screamed, clawing at the grain, but her arms sank in deeper with every frantic motion.

There was no response, just the din of the auger and the echo of her own screams and of whirring grain.

"Stop moving!" Eli yelled from the top. "You're sinking faster!" Olivia forced herself to still, her chest heaving as the collective weight of kernels pressed against her.

A hand reached out and she latched on. Kyle, hanging from the ladder affixed to the silo wall. Her nails dug into his wrist as he strained to hold her. The grain shifted ominously below, a soft, rumbling groan that sent fresh terror surging through her veins. She felt herself sink another inch.

"Come on!" Kyle yelled, his knuckles white as he gripped her forearm.

Olivia choked out a sob as her boots scraped something solid—the auger blade far below.

"We've got you!" Austin's voice. She glanced up, swallowing and choking on bits of grain and dust, and saw both of them there, Austin on the ladder holding Kyle steady from above.

Her pulse thundered in her ears as the boys hauled her upward, the grain rippling and collapsing where her body had been buried moments before, and she grabbed the ladder.

"Ow," Kyle breathed, shaking out his hand. "That hurt."

Olivia shook her head and coughed. "Thanks."

"Can you climb?" Austin called down.

"I'm gonna have to. Let's go."

Her arms and legs trembled as she collapsed on the snow covered rooftop, gasping for air. She barely had time to catch her breath before the flannel red-eye, lunged at them. He snarled, swinging a crowbar wildly.

"Get back!" Austin screamed, now wielding a loose pipe from the ground and swinging it at the man. It connected with a dull thunk, but he barely flinched.

The red-eye lunged and Kyle stuck out his foot and tripped him up. Olivia dove out of the way. He teetered on the edge of the silo's opening and his glowing eyes widened as he stumbled back and fell into the auger churning grain bin, his weight pulling him under immediately as the crunch of bones snapped above the biting wind.

Olivia winced, heard the others make noises of revulsion, and collapsed to her knees, chest heaving. But relief was short-lived. A shotgun blast tore through the air, buckshot spraying sparks around them.

"Move!" Casey shouted. Olivia saw him taking cover behind an HVAC unit as Crawley fired again.

Olivia hesitated a moment. "What about—"

"Go, I'll deal with him," he yelled.

She grabbed Eli by the arm, dragging him toward the catwalk that spanned the gap between the silo and the mill's rooftop, and the others followed.

The wind tore at them as they crossed, the metal beneath their feet slick with snow and ice.

She looked back and wished she hadn't. Crawley's glowing eyes locked onto hers.

6

Casey gritted his teeth as another shotgun blast ricocheted off the pockmarked HVAC unit.

Crawley was methodical, circling closer, his boots crunching against the snow-covered rooftop.

Casey's mind raced. The Ruger only had two bullets left.

Crawley paused, reloading, his glowing red eyes scanning the rooftop.

"Benson," he called out, his voice eerily calm. "You think you can protect them? You can't even protect yourself."

Casey didn't answer. He steadied his breathing, his eyes fixed on Crawley's head as he rose slightly from cover. Crawley raised his shotgun, aiming for the catwalk where the kids were crossing.

Casey fired.

The bullet hit Crawley in the chest.

But he was still standing, and raised his shotgun again and fired, his body swaying like a puppet on strings.

Casey didn't hesitate.

He fired the Ruger's last bullet.

This time, Crawley's body crumpled, the shotgun falling in front of him. His glowing eyes dimmed as he fell backward, disappearing into the snowy alley five stories below.

Casey lowered the gun, hands shaking.

7

All was silent atop the silo roof, the snow falling thick and fast and not letting up, muting the world in an eerie hush.

The PRINCE sign loomed behind them, two of its letters shattered by buckshot and flickering in odd electrical spurts.

Casey stood at the edge, staring down at Crawley's crumpled body far below on the utility road. Even from this height, he could see the trail of blood pooling around the man's head, his face frozen in that unsettling, maniacal grin.

"SHIT!" Kyle blurted, his voice echoing in the night. "You shot him."

"Glad you noticed," Olivia muttered, her breath visible in the icy air. "But yeah . . . holy shit."

The heat of life and death mingled with the bitter cold. His face throbbed and his knuckles ached from the earlier brawl. He turned away from the edge, trying to steady himself as the muffled shouts of the trapped men below rose through the open silo hatch.

"We need to get down from here," he said, his voice clipped. "Now."

Just as he turned toward the staircase, a deep groan and a hissing scrape like a blade on metal carried over the snowy expanse. Everyone froze.

"What the hell was that?" Olivia whispered, his eyes wide.

They turned toward the sound. Across the river, the old high school. Dark, boarded windows of the gymnasium pulsed with uncanny red light, like a heartbeat in the storm. The streetlights on Main all flickered violently.

"I think we know where Millie is," Austin breathed.

8

The storm raged around them as they descended the silo's staircase.

Each step groaned beneath their weight, the steel trembled with a threat to give way under the combined weight and pressure of the night's chaos.

They went through a door and crossed to the factory floor, alive with the eerie hum of machinery, automated lines creaking and whirring as though oblivious to the carnage that had unfolded. Lights flickered erratically, throwing long shadows that stretched and twisted like specters against the cold concrete walls.

Casey led the way, his hand gripping the railing, his every nerve on edge.

As they reached the final turn, his flashlight caught the body of a man draped across a conveyor belt, his head hanging at an unnatural angle. An innocent man caught up in this and slaughtered mercilessly, probably by Crawley. Jack Thompson and Janus were just as complicit. Blood trailed from his temple, pooling on the metal surface below.

Casey swallowed hard, his mind awash with doubt and guilt. He'd been forced to kill men tonight. Granted they were possessed by that Red glow, but he already stood accused of shooting a fellow officer. What court would ever believe his defense? Crazed mill workers and curses wouldn't exactly hold up under cross-examination.

They reached the ground floor, the dim light casting their faces in stark relief. Casey raised a hand, signaling the kids to hold back.

"Let me check first," he muttered.

He cracked the factory door open, the icy air biting his face as he peered into the night. The storm was relentless, wind howling and whipping snow. Crawley's body lay crumpled on the utility road, a discarded marionette, his face frozen in a grotesque grin.

Main Street was deserted, eerily still except for the storm's fury. Between the power outages and the road conditions, and the call to stay inside for fear of the deranged former Westville cop on the loose, no one was liable to be out and about.

But where were Reynolds, Hart, and DeYoung?

The festive glow of Christmas lights strung along lampposts clashed violently with the scene. Wreaths adorned with cheery red bows swung wildly in the gale, while snow-laden garlands sagged from their anchors.

Casey took a breath and glanced back at the kids, who stood huddled together, their faces pale and taut with fear.

"Come on. We have to get to the station."

A couple hard fought blocks later, they stumbled in, snow swirling in behind them before Casey slammed the heavy glass door shut.

The air inside was heavy and still, carrying none of the usual hum of activity or the soft crackle of police radios. Instead, the only sounds were their labored breathing and the faint whistle of the storm outside.

Casey flicked the light switch near the door. Nothing happened. He muttered a curse under his breath and turned to the kids.

"Stay close," he ordered, pulling his flashlight from his belt and clicking it on.

9

The beam of the flashlight cut through the darkness, illuminating the front desk and rows of filing cabinets.

Papers were scattered across the floor, fluttering slightly in the draft from the storm. Olivia's stomach churned. Something about the quiet felt wrong—too still, too heavy. Her breath came in quick bursts, fogging the air in front of her.

Casey motioned toward the supply room at the back of the station. "Grab anything useful—flashlights, batteries, flares. But stay together."

Olivia nodded, trying to steady her nerves. Austin and Kyle shuffled behind her, their faces pale and uncertain. She could see the tension in Casey's shoulders as he led them deeper into the station, his flashlight sweeping across overturned chairs and the shattered remnants of a coffee mug near the break room door. The air seemed colder here, as if the storm had seeped inside.

When they reached the supply locker, Casey knelt down and pulled it open. He grabbed a box of bullets and began reloading the silver revolver before grabbing another wheel preloaded with bullets, from what she could tell. Olivia noticed his hands trembling slightly, though his expression remained determined. He pulled out extra flashlights, handing them out to Olivia and the boys.

Kyle looked expectantly at an all black pistol Casey had pulled from the locker. "Can I . . .?" he asked, his voice barely above a whisper.

Casey gave him a sharp look. "Can you handle a gun?"

Kyle hesitated. "Dad's taken me to the range a few times. I'm decent."

"Decent at the arcade," Austin muttered under his breath, earning a glare from Kyle.

Casey shook his head, pulling out a bright orange flare gun instead. He handed it to Kyle, who frowned.

"What am I supposed to do with this?"

"In case of emergency," Casey said, his tone leaving no room for argument. He looked at Olivia. "You good?"

Olivia nodded, gripping the flashlight tighter. "What now?"

Before Casey could answer, she glimpsed something glistening near the hallway—a dark smear on the floor, trailing toward the chief's office. Olivia's heart skipped a beat, and before Casey could stop her, she started forward.

"Olivia, wait!" Casey hissed, his voice low but urgent.

She didn't listen. Something pulled her forward—a mix of dread and determination. The blood trail led to a door slightly ajar. She pushed it open, the hinges creaking in protest.

Inside, her flashlight illuminated a horrifying sight. Chief Hart was slumped against the wall, his chest rising and falling in shallow, labored breaths. Blood soaked his uniform, pooling beneath him. A deep cut on his right arm.

His face was ashen, his lips trembling as he struggled to form words.

"Frank!" Casey rushed to his side, kneeling to support him. "What happened?"

Hart's eyes flickered open, unfocused but struggling to find Casey's face. "Travis," he rasped, the word barely audible. "It . . . it was Johnson."

"Travis? He did this to you?"

Hart gave a faint nod, his hand twitching toward Casey's arm. "Not . . .

himself . . . Couldn't stop him . . . " Hart nodded toward Casey. "You were right son . . . I'm sorry."

"Where are Reynolds and DeYoung?"

"Off joining the manhunt . . . with the Sheriff's Office. We thought he was still in Iron Falls . . . but . . . "

"Just hang in there, Frank. We'll get you help."

"Go after him. Don't—let him hurt anyone else . . . "

His head slumped forward. Casey shook him gently, but Chief Hart's breathing had slowed to nearly nothing. Olivia hovered near the edge of the desk, her chest tightening as the stillness in the room pressed against her.

"Is he . . ." she began, her voice trembling.

"No," Casey said, though his tone carried the weight of uncertainty. "But he'll need help—and fast." He leaned over the Chief, examining the blood-soaked makeshift bandage Hart had tied around his wound. Casey's hands, steady but urgent, tried to adjust it.

"I can help," Eli said, stepping forward despite his limp, clutching the edge of the desk for balance. His face was pale, but his eyes were sharp with determination. "We need to stop the bleeding. I learned tourniquets in Scouts."

Olivia blinked at him, unsure if relief or fear for his confidence should win out.

"I need a shirt or something."

Austin yanked off his sweater and removed the t-shirt beneath, thrusting it toward Eli.

Eli dropped to one knee beside Hart, carefully maneuvering the shirt into place. "Lift his arm."

Casey complied, moving the Chief's arm as gently as he could while Eli folded the fabric into a wide strip.

Olivia watched, nerves prickling as Eli worked. He twisted the shirt into a band, looping it securely around Hart's upper arm, just above the injury. He looked around, expression turning desperate. "I need something to twist it with. Anything strong and thin."

Casey rummaged in a nearby desk and produced a screwdriver. "This work?"

Eli nodded.

He slipped the screwdriver through the fabric loop, twisted it until the shirt tightened. Hart groaned faintly, a low sound that made Olivia wince.

"Almost there," Eli said, his voice strained as he tied it off to hold it in place. He leaned back, inspecting his work. "That should slow the bleeding. Now, he just needs to stay warm."

"First aid badge eluded me," Kyle muttered. "Nice work."

Eli shot him a nervous, sheepish grin, the first time his expression had shown any sign of light since they descended the elevator at the mill.

Casey opened the gun safe in the chief's office, producing an all black shotgun. "We have to go," Casey said, standing and glancing out the window toward the high school. His voice was grim, resolute. "You all stay here."

"I'm coming," Olivia said before he could argue.

"Me too," Austin added, stepping up beside her.

"Wait—you expect us to stay here by ourselves?" Kyle asked, his voice rising in disbelief. He gestured at the unconscious Chief and the lingering scent of blood.

"In case of emergency," Casey said, gesturing to the bright orange flare gun resting on the table.

Kyle grimaced but didn't argue further.

Casey, Olivia, and Austin moved quickly toward the exit, the cold seeping into Olivia's bones as the storm outside howled in renewed fury. The cruiser sat parked out front, its roof already blanketed in a thick layer of snow. As they piled in, Casey scanned the surrounding area, his senses on high alert. Olivia watched him grip the wheel, his knuckles white, his gaze sharp.

Casey slammed the car into gear. The tires skidded briefly before catching traction, and they roared down the desolate street, snow spraying in every direction. Olivia gripped the door handle, her heart pounding as the cruiser skidded around a corner, he glanced back at her and their eyes met. They both knew.

It was time to end this.

10

Punching into the old high school parking lot by the river, the headlights of the cruiser illuminated the round brake lights of Aly's Beetle parked by the brick of the gymnasium exterior and further, near Joe's pick-up and a frost-laden array of demolition equipment and yellow construction vehicles.

Casey slammed on the brakes, opened the door, and jumped out. The kids followed suit.

"You two stay put," he said, stepping toward the double entry doors.

"What if you need backup?" Austin asked.

"Let's hope I won't."

Olivia stepped forward as if to argue or assert herself. Instead, she said, "We'll be here. Just find them."

Casey nodded and walked inside, flashlight in one hand and Ruger in the other. He hated the man who owned the gun, but the revolver felt better in his hand.

The hallway was dark, only a dim, erratically flickering series of emergency lights and the red exit signs at either end. A version of *'Silent Night'* echoed from the crackling thin old PA system as glass, drywall, and random debris crunched beneath his boots. He came to the middle of the hall and turned left into the gymnasium doors.

Casey shined his flashlight on piles of bones laid across tarps. Skeletons picked apart. The skulls all notably missing. There were animal bones too— deer, he thought. There was a musty stench and the iron tang of old blood.

Then he saw the gaping hole in the gymnasium floor. It could have been part of the demolition, but it looked oddly haphazard and out of place. He walked further in, guiding his flashlight over it. Inside was another body, emaciated and brown with decay but intact, arms tied and a cloth wrapped around the mouth.

A rustling prompted Casey to jolt and look up.

Joe stood there facing him, his right hand stained with blood, his brow, low and flat, staring into nothing but at the same time right at Casey, or right through him.

"Joe," Casey breathed. "What is this?"

He stood there, silent, unmoving, and the closer Casey stepped he saw the darkness beneath his friend's eyes, and something else in them. A glint of red.

Casey glanced left and saw Millie laying there in a nightgown, her arm and hand bleeding.

"What the hell did you do?" Casey yelled. He moved for Millie. That was when Joe raised his head, a sibilant head splitting hiss made Casey double over.

"This can't be stopped." It was Joe's voice but another one too. Deeper, wrathful.

Casey righted himself, the initial brunt of the sound ebbing. "It ends tonight," Casey said.

Joe glanced at the gun in Casey's hand. "Are you going to shoot me? Your best friend?"

"I don't want to hurt you, Joe. But I'm getting Millie out of here."

Joe snorted. Then laughed, bellowing which turned into a scream that sent a chill running down Casey's spine, his eyes wide and full of rage.

Casey ran toward Millie, and Joe walked forward in slow deliberate strides. He stopped and trained his gun on Joe.

"Don't make me do this," Casey whispered.

Joe didn't respond. He kept moving toward him, wielding a jagged edged ivory knife. The same one Crawley had that night. He was sure of it.

"Drop it!" Casey yelled, his throat tight, desperate to do anything but shoot his friend.

His finger flicked to the trigger.

Before he pulled, Joe seized, clasped at his neck, and stumbled.

Casey saw the figure behind him.

Aly stood, syringe in hand as Joe tumbled down to the ground.

"You can't . . . stop this . . ." Joe hissed. "No one can."

His eyes closed.

Casey swore and ran to Aly, who was trembling. "What happened?"

"I don't know," she said, shaking her head. "I was supposed to meet Erin today and when she didn't show I thought I should check on her. Found her at the house. Millie and Joe, nowhere to be found. The power was out, and the phone line was cut, so I was driving to the station for help when I saw Joe's truck."

Casey knelt down to Millie, checked her breathing and pulse. "Help me get her up."

He pulled Millie to her feet, Aly taking her beneath her other arm. Something hung around her neck. Before Casey could inspect it Millie groaned, her eyes fluttering open, and mumbled something.

A blood red glow slowly filled the room. Casey turned and saw the source. From the hole in the middle of the room, a red glowing orb arose, its crimson, mirror sheen bending and blurring the air around it. It hovered there, the static hiss returning, and he winced against it. He felt Millie tense too, and she whispered something.

"Ska . . . dega . . . mutc . . ."

The orb started to shift and shimmer, the piercing sound of the hiss growing louder. It shot across the room in an eye-blink, straight into the effigy of bone and rotting hide.

There was a silence heavier than lead, until red light shimmered throughout the figure, and it jutted and jerked into motion, raising itself up onto two skeletal legs crawling with bits of red and black sinew. Long claws of bone protruded from crooked arms, a surreal array of skulls and antlers, and scarlet emanations in empty eye sockets.

Then came the screech.

11

Olivia pressed her hands to the icy window of the cruiser, her breath fogging the glass as she strained to see through the swirling snow. There was a screaming howl—and it wasn't the wind.

"What was that?" Olivia asked.

Austin shook his head. "Don't know," he muttered, bouncing his knee anxiously. "But what's taking so long?"

Olivia clenched her fists, the unease in her chest growing heavier with each passing second. The storm howled around them near the empty side street, dead Christmas lights from the outage swinging wildly in the wind.

Then she saw movement at the entrance.

"There!" she yelled, shoving the door open and stepping into the storm.

Aly ran forward, Casey behind her carrying a limp body. Millie's gown was smeared with blood, her face ashen, but her chest rose and fell in shallow breaths.

"What happened?" Olivia asked frantically.

Aly tried to respond, but before she could, the air split with a deafening crack. The front doors of the high school exploded outward in a hail of glass and twisted metal.

Olivia froze.

The creature that emerged was nothing she'd ever imagined. Towering above the snow, its jagged claws scraped against the ground as it moved. A monstrous amalgam of bone and skin, crowned with a deer skull and flanked by human ones, every socket blazing red with hot embers, emitting a shriek that tore through the night—a sound of grief and rage, and of that unending hunger.

"Skadegamutc," Austin whispered, stumbling backward.

12

Casey shouldn't have known what he was looking at. But he did.

It was what had been haunting Westville—the source of everything.

He raised the Ruger in a two-handed stance, his heart thundering as fast as the hammer mechanism. He emptied the cylinder.

If any bullets hit their mark, the creature didn't show it, apart from swirls of iridescent air mingling with the snow, like the sheen of oil in water. He thought of the red doors.

This thing was 'in-between' reality and something else. He wouldn't be able to hurt it. But from what he'd seen it do to the building, it sure as hell seemed to be able to hurt him.

He discarded the useless pistol.

It tore toward him, its long, contorted limbs crossing the parking lot in monstrous strides. Casey turned for a split second to see the kids and Aly scrambling toward the road. They were clear.

Good.

"Here!" he shouted, waving his empty pistol in the air. "Come on, you ugly bastard!"

The Skadegamutc's glowing eyes locked onto him, and Casey darted to the side as its claws swiped down, shattering the pavement with a sickening crunch.

The force of the blow nearly knocked him off balance, but he righted himself and sprinted toward the river. He slipped on the icy pavement, catching himself just in time. The creature was gaining with every stride, its unnatural limbs propelling it forward. Casey's chest burned, his breaths coming in ragged gasps as he pushed toward the boat launch.

If he could get it onto the ice, maybe—just maybe—he'd be able to stop it or slow it down.

The dock came into view, the aluminum glinting. Casey sprinted onto it, the structure creaking under his weight. He turned, ready to face the monster again.

But it wasn't there. His heart stopped as he scanned the parking lot, the thing's glowing eyes no longer visible. There was only a strange oil-like afterimage swirling in the air.

Then a diesel engine growled to life to his right as bright headlights pierced the snow. He raised his arm over his eyes just in time to see the winter dark silhouette of a bulldozer roaring toward him.

13

Olivia had only driven a car twice in her whole life. Neither of those times had it been a police cruiser, during a blizzard, or while being chased by some undead monster.

First time for everything.

She slipped all over the street, much to the protest of the others in the back, her sister cradling Millie's head and Austin holding her friend's legs awkwardly in place so she wouldn't go flying.

They careened over the curb and into the station parking lot.

"We have to get her inside!" Aly yelled.

Austin opened his door, and together they pulled Millie's limp and pale frame out of the backseat. There wasn't time to think. She wouldn't lose her now. Not after everything.

They made their way to the station garage door over treacherous icy cement.

The screech came sudden and shrill, and Olivia's heart leapt into her throat.

She turned and saw it there behind them, too many eye sockets burning red in the night, the cruel crown of twisted antlers basking in the glow. Its arms raised, claws reaching into the frigid dark.

"Go!" Olivia screamed, some madness impelling her to step toward the thing.

Kyle stepped up next to her out of nowhere, raised the bright orange flare gun as he winced, and fired off a blinding bright projectile.

It struck true, and the creature writhed and screamed with what sounded like a hundred human screams at once, all agony and rage echoing in the cold silence. The sparking fire of the flare spread for a moment across its torso, until with all the suddenness with which it had appeared, the creature flashed from view right before their eyes, leaving behind only a glistening iridescence.

"Emergency," Kyle breathed.

"That worked," Olivia said, matter of fact, out of breath, and shaking all over.

Aly came up from behind them and pulled Olivia inside.

Ahead, Austin and Eli had Millie over their shoulders. They got her settled inside on a holding cell bed.

Aly knelt, examining the fresh cut on her arm. It bled, and Aly started wrapping a bandage around it to stave it off. Millie was pale, quavering, and her head was darting back and forth, her eyes closed but lids fluttering. Around her neck was the gold chain. The watch.

Olivia pulled and grabbed it, stained with dark old blood—and some newer. She held it in her hands and felt a thrum through her, saw the air blur around it with an iridescent sheen.

The converged object. She had been right. "And time," she recited, the line from the journal. "Always time."

"It's like she's having a nightmare," Austin breathed.

"I'm going after Casey," Aly said. "You stay here with Millie. Keep every-one safe."

"But—"

"Please, Liv. She needs you."

Olivia looked back at Millie and knew Aly was right.

"Be careful."

Aly nodded. Kyle caught her as she ran out and offered her the flare gun. "It worked before. Maybe burning it would work again."

Aly nodded, and gestured to the gun. "Only one shot. You keep it."

She went to the storage locker across the hall and grabbed a fresh one along with a couple road flares.

Olivia moved over to Millie, her movements more erratic now, sweat bead-ing on her brow and fast whispering murmurs coming from her lips.

Olivia could only make out one word:

Seethe.

14

Snow swirled violently across the riverbank, each flake a jagged shard against Casey's skin as he sprinted toward the Slate River. Behind him, the roar of the bulldozer's engine tore through the night, a guttural growl that refused to be drowned out by the storm.

Casey glanced over his shoulder, his eyes widening as the headlights of the massive machine lit up the swirling snow. Travis Johnson sat in the cab, his red-glowing eyes burning with an unnatural fury, his hands gripping the con-trols with inhuman determination.

"Come on," Casey muttered, his boots skidding on the icy path leading to the frozen river. He had to make it. There was no way he could outrun the bull-dozer forever.

The river's surface stretched out before him, a deceptive expanse of smooth, snow-dusted ice. He hesitated for a split second. It wasn't safe. But neither was staying here.

The blade tore through the snow behind him, throwing up chunks of ice and dirt. Casey made his decision.

He darted onto the frozen river, the ice groaning beneath his boots with each step. The bulldozer followed, its massive treads crunching onto the edge of the ice. The weight of the machine sent cracks spider webbing outward, but Travis didn't stop. He pressed forward, the engine's growl growing louder as the bulldozer picked up speed.

Casey ran faster, his boots slipping as the ice trembled under the weight of the machine. His heart thundered in his chest.

A deafening crack split the air, echoing across the river.

Casey risked a glance back and saw the ice buckling beneath the bulldozer's front treads. The massive machine lurched, its weight driving it downward. Travis didn't react. His glowing eyes remained fixed on Casey as the bulldozer tilted forward, its blade slamming into the ice.

With a final, earsplitting groan, the ice gave way. The bulldozer plunged into the freezing water, the engine sputtering and choking as it disappeared beneath the surface.

Casey staggered back, his chest heaving. The cold bit into his lungs, but he forced himself to keep moving, his boots crunching through the snow as he made his way back to the parking lot.

As he neared the road, a hand clamped onto his shoulder, yanking him backward. Casey twisted, his fist flying instinctively, but it was caught mid-swing. Travis stood before him, water dripping from his soaked clothes, body quavering and steam rising, his eyes blazing brighter than ever.

"You can't kill me," Travis growled, his voice a guttural rasp that seemed to echo from somewhere far away, in whispers and screams, his crimson eyes searing into Casey's. "You see Red . . . Red sees you."

Travis shoved him forward. Casey stumbled, his knees hitting the frozen ground. And when he looked up, a towering form loomed above him.

The Skadegamutc's grotesque body seemed to pulse with life, the red glow emanating from its many eyes, casting monstrous shadows across the snow. Its claws glistened in the light, each one as long as a man's arm.

Casey braced himself, his fists clenching as he prepared for the inevitable strike. But the creature didn't move toward him. Instead, it turned its baleful evil leer on Travis.

"No!" Travis shouted, his voice cracking with desperation. "I did what you wanted!"

One of its six-pointed claws drilled straight through Travis's chest without ceremony.

Any scream he made was short-lived, cut off as the creature began to draw the crimson light from him. Casey watched in horrified fascination as the glow faded from Travis's eyes, his body withering in a swirl of the oil-iridescence until nothing remained but a shriveled husk.

The Skadegamutc dropped him, the brittle remains crumbling into the snow, as fresh oily tendrils of black and red sinew wreathed themselves over the bony limbs of the creature.

Casey staggered to his feet, his heart pounding as the Skadegamutc turned its attention back to him. Its many glowing eyes locked onto him, and it began to move, its claws scraping against the ground.

The roar of an engine shattered the tension.

Casey barely had time to dive out of the way as the cruiser careened into the monstrosity, its massive form slamming into a snowbank and a pile of rubble from the nearby building. The impact sent a shower of snow and debris into the air, burying it.

Casey scrambled to his feet, turning to see Aly behind the wheel of the cruiser, her knuckles white as she gripped the steering wheel.

"Get in!" Aly shouted, throwing the passenger door open.

Casey didn't need to be told twice. He climbed into the back seat, grabbing the shotgun from the floor. "Go!"

The cruiser sped off, skidding onto the icy street.

15

"What's wrong with her?" Olivia shouted, looking to Eli as Millie continued to thrash and writhe, yelling things that they couldn't understand.

"I—I don't know . . ." Eli gulped. "The bleeding from her arm has been stopped, but maybe she's been injected with something or had some sort of infection."

The poor boy was crying.

She leaned in toward Millie and grabbed a hold of her shoulders. Millie growled when she did, and her eyes flashed open, her teeth gritting as they revealed red.

Olivia's chest clenched, and her stomach felt sick. She heard the whispers. The static hiss.

Then she realized.

"She's connected to it."

"Connected to what?" Austin asked, shivering next to her and shirtless, his sweater and shirt caked with Millie's blood.

"The Skadegamutc. The watch. All of it." Olivia swallowed and leaned in closer to her friend. "Mil, it's me. It's Liv."

Millie snarled, her head jerking side to side.

"You don't—" Olivia drew a deep breath. "You don't have to live in this nightmare anymore. You can fight it."

But could Casey and her sister fight that thing?

Millie's body convulsed again, her back arching off the cot as though an invisible force was trying to tear her apart.

Olivia gripped her shoulders tighter, her knuckles whitening. The faint static hiss that had been haunting them grew louder, the sound filling the room with an electric charge that made the hairs on the back of her neck stand on end.

Austin, pale but resolute, stepped closer. He glanced at the glowing watch on the desk then at Millie. "It's the pact. Blood bound their family to the Skadegamutc. If we break that connection—"

"How?" Olivia snapped, the roar of the static nearly drowning her out.

Millie's eyes flew open, crimson light pouring out in streaks that painted the room in eerie red. Her lips parted, but when she spoke, the voice was not her own. It came in overlapping tones—childlike, mournful, wrathful—a chorus of souls entangled in torment.

"Blood binds the guilty . . . Blood makes us *Seethe* . . ."

The air grew heavier, a weight pressing down on her chest.

Millie's eyes latched onto the pocket watch. Her hand shot out with unnatural speed, fingers curling around the tarnished metal. Olivia tried to pull it away from her but it was no use. Millie gripped the edges of the metal timepiece so hard Olivia saw her knuckles whiten and shake, as fresh blood dripped down its surface from the reopened slice on Millie's hand.

Then the watch began to vibrate rapidly, a shatter of glinting air around it like a mirror shattered in the sun, pulsing in rhythm with hissing static.

"Millie, stop!" Olivia cried.

Millie's scream cut through the air, a jagged blade. It wasn't just sound but a wave of force, tearing and ripping.

Olivia and the others stumbled backward, clutching at their ears as the already sparse and faint station backup power flickered. Lights sizzled and exploded, plunging them into chaos, tiny pieces raining down.

The pressure in the room spiked, as though reality itself was tearing at the seams. Across the hall and in the lobby, windows shattered outward in violent bursts, shards of glass cascading into the snowstorm outside.

"Millie!" Olivia yelled over the deafening roar. She lunged forward, grabbing her friend's hand despite the searing heat radiating from the watch. "I'm here! You're not doing this alone!"

The crimson glow in Millie's eyes intensified, bright enough to burn. Her voice deepened, layered with anguish and fury, reverberating through the walls. The air blurred, like warping heat haze in the dead of summer. The sound of the static reached an unbearable crescendo, and then—silence.

The watch was gone—vanished—and only traces of shimmering, iridescent air remained, swirling and dissipating.

For a long moment, the only sound was Olivia's ragged breathing. The pressure lifted, leaving the room eerily still. Millie collapsed back onto the cot, her chest rising and falling in shallow breaths. The glow in her eyes faded, replaced by exhaustion and pain. Her fingers loosened their grip on the watch, letting it fall to the floor with a heavy clink.

Olivia leaned in close, brushing sweat-dampened hair from Millie's face. "Mil . . . are you okay?"

Millie's voice was barely a whisper, and she couldn't make it out.

Eli, who had been pressed against the far wall, straightened shakily.

Millie turned her head slightly, eyes tired and pale blue.

"It—can't hide anymore."

Austin's face paled, his voice trembling. "Does that mean we can . . .?"

Eli's eyes widened as the realization clicked. "That's it—it could be vulnerable now! No more half-existence. It's here, in our reality, bound by its laws."

Austin nodded slowly, his voice steadier now. "It can be killed. Just like anything else."

"With fire," Kyle said.

Olivia felt a rush of adrenaline course through, and she radioed the cruiser.

16

For a moment, Casey dared to hope they'd left the creature behind.

The snowbank exploded outward, and the Skadegamutc emerged, its macabre form rising into the night.

"Drive faster!" Casey yelled, racking shells into the shotgun.

Aly swerved around a corner, the tires barely gripping the icy road. The creature was gaining on them, its glowing eyes piercing through the storm.

Casey rolled down the window, bracing the shotgun against his shoulder as he took aim. The first shot rang out, the recoil slamming into his shoulder. It barely slowed the creature down.

Aly's knuckles were bone-white on the steering wheel as the cruiser fishtailed down Main Street, headlights slicing through the storm. Casey sat beside her, his shotgun resting in his lap, reloading with trembling hands. His ribs screamed in protest every time the vehicle jolted.

"Keep it steady!" Casey shouted over the roar of the engine and the howling wind.

"I'm trying!" Aly snapped, jerking the wheel to avoid a drift of snow that had overtaken the street.

Behind them, the shadow of the Skadegamutc loomed, its towering form barely visible through the swirling flakes. A red glow pulsed in its eye sockets, illuminating the crooked antlers jutting from its grotesque head.

The creature's guttural screech cut through the storm, rattling the windows of the cruiser. It moved with terrifying speed, its claws tearing through snowbanks as it gained on them. Casey twisted in his seat, bracing the shotgun against the doorframe. He aimed and fired. The blast lit up the storm for an instant, the buckshot cracking into one of the skulls near its head.

"You hit it?" Aly asked, her voice tight with fear.

"Yeah," Casey said, reloading. "But it's still coming."

The cruiser barreled down Main Street, the Christmas lights strung between lampposts casting fleeting patches of warmth against the icy darkness, all of which were pulsing wildly between dim and blinding, as if a constant unstable power surge was flowing everywhere.

The street ahead was empty, eerily quiet save for the howling wind and the cruiser's engine. Casey glanced backward and out each side of the vehicle, their macabre pursuer nowhere to be seen.

"Where is it?" Aly asked, voice trembling as they pulled into the parking lot of Fischer's.

Casey tightened his grip on the shotgun, his eyes scanning the darkness. They got out of the cruiser slowly, the cold night air and blur of snow less of a covering and more like any given flake might materialize into skin, bone, and claw.

The radio squelched, and Casey reached inside and grabbed it, thinking that finally some backup might be on the way.

"You guys hear me?" Olivia's voice.

"We're here."

"It's fire. You can hurt it now. But it needs to be burned!"

A deafening screech cut through the night, and their eyes were both drawn up to the gleaming white steeple above the brick of the United Methodist Church, one long arm and its six claws wrapped around and scraping into the structure like a knife into bone. Its scarlet stare froze Casey with terror, until he managed to snap out of it and push Aly away and toward the restaurant entrance.

"Inside!" Casey yelled.

He raised the shotgun as the creature leapt down from the steeple, skidding chaotically down the slant of the roof in a scrape of shingles and snow, landing with a crash on the parking lot surface. It darted with terrifying speed across the road.

Casey squeezed off two shots before spinning and running through the restaurant door. He slammed it shut, pressing himself against it, only to be flung backward as an arm and claw reached. Casey scrambled back upright. It was too big to get in and reach them, but its other arm broke through the glass clasping and stabbed at the ground.

Aly pulled on Casey's arm, near hyperventilation as she breathed and swore.

It pulled its arms away, out of the door and back through the shattered glass of the window. They heard it moving around, looking for a way in.

"How about that idea?" Casey said.

Aly swallowed, pulling out two road flares, and relayed how Kyle had fended it off earlier with the flare gun.

Aly headed for the kitchen and spurred into motion, turning on the stovetops. They clicked and hissed as the alarming smell of leaking propane filled the restaurant.

A harsh crack and creak from above them. The rooftop groaned wherever the creature stepped.

Multi-colored Christmas lights that hung from the awning flickered and went dark. The ceiling collapsed, a heap of gray skin and jagged bones breaking through, the angular skull and its maw snapping, the array of antlers breaking the glass display cases of clowns.

Casey raised his shotgun but hesitated. The gas was filling the room all the more.

Casey grabbed Aly's arm. "Get out the back, get as far away as you can."

"I'm not leaving you here."

"And I'm not letting you get killed."

The Skadegamutc broke through the glass door of the restaurant, shards scattering across the tiled floor like jagged stars. Its shadow loomed immense and unnatural against the backdrop of the snowstorm outside, twisting as though it contained a dozen writhing figures. The thing's claws scraped against the walls, leaving deep gouges in the wood paneling, and its buck skull split in a toothy grin that seemed curved and stretched wrongly. Casey barely had time to raise his shotgun before it lunged.

The blast of the shotgun reverberated through the air, but the buckshot seemed to slow the creature for only a moment. It howled—a sound that reverberated in the chest and churned the stomach. A claw lashed out, striking the shotgun from Casey's hands and sending it clattering across the floor.

Before he could react, its claws were on him, pinning him against the wall. Pain lanced through his shoulder—the same shoulder that had been stabbed by Crawley—as the talons pierced his jacket and bit into flesh, warm blood soaking the fabric. Looking into the deer skull with its unnatural dead grin and those leering red sockets he sensed it reveling in satisfaction.

It knew, somehow. And he heard it then . . .

The guilty one . . . You are the guilty one . . .

"Get out of my head!" Casey yelled and struggled, his legs kicking against the air as he tried to gain some leverage, but the creature was unyielding. Its other hand reached for him, bony fingers curling as though to crush his skull, when Aly's voice broke through the din.

"Let him go, you bastard!" Aly stepped forward, gripping a length of broken chair leg like a club. Her face was pale, but her eyes were blazing with determination. She swung the makeshift weapon with all her strength, aiming for the creature's head.

It reacted instantly, the free arm swiping through the air, striking Aly with a force that sent her flying backward into a row of booths. She crumpled to the floor with a gasp of pain, the chair leg rolling out of her hand.

"Aly!" Casey shouted, his voice raw with panic.

He thrashed harder against the creature's grip. The Skadegamutc turned back to him, its hollow eye sockets glowing with a sickly, burning red light. Its grip tightened, and Casey could feel his breath being crushed out of him.

Then, from the shadows near the kitchen, a figure emerged.

Joe Thompson stepped into the light, his face pale but his expression set with grim resolve. His eyes flickered with the same red glow that filled the Skadegamutc's sockets, but it was different somehow—fighting against the light instead of succumbing to it. A strange, crackling red aura surrounded him, misty tendrils curling from his skin. In his right hand, he clutched the ritual bone knife, its ivory blade glinting in the red light and the sparking electrical in the ceiling through torn out tiles.

"Let him go," Joe growled, his voice rough and layered with an unnatural echo.

The Skadegamutc hesitated, its head tilting as though it recognized him. Joe didn't wait for it to react further. With a roar that was both human and something else entirely, he stabbed the knife down in a brutal and swift two-handed arc.

The blade connected with the creature's arm, and Joe twisted and tore with his weight, separating it at the elbow with a wet, sickening crunch. It screeched, a piercing, inhuman sound, and its severed arm fell to the floor in a heap of blackened, writhing sinew.

Casey dropped to the floor, gasping for air and clutching his bleeding shoulder. Joe stepped over him, standing between Casey and the creature. The nine-foot frame of skin and bones reeled, clutching its stump, but its hollow leer fixed on Joe with renewed fury.

"Casey," Joe said without turning around. His voice was calm and detached, despite the chaos. "Take Aly and go. Get out of here."

"Joe, I can't—" Casey began, but Joe cut him off, his tone brooking no argument.

"Take care of my Millie girl." Joe's searing eyes met Casey's for a moment, and in that instant, Casey saw everything. The guilt that Joe carried for what he'd allowed to happen. The love he felt for his daughter. The knowledge that this was the only way he could make amends. There would be no coming back for Joe.

Casey tried to rise, tried to argue, but Joe turned and shoved him with supernatural strength. The force sent Casey sprawling across the floor toward Aly, who was beginning to stir. Before Casey could get up, Joe snatched the road flare from Aly's fallen bag and turned back to face them.

"Go!" Joe shouted, his voice filled with authority and something else—a primal, otherworldly power that left no room for hesitation.

Casey scrambled to his feet, grabbing Aly under the arms and dragging her toward the back exit. He cast one last glance over his shoulder as Joe rapped the flare against his thigh, igniting it in a blaze of bright, red-orange light.

The last thing Casey saw before he shoved the door open was Joe, the flare blazing in one hand and the bone knife in the other. A screeching howl followed them into the night.

The explosion came seconds later.

The force of it knocked Casey and Aly off their feet, the heat of the blast rolling over them even in the frigid air.

Casey shielded Aly with his body as debris rained down around them, the snowstorm turning into a swirling maelstrom of ash and embers. He turned his head to look back at the restaurant, now a towering inferno. Flames licked at the night sky, casting flickering shadows across the snow-covered ground.

Out of the flames stumbled a figure. Its skeletal frame, wreathed in fire, staggered forward. Its movements were jerky and uncoordinated, its once-formidable presence now reduced to a shambling husk. Casey rose to his feet, shotgun in hand, the barrel aimed at the orb. His finger tightened on the trigger, and the shotgun roared one final time. As it collapsed to its knees, its burning flesh and bone crumbled into ash and an iridescent mist.

A glowing red orb, pulsating like a heartbeat, rose from the remains of the creature. It hovered in the air for a moment, its light pulsing brighter and brighter as if searching for something, erratically shunting side to side, and shot away into the snow-strewn dark sky.

For a moment, there was silence, broken only by the crackling of the flames. Then, in the distance, the wail of sirens grew louder. Emergency vehicles, county sheriff's cars, and unmarked federal SUVs arrived in a flurry of flashing lights and shouting voices. Reeves and Lochlear stepped out of one of the SUVs, their expressions grim as they surveyed the scene.

Casey stood in the snow, gripping the shotgun, as Aly leaned against him for support. The two locked eyes, a silent understanding passing between them.

As Reeves and Lochlear approached, Casey lowered the shotgun and looked back at the burning remains of the restaurant. Somewhere in the flames was Joe. What remained of him, burning.

"She'll be alright," he whispered to no one. "She will."

All that had happened in the last hours shot through his brain as he watched dying flames doused by firetrucks. Casey held onto the hope that—for once—the nightmare had truly ended.

But when he caught Lochlear's solemn countenance from across the lot, he knew this afterglow wouldn't last nearly long enough.

THE BELIEVERS

1

The stark interview room hummed faintly with the ambient buzz of harsh light and the low drone of HVAC.

Lochlear sat back in his chair, fiddled with his glasses, squinting at the papers on the table with suspicion as if they weren't telling him everything. The unintentional skepticism wreathed in the wrinkles on his brow reminded Casey a little of his father—a rare humanization of Lochlear who had thus far seemed nothing more than an unfeeling, overly fastidious bureaucrat.

Casey leaned forward to break the silence. "Are we done here?"

"Nearly," Lochlear droned. "I'll draw up a few more things for you to sign, and we'll get you on your way. I appreciate your cooperation."

"Wasn't exactly how I planned to spend my New Year's Eve, but sure."

Lochlear stood, taking off his glasses, turning toward the interview room door. "Oh, one more thing," he said.

"Forgot to ask me my favorite color? Childhood snack?"

A rare smirk ghosted across Lochlear's face. "Agent Reeves will be taking up a post in the Westville area for the next several months. She'll be your new contact."

Casey's fist clenched. He wasn't exactly surprised. Given the way the interviews had gone and what Lochlear had outlined, he'd known this was coming, knew the D.C.B. would want to keep a close eye on Westville.

"And what if I don't agree to be your lapdog or at Reeves' beck and call?"

Lochlear flipped back through the swollen file folder he carried, and slapped a thinner but by no means lightweight blue folder back down onto the table.

"Then we'll need to talk about a more official procedure to deal with the deaths of the men at PRINCE Milling. Many of them were shot after all."

Casey's blood drained from his face and channeled heat throughout the rest of him. "You're blackmailing me for defending myself and those kids?"

"The Bureau is prepared to ensure a blanket statement involving a tragic accident at the mill to account for these men. But we need your cooperation."

Coercion was more like it. But what choice did he have?

"Are we clear on that count Benson?" Lochlear asked.

"Crystal."

"Good. With an event of this nature, we need to carefully monitor the area. Often with ley line anomalies of this nature there can be—let's call them aftershocks."

Casey straightened, narrowing his eyes. "What kind of aftershocks?"

Lochlear hesitated, as though weighing what he could share. "Residual energy. Fluctuations. Dimensional entry points that shouldn't exist."

"The Chasm," Casey said, picturing the pipe and the Janus warehouse.

"Heiser's term. But yes."

Casey wiped his hands over his face and swore. "Bastard was right about all of it."

"Unfortunately, he usually is," said Lochlear.

"Is the good doctor is being reinstated?"

"We'll see." Lochlear's expression remained neutral. "Need to know basis."

The door behind Casey next to the one-way glass cracked open.

"In fact I am." Casey shifted to see Heiser waltzing in, wearing a brown sweater vest and slacks. "I appreciate the vote of confidence, Mr. Benson."

Lochlear eyed Heiser. "I wasn't informed you would be listening in."

"Need to know basis, I suppose."

Lochlear sniffed. He looked at Casey. "An agent will be in soon with the paperwork."

He stepped out. Heiser came alongside the table and stretched out his hand. Casey stood and shook it, recalling the first time he'd come to his door. Recalling the impossibility of what he'd said that night.

And yet here Casey stood, having experienced all of it.

"Quite a ride," Heiser said, settling into the seat Lochlear had vacated. His tone was casual, but his sharp eyes betrayed a keen interest in Casey's reaction.

Casey snorted. "Ride's one way to put it. Nightmare's another. You want to fill me in on what Lochlear meant by 'aftershocks'?"

Heiser folded his hands on the table. "I'd say Lochlear's term was . . . optimistic. 'Aftershocks' imply a temporary disturbance, something that will settle in time. That would be preferable for the Bureau, and for everyone. Keeps things quiet. But when a dimensional breach of this scale occurs—especially one involving a Class 3 entity—it's rarely that simple."

Casey frowned. "So, what does it mean? That thing—it's . . . gone, right?"

Heiser tilted his head slightly. "That's a complicated question. What you confronted wasn't any one thing, but something that had been feeding off this town for generations. An amalgam of beliefs, fears, and other things, harnessed by RE-728."

"The Red," Casey breathed.

He steepled his fingers, and nodded. "It anchored itself in Westville."

Casey's jaw tightened. "Through the Thompsons. Whatever pact they made."

"And through everything that followed," Heiser confirmed. "The whispers passed down through generations. Fear spreads. Grief lingers. Rage festers. That's what gave it a foothold."

Casey swallowed hard, picturing the Thompson family pocket watch. All those years, ticking away. A time bomb in the background, behind the shining veneer of PRINCE Milling and Jack Thompson. He felt a stab of pain in his shoulder and saw a flash of red.

And he thought of Joe, and felt a pang of deep sorrow.

"What happened to the watch?"

"As far as we know it's gone. Perhaps lost to the Seethe or elsewhere when Miss Thompson broke the bond. Or at least, that's what we believe may have occurred. But the ritual knife was found in the fire wreckage, and is being contained at a secure location. These types of converged objects are dangerous weapons, powered by belief." He met Casey's gaze. "And belief, Mr. Benson, is a powerful thing."

"Not to be a broken record, but I need to know," said Casey. "Powerful enough to come back?"

Heiser let out a slow breath. "It's possible. When something crosses between planes, it doesn't do so cleanly. It's not a closed system. Think of a tide carrying debris—sometimes it washes back out, and things get left behind." He hesitated. "And sometimes, something else slips through."

Casey shook his head. Every answer he got was a bad one or a complete non-answer. "Reeves and her team. Lochlear said they took control of that site. Shut it down."

Heiser nodded.

"Janus had its hooks in Westville through PRINCE Milling for a long time," Casey said. "Doubt they'd stop now."

"They may not." Heiser's expression turned grim.

The room fell silent for a moment, the distant hum of fluorescent lights and the muffled voices of agents outside the door the only sound.

"Before you go," Heiser said, "I did want to go over the results of your medical evaluation."

Casey tensed. "What about it?"

Heiser exhaled, folding his hands in front of him. "It could be a combination of factors—your past head injury, for one."

Casey frowned, his fingers unconsciously drifting to the faint scar along his scalp.

"But more than that," Heiser continued, "you've spent most of your life in Westville—a town sitting directly atop a ley line confluence, a known 'thin spot'. That length of exposure alone could account for some of it."

Casey narrowed his eyes. "Could account for *what*, exactly?"

"The symptoms of the way your brain processes Seethe resonance."

Casey's stomach turned, thinking of his migraines. Of those strange flashes.

Heiser inclined his head slightly. "Some people go their whole lives standing at the edge of thin spaces and never feel a thing. In fact I expect you'll find many of those who had direct encounters with these trans-dimensional phenomena will remember it like a dream. Maybe starting to forget over time."

"Somehow I doubt that," Casey said, though he'd already seen it. Through the way Olivia seemed to remember her experiences so vividly, while the others could only recall sparse details about what happened in the pipe. He'd seen some of the others' interview transcripts on a break when Lochlear wasn't looking. They knew what they'd been through, but somehow couldn't describe the details of that thing, or what they had seen.

Casey saw it in his head, clear as day.

"Others develop mental ailments," Heiser continued. "They can suffer from various states of delirium."

Casey thought of his mother. Of Francine Meyers. Dementia was its own animal, but was there a connection? He didn't get the chance to ask before Heiser continued:

"Your mind responds somewhat uniquely. It syncs with the Seethe's resonance at times."

Casey let out a short, humorless laugh. "So, what—you're telling me I'm some kind of human lightning rod for all this?"

"Telepathic *sensitivity*," Heiser corrected. "You're not reading minds, Casey. But your brain is wired in such a way that it registers disruptions in the dimensional framework. It picks up on morphic resonance shifts and interprets them in ways most people never could. Just be grateful you're not psycho-kinetically sensitive. Many of our field agents are and use it to their advantage, but it's much harder to control and comes with certain . . . baggage."

Casey didn't have the slightest clue what that vague statement meant, but at this point it was Heiser, and he'd grown accustomed to the man dancing around disclosure.

The door cracked open, and an agent stepped in carrying a thick folder, apprising him of the final documents to review and sign. Casey took the folder, flipping it open. Legal jargon thick as tar—non-disclosure agreements, waivers, acknowledgments of cooperation. Bureaucratic chains meant to keep the whole affair under lock and key.

"Lochlear was right, you know," Heiser said, as Casey began scribbling out signatures.

"What about?"

"Westville needs to believe things can go back to normal. And you need to help facilitate that."

"And if people don't believe it? What if they can't? If I can't?"

"Let's hope we don't have to have that conversation."

As Casey looked back down and continued signing, Heiser stood, adjusting his sweater.

"Well, I'd best be on my way. It's been a pleasure, Mr. Benson. I imagine we'll cross paths again."

Casey looked up, his pen hovering over the last page. "No offense, but I'd rather we didn't."

Heiser chuckled. "All a matter of perspective."

2

When Casey stepped out into the hall, he was led out to reception, the panoramic windows displaying the Chicago skyline and blasting him with gray-white daylight, a cover of cloud sailing over Lake Michigan. He spotted Lochlear down the hall, who gave the slightest of nods. Casey waved goodbye like you would at the end of some awkward encounter with an old high school ex.

That made him think of Aly, and he couldn't help an ironic smirk coming on. Things weren't settled with them—with whatever they were—but after everything they were closer, and they were better. Maybe there'd be something to it after all.

Casey pressed the down button, illuminating pale yellow, and watched the ascending red digital numbers with growing intent. He felt his body tense and looked away.

"Officer," said a familiar, brash voice. Agent Sarah Reeves was walking briskly toward him, catching up down the hall.

"Thought I had at least a day until I heard from you," Casey said.

"Lochlear filled you in. Good. I'll be needing your cooperation moving forward as a liaison to the department."

"Sure," Casey said. "First things first, we need to get our department together."

"How is Chief Hart?" she asked.

"Forced into an overdue retirement."

Reeves frowned, and her face grew pale. "He didn't make it then."

"Bad phrasing," Casey said quickly, catching himself. "He's okay. Just was the push he needed to pass the reins. Reynolds is taking things on for now."

Reeves nodded. A faint smirk crossed her lips as she assessed him with those sharp hazel eyes. "Well, for what it's worth you wouldn't be a bad fit."

"Thanks for the vote of confidence," Casey said, the elevator dinging behind him. Casey stepped through the open doors and turned to press the button for the ground floor only to find it already illuminated.

"Be seeing you then—sooner than you'd like." Reeves turned and strode down the hall at her usual determined clip, copper hair in a tight bun with a gold geometric barrette.

Casey glanced at the yellow glowing 'L' button again.

He thought of that moment in the Janus facility, when he'd felt pulled to the side out of the way of gunfire.

He thought of the term Heiser had used, and he knew.

'PK.'

Psychokinetic.

The elevator shut.

3

Casey had made the drive back to Westville from Chicago too many times to count.

Coming back had always been a strange cocktail of relief mingling with reluctant dread, borne of seeing people he didn't want to or being reminded of the reasons he had wanted out of town in the first place.

Now, he found himself pressing the pedal down harder. He *needed* to get back. Maybe he even wanted to. Any dread he felt was a different creeping kind; the feeling things would happen again and would keep happening.

Aftershocks, Lochlear had called him. He couldn't afford to check out and abandon the town now. Least of all the people in it he cared about most.

When he pulled across the bridge north of town, the rigid metal downspouts and ribbed siloes of PRINCE Milling gleamed in the cold gray light of New Year's Day. A crane stood motionless and abandoned, staged to remove the shattered sign and tend to the damage done.

An official story had been woven, one which Casey had been given a copy of and was encouraged to memorize in order to ensure he made good on navigating the many NDAs he signed when leaving the federal offices. It stated Joe Thompson and two others were killed while trying to attend to a malfunction with one of the silos.

The other men who had been possessed by the Red weren't mentioned in the report, including Ethan Crawley. Jack Thompson's plan—whether under direction of higher ups at Janus Global or not—had worked. Men looking for a new start coming off of troubled addiction-riddled pasts were given new names and encouraged not to interact beyond what was necessary with others in the mill, who would be told they were simply 'laid-off' over the holidays.

As for Jack himself, he was under federal investigation. Lochlear had brought Casey in on the fact that he was willing to give up key information on Janus operatives and collaborators. Temporary immunity for the man who already has it all. Or had it all. Word was they were at their cottage in the Upper Peninsula, and Casey doubted he or Mary would be showing their faces in Westville any-time soon—save for Joe's upcoming memorial.

The explosion at Fischer's was being pitched as purely coincidental and accidental. An electrical fire sparked by Christmas lights serendipitously short-ing out and spreading to the kitchen, grease and propane accelerants for the inferno—on the same night chaos had broken out at the mill.

Casey would have liked to think that people were smart enough to see through all of that but couldn't shake the feeling that maybe Lochlear was right.

"Truth is relative, and people will believe what's most palatable. Until they are presented with irrefutable evidence. It's the Bureau's job to make sure that evidence remains . . . undisclosed."

At least Howard Meyers had been ostensibly cleared of being involved with what happened to Millie. Though Casey was sure that he'd go down in infamy either way. Townies had a way of not letting others forget what happened, as well as what never had, but was so thoroughly rumored it didn't matter.

In fact, as he thought about it, that sounded a whole lot like Heiser's collec-tive belief theory.

Casey turned onto Main Street, cruising West on M-12. The lumber yard, gas stations, and pizza joints he'd passed *ad nauseum*. The same old town with a brand-new set of problems, seen by a few, unseen by the many. Before he turned up the hill for Aly's place, he stopped at the red light and glanced over to the sign on his left on the corner.

'Welcome to Westville, est. 1831'

This town had changed—and so had he.

But he wasn't going anywhere.

A car honked behind him, stirring Casey out of a momentary trance. He pressed the gas and banked right up the hill toward Aly's place.

When he pulled into the drive he felt the tension slowly beginning to uncoil in his gut.

He stepped out of the car and into the bitter air. Before he got to the front door, it opened, and standing there was none other than Liv Fischer. She looked at Casey with knowing green eyes. They'd seen too much together for there not to be an unspoken understanding between them.

"Aly wasn't sure you'd come," she said, matter of fact.

"Never one to miss a party."

Olivia snorted. "Could have fooled me."

"Liv, who is it?" Aly stopped when she got to the door. They hadn't seen each other since Christmas Eve morning, when after getting cleared by the medical teams on site following the explosion at the Cafe, Casey had been ordered to Chicago for immediate debriefing courtesy of Lochlear, and Casey promptly had told him to screw himself before wising up to the fact that he preferred not to be taken into custody by force and in contempt of whatever secret laws they operated under.

"You're back," Aly breathed.

"Yeah. Feds had enough of me I guess."

There was a silent pause between them, Liv glancing back and forth.

"Well, I'm going to leave you two alone. Mil is waiting for me to start the movie."

Casey felt his throat tighten.

"Millie's here?" he asked, as Liv walked back inside.

Aly nodded. "Erin asked if she could stay here a while. With all that's been happening and preparations for the funeral it seemed best."

Casey craned his neck inside, saw the back of Millie's blonde hair as Liv sat back down beside her friend on the couch.

"Has she . . . said anything?"

Aly shook her head. "Nothing new. The doctors checked her out and gave her the all clear. Did a psych eval too."

Something told Casey a shrink wouldn't help. Not after what she'd seen. What they'd all seen.

"You coming in?" asked Aly.

Casey nodded and stepped inside. He walked into the kitchen, greeting Kathy along the way. They talked about the restaurant briefly, and the surprisingly expeditious response of the insurance company. Something Casey had insisted the feds helped speed along using whatever flimsy sway he had in all this.

Then, he turned to see Millie standing there. Beneath her blue eyes hung darkened rungs, her face thin and her sweatshirt billowing over her slight frame.

Casey swallowed the collected burden of the past months, not knowing what to say. There was nothing that would bring any justice to what she endured—even if she blessedly didn't remember much of her ordeal.

"Hey nutcase," she said, voice raspy.

"Keep calling me that," he said, "and I just might start to believe it."

She stepped forward and wrapped her arms around him. She felt paper thin and feather light, but he knew there was so much more under the surface weighing down dark and heavy.

Just like him. But she was here. She was safe.

When Casey let her go and watched her sit back down on the couch next to Millie, he felt the worry, weight, and guilt pull away from him too. If just for a moment, he felt what it was to be free of all that. And he was. Almost.

He turned toward Aly.

"Hey, I'm sorry. There's something I need to do."

"Oh," she said. "Yeah, sure."

"But I'll be back. Promise."

She smiled. The way she did that said to do what he needed to do. He grabbed his coat, but impulse pulled him toward her and he caught Aly by the arm as she turned toward the living room. He kissed her cheek, holding her emerald eyes for just a moment.

Then he headed for the door.

4

Andy and Beth Hopkins still lived in the same house, on the hill of Forest Street.

Casey got out of his car, breathed warm air into his hands, and tried to stop himself from shaking. This had been a long time coming.

He knocked and waited. And when Beth answered the door, visibly confused as to who he must be and what he could possibly be there to sell on New Year's Eve, he said:

"Mrs. Hopkins. My name is Casey Benson. I want to talk to you about your son."

5

Olivia stared into the dying embers of the hearth, their faint orange glow flickering against the remnants of confetti and scattered noisemakers.

Kyle was sprawled on the recliner, one leg dangling off the side, his breathing slow and steady. Austin was curled up in a sleeping bag on the floor near the hearth, his arm draped over his face. Eli had claimed the corner of the couch, his notebook clutched loosely in his hand, his head tilted at an awkward angle and his left, braced leg stiff and straight on the footrest.

A few crumpled Little Debbies wrappers lay among them, adding to the chaotic remnants of their subdued New Year's Eve celebration, including but not limited to the creme de la creme, O.C.P.

Millie, who sat right next to her on the couch with knees pulled up to her chin, hadn't touched hers. It was surreal that she was here. That after everything, she'd made it.

"I'm sorry," Olivia blurted, her voice stark against the quiet crackle of the fireplace in the downstairs living room.

Millie shifted on the couch, glancing at Olivia. Her face was pale but calm, framed by her slightly mussed blonde hair. "You don't have anything to be sorry for."

Olivia turned toward her, her hands gripping the edge of her knees tightly. "That night . . . I should have been with you."

Millie shook her head, her blue eyes soft but firm.

"Mom told me what you did. How you called the house three times or more a day to check if the police had found anything. How you went out into the woods just to look for me. And there's—" Her voice broke. "All the rest."

Olivia swallowed hard, her vision blurring slightly. "I was afraid . . .it was my fault."

352

"It wasn't," Millie said, her voice steady despite the weight of the words. "What happened to me was—" She trailed off.

Olivia felt her chest tighten and Millie's voice trailed off.

She glanced around the room. She didn't know what to say.

Thankfully, Millie didn't remember being taken by her own father that night to the high school. All she knew was what everyone else had heard in the news and by word of mouth—that Joe Thompson was tragically killed in an accident at that mill. Olivia hated that there was a secret between them. Something in the way that she didn't see being rid of anytime soon.

"Is it going to be alright?" Millie finally asked, tinged with doubt.

The truth was too painful. And Millie deserved better than that, after everything. So Olivia stayed silent for a moment, put a hand on her friend's bony shoulder.

"Yeah, it will. Alanis says so."

Millie's lips quirked into a faint smile.

The clock on the mantle read 1:38 a.m., the muted tick of its hands marking the slow crawl toward dawn. Millie stood, her movements languid but deliberate.

"Guess we should try to sleep at some point."

Olivia nodded absently, watching as Millie padded up the stairs, leaving Olivia alone in the dim light of the room. The fatigue clawed at her, but she couldn't move just yet.

The hearth embers flickered weakly, casting shadows across the sleeping faces of her friends. For the first time in weeks, she felt a faint glimmer of peace—not enough to dull the weight entirely, but enough to steady her.

Things weren't the same, but they'd keep going. Keep changing. Together.

Whatever came next.

Olivia stood, her gaze drifting toward the other downstairs bedroom, the door slightly ajar. The room where her dad died.

Her feet carried her toward the door. Olivia paused at the threshold, staring inside. The bed was gone, replaced with neat stacks of boxes and a stray chair. The space felt hollow, an echo of a life that had slipped away. She heard a distant echo of *'Baby I Love Your Way'*, saw a whisper-thin image of her dancing with him that summer night in the now ashen kitchen of the restaurant.

The two words she'd never gotten to say hung heavy at the back of her throat. Words she finally felt ready to say.

"Bye, Dad," she whispered. The words hung in the stillness for a moment. She reached out and gently closed the door, the latch clicking softly.

6

The Fischer household lay silent, blanketed in the hushed weight of winter sleep.

Millie slipped out of her friend's bed, her bare feet sinking into cold snow. She moved past Olivia, who was sprawled on the floor in a sleeping bag dead to the world, snoring.

But Millie couldn't hear her.

All she could hear was the static clawing at her mind and the growing rush of blood in her ears. Beneath it all, faint but growing, came the familiar, terrible groan—the sound of a thousand bones bending, creaking, breaking.

Her movements were mechanical, each step carrying her forward without her consent through the snow-covered hallway. She drifted through the Fischers' living room, and walked toward the wide open front door, moonlight spilling through in the shape of the doorway, frosting the brown and tan wallpaper and wooden baton boards with a surreal glow. She waded through billows of deeper snow as air bit against her skin, seeping to the marrow as she stepped onto the porch.

The night stretched before her, the spiking branches of the trees clawing at the starlit sky. Her breath rose in puffs of vapor, encasing her face in ghostly mist. Millie drew in a slow, shuddering breath, slicing down her throat, feet numbly burning atop the snow-covered concrete.

Then she saw it.

At the edge of the tree line, shimmering, rippling and folding waves, like pavement on a blistering summer day. It pooled and twisted, colors shifting in iridescent hues, mesmerizing and wrong. At its center, a red glow pulsed—a deep, searing crimson, alive and malevolent. The glow seemed to throb in time with the blood pounding in her ears.

Her lips parted as if to speak, but no sound came out. The hissing static swelled, filling her mind until it drowned out everything else.

Millie shot upright in bed, her chest heaving, cold sweat clinging to her skin. The room was dark and still. There was no snow in the house.

For a moment, she could only sit there, frozen, her fingers gripping the blanket as she tried to calm her breathing. The dream clung to her, vivid and oppressive, a shadow that refused to fade in defiance of the dark.

She glanced toward the couch just outside the bedroom. Olivia was sprawled across it, snoring, utterly undisturbed.

A dream, Millie told herself. *Just another nightmare.*

She sat on the edge of the bed, running her hands over her face, her fingers brushing against the scars on her forearms. Her eyes traced thin, pockmarked trails where the needles had pierced her skin again and again.

And there was the thicker, jagged scar. The one that no one would tell her the truth about. They'd tried to hide it, but she knew. Some deep part of her remembered tears streaking her father's face. The tremble in his hands. The crimson sheen in his eyes as he turned away.

A shiver ran through her, and she glanced up sharply when she heard it.

The hissing.

It started low, faint, as if coming from somewhere far off. But it was there, unmistakable, threading through the silence. Her pulse quickened as the sound grew louder, more insistent. Millie stood, her movements hesitant, and stepped into the bathroom. She reached for the light switch.

Millie's breath hitched as it grew louder, drowning out her thoughts. She gripped the sink harder, her knuckles whitening. She forced herself to look back into the mirror, hoping it was just a trick of the light, the stress, or her imagination playing cruel games.

But the red glow in her reflection didn't fade. It sharpened and stared back, unblinking, the glowing red orbs fixed on her as a single tear streaked down her cheek, and she felt its warm trail.

Her mirrored image leaned closer, the glowing eyes brighter now, vivid and alive, filled with an unnatural hunger. It wasn't just her reflection anymore. The air in the bathroom thickened, a suffocating weight pressing down on her chest as frost crept along the mirror's edges. Spreading veins. Her heart pounded in her ears.

Behind her, the bathroom light flickered. The wind outside rattled the windowpane.

And then it stopped. The wind, the rattling—everything. The silence was so sudden, so complete, it was as if the world itself had paused, holding its breath.

Her reflection leered with those red-eyes, lips curled into a faint, knowing smile.

It was her, but it wasn't.

Something *in-between*.

The frost on the glass of the window cracked, a sharp sound that echoed in oppressive stillness.

Millie shut her eyes, not wanting to see. Not wanting to let it see her—not again.

Then, came the whisper.

AUTHOR'S NOTE

In many ways, I suspect this book has a lot in common with other authors' first published works.

Like all works of fiction, it came from a deep well of imagination—one filled from childhood and drawn upon throughout the process, giving life to the story.

I started my writing journey in earnest five years ago. It was something I'd always thought about doing, but I had never made the full commitment. Ideas would come in fits and starts. But the more I caught myself saying, 'I wish I'd written that'—after watching an incredible movie, finishing a harrowing TV series, or lingering in the resonance of a novel—I knew I had to stop putting it off and start writing.

At first, I was exclusively writing fantasy. And because I have a penchant for big-picture thinking, I didn't just start with one book in mind, but a series—then connected series in a universe. All of which, believe you me, is still forthcoming.

But then Westville came crashing in and wouldn't let me go, the oft-repeated (and slightly trite) writing advice 'write what you know' tilting just enough through the lens of my hometown of Lowell, MI, to 'write where you know.'

That's when I knew this was the story I had to tell first, and where my 'first book' experience perhaps starts to differ.

When you spend enough time in a place, it gets under your skin—it sinks right to the marrow of your being. Maybe that's why a fictionalized 90s version of Lowell, infused with the kind of eerie, liminal dread I love in mystery and horror stories, felt so right.

I almost wrote just now that it: 'came easily'—but I don't think any writer can genuinely say that about bringing a novel from conception to birth.

In fact, there was a moment when I nearly put Westville on hold, back when I was first releasing its serialized version on Substack. My dad was actively losing his battle with cancer. But something told me—maybe it was him in his own way—to press on.

So I did.

And here we are. Here you are, having finished your first foray into Westville. I'm glad you made it to the other side, and I hope you found something worth carrying out with you.

I want to take a moment and express a sort of gratitude that runs just as deep as the memories of childhood locales.

To the people who have encouraged me throughout my life to keep creating—thank you. There are teachers, friends, and family too numerous to name, but I'll name the ones who have been my greatest encouragers, who fostered belief in me from the start: Thank you, Mom and Dad.

To the very first readers of Westville on Substack and those who read the early drafts—thank you for immersing yourself in a work-in-progress. Your early hunger for this story, even with all warts and jagged edges, gave me the drive to carry on.

To the town and community of Lowell, MI—for whom Westville is a love letter—thank you for shaping me in ways too many to count, and for the incredible support behind the launch of this book.

There was a novel dedication I saw once in which the author wryly pointed out that, were it not for his wife and kids, the book would have been finished two years sooner.

Sure, there's some truth to that.

But what would be the point of creating any meaningful work without the people who mean, and who simply are 'the most'?

To my daughters Emery and Reese, endlessly playful and creative, to my only son Archer, and to 'my one', Jessica: Nothing works without you. Including this story.

And to you, dear reader—thank you.

I'll see you in Westville.

ABOUT RYDER

Ryder grew up in Lowell, Michigan where he still resides with his family of five. He is the author and creator of the 'Westville' series and the forthcoming fantasy universe, 'Remnant Divine'. He is also the founder of Remnant Heart Publishing, a small imprint bringing creative vision to life.

Connect with him at ryderjones.com, westville.substack.com or on Instagram: @ryderhamiltonjones